Closure

Sarah Harris was born in 1967 an[...] School of Economics in 1988. She has worked as an assistant producer on BBC Television's *Newsnight* and as a press officer for the Liberal Democrats. She now writes full-time and lives in London. *Closure* is her second novel.

Acclaim for Sarah Harris's first novel, *Wasting Time*:

'As insightful as Nick Hornby's *High Fidelity*, but much funnier . . . Laugh at the jokes by all means and enjoy the fast-paced writing, but be prepared to cringe with recognition as Harris sticks her stiletto of satire into the characters.' *The Times*

'Sarah Harris is one of the cleverest, sharpest – and angriest of [her] breed . . . A brilliant piece of jabbing satire.' *Mail on Sunday*

'Funny and perceptive.' *Daily Express*

'Harris has painted a bigger and better picture of young working women in London than many of her contemporaries, Helen Fielding included.' *The Big Issue*

'The characters are real as only fictional characters can be . . . I hope it will earn Sarah Harris a sizeable following.' *Sunday Telegraph*

'Very funny, perceptive and with a refreshing turn of phrase, this is one book that you'll find hard to forget and will recommend to everyone.' *Prima*

CLOSURE

Sarah Harris

HarperCollins*Publishers*

This novel is entirely a work of fiction.
The names, characters and incidents portrayed in it are
the work of the author's imagination. Any resemblance to
actual persons, living or dead, events or localities is
entirely coincidental.

HarperCollins*Publishers*
77–85 Fulham Palace Road,
Hammersmith, London W6 8JB

www.fireandwater.com

A Paperback Original YEAR
1 3 5 7 9 8 6 4 2

A catalogue record for this book
is available from the British Library

ISBN 0 00 651394 8

Typeset in Meridien by Palimpsest Book Production Limited,
Polmont, Stirlingshire

Printed and bound in Great Britain by
Clays Ltd, St Ives plc

For Claudia

With thanks to David Rowan; the Harrises – Lionel, Vivienne, Judith and Daniel; Fiona McIntosh, Yvette Cowles, Claire Round, Anne O'Brien, Jennifer Parr and the team at Harper-Collins; and especially to Jo Frank, my agent at A. P. Watt, and Rachel Hore, my editor – all of whom have helped me to achieve closure.

Chapter One

She had smoked what she hoped would be her final cigarette,
stubbing it out on a street sign saying Dove Road, inside the
O. For some time now, she had been searching for Notting
Hill Terrace, walking up and down similar, parallel roads, and
smoking. Finally, and although she didn't believe in maps,
thinking of them as a man's accessory, she consulted her
London *A–Z*. Apparently Dove Road grew into Allison Street,
which became Simeon Square. That backed on to Notting Hill
Terrace, and there Anna had a four o'clock appointment to
see a flat. So at least she was in the right vicinity.

As Allison Street did indeed become Simeon Square, she
lit what she hoped would be her absolutely final Silk Cut,
stuffing her trouser pocket with the empty cigarette packet.
She wouldn't be tempted to buy another box. Anna saw
temptation instead in the call box at the end of the square,
which offered her communication with Him.

She had hoped that this morning's telephone conversation, during which she had called Him a 'selfish, fucking
bastard', would be the last. But it hadn't been easy, finding
His new girlfriend's number. Besides, He had been the one
to suggest, weeks ago, that she should see this flat in Notting
Hill Terrace.

He had said that someone called Sonia – a friend of a friend of a friend – was looking for a flatmate. He had given her Sonia's telephone number, urging Anna to call.

And then, He had ended their relationship.

It was fate, she felt, that the phone box was empty, as the streets were littered with a Lowryesque crowd coming back from the Portobello Road market. She had just been a part of that crowd, sitting with a glass of milky coffee at an outside café, and listening to an argument in Spanish. She had had only a smattering of understanding, but it had been a colourful, couple's row, and Anna had found it more entertaining than her Saturday supplement. *'Que eres una puta de madre . . .'*

It was fate, she felt, that the call box was there at all. Anna went inside, feeling in her pockets for change, and half-hoping that the telephone would be for emergency calls only. She had phoned Him six times this week. (On the Sabbath, she had shown enormous restraint.) And yet, and yet, she did want to hear His voice and, on a more general note, to be back in a relationship.

Oh, she knew that she was weak. Although, for that, Anna blamed her parents. For the end of her relationship, Anna blamed society. If only the traditional family structure hadn't broken down before she had had time to enjoy it. If the relationship had begun fifty years ago they would be married by now. They would be living in a sizeable house, with bay windows, and built-in children. Their house would be within driving distance of a family-run grocery store. There, they could buy all of their requirements.

In actual fact, she blamed Him for everything. He had been unnecessarily cruel, saying that Anna would never call this Sonia about her flat in west London. That she would be living with that depressive Myrna, and working at Radio Central as

2

an operator (His new girlfriend was an opera director) until the day she died from some whingeing 'women's disease'.

He blamed all women for Anna's behaviour.

A gallery of prostitutes' cards was jammed inside the crack between the phone and the wall, and the sight of them made Anna feel, for some reason, uncomfortable. But a single, tiny phone call wouldn't hurt anyone, she reasoned. Except perhaps herself.

The receiver had a shot of spit on it, which she wiped off with her sleeve, hearing Him say, 'Hello?' and realising, with a sigh from every one of her organs, that the 'hello' had been irritable, as if she had interrupted Him writing His novel or reorganising His wardrobe. Nonetheless, she pressed on.

'Hi, it's me,' she said, putting the receiver quickly back to her ear. 'Anna,' she went on, unstoppably, disliking the sound of her own name. 'Look, I called to say I was sorry about this morning. Calling you a . . .'

'Oh, for God's sake. What is this all about?' He said, interrupting her just as she realised that she had something important to say. 'Will you give me a break? Anna, please.'

'I'm sorry.' She scratched the eczema on her neck, which always erupted, like a bad temper, during any difficult situation. Her cigarette was a stick of ash now, and she knew that He was furious, as if Anna had interrupted Him in bed with His new girlfriend. Only, at least He had used her name. She liked the sound of it in His mouth.

'I mean, *Anna*.'

She dropped the cigarette, treading it flat, and said into the receiver, 'OK, look, I'm sorry. Honestly. I just wanted to have a conversation about us. In person. Not like this, you know. From a phone box . . .'

'Why are you in a *phone* box?' He asked, and she was

pleased that she had managed to arouse, at the very least, His curiosity.

'I'm in Notting Hill.' It was important that He knew about Anna's new beginning. 'I'm going to see this flat you told me about. You know, you gave me someone called Sonia's number? She was a friend of a friend of Josh's?'

'You don't know Josh,' He said sharply.

'I met him at your part . . .'

'Anyway, I thought that Sonia didn't want a smoker.'

'You *know* I gave up smoking.'

'In between *cigarettes*, you did.'

He paused for Anna to appreciate His 'joke' and she laughed, softly this time, in order to appear feminine and easy-going.

'And what about *Myrna*? You not going to live with the *bee-yoo-ti-ful* Myrna any more?'

'Don't be so nasty. And I don't know . . . I mean, this flat sounds wonderful. You know I'll be near you? Actually, I'm on the District and Circle line this afternoon, so I could come round after I've seen the flat if you . . . ?'

How easy it was to lull Him into conversation. Before He knew it they would be a couple again and eating croissants in bed on a Sunday morning, after sex.

'Anna, *no*.'

'Look, all I want is to talk. That's all I want. To have a final, face-to-face conversation.'

'We've had three *thousand* fucking final conversations . . .'

'I know but . . .'

'Also . . .' He lowered His voice to a whisper. 'My *girl-friend's* here.'

'Oh, fuck you.'

Anna prided herself on the fact that, at the height of

4

their conversations, she was always the one to put the phone down. As she put it down now, prostitutes' cards flew everywhere. They fell on to the floor, in a colourful mess; but one stuck fast. It read, *'Personal assistant Astrid – available for punishment during Office Hours'* and, for a moment, Anna thought about offering a more competitive service. Her own card could read, *'Phone-in operator Anna – available for punishment 24–7.'*

She walked along, needing a cigarette, and wondering whether she should simply turn round and go home. But, by now, Anna had reached Notting Hill Terrace, and she couldn't help but admire the buildings. She had forgotten that London hid such streets. The cake-shaped cream houses. The thick, iced paint. The whipped flourishes, purely for decoration.

She rang Sonia's doorbell, flattening the bulge of Silk Cut in her pocket.

Until now, Anna had thought that flats such as Sonia's, filled with African wood carvings, naked statues of bronzed abstracted women, cashmere and Turgenev, lemons, linen, muslin and Liszt, existed only in the pages of furniture catalogues.

But there it was – all that flesh-coloured upholstery. Sonia, fresh from the gym, apologising for having kept her waiting. ('You're Anna, yes?') Anna trying not to gush, telling Sonia it was a stunning hallway. ('Yes. We spoke on the phone?') Sonia saying she had had to have a shower after her *workout*; Anna saying yes, telling Sonia it was a lovely street. ('Wow,' was all Anna could say when she saw the living-room.) Sonia saying, *'Shit,'* her record had stuck; Anna saying, 'Shit,' but it was beautiful music. She had heard it outside.

'Yes, I love Liszt,' Sonia said, going to her old-fashioned gramophone and lifting out the record, as if it was a child that had been hurt. Sitting on a broad cashmere cushion, Sonia examined the vinyl for scratches as Anna sat down, trying desperately to deflate the packet of cigarettes in her pocket.

'This is lovely. So *bright*,' she said, wanting to remind Sonia that she was there.

She had sunk low into the cream sofa, as it had a depth she would never have imagined, feeling suddenly, terribly, ordinary. Sonia, by contrast, looked extraordinary – all blondeness, and tall fragility.

Until now, Anna hadn't minded her own ordinariness. She had done her utmost, in fact, to appear ordinary – dutifully following fashion, and buying white, for example, if that was the new black, or for that matter the new red, or lilac, or grey. She liked to fit in. She was wearing camouflage combat trousers now, although the army colours drained her pale English skin. She had on her fashionably flat shoes, despite her height, and was feeling clumsy and short beside Sonia, who was wearing last season's white, with confidence.

'So, what's your position at the moment?' asked Sonia.

'I'm an operator.' Anna picked up the Turgenev novel which sat on the coffee table, in an effort to appear curious. 'For Radio Central. You know, the phone-in station? I've just been moved from the Jimmy Salad show – the showbusiness one? To Pammy Lowental's problem hour. I imagine it'll be quite different.'

Oh, to be able to show off such a bookshelf as Sonia's, thought Anna, smiling, she hoped, wryly. It collected mainly classics. The odd contemporary novel sat securely among those lines of operatic CDs, and even works of philosophy.

6

Sonia's life sang with the soft sounds of sitting on cushions. It would only be a matter of time before Anna could have it all. In an instant, she would rent not just a room in a flat, but all of its contents.

'No, I meant, where d'you live?'

'Oh, sorry. No, I mean, north London. Finchley Road.'

'Finchley Road?'

'Yes, but at the Swiss Cottage end.'

'Swiss Cottage? Oh dear,' said Sonia, as her telephone rang. But had she misunderstood Anna's point? 'I'll just get that,' said Sonia, as the telephone urgently rang on.

'Yes, of course.'

Sonia went to the phone, and Anna caught her eyes in a full-length mirror, which stood – as if it had been observing her for some time – in the right-hand corner of the room. How she wished, walking to the sofa, that she had broken in her combat trousers. Because it was clear from her reflection that Anna was wearing them for the first time.

Sitting down, she couldn't help herself, standing up to look in the mirror again, as she didn't trust her appearance, which altered from one photograph to the next. Still undecided as to whether she was to suffer plain, or to grow vain from pretty, Anna's value could, like the Brazilian real, go down in the time it took her to complete a bus journey.

Secretly, she was certain of her allure. Surely, all women were? That was what kept her going, from one cosmetics counter to the next. Lurking deep down, in those average penny-brown eyes – thick under that lank, puppy-brown hair – lay an extraordinary loveliness. Now, Anna just had to find the right shade of lipstick for her skin-tone, the most flattering trousers for her legs, the most

7

vitamin-enriched shampoo for her hair. Then, as if over-night, her beauty would emerge from an old blanket of blemishes.

For now, however, Anna would have to settle for being visually slightly above average. Over the last ten years, she had conducted an informal survey on the London Under-ground. Using a fairly large sample, she had scored an average of sixty per cent. Six out of every ten women using the tube were plainer than Anna was. Just four, or forty per cent (fewer than half), were more attractive.

There were days, of course, when Anna Potter looked half-dead, her hair almost mousy. Then, the pores in her skin grew huge, opening up to let in Underground dirt, trapping the filth in her face, and snapping shut. On such days, most of the women on the tube were beautiful. Among them, she felt a freak, low enough to eat her breakfast on the train, leaving her wrappings behind. On such days, she did not conduct her survey. The sample, Anna reasoned, was unrepresentative.

Alternatively, there were days when she could pass more than fifty women before finding one as pretty as she was. Oh, how her fingernails had been filed. Delicate, pretty, features. Despising those women loathsome enough to be eating in public, leaving their rubbish for her to tidy up. On these days, people looked at Anna as if she counted.

'Sorry about that,' said Sonia, coming back into the living-room.

'Oh, that's fine,' said Anna awkwardly.

There was a pause.

'So, do you want to see around the flat now?' asked Sonia, and they saw the second bedroom first, flicking through Sonia's on the way, everything fresh cotton and cashmere; no fat duvet, dimpling. No plaited, washed-pink knickers sticking out of the mouths of the drawers, like tongues. The room that Anna hoped to rent was white lashed with yellow; a chair here, a bed there, a burnt-wood wardrobe.

'I really do like it. It really is lovely. That's a good big wardrobe. Oh, there's space there for shoes. I mean, a shoe-rack. I don't think I've ever had a shoe-rack . . .'

Sonia glanced at Anna's clothes, which she knew then were far too drab, as she led her to the bathroom, which smelled of nothing, not even baths, nor the many expensive scents jumbled together in a basket. Possibly because, as had been quickly pointed out, the toilet was kept in a separate room, its paper plain, rather than her own cheap stuff, which blushed pink. Its reflection could be seen in a huge glass mirror, which also revealed Anna.

She could not help herself, opening Sonia's bathroom cabinet to see if it was similar to her own, at home, which spilled out everything. Her flatmate, Myrna, had so many medicines. Anna had so many clinically tested day creams.

'How much room . . . ? D'you mind?' Anna said, and Sonia 'No, go ahead.'

Naturally, Anna knew, closing the cabinet on Sonia's four supermarket own-brand products (of which even the supermarket branding was unfamiliar), that, as soon as she arrived home, she would bin all of her bathroom things apart from the toothpaste, a toothbrush, dental floss, unperfumed soap, anti-perspirant deodorant, and a bright white flannel. If, indeed, she owned a flannel.

She would begin to floss on a regular basis.

The broom cupboard in the hall had brooms in it rather than old clothes and unwanted Christmas presents, unused sale items and large floppy hats that Anna hoped would transform her into, if no one else, Annie Hall. The cord of Sonia's vacuum cleaner had been perfectly wound. It stood in sharp contrast to Anna's Hoover at home, which leaned lazily against the television, and had a cat's cradle of a cable.

Anna's cleaning woman hadn't gone near the Hoover for months. She complained that the dust-suction irritated her asthma. She had made a point, too, of saying at her interview that she would not pick up dirty underwear.

'Oh, that's fine, we don't have dirty underwear,' Anna had replied, ridiculously. But she didn't like to be in the position of having to ask someone to carry out mindless, household chores. As her flatmate, Myrna, had pointed out, the woman had had a hard enough time escaping the civil war in Sudan, and giving birth en route to Britain, without having to worry about Anna's smalls.

Anna was now in the kitchen, admiring Sonia's oven. ('Oven,' Sonia had said, pointing.)

'Dishwasher, microwave, freezer, kitchen roll, waste disposal, etcetera,' continued Sonia, indicating the fully fitted camouflage of cupboards.

'Wow,' said Anna, opening doors and pulling out drawers at random. 'It's got everything.'

She opened the ice-metal of the fridge door, its handle reminiscent of the start-up levers on fairground rides, finding the cold breath of shelf upon shelf, illustrated with the fresh colours of a children's book. Everything shivered wet: the red-skinned Edam cheese, like a child in a swimsuit; the splashing skirts of washed lettuce; the tanned chicken legs; the cherry tomatoes; the live yoghurt; the crate of green-bottled beer.

Anna smiled at the eggs, which sat patiently in the egg tray. She felt like climbing inside, sitting cold, twisting in

10

the shower of still water which came on tap. But instead she half-knelt down, to open the vegetable drawer.

'Just wondered . . .' she murmured, thinking of her own stinking vegetable drawer in her fridge at home, painted green, with shards of broken cheese and brushes of bald broccoli. One of its dirty stalks had lain in Anna's bottom drawer for several years. Three stale cloves of garlic sat there too. Even Myrna was afraid, by now, to pick them up.

'So *nice.*'

She couldn't help but admire Sonia's stack of knives. They hung from the wall in order of brutality, beginning with meat cleaver and finishing with fruit peeler, like weapons patiently waiting for some domestic fracas. And, beside them, Sonia's friends. Plastered in photographs across a cork board, they were, to a body, beautiful. Anna would have admired them too, protocol permitting. Barely could she see any cork.

Ordinarily, of course, such people existed only in advertisements. Anna could imagine peeling back the images to find bottles of, say, salad dressing. They wore ski jackets, sporting cartons of drinking yoghurt, all of which had continental names. They clutched each other, as if afraid ever to fall apart.

Her own friends wouldn't have formed such a good-looking group. All together, in one place, they would have looked odd, as if each one didn't quite belong. Some of Anna's friends behaved as if it was still the early seventies, discussing communism as if it was alive and well and operating in an undivided Soviet Union. Even in the summer, they wore long overcoats.

Others of her friends acted as if it was the mid-eighties; they talked about sure-fire enterprises, or fluctuating house prices, in an overbearing manner. (How would Roo look

11

in a group photograph? So *pushy*, she would stick out, like celery in soup.) Not one of her friends ever made the effort to blend in.

'Where was this one taken?' Anna asked Sonia now, referring to the largest and most colourful photo, which took up a great deal of cork.

'Oh, just in the pub. But it's taken by a professional photographer – a colleague of mine.'

'You're a photographer?'

The photographs had a depth that Anna wouldn't have thought possible. They were shaded in such a way as to make them appear three-dimensional. She would have liked to have photographed Sonia's photographs.

'Yeah. But I specialise in single portraits, so I didn't want to take this one. I wanted to be in it. Anyway, I wanted a photo of the gang – so it needed someone with a different eye.'

Anna's tongue found a hole in her tooth. She hadn't had a gang since primary school, when she had handed round those home-made laminated membership cards, and persuaded her parents to buy the obligatory gang dog. The Secret Society. Barbara and Don, feeling guilty at their inability to give Anna a sibling, had agreed to buy her a dog. It was only unfortunate that it had had to be put down, Anna's mother always forgetting to feed it.

She couldn't even imagine rounding up her friends for a satisfying group photograph. They would all fight to sit at the edge of the scene. No one would touch anyone. Individually, they were fine. But as a whole . . . ? In her *local* too, where the landlord still hadn't learnt Anna's name, although she had been drinking there regularly for the last ten years.

'And they all came? I mean, they were all free?' Anna

asked Sonia, fascinated. She had never seen such together-ness since infant school.

'Well, we hang out together all the time.'

Anna pictured her own friends, from all corners of her life, gathered together for a photograph. (They would all behave as if they had only just met, asking, 'You're . . . ?') Roo, wanting to leave immediately. 'Oscar's about to turn from back to front. Got to collect Daisy from Tumble Tots.'

Myrna – Anna's flatmate – not wanting to stay for a *photo*. (Really quite fat now, she wouldn't want to know.)

Roo, arguing that she couldn't hang around forever, wait-ing for Anna's ex. Anna really should try and forget about Him. She needed a man who cared about more than just a woman's appearance. Or her career.

Of course, Roo knew what she was talking about. She had reached the finishing line in terms of relationships – Roo being married, with two children and stains of puréed carrot and formula milk where shoulder pads had once been. 'I wish I'd never introduced you to Him now,' she would say, preparing to leave. 'And I'm sorry about this photo, Anna,' she would say. 'But you'll understand, when you have kids.'

All Anna knew was that Roo was going through a clingy stage.

'So, was anyone *not* able to come?' insisted Anna now, to Sonia. 'I mean, it's hard to get people together, isn't it? People are so busy . . .'

'Is it so hard?' asked Sonia, puzzled. 'I mean, I just asked them, and they came.'

Justine would not heave herself out of bed for anyone. 'I'm not coming *north*, Anna,' she would say, wearily sniff-ing her coked-up nose. 'What did you say you wanted? A photograph?'

Justine lived on the other side of London, along the Central line, renting a kind of a commune, with the benefits of Ecstasy and income support. She was in the process of setting up a nightclub in Soho, and couldn't see anyone during the day.

She couldn't see Anna during the day. Even during the night, she was always doing something else. She was always too *shitfaced* to answer Anna's calls. ('Sorry I didn't get back to you.') In fact, Anna hadn't seen her for two months, but she was still on Anna's British Telecom's priority call-list of Family and Friends. Well, Anna had known her since primary school.

She was at No. 5 on Anna's bedroom phone speed-dial, too. She was just behind her Australian friend, Liz, who was at No. 4. Anna's parents were at No. 3. Roo was at No. 2. He remained her No. 1.

'Is that your boyfriend?' Anna asked Sonia. Plaits of muscle were visible in his thick, beef-brown arms. The man's eyes were huge and army-green.

'Yup,' said Sonia, laughing and glancing at the man in the photograph, who was gazing at her with such affection. He looked perfect. What was more, Anna couldn't imagine him ruining all that masculinity by speaking.

'He's *gorgeous*,' Anna admitted. 'Is he a model?'

'Oh no, he's an academic. I was photographing him for the cover of his biography.'

'He's written a biography?'

'Yes. On Flevidor Lichieuvies.'

'Right,' said Anna, as if *Flevidor* was well-known to her. 'And this *gang* of yours?' she added, unable to help herself. 'Does it include Josh?'

'Josh?' asked Sonia, puzzled.

'A friend of Josh's told me about the flat?'

14

Sonia was thinking, her brow furrowing into perfectly straight lines.

'Oh, you mean *Andy*,' said Sonia finally. 'Andy's fine, but he's not really part of . . . Do you know Andy?'

'No,' admitted Anna. In truth, she didn't even know Josh.

'He's a bit . . . I mean, the rest of us are so . . .'

'So close?' said Anna, wistfully.

'Yeah.'

Anna imagined her closest friends together, in one place. Her flatmate, Myrna, congratulating Roo on her success in journalism. *But Myrna couldn't exploit people like that for a living.* Roo saying she thought Myrna brave, prepared to be unemployed in this day and age. *But Roo couldn't cope without a job; she would feel such a failure.* Myrna admiring Roo, for staying so thin. *But Myrna couldn't starve, or spend her life at the gym.*

Roo envying Liz's singleness. *But what did Liz do in the evenings?* Liz envying Roo being married. *But what did Roo do with him in the evenings?* Roo admiring Liz's assertiveness. *But didn't Liz feel humiliated, giving strange men her number?* Liz wanting Roo's children. *But didn't Roo feel trapped by the two of them?* Roo wanting Liz's life without children. *But didn't Liz worry that she'd never, ever, have children?*

Anna knew that she was wasting too much of Sonia's time, looking at the photographs. But she wanted to ask Sonia where all of her friends had bought their clothes. And, while she was on the subject, their hair and that tanned skin. At the centre of each snapshot, Sonia stood, or sat, or lounged around. In all of them she wore the same blue, baby-doll cashmere cardy, which looked as if, at any moment, it might fold itself up.

'Is that your mother there?' asked Anna, still studying the photographs. She saw a glamorous, although older, woman, nestled into the gang.

'Yeah. I wouldn't have had a photo taken without Teddy,' smiled Sonia. 'She'd go ape.'

Anna checked Sonia's face to see if she was joking. She could think of no greater nightmare than her own mother turning up to the pub in the middle of Anna's group photo. And, of course, with her mother – or should she say Barbara – would come Anna's short and balding father. Although they would come in separate cars.

His and hers.

They would barely speak to one another. *Barbara* would sit there, saying it didn't matter if Anna's boyfriend didn't show up. 'We can just get a lovely photo of you, by yourself, Anna, in that colourful army uniform.'

Don would mutter, 'Why do you want a photo anyway, Anna? Don't you have better things to do with your time?'

Looking around the pub, Barbara would say, 'A *pub*. Well, isn't this exciting?' Then she would trill, 'Anna. Do they do anything without alcohol in?' Eventually, she would order herself a hot chocolate from the bar.

Everyone would hover around the table, as if they had just arrived. Embarrassed by Anna's parents, they would all be doing their utmost to leave.

Anna would be trying, as in dreams, to make herself heard. 'Please sit back down, Mum,' she would say. 'I don't want a photo of *me*. This is absurd.'

'Couldn't you have worn a prettier outfit?' her mother would ask. Suddenly, she would shrill, '*Anna*,' pointing at a drunk and middle-aged man. 'Is that The Boyfriend we've heard so much about?'

He would arrive, just as everyone was leaving.

'I'll give you a ring, Anna,' Roo would say. 'When I get back from that all-expenses-paid trip to Spain.'

'D'you mind moving out of the way, Sonny Jim?' her father would ask Him.

Anna would try to encourage Him to leave.

'That chap seems to have latched on to *you*,' Anna's mother would tell her. 'Leave him there, Anna. I don't think he's doing anyone any harm.' Then, as He rose, Barbara would sigh, '*Ahhh*. You look so *happy*, Anna. Sitting there all on your *own*.'

'No, I don't think it would work somehow,' said Anna.

'What?'

'A photo. Never mind. *How* long have you lived here?' she asked Sonia, who was sighing at the ringing phone.

'I think I'll leave that to the machine. We've lived here a couple of years. I suppose we bought at a good time.'

'We?'

'My sister and I.'

'What's happened to her?'

'She's married.'

'Ah.'

She had expected Sonia's answer. From this flat, all things were possible. Anna wondered whether she could stand there forever. There was a pause, which Anna fancied as intimate. But Sonia's message was playing on her answer-phone, and interrupting their shared silence. '*Please leave a message for Sonia or Lucy after the tone.*'

'*Hi Sonia, it's Maddy. I need your advice. I can't get this exhibition together. Ring me.*'

'Luce and I were very close.'

'Your sister?'

'Yeah. I mean, I don't know about you, but I think

17

it's important with a flatmate. To get on. That's why the rent's so low. I don't want to live with someone who's *already* a friend. Because, that way, there's an agenda already in place.'

'You're right,' Anna agreed. 'I think it's better to . . .'

'I mean, of course, there *does* have to be a recommendation.'

'Well, of course,' said Anna quickly.

'But that doesn't mean . . . I mean, I think a flatmate should be someone that, in different circumstances, I would have been friends with anyway.'

'God, yes, I agree,' Anna said warmly, ready to move in right away. Now that Radio Central had promoted her, to be an operator on *Problem Call*, she could almost afford Sonia's 'low' rent. She could leave her tip of a flat in Swiss Cottage, taking the place of Sonia's sister, having a laugh with Sonia, getting close to Sonia. Absorbed into Sonia's life, Anna would have no further need of her own. 'I mean, definitely.'

'So. That's the whole flat,' said Sonia, as she led her back into the living-room.

'I really love it.'

'Good. Bloody hell, is that the time? I've got to go to the market.'

'Oh, right, yes. I'll go.' Anna busied herself with her duffel bag.

'No, no, stay. It's fine. Only Leo's invited Flevidor and some of his friends round for supper here tonight.'

'Here?' Sonia seemed genuinely to want her to stay; so Anna put her bag back down. It slumped on the floor, like a frightened, small animal.

'Yeah.'

'And you don't mind?'

'No, I love cooking. Trouble is, everyone knows it.' She laughed. 'They take advantage of me.'

'Yeah, same here.'

'So what sort of thing do *you* do in the evenings?' Sonia asked Anna, who could never remember how she filled her spare time. In between watching television, she didn't seem to have any.

'Well, whatever. Tonight, I'm going to a party, for example,' Anna said, deciding to go to Roo's cousin's party.

'Oh, right. What about during the week?' Sonia had sat down, putting her feet up on to the glass table in front of her. She was so fragile that it made an incongruous image; she looked like a ballerina on a fag break. 'I mean, d'you belong to any club?'

Again, Anna thought of the Secret Society.

'What do you mean?'

'Well, like Blacks?'

'Oh, no.'

'Soho House?'

'I mean, I don't belong to a club.'

'Oh. So what d'you *do* then? In the evenings.'

'Oh, well, go out. Or stay in. Watch TV.'

'Right.' Sonia appeared to be disappointed, and Anna wondered whether to invent a hobby. Yoga, for example. Or aqua-aerobics.

'What do you *watch* on TV?' asked Sonia.

'Oh, you know,' Anna said, although Sonia clearly didn't. '*Seinfeld* . . . Alan Partridge . . . *Friends* . . .'

'Actually, I must admit I haven't seen any of those programmes . . .' said Sonia.

'And documentaries,' added Anna, thinking quickly. 'Current-affairs programmes. *Panorama* . . . *Horizon* . . . *World in Action* . . .' she said.

'I mean,' said Sonia, 'I don't have a television.'

Anna looked around. She had wondered why the living-room looked so distinct – certain items, such as the stereo system, the books, even the pictures on the wall, outstanding; haughty; behaving as if they were anything other than music without pictures, pictures without movement, or words without sound.

In Anna's flat they would have been put in their place. There, the TV dominated. All other objects paid homage to it, finding their reflections slighted in its glare. Those objets d'art standing spoiled by the clean fireplace would have been, in any other environment, just a back-up, and there as entertainment only during the ad-breaks of Anna's soap operas or Myrna's *Crimewatch*.

'You don't have a TV at *all*?'

Anna and Myrna had a television in every room, save for the toilet. There, they had an emergency pile of monthly women's magazines.

Sonia said slowly, 'No. But I don't mind if someone wants to bring one.'

'I would want to, I think,' said Anna, feeling suddenly insecure.

'That'd be fine. I'm not fanatically against. I just haven't thought about getting one.'

Anna thought about TV a good deal. The Potters had been the first family in the street, back in 1970, to buy colour. Her parents had bought that life-sized TV to keep their daughter company.

She had stayed home from school, ill, to watch *The Sullivans*. Otherwise, Anna would have missed all of the wartime episodes. How could her mother expect her, after a bout of flu, to be up and about, and missing Kitty? She would have lost the plot. Of course she had malingered.

20

She had had to hear the verdict on a prolonged case on *Crown Court*.

Warm feelings during *Fingerbobs* and *Sesame Street*.

It was important, during a foreign holiday, to be near a camping centre. Then, Anna could watch TV. She could watch *The Brady Bunch* in Italian, with subtitles if lucky; otherwise, it was fine ('no, no, you go ahead') if her parents went to the beach without Anna, so that she could work out what the Waltons were saying when they were dubbed into French.

'I *would* need a TV,' she said decisively.

'Well, that's fine,' said Sonia soothingly, as Anna took a pen out of her duffel bag. She felt more secure holding some sort of a prop.

'So tell me. What do you do, again? I mean, for a living?'

'Well,' said Anna, wondering whether she should lie about her job at Radio Central. She put down her pen on the side table. 'I'm a phone-in operator,' she said, settling for the truth. 'I sort out the calls that come in, and pass them on to the presenter.'

'That sounds interesting,' said Sonia, blankly.

'Tell me about what *you* do. What photographs . . . ?'

'So, which programme did you say . . . ?'

'Well, I've just been moved, actually. From Jimmy Salad's showbusiness hour, to the Pammy Lowental show. I start on Monday,' she said.

'Jimmy *Salad*?'

'Yeah.'

'No, I haven't heard of him. And . . . did you say Pamela Anderson?'

Anna apologised for laughing.

'No, her name's Pammy *Lowental*. And she's no Pamela Anderson.'

'So, what sort of programme is it?'

'*Problem Call?* Well, it's a problem programme. People phone in for advice.'

'A *problem* programme?' said Sonia, as if the word 'problem' had only just occurred to her. She appeared to need to laugh.

'It's considered a promotion,' said Anna, smiling feebly. 'I mean, it goes out during the day.'

There was a pause, then, to Sonia's clear relief, the phone rang again. 'Oh God. Look, I'll get that. So, unless you've got any questions . . . ?'

'No,' Anna said, standing up and seeing herself, once more, reflected in the mirror. She seemed terribly small. 'That's fine. Thanks.'

'Hello, Biba . . . ?' said Sonia, who had picked up the phone.

Anna picked up her bag, smiling at Sonia as she passed her in the hallway.

'Biba. Hang on a second. Look, I've got your number.' At least half of that was to Anna, who had found the social prop of the door handle.

She reached for it, saying, 'Yes.'

'Sorry I can't let you know now. But you know how it is.'

'Of course. Thank you.'

'No, thank *you*.'

Anna walked out of Sonia's flat, leaving behind her pen, thick and expensive with bottled ink, on the side table.

'Damn,' she thought, standing in the communal hallway. But the door was still on its latch, so she went back in, knowing that she would need that pen if she was to start as she meant to go on, at *Problem Call*, on Monday. And she was just about to call out, 'Sorry, Sonia. It's only me. Just left my pen behind,' when she heard Sonia on the phone, talking about Anna Potter.

'Some friend of *Andy*'s. An Anna Potter,' she was saying.

'No. I don't think . . .'

'No, that was Anna *Suter*. Idiot . . .'

Anna remained still, hanging on to the door handle. She heard Sonia laugh.

'It's just funny, that's all.'

'No, the idea that she's anything like Anna *Suter* . . . No, she just wasn't right, anyway. It's a shame, because when I spoke to her on the phone, she sounded fine. She's got this *problem* . . .'

Anna, of course, had to forget about her expensive pen, finding her way out. On the front steps, going down, she just wasn't right somehow, falling over, spilling her bag on to the bottom step, throwing out her plastic purse, her travel pass, her spare sanitary towel. Anna had never, she realised now, been sophisticated enough to cope with the instructions on tampon packets. Picking up her empty sandwich wrapper – the mayonnaise melting on to the Cellophane – Anna just wasn't right somehow.

She had tried her damnedest to be likeable – answering Sonia's questions, smiling, hiding her ugly eczema, and pretending interest in Liszt and Turgenev – yet she had appeared to have *a problem*.

Now Anna saw that she had hurt her leg. She rolled her trousers up to find a playground stain of blood on her knee; it looked like bleeding concrete. But the concrete cut didn't surprise her. Anna often found herself mixed up in metaphors. The sky would compete in its charcoals with her black moods. She would ladder her tights at critical career points. Or hear children singing as she received good news. As He had ended their relationship, a woman of her age had

23

fallen, painfully, on to the pavement opposite them.

'No, I'm fine,' she had heard the woman say to someone only trying to help.

'No, I'm fine,' Anna had heard herself tell Him.

'No, I'm fine,' she said now, to a man just passing by.

Chapter Two

Finally, Anna was home. Finchley Road. For the last hour, she had been trapped on the tube, staring at an advert for a cosmetic surgery clinic, and wondering why Sonia had said, 'No, she just wasn't right.' There had been a delay at Paddington. Anna had used the time, sitting, stuck, on a tube, to analyse Sonia's words, 'She's got this problem . . .' What was Anna's problem? Was it her appearance? Or her career? Her life?

She stood at a pedestrian crossing, waiting for the lights to change, and wondering about her problem. What could it be? Anna had such a long list of problems; they were hard to whittle down. Job. *Him*. Justine. Damaged hair – although, for that, she blamed her hairdresser. Myrna. Her mother, naturally.

Money.

Men.

The fact that, for too long, Anna had been waiting for the lights to change. (She considered risking her life, and crossing that motorway of a main road anyway.)

Her parents were, of course, a problem. Liz. Her car.

Cars, in general.

Carbon monoxide poisoning.

Finchley Road.

Finally, the lights changed, and Anna crossed, thinking that, of course, Finchley Road could never be Notting Hill Terrace. For too long, in fact, Anna had been living in this filthy, concrete rectangle of the city. Sweet-sounding Swiss Cottage, where cars collided on the one and only street in a rush to leave. Swiss Cottage, where no one was fooled by the name.

Anna walked on, reaching her stretch of road, off the main thoroughfare, where the numbers became confusing. He had been the one to point this out, after that momentous first visit to her flat. (They had made love for the first time, that night.) He had not been able to find Anna's part of the Finchley Road. Did Anna know that it fell on the crease of the London *A–Z*? It was not on the road itself; He had had to ask for directions.

Lying in bed, that night, He had said, 'Why do you want to live here anyway?'

Oh, Anna knew that she shouldn't have agreed to 113B – although, for that, she blamed her flatmate. Myrna had chosen it. She had said that the flat had a living-room, and Myrna had seen a few that hadn't. Plus, the area was very well served by public transport.

Anna's mother, who had wanted her daughter to move back into the family home, had nevertheless interrupted to say that Swiss Cottage might not have been Belsize Park, but then neither was it just another part of the Finchley Road. The area had an identity all of its own; Anna and Myrna should take the flat. It was absolutely fine for their short-term needs.

But Anna's needs had plainly changed, and she felt, now, as if she was seeing the house for the first time. 113 was old, and ugly. It was only half-painted, and covered in the braces of scaffolding. Anna decided that she would speak to the landlord. She would ask him when he was planning to finish re-decorating.

She felt in her pocket for her keys, finding only the empty, squashed box of cigarettes. It was Myrna who usually dealt with any problems concerning their house. She handled all things domestic. Anna took on the traditionally male role in any functioning living arrangement, going out to work on behalf of Myrna, who was at the moment between jobs.

So, when – in June – the landlord had explained that he was going to start a re-decoration project on his 'invest-ment', Anna had asked him to speak to her flatmate. And the landlord had explained to Myrna that there might be some 'upheaval' but that it was time to 'get the illegal Pakis out of the house and start restoring, redoing, renewing'.

Myrna, had replied that a) there were no Pakistanis living in the building, and that b) the word Paki was pejorative; and that she, for one, would not tolerate racist abuse. It was men like him who had ensured the rise of National Socialism in Germany. Who had stood by, watching millions sent to the gas chambers. Babies' heads smashed against walls. The elderly, digging their own graves. Could he, in fact, leave her flat? Now?

In July, as the shock of a hot English summer had arrived, so had the decorators. A man wearing overalls had peered into Anna's bedroom window. Full mugs of milky tea had appeared on window-sills. Brushes had been left to moult in the sticky sun and, for a few weeks, the edges of Anna's house had melted with fresh cream paint. At last her life was having its longed-for makeover.

But then August started, and the building work stopped. Their landlord had run out of 'capital' and, for the last month, nothing had happened. It was now the start of

September, and, still, half of the house was all pock marks and scabs of grizzled paint. The re-decorated half showed up the other half, and made the whole look ugly.

Anna searched in her bag for her keys.

As she was feeling for her key-ring, a stranger came up behind her. He let her into the building, and Anna tried to place him. Perhaps he lived on the top floor? Although few lived in Anna's building for longer than five weeks. Inside the house, flats were let, then were illegally sub-let, then were sub-sub-let to refugees.

Anna was on nodding terms solely with the elderly woman who lived in the basement. Once, after she had invited the old woman in for a cup of tea, they had almost become what Anna might call friends. Anna had sympathised with the woman, whose daughter had died last year.

'Your children shouldn't go before you do,' the woman had said sadly. 'It's not the natural order of things.'

'I'm sorry,' Anna had said, offering her a Rich Tea biscuit.

'Oh no, don't be,' said the woman, taking her hand. 'I'm grateful to you just for talking. Nobody knows their neighbours now, do they?'

Anna had helped the woman back to her own flat, feeling good about herself. Suddenly, she had felt part of society. She had felt a glow not felt since the World Cup, the demonstrations against the introduction of a community charge, and the death of Princess Diana. A glow that people no doubt felt throughout the war. Because, despite the passage of time, Anna still believed in the Blitz spirit, certain that it could be felt again, when all the out-of-town hypermarkets shut down.

'You know, Myrna, I think we should both befriend her,' Anna had said.

'What's the point?' replied Myrna, reading a biography about an American serial killer, and eating a Tunnock's tea cake.

'Because she's interesting,' said Anna. 'And, anyway, man is a social animal.'

'Yeah, but woman prefers to stay in, watching Jerry Springer.'

Anna had been invited back to the old woman's basement flat, deep down in the bowels of the house. Again, the woman had talked about her daughter. How she had played lacrosse for England. Of her daughter's taste for foreign foods, such as garlic. Did Anna know that she had died last year?

'I did. I really am sorry,' said Anna.

'Why are *you* sorry?' snapped the woman. 'You didn't kill her.'

Tea was a bag from which all life had been wrung, and dumped unceremoniously into Anna's cup of hot, smoky water. As Anna talked about the gym that was opening along the Finchley Road, and the fact that a payphone was about to be installed in the communal house corridor, the woman's eyes had filled with tears.

Anna's cup had wobbled nervously on its saucer.

Suddenly, the woman had asked for her teabag back. It had been as if Anna had had the bag for years. Why, she had asked, did Anna have her television on all the time? Was Anna's flatmate *deaf*? Her own hearing had gone, and that was Anna's fault. That, and the fact that her ceiling was falling down. Did she and her fat flatmate have to walk so heavily?

The stranger flicked through the letters on the shelf. Anna stood behind the man, waiting for him to finish. She wanted to check the pile too, as He had promised to return all of Anna's possessions.

'Sorry. So many of them,' said the stranger at last, smiling at Anna. She returned his smile, and started to flip through the pile of unclaimed letters herself. The pile grew each day, as their postman daily stuffed their box with letters that weren't properly addressed. The postman must have known that the house was filled with asylum-seekers, who couldn't complain; Anna who simply wouldn't; and Myrna, who felt that there were more important problems in the world than an erratic postal service.

There wasn't a single letter for Anna, who wished that she was 'Sally Foster, London, NW3'. The back of the letter read, 'Sorry about this address. It's all I know of Sally, except that she's beautiful, and that I met her in Italy. If undelivered, please return to Alex Bedford, 15 Turner Road, Leeds. P.S. Take pity on me, Postman, I think she lives on Finchley Road.'

For one moment Anna thought about returning the letter. Such an apparently motiveless act could persuade *Alex Bedford* to fall in love with Anna. They would have the type of romance realised only in the movies. But Anna thought better of it, allowing the letter to fall, with all the others, behind the radiator in the hall.

Myrna was out, at one of her all-day evening classes.

Three years ago, Myrna had been made redundant from her job, marketing boxes of British Variety biscuits. After such a social, interactive office, she had felt lonely, stuck indoors all day, and had signed up for several classes at the Adult Education Institute.

The classes had filled a void left by the early finish of daytime television. Myrna had enjoyed being back in the breezy classroom, painted high-pink. At work, she had had constantly to come up with ways of marketing someone else's product. But at the Adult Education Institute, no one forced her to show enthusiasm. She could stare dully out of the window.

She could feel less redundant.

As at school, people cared enough to comment on Myrna's work. They gave her A grades, and talked about Myrna's brain. Finally, she saw that school rules had been put in place for a reason. No one ran in the corridors, barging into her. 'SorryButI'veGotToGetToThatMeeting.'

It was only last year that Job Centre form-fillers had begun to ask Myrna some questions. Why was Ms Lomond not filling in job applications? Had Ms Lomond stopped looking for a position in marketing? Was she still available for interview, on request? Could she please cut down on the number of classes she was taking? Did Ms Lomond realise that her housing benefit could be stopped, at any moment? Her income support?

Just one more module, Myrna had begged.

Anna smelled chocolate, and felt hungry. She went to the freezer, and took out one of her ready-meals-for-one. Today, haddock in mushroom and cheese sauce. The phone rang just as Anna was piercing the plastic several times with a fork.

'Hiya. I'm ringing about tonight's party.'

'Oh, Roo, look, I really don't want to go.'

'Yeah, but you'll enjoy it once you get there. I know you.'

They had been friends through many a bad hairstyle, meeting during their first week at Arndale Polytechnic, in the ladies' toilets. There, Roo had lent Anna her lipstick. Tickled Pink.

From then on, they had shared everything of Roo's. Anna had used her friend's milk – labelled *Keep off* and *It's still theft* – which Roo kept in the Graystone hall of residence fridge.

She had shared Roo's recipes for tuna pasta (add one tin of tuna to one pan of pasta) and baked potato with cottage cheese (add one baked potato to one pot of cottage cheese). Oh, and all of Roo's friends. 'You're *Roo*'s friend, aren't you?' Anna had been asked, even in her third year.

After college, Roo had worked as a receptionist at Radio Central.

By the time Anna had decided it was time to get a job, it was the year of the Lost Generation, and most graduates were 'resting' – either as actors or accountants. Anna had enrolled in a course at the London School of Beauty and Fashion.

But she had left after a term; after that, acting in a profit-share fringe production of Langland's *Piers the Ploughman* – although there hadn't been any profit. Anna hated, now, to think about that one review. *(Anna Potter, playing Envy, was particularly infuriating.)* The play had shut down after two weeks. *(Whoever led her to believe that she could act was cruel and vindictive.)* Roo had been the only one of Anna's friends to have found what Don Potter would call a proper job. She had been working as an operator on Jimmy Salad's phone-in show, securing Anna her old job as a receptionist at Radio Central.

It had been Roo who had suggested Anna to replace her on the Jimmy Salad show – she had left to become a journalist. And so Anna had stepped into the spiky shoes of Roo.

Sometimes Anna wondered what her life would be like, without Roo there to tell her what to do. She had taught her how to breathe in difficult situations. How to have multi-orgasms. To have a pen on her at all times. To back everything up with a fax.

She had introduced Anna to Him; and, now, she was insisting that Anna come to the party tonight. She should finally meet Tom, who was not only single but tall. Anna could do so much better than watching Saturday night TV game shows with Myrna for company. She could do with this tall man called Tom.

Anna tried to argue that she didn't need to go to Roo's cousin's party. Indeed, any party. She was tired. She had had a full day. There was a haddock in her oven. And Myrna needed Anna; she was depressed. Anna, anyway, wanted only to watch Cilla Black on the television. Cilla always cheered her up.

Roo would cheer Anna up. Besides, Tom would be expecting her; and Anna just wanted to stay in and mope about Him. And Myrna was always depressed. There was nothing that Anna could do for her any more. Perhaps Myrna should try Prozac?

Oh, Anna should stop being so sensitive on Myrna's behalf, and wear that DKNY skirt, which Roo had chosen for her. It looked great. Roo had some news. Could Anna be at her house for eight? No, she couldn't tell Anna now. Not over the phone.

No, no. Anna *must* come to the party, if she ever hoped to find a husband. Oh, she should stop being so defensive. Roo had been joking. But, seriously, they weren't at poly now. People their age didn't have proper parties. Not without tablecloths, and couples, and mobile phones, so that they could keep in contact with the babysitter.

And so Anna agreed to drive over to Roo's house, although she was not in the mood for Roo's five-year-old daughter, Daisy, who, last week, had laughed at Anna's shoes.

33

'They're ridiculous,' she had said, as if trying out a new word for size. 'Mummy says you dress like you're a teenager and if you leave it much longer you won't have any children.' She had paused, as if to allow Anna to reflect on her words, before saying, with horrified indignation, 'Why is your hair all straggly?'

Roo had praised Daisy for the proper use of the word 'straggly'.

Just twenty of the thirty-five minutes' cooking time needed for Anna's haddock in mushroom and cheese sauce had passed by the time Myrna arrived home. By then, Anna had lost all patience with her instant meal, switching off the oven.

'You forgot this,' said Myrna coming into Anna's bedroom with Anna's ready-meal. The cooked haddock was swimming in a frozen sea of mushrooms. 'Whatever it is.'

'I don't want it any more. I've got to get ready. I'm going out – to this party.'

She did go out without make-up, sometimes, but only to bring in the milk. Really, Anna was waiting for a man to say that she was more attractive without it. Then she would stop wearing the foundation. Concealer, the shape and shade of a cigarette stub. Eyeshadow, used since the early eighties. Blusher. It did so irritate her eczema.

'By the way, can you remind our lovely landlord about the house?'

'What do you mean? What about the house?' Myrna sat on Anna's bed, and wrapped herself in the duvet.

'The painting?'

'The outside?'

'Yes.'

'Maybe it's Maybelline,' sang Myrna. 'So, do you *like* these

34

things?' she asked, dipping the wand in and out of Anna's mascara.

'What d'you mean?'

'These singles events?'

'It's not a *singles* event.' She snapped shut her Eye Kit.

'Oh, I thought that was why you were going? Isn't it to meet Mr Right?' said Myrna, pretending confusion.

Anna knew that this was all part of her flatmate's trickery. Her aim, as per usual, was to persuade Anna to stay in, and watch television with her.

'Very funny.' She unscrewed her lipstick.

'So do you still enjoy these "parties"?' asked Myrna, affecting the manner of a bewildered high-court judge from a 1970s comedy show.

'Yes,' she said, irritably, trying to remember the last party she had enjoyed, so that she could use it as an example. 'And no,' she admitted.

'I mean we're thirty-one. How many men are there left at these events?'

'Well, apparently, there'll be a Tom there tonight. Why don't you come with me? He might have a friend for you.'

Myrna's eyebrows went up at that. 'Oh *yes*, Anna,' she said. 'Let's turn ourselves into characters from an American sit-com. We can go on dates every week. They can end in a really comic way.'

Myrna felt that she could do without sex, in a television age. Gregory, who had fallen for Myrna in a dramatic way (he had graffitied her name – *Myrna Lomond* – on the undercarriage of a bridge), had found this out to his cost. They had met at an evening class. Myrna's life drawings were, Gregory said, intriguing.

'You're the only woman I've ever met,' he had said, 'who knows how to draw the penis.'

35

But even Gregory, who was interested in women for their minds, had found Myrna's lack of enthusiasm depressing. He, for one, loved life. Whereas Myrna thought it might go away if she didn't get out of bed in the morning. Besides, as Gregory had said, even Gregory needed sex.

'God, I feel unhappy,' said Myrna now, her voice sounding as if it was being played at the wrong speed.

'What's wrong?' asked Anna, still trying to blend in her foundation.

'Well . . . Just that gang who raped that woman in the cave.'

'Oh.'

'And Kosovo.'

Anna did not have the stomach to ask what was happening in Kosovo. Myrna was always happy to supply her with the details of any war. The skin dripping from skulls. The women raped with baseball bats. The children savaged by Alsatians. Bodies taken apart, their organs found in black sacks. Men hung upside down and bled to death.

'How are you getting there anyway?' Myrna was terrified of most modern-day things. She referred to Anna's car as a 'killing machine'.

'Car.'

If Anna left the washing-machine on at night, it would flood, said Myrna. It could electrocute them. God knows what was happening to them whilst they slept. Electric cables gave them cancer, as did Anna's cleaning woman, with her hygiene products and her mobile phone.

Fruit was filled with pesticides. It might be rare, but light-ning *killed*. How could Anna party, after the Holocaust? Did she *know* what was going on in the Middle East? Did Anna realise the extent of Saddam's chemical weaponry?

'Just be careful,' Myrna had said, as Anna left the house.

'God, it's cold out there.'

'That's just what I'm trying to tell you,' said Myrna. 'Remember, if you run out of petrol, don't get out. Just lock the windows and *scream*.'

And so Anna drove all the way to the Hastings household, in Tufnell Park, steeling herself for Roo and Warren's arguments, Daisy's honest brutality, and the stench of Oscar's nappies, Waitrose-bagged and waiting to be binned in Roo's hallway.

Roo, wrestling Oscar into a grey Babygro. 'Do you love Mummy? Love Mummy lots?' Warren, spreading out his *Master Atlas of Great Britain* on the desk. Roo, shouting at Daisy, who was screaming out from her bedroom, 'Shut up, Daisy. Warren, Anna wants to get to Shepherd's Bush. Not Scotland.'

Warren suddenly becoming bored, and slamming shut the book.

Roo saying, 'Don't go into Daisy's room. She's *got* to know that the world doesn't revolve around her.'

Warren picking up a surprised Oscar, sailing him through the air. 'Well, of course, darling. We all know that the world revolves around Roo.'

Roo suddenly angry, and moving the jaws of a crocodile glove puppet up and down in front of Oscar. Warren saying, 'Leave him alone. He's enjoying this,' and swinging Oscar to his left from side to side. Roo running after Warren and Oscar with the glove puppet. Oscar lying on top of Warren, and laughing. Roo saying, 'That's just wind. He *loves* Crocky.'

Now that they had kids, Roo and Warren had a focus for their arguments. Before that, their rows could be about anything, including what their rows had been about. Roo telling Warren that he should lose that stomach. Warren

37

telling Roo that she was the cause of his irritable bowel. Roo drinking all of Warren's soya milk in the fridge.

They competed in their careers: Warren, who worked in the City, felt that it all came down to How Much One Earned. Roo, who was an arts reviewer for *Mz* magazine and wrote a column – 'The Voice Of Ordinary Women Everywhere' – felt that income was macho. Her husband thought too much about that sort of thing. She had written about that, as well as about all other of her private feelings, for the emotional pages of *Mz* magazine.

Roo kept her cuttings book on display, yawning whenever Warren talked about his day. Warren felt that his wife's family – the Longworths – were lower middle-class. How lucky it was for Roo that she hadn't lived under a feudal system. She could not have survived. Not without the Hastings name. 'One only has to meet the Longworths,' he would say, in the manner of a character from a Victorian novel, behaving as if, rather than simply taking his name, Roo had stolen it. How lucky it was for her that they were now in a classless society.

'Come the revolution,' his wife would mutter.

Now according to Warren, Daisy was a daddy's girl. Whenever he came home from business trips, Daisy would throw herself at Warren, screaming, 'Daddy, Dad . . . What have you bought me? Now that you're back, can we have cake?' He took Daisy to McDonald's, built baby Oscar a toy farm from a highly complicated instruction manual.

Warren felt that the father/first-born-son relationship was special.

The mother, realised Roo, was paramount. Oscar and Daisy had come out of her body; it was as if they were a part of her digestive system. ('Well, you *treat* them like digestive waste.') No matter how much Warren did, she would be

38

forever umbilically tied to Daisy. When her husband hurt Daisy, that hurt *her*. For example, their daughter had cried when Warren had refused her a new dress from The Gap; and so too had she.

She had been the one to purée all of Oscar's food.

'You treat our children as if they were Tamagotchis,' Warren said. 'Feeding, washing, changing. When what they need is active play.' Besides, he had taught Daisy to read. Warren paid all of the Hastings' bills. But Roo had soothed Oscar's chicken-pox. *She* had taught Daisy all of her gross motor skills.

'Why not let Anna just follow us?' Roo asked now.

'No,' said Warren. 'We'll only lose her.'

'But we have to wait for the babysitter. What if we miss Tom?'

'I tell you what. Why doesn't Anna decide who to have sex with?'

'Why should she? *I* can't.'

'Look, d'you want another row? I'll always win.'

'It's not *about* winning.'

'Oh no, don't tell me, it's about taking *part*.'

'Why do you – always – have to *start*?'

And so, there was Roo wondering aloud whether Oscar would ever recognise his daddy, what with so many of Warren's business trips. Did anyone actually speak Latin – Warren's university degree – or was Roo missing something here?

Warren *merely* saying that Anna should arrange her own relationships. Then, one of them might work out. Or didn't Roo learn that, or indeed, anything else, at the University of the A4 Intersection Near Broadstairs? Oh, sorry – Arndale Poly. Whereas Warren, as he felt he should remind everyone, was an alumnus of a 'proper' university.

Anyway, Roo was only truly successful at having Warren's beautiful kids.

'Well, good,' said Roo. 'Because I'm eight weeks pregnant.'

'You're *what*?'

('Oh, *congratulations*.')

'How *could* you?' said Warren.

('Was that what you wanted to tell me?')

'I don't believe it.'

('I should, er, go.')

'Didn't you bloody well *think*?'

'Didn't *I* bloody well think?'

And so began another Battle of the Hastings.

Chapter Three

If she turned left at the traffic lights, Anna would find
Peterborough Road, and the party. ('It's just that I thought
you were using a *sponge*,' Warren had shouted at Roo.) The
party was at 13 Perceval Road, behind the Peterborough
Arms in Shepherd's Bush. It was simple to find, Roo had
said, glaring at Warren. Anna should drive along Spencer
Street, cut through Tracy Street. She should take a left at
Peterborough Road. It was very clearly signposted. ('Oh,
and contraception is my bloody responsibility, is it?')

Warren had argued that Anna should miss out Spencer
Street altogether. Instead, she should take a right at the
weak bridge sign on Tracy Street. That would lead her to
Peterborough Road. Spencer Street, Warren had reminded
his wife, was murder on a Saturday night.

('Well, what d'you want me to do? Get rid of it . . . ?'

'I'm not *saying* that.'

'Because it's fully formed, Warren. I mean, even at this
stage it has a rudimentary brain.'

'So – poor thing's like its mother then.')

There was a no left turn sign at the traffic lights, and
Anna pulled up outside Mothercare. She could smell the
dense, black smell of other people's exhausts. It was dark,

and she fumbled on the floor for a London road map. Then she remembered that her father had fixed the car light. A retired civil engineer, Don was an expert at fixing things.

Switching on the light, Anna found *The Royal London Road Map*. She thumbed through it without much enthusiasm. If only her father was there to help her now. The map was falling apart, west London hanging by a thread. Dad would tell her what to do.

Hammersmith came out in her hands.

She wondered whether simply to turn round and go home. But what if Tom turned out to be the man who helped her to sleep at night? Still, Anna had had to compromise even with this dream-man, thinning his hair and ageing his skin. Even in the dark, deep under her duvet, that fascinating, youthful, imaginary male was beginning to seem fantastical, alongside Anna.

She recognised him in a way she often did English people abroad – half-relieved to see another fair-skinned, polite type, and half-repulsed by all that Britishness, in that it reminded her of home. He was her anti-dream-man, adjusted. An even paler imitation, in fact.

Their eyes met reluctantly across a room crowded with pretty, animated men in skinny-ribbed t-shirts and sullen women ironically wearing hair accessories. He smiled at her. And Anna smiled back at him, but only in an effort to appear happy. He was even less handsome than she had imagined him. His hair, for example, was between colours. A shade less than blond. A shade fairer than brown.

Everyone else was oh-so young. A generation had grown up whilst Anna had been indoors these last ten years, watching television. They all appeared to be at ease with themselves. Ethereal-looking. Anna felt as if she had drifted backstage midway through a student production of *A Midsummer Night's Dream*. Again, she caught the eye of Anti–Dream-Man (adjusted to fit the brutality of reality), who was acting as awkwardly as Anna felt.

Now, she was going from room to room, hoping to find Roo, and realising that she too had felt young enough until this evening.

She had always, for example, felt far more comfortable with schoolgirls, hogging the back carriage of the train, than when surrounded by any of Roo's married, mother, mortgaged friends.

But she was now turning into her mother. Seeing a woman in a bra-top and slip, she thought à la Barbara, *Lovely, dear. But why are you wearing your underwear?* In another room, wallpapered with speakers: *Lovely music, dear. But can you hear yourself think?* By the time Anna reached the dining room, and saw people sniffing the powdered lines of cocaine laid out on the table, she was thinking, *Oh dear. In my day* . . . And that was it for Anna.

That was her mother's favourite expression.

In Barbara's 'day', women put themselves in the path of men. They made it their business to find husbands. Marriage, as they knew, buttered one's bread. Couldn't Anna, she would ask Anna, find anyone? Well, if she was going to be so picky. In Barbara's day, you married someone and that was it.

Anna had said, 'But surely you loved Dad when you married him?'

But no, in Barbara's day, one didn't fall in love. Not then. She had loved Your Father's Friend Antony, anyway. Surely Anna knew Antony Haverstock? Balding? Shiny head? Short, rather fat legs?

In Barbara's day, it did not matter if the man was attractive

43

or not. One married the man anyway. The reason she hadn't married Antony, was because Antony preferred Audrey. Barbara had said this as if she was saying, 'Antony preferred margarine.'

Now Anna knew that, by thinking *In my day*, she must finally have had her day. In Anna's day, for example, there had of course been cannabis – but drugs had moved up a class or two since then. Although Justine Quealy, who had been an art student in London, would have argued that, even in 1986, it was only a matter of knowing where to look. Anna had hung out with the wrong sort of people.

Anna had always lagged behind little friend Justine. At thirteen, just as she had formed buds, bursting through her childish vests, Justine had bought a cup-size B.

'Don't worry. That's just nature's way,' said Anna's mother.

She had dreamt of waking up as Justine, or at least the type of girl to be able to use the word *fuck* naturally and in context. A girl like Justine, who had a tattoo, and was brave enough to try out tampons. But even Anna's boyfriends had been imaginary. She spoke only the language of romantic teenage magazines.

Which Boy's Type Are You?

*If you ticked mostly Cs, you don't care **what** the boy's like. **The Flirt** has oodles of Zip and Zing. Stud or shy, it doesn't bother you: you'll be there, oozing summer fun, and chatting up **all** the fellas!*

While Anna, at her first mixed-sex party, had oozed summer fun, Justine had lost her virginity. Skinning up her first spliff

44

with party host Russell Cocker, she had laughed at Anna, for whom danger lay in the fruit bowl. A fruit bowl stirred in with alcohol.

'Have a fucking drink,' said Justine.

'I *can't*,' Anna had wailed, as her friend swigged Russell Cocker's cider and smoked spliffs. A hazy image of adulthood came to Anna. It involved grown men clinking crystal. It involved grown women, sitting around a fondue set, dipping.

'Sorry,' said Anna now, as a man elbowed her in the ribs. She was trying to find the kitchen, and Roo and Warren. But there were too many people in this long, narrow hallway.

'*Roo.*'

It was at times like this that Anna wished Roo had a different name. Or even that she had kept the full-length Rosemary. Calling out that name, Anna felt like some children's television presenter addressing her silly, ne'er-do-well puppet. At other times, Anna wished that her own name could be shortened. She would have felt more loved had complete strangers called her Pixie, say, or Squirrel.

Roo didn't hear Anna, anyhow. She was talking to a man in a brown suede jacket and a seventies shirt.

'I'm a Webmaster,' he said, as Anna stood there, ignored by Roo.

'Oh *really*?' Roo giggled. But she was only flirting because Warren was within hearing distance. The conversation was for her husband's benefit, rather than the Webmaster's. That was clear – to Anna at least.

'I really can't believe you're *thirty*. You look *eighteen*.'

'Tell that to my husband.' She looked at Warren, who was busy drinking beer, and being bored against the oven. 'I'm just old. The only men who'll look at me are obstetricians.'

'*Noo*,' said the Webmaster, spluttering with laughter, and lager. 'And don't tell me you've got children?'

'Yeah, I'm just some huge mumsy type now.'

'*Hardly.*' His eyes ran the outline of Roo's body.

'Yeah, well, after two-point-four children . . .'

'Point-four?'

'I'm actually pregnant.'

Roo looked satisfied, as if she had just realised that she was about to beat the national childbearing average. Warren belched.

'I don't believe that,' said Webmaster, shaking his head. '*Pregnant?* Wow. A mother. You don't look old enough.' The fact of her being pregnant did not put him off. Not now that he was in his stride.

'Well, we're looking younger and younger, us mothers,' said Roo, examining her wedding ring as if it had suddenly appeared. 'We're like policemen.'

'Hell-*o*?' said Anna, now feeling that it was her duty – if only for Daisy and Oscar's sake – to interrupt this dangerous flirting-by-numbers game.

1) Roo tosses hair, giggles, and tucks her chin slightly down.
2) Webmaster arches his back, stretches his pecs, laughs loudly, and tugs his collar.
3) Roo tells her obstetrician joke and bends her head coyly to the side.
4) Webmaster 'accidentally' touches her with his right hand.
5) Roo describes herself as 'huge', even though she is so thin that all her fat looks as if it has been sucked out of her by machine.
6) Webmaster gazes at her as if he is unable to imagine

46

anything going in or out of Roo's body, let alone a) a husband, and b) two children.

7) Anna isn't going to wait to find out.

'Oh, it's you,' said Roo, reproachfully.

Anna had guessed that she had done something wrong. She had felt the vibes; and the feeling was familiar, because, despite all of her experience, Anna still felt her failings as Roo's friend. She knew that there was more expected of her. Roo was a better friend than she could ever be – on hand with the white wine and the Belgian chocolates whenever there was a crisis on.

She was warmer, too, and generally more tactile than Anna, who hated to be hugged unless it was clearly a part of sex, and a definite precursor to penetration. Yes, Anna was inhibited. Although, for that, she blamed her mother. Barbara had never been one for showing affection, saying that she preferred to leave 'all that rubbish' to the younger generation.

'*So*. Have you met Tom?'

'How could I? I don't know him. By the way, you gave me such odd directions . . .'

'I *knew* you'd blame my directions.'

'Is Tom here? Oh, and congratulations again – about the baby.'

'Yeah.'

Roo turned away from the Webmaster and spoke more quietly.

'Anna, d'you really think it's good news?' she said.

'Of course I do.'

'I just wish Warren did.'

'Oh, he will soon,' said Anna, smiling hopefully at Warren. 'If I know Warren.'

47

'Anyway, hurry up. I'll introduce you to Tom.'

'Can't I get a drink first?'

'You're not going, are you?' the Webmaster asked, as Roo picked up her plastic cup of wine. It looked warm, like a urine sample.

'Yeah, nice meeting you,' she said casually, as if the Webmaster should have known that she had been flirting only to keep her hand in. It had hardly been subtle. Roo was pregnant, for God's sake. She said all this with her stance – which was that of a heavily pregnant woman. (Hands on back, stomach out.) 'Right, Anna, let's go.'

'I want to get a beer first.'

'Oh, Anna, *please*. We'll miss Tom.'

Frankly, Anna was feigning awkwardness only to lend her meeting with Tom some romance. A delayed introduction, à la *Sleepless in Seattle*, might at least exaggerate the moment when they were finally introduced, and add to it some dramatic tension. Because, otherwise, it was all so inevitable. Tom would be beautiful, and fragile, and creative, in an off-the-wall way. Everything, in fact, that He had been.

'Oh OK, I'll meet this Tom first.'

The only difference would be that, with Tom, the relationship would reach some sort of a conclusion. She would marry him, and they would visit garden centres together. Shopping complexes. They would have four children – all variations on herself; and, eventually, they would die, plotted in the same yard. They would have matching headstones. At that point, even Anna's mother would allow her to rest in peace.

Roo led Anna along the hallway and into the living-room. She stopped to look around, saying, 'Yeah, there he is.' And, yes, Anna had been right, because Roo was leading her towards a man very like Him – his cheekbones visible across a crowded room.

She said 'sorry' to Anti-Dream-Man, who was in her way.

'*Tom*,' said Roo, grabbing Anti-Dream-Man's arm.

Anna had to admit it, she had been excited at the prospect of meeting the man with the cheekbones. So, Anna had to admit it, she was now disappointed. Tom was so ordinary. (Of average height.) His face was instantly forgettable, in fact; and his blond hair clearly erred on the side of brown.

Yes, Tom was the quiet friend of the movie's hero – his role to offset other people's good looks. 'Other people' such as Cheekbones, who was grinning at either Anna, or at Roo. She only wished that she knew at whom.

'So, Tom, I was telling you about Anna's . . .' started Roo, tailing off as if she had suddenly lost all interest in Anna. 'Oh, there's my cousin,' she said, leaving Anna to stand there, awkwardly, staring at a line where the wallpaper met, and wishing herself at home, with Myrna. Cheekbones, meanwhile, had vanished.

'Oh shit, sorry,' said Tom, as someone pushed past him, spilling his drink on to her sleeve.

'No,' said Anna. 'My fault. Sorry.' She wiped the wet patch wondering why she was always the one apologising. No doubt if Stalin appeared in front of her now, begging forgiveness for his crimes against humanity, Anna would interrupt him to say, 'No, no. I'm sure it was me. *Please* – put it down to my period.'

'So, you're Roo's friend?'

'Yeah. From poly.'

She wondered whether to explain why she had failed to go to university. As a rule, whenever she mentioned the word *polytechnic*, Anna went into long explanations about her inferior Victorian-state-school education, or the examination board's unusually strict marking policy. Sometimes, she referred to the headmaster's drinking problem. But, on this occasion, she did not even go on to explain that, since she had left Arndale Polytechnic, it had been awarded university status.

He did not seem overly interested.

Anna was wondering whether to leave him, muttering something about needing the toilet, but a man interrupted her thoughts, holding out his cigarette to them, and saying in a German accent, 'Will you fire me?', to which Tom replied,

'Nope. Don't smoke. As from today actually,' which was a quaint enough coincidence to persuade Anna to stay put.

'I gave up smoking today too.'

'Will you *fire* me?' Tom repeated, looking after the man. He turned back to Anna, saying 'Must be young people's vernacular.'

'Is that what it was?'

'Yeah. You need a phrase book at this party.'

'Clearly.' (She did like his smile.)

'Don't worry. I'll interpret for you.'

'Thanks.' (Although Anna suspected that all smiles were likeable.)

'Here's a test,' said Tom. 'If a young man approached you at a party, saying, "Will you fire me?", would you a) light his cigarette, b) set fire to him, or c) dismiss him from his present employment?'

At that point, Anna, too, began to smile.

Neither of them could hear themselves above the music. Anna thought about leaving Tom, to find Roo. But Tom had asked Anna whether she would like to go outside. She

50

had said yes, so he was now leading her through the kitchen, and past Roo and Warren, who were arguing over who had been to blame for their argument.

'Look, it's my fault – I must be just so fertile.'

'Oh no. I'm sure it's *me*. Fertility's always run in my family.'

Ripping two cans of beer from the plastic pattern, Tom led her out of the stiff kitchen door, into the back garden, and a smell of end-of-summer grass, which reminded Anna of Russell Cocker's thirteenth birthday. 1980. A wet, green smell. Charlie, fishing his wet tongue around Anna's metal mouth.

Now Anna half-expected to see teenage boys pissing in the garden, sopping the pink roses. Paul Mowbray, puking on the rhododendrons. The reassuring underarm smell of her Mum anti-perspirant deodorant. But it was only Tom, asking, 'Are you OK?'

Because he was dying for a cigarette.

'Yeah, I am too. Mind you, I've got a few years left to smoke . . . If you give up at thirty-five, it's as if you've never smoked. Your lungs are clean at forty.'

'Where did you read that?'

'The *Lancet*.'

Myrna subscribed to medical magazines, because, that way, she could keep up-to-date with all the latest diseases.

'So, really, I ought to pack in as many as I can. Because I'm thirty-one.'

'Well, I've got two years' grace then. I'm thirty-three.'

'But, neither of us has any, so . . .'

'So it's all academic,' admitted Tom.

But Tom wasn't going to give up that easily; he knew that the party hostess smoked. So, he went in search of Roo's cousin. And Anna and Tom's evening together might have ended then, as his cigarette hunt provided her with an opportunity to escape. Indeed, Anna thought of running away to find the toilet, as she had done at thirteen. But, at thirty-one, she didn't have the energy.

At thirteen, she had run away from Charlie, whose hand had crept inside the folds of her ra-ra skirt. 'No. Not that,' said Anna, remembering the words of her agony aunts, Cathy and Clare. *Try not to go Too Far. Never go All The Way. Remember, Personality Counts. Whatever The Boys Might Say* . . .

Anna had run away, sitting for some time in the upstairs toilet. She had dreamt up schemes of shattering the frosted glass, bolting through the tiny window, and escaping through the pink-rose patio. Sipping the half-inch of cider in her cup, she had heard a voice outside, chanting, 'Anna Potter's a *virgin*. Metal mouth's a *virgin*.'

Tom returned with an open, half-empty packet of Silk Cut, tossing it over to Anna and saying, triumphantly 'Half-full.'

She dragged on a cigarette, her lungs inflating. 'I'll just have the one,' she said, looking over the garden fence at a washing line of swinging white lingerie. 'I really am giving up tomorrow.'

'Oh, right. Well, I'll smoke them then. I went through a lot to get these. I had to persuade . . . Apparently, they're bad for my health. Oh, and for the environment as well – according to all those coke-heads in there, anyway.'

'It's become like snuff, hasn't it?' said Anna.

'Yeah, an old people's drug . . . God, I don't even know why I'm here,' he sighed.

'So, why *are* you here?'

'Why am I here? Well, it's my assistant's party, and I

wanted to feel young again. For too long, it's been dinner parties and . . . I feel so ancient.'

It was Anna's turn to say something. Eighteen years on from Russell Cocker's party, and personality finally counted. 'What do you *do*?' she asked eventually, but Anna would have preferred to be judged, not on her character, but on the womanly shape of her Wonderbra.

Because, at thirteen, she had lost her Zip. Not long after that, she had lost her Zing. Her oodles of fun were probably still lying, spent, there in Russell Cocker's living-room.

'I'm a teacher,' said Tom, which led them to discuss careers, and Tom brought up the subject of 'bloody education policies', which led them to discuss politics. Tom said that the trouble with the British was that they would never elect anything other than a Conservative government. Even if it was called New Labour. 'Yes,' she said. But that was because of their first-past-the-post electoral system, which Anna blamed for turning Britain, effectively, into a one-party state.

He looked at her quizzically.

Of course, she usually pretended ignorance about politics, purposely mixing up her political parties, careful that no one should find out about her father, and what he did in his spare time. At her left-leaning polytechnic, Anna would have been a pariah had anyone known that Don Potter was a Conservative Party agent.

There, she had said it. She had been brought up in a household where local by-election results were followed as closely as football scores might be in, say, Tom's home.

Tom laughed, saying that, no, he had been brought up in the same way – although his father was active in his local Labour Party.

Oh, Anna would have preferred that. It would have

helped her credibility, no end, on student demonstrations. As it was, she had always had to behave as if she had never met Margaret-Thatcher-milk-snatcher, or suffered the shame of her father speaking at Conservative Party conferences.

Oddly, Tom was impressed by that. It was as if, although he had always been an avid Arsenal supporter, he couldn't help but be interested in Anna's father, who was the equivalent of a Chelsea centre-forward.

'Are you warm enough?' he asked, squeezing his empty can of lager into a female hourglass shape.

'I'm fine,' said Anna. 'This is my boyfriend's jacket. Well, my *ex*-boyfriend's. We've just split up. So, at least I came away with *something*.'

That led the conversation on to relationships. He said that there hadn't been any women for a while. Anna talked about Him. Then, at the risk of boring Tom, Anna brought Him up again. How He had hated aftershave and big cities. How, underneath all that 'front', He could be lovely.

'You're still into this man then?'

'I know – I talk too much about him.'

'That's fine. You talk about Him as much as you want.'

So they talked about His writing and His sensitivities, until Tom said, in a teacherly voice, that Anna might like to go easy on the grass.

'What?'

'Well, you're pulling it out by the handful.'

For some reason, that reminded Anna of her ex-boyfriend. So they talked some more about Him. How, underneath all that charm, He could be evil. His refusal to see Anna on Friday nights. His other women.

'And you thought that that was a good basis for a relationship?'

'Well, of course not. But what *is*, d'you think?'

'I don't know. Staying power?'

'Ah, but Roo and Warren have that,' said Anna, still pulling up strands of grass.

'You know, they've been together for *sixteen years* . . . ? I mean, if you don't count Roo's other boyfriends, in between. Or Warren's women. Before they were married, I mean. Sixteen *years*. So, staying power can't be everything.' Sometimes Anna thought that their relationship was based entirely on sex.

That sounded good to Tom.

That might have led them to discuss sex. But Anna thought that the conversation had gone far enough. She was so tired. She should get home. Yawning, as if to underline her point, Anna picked up her duffel bag as, behind them, the house flickered with sounds.

Tom said that he had to make a move too. Anna looked up at him wondering whether – if push came to shove, tomorrow – she would be able to pick his face out of an identity parade. But she doubted it. He had no distinguishable features.

Tom said that he would call a cab. But, first, he would walk Anna to her car.

'It's the blue one. Ah, there.'

Would she, er, give him her telephone number? They should meet up. It would be nice to hear more about her *ex*. And Anna scrawled down her number on the cover of a schoolgirl's exercise book. But only because, as per usual, she had a pen handy.

The problem with Tom was that he was so ordinary. Plus, as he must have realised, being a chemistry teacher, there had been very little chemistry.

*   *   *

That night, Anna dreamt that she was back at poly.

'D'you think Tom *liked* me?' Roo was saying.

'I wouldn't have thought he's your type.'

'I know. What shall I *do*? He was all over me.'

'Was he?' Anna said, doubtfully. And quickly: 'I mean, I didn't see.'

'Why didn't you introduce us before?' she dreamt Roo saying.

'I did. But you liked Him then. You know? My *boy*friend?'

'Oh God. I don't know what to do. Was Tom a bit, well, common, or was that just me?'

'Look, Roo, there's something you ought to know . . .'

'You've *got* to have a party . . .'

'I'm going to marry him.'

'*You're* going to marry him?' she said, her voice acquiring an urgency. 'Anna, give me his number. I've *got* to call him.'

Chapter Four

Anna still stank of cigarettes. At Saturday's party, she had only smoked one. On Sunday morning, she had resisted buying a new packet. But in the afternoon, and purely by chance, Anna had discovered at the bottom of her Memory Box a half-empty box of Marlboro. Of course, the tobacco had been stale – they had been her first ever post-coital cigarettes, circa 1986.

They had belonged to the director of her polytechnic play: Oscar Wilde's *A Woman of No Importance*. The director had given Anna the leading role, taking her virginity. Not long after that, he had taken her to the cinema.

But by then they had both known it was over. 'I think we'd both agree that it's over,' he had said. 'Not time wasted, though,' he had argued. 'I got so much out of my relationship with you.' Anna had got, for her Memory Box, those Marlboro cigarettes, a gift compilation of his favourite songs, and two cinema ticket stubs.

Her second sexual relationship had left Anna with a *Piers the Ploughman* script and a foil-wrapped chocolate heart, the price label still affixed. *30p*.

Her third sexual relationship had added to her Memory Box a photograph of her boyfriend in his army uniform, a kibbutz entertainment programme, and a love letter. He had typewritten that he respected Anna too much to 'let it go on and on'. Besides, he had been sleeping with another woman.

Anna's fourth sexual relationship had generated more. There was the man's toothbrush clogged up with Colgate, the key to his flat in Finsbury Park, a 1,000-lire note, a Mardi Hotel serviette, a 1993 Valentine card, the dregs of his shampoo for Fine But Dry hair, a 1994 Valentine card, a chipping from a china mug that he had thrown at Anna in an argument, a drunken note, in which he had pleaded with Anna to 'get back with him', a proper, posted letter in which he had begged Anna 'not to split up with him' (*Love*, he had written, *is forever*), and a beermat with *To comemorate getting back with Anna* scribbled across the Carlsberg logo. By then, it had not mattered that Bryan had not known how to spell the word *commemorate*.

Finally, another letter. A letter that Bryan 'hated writing'. But he was afraid that he didn't love Anna any more.

Her fixth sexual relationship had left Anna with a cloakroom ticket for a Spanish nightclub, his Spain-to-Britain plane ticket, and a packet of condoms. Judging by the number left in the packet, that relationship, too, could not have lasted long. Anna had imported Alfonso after a beach holiday. But he hadn't looked as good once she had got him home.

Now she remembered him only in bed. His left eye full of the junk of sleep. The skin on his stomach, bitter-chocolate from the Spanish sun. The blanket-stitch of hair from belly-button to groin.

Number Six had left Anna with his business cards. Number Seven, a brown paper bag which read: *Danny Quin – a name in quality fruit*.

Yesterday, Anna had packed away all of her memories of Him. The tickets for the opera, the theatre, the ballet. The dog lead – found on their fourth date, the trinkets from their Winchester weekend away – a complimentary shower cap, a tiny bottle of all-over body moisturiser, a bath-flannel, and an emergency sewing kit.

He had been Anna's eighth relationship. Any more, and Anna would have to start lying about her sexual history.

Monday morning, and today being the start of her new job, and a new Anna Potter, she couldn't help calling. She wanted Him to know about her Absolutely New Beginning.

('So am I going to get Sonia's knickers off?' He asked.

'What?'

'Well, are you going to move in with her?'

'What? So, let me get this straight? You wanted me to move in with Sonia so that I'd *introduce* you . . . ?'

'*Re*-introduce me.'

'You fucking *bastard*.')

Of course, that call led to another cigarette, stamped out in a mug which read World's Best Dad.

The mug had been a Father's Day gift, which Myrna's father had returned.

'Do you want this?' Mr Lomond had asked Myrna, last year. 'Only I'm clearing out the loft.'

Monday morning, and today being the start of a new job, Anna's father, Don, telephoned to wish his daughter luck. 'And to say, luck doesn't come into it any more,' said Don on the telephone. 'It's hard work that's wanted now.' She could hear him puffing out his chest. 'This Pammy Lowental will want to see if you've got the stuff, because *Problem Call*'s a whole new ball-game. You're going to have to be on the ball there, Anna. It's a tough world out there. You can never, ever, stop building up your CV . . .'

Anna heard the smack of mail falling on to the doormat. 'Hang on a sec, Dad. It's the post,' she said, wanting to check whether there was anything from Him. He had promised to return all of her love letters.

'Yes, I sent you something,' said Don, who regularly sent job adverts to Anna. Job adverts that Myrna would collect.

'An effective communicator, you must be able to produce a high standard of work under pressure . . .'

'This is an exciting opportunity for a dynamic manager to head the unit . . .'

'Are you the highly motivated professional we're looking for . . . ?'

Delightedly, Anna found a plump parcel addressed to her, returning with it to the phone. Delightedly, because she didn't receive much post – although for that she blamed the postman.

'Anyone would think this was my first job,' she said, picking up the phone again, and studying the unfamiliar handwriting on her parcel.

'Well, that celebrity programme was all very fun and good,' said Don. 'Late at night and all that light-heartedness. But this is reality now. You won't be able to prance about in this job. Around lunchtime, people will be listening . . .'

'I don't prance, Dad,' said Anna, trying to open her parcel. She hadn't pranced for days.

'Oh yes. A joke. Well, fine. I've *always* thought you could do something research-wise . . . So I've been cutting out some articles, which I think you'll find useful. They're all problem pages. I found them in magazines and newspapers. What they'll do is to show you how different agony aunts reply. Show you how many solutions there are. You can *impress* this Pammy.'

60

'You really didn't have to bother, Dad.'

'Well, maybe you should bother a bit more, Anna. Maybe life is *about* bothering.'

Her father had spent his life bothering. He was a Conservative Party agent in a Labour stronghold – one of Labour's safest seats in the country – and proof that, frankly, anything was worth the bother. Because, as Don wouldn't tire of telling anyone, he had seen the local Conservative Party take a bigger share of the vote, year-on-year, with every single election.

'Anyway, I'll see if I can find some more problems for you.'

'Don't worry. You've given me more than enough.'

There was silence. Meanwhile, Anna found a pair of scissors, and cut open the parcel. ('Ah. A joke,' said her father, finally. 'Fine. A joke.')

Anna's bubble-wrapped pen fell out. ('Well, that's fine, Anna. That's fine.') There was a note too. *You left this behind. I let the flat to a friend in the end. Sorry. Hope all's well. Love, Sonia.* ('Let's all joke,' said Don sadly. 'Let's all just make jokes.')

All of the long, polished corridors looked the same. The top floor, where *Problem Call* was recorded, looked to Anna very much like any other. The coffee machine was the same as it had been on floor three. She was still able to have her A6: the coffee first, then a squirt of milk, then an avalanche of sugar.

Not one of the pine-wood doors said *Problem Call*. For all of her years at Radio Central, Anna was lost. She kept on passing the same glass-panelled office. A woman watched Anna pass by, and pass by, and pass by.

'I'm looking for *Problem Call*,' said Anna, but the woman couldn't hear her through the thick glass.

'I can't lip-read,' she smiled as Anna came into her office. 'These days, everything's double-glazed.'

'D'you know where the *Problem Call* office is?'

'A-*ha*,' replied the woman, delightedly, pleased to be of service to somebody. She tore open a Snickers bar with her teeth.

She must have been up here for years, thought Anna. Imprisoned behind all that glass. The woman took a bite of chocolate, and crumbs of peanut fell on to her desk.

'Well, you've found *accounts*,' she said.

'So d'you know where . . . ?'

'Of course. They don't make it easy, do they?'

'No,' agreed Anna, smiling in an effort to appear kind.

The woman took out a pad of A4 from her bottom drawer. *She's going to draw me a map*, thought Anna. The woman tittered and muttered, 'I thought I was having another relapse, seeing you walk past all those times.'

'It's OK. I'll find the way.'

She was beginning to feel uncomfortable.

'Oh, no, it's a pleasure,' said the woman, taking another bite of her bar. 'I'm just glad I'm not going *mad*.' She tittered. 'Again.' The word stayed there, between them. 'Ho, hum,' said the woman airily, as if people were going mad again everywhere. What could one do? 'Well, here you are. If you get lost again, I'm always here. Just ask for Sarah.'

Anna smiled, instantly forgetting the name. She took the map. Then she asked directions from another passer-by, who happened to be a tall and beautiful man in a soft, green suit.

'Excuse me, I'm . . .'

'Lost?' interrupted the dark and softly-spoken man.

He was able to show Anna the way. 'So, why do you need *Problem Call*? I'm Sean, by the way.' Sean put out his hand for her to shake, explaining that Anna would first have to pass through two other open-plan offices. Anna shook the firm hand, and followed Sean through the Development Unit. 'They come up with so-called *ideas* here,' he explained quietly in Anna's ear. 'Although any secretary worth her salt has such ideas in a day.'

Sean smiled at a group of secretaries.

'I've been at Radio Central for years, actually, as an operator,' said Anna, trying to keep up with his pace. 'It's ridiculous that I don't know my way around,' she muttered, as he led her past the controller's office.

'Oh, that's fine. I don't know why Duncan gets an office of his own,' said Sean confidentially. 'Everyone should be made to work in open-plan.'

'This is really out of your way.'

'No, not at all. I'm guest-presenting *Problem Call* this month. So I'll be working with you, I suppose.'

'You're presenting with Pammy? Oh, right. What's your surname?'

'Just for a month. They're doing my special subject. Closure,' he said, grinning. 'And it's Harrison,' he said, reaching a door that read *Problem Call*.

Sean Harrison.

Pammy Lowental was sitting on a large desk. Her swinging, fattish legs were caked in American-tan tights. 'Take your time,' she said slowly, as Anna put down her cup of coffee.

'Er, is this my desk?'

'Well, I don't know about Jimmy *Salad*,' said Pammy, in a vaguely American accent. 'But we tend to hot-desk it at *Problem Call*. We're not territorial here. Although don't sit *there*, honey. I call that the office thinking desk.'

'Oh, right.'

'Come sit here with me. Pull up a chair. You can shadow me this morning.'

Anna picked up her flimsy cup of coffee. She knew that hot-desking meant that, with the exception of management, no one would be able to find a seat. She dragged a chair to a desk that was clearly Pammy's.

There was no mistaking it. Everything was branded. The cuddly bear, for example – Pammy's name knitted through its stomach. The stapler with Pammy's name plastered on top of it. Had Pammy been any more 'territorial', her desk would have been surrounded by a moat and defended by armed forces.

'So, Anna. Perhaps you'd like to start by telling me why it is that you're late? On your very first morning? Because it's not the best foot to start out with, is it? Hmmm?'

'Well, I . . .'

'No, *go* on,' Pammy interrupted, raising her hands and dropping them back down in her lap. Her eyes glazed over. 'I'm *ever* so interested.'

Rather than breasts, Pammy had a bosom. Anna could not imagine the huge shape in the sweater separating, except by brutal force. And no one would dare to use force with Pammy Lowental. Anna tried to escape the bosom's glare by looking up at her face. But there was that dull, hard-red lipstick. Then the mouth, which looked as if it had been kept for a fortnight in the freezer.

'Well, I couldn't . . .' She couldn't think of a suitable excuse.

'You see, I am concerned, Anna. That you should be late into work on your first day. I don't think that shows respect to *me*. To the programme. But most of all, I don't think it shows an ounce of respect to you.'

She sounded as if she was about to burst into tears,

or song. Of course, Myrna would argue that Anna had a problem with authority figures. But listening to Pammy, whose tone was polite to the point of hysterical, Anna felt that, in truth, authority figures had a problem with Anna.

Was she – they would ask – listening to them? Could she wipe that smirk off her face? Hello – was Anna a part of this meeting? Did she think liver just jumped into a frying pan and cooked itself? It was only a tiny injection – she was behaving like a baby. They weren't speaking for their own benefit.

'Now, I know you have experience with phone-ins generally. Although I don't have much time for the Jimmy Salad show. Or for Jimmy *Salad*, come to that. But I have my own personal reasons for that. No. The difference between my show and Jimmy's is that the people who ring me up are in *trouble*.'

Pammy lingered over the word 'trouble' as if she was enjoying the sound of it.

'*Problem Call* is *not* entertainment. The callers need to be treated with respect. Anna, I might be your boss. But I too deserve a little respect. I too am a *human being*. Just because I am senior to you, on this programme – in this situation – does not mean . . .'

Anna gazed, absentmindedly, at the bridge of shiny hardback books above Pammy's head The faded photograph of her new boss, standing beside Shannen Doherty. *Pammy meeting the stars of Beverly Hills 90210*. Beside it was a photograph of her shaking hands with a former Prime Minister. *Pammy meeting John Major. Hove. 1992*.

Care-givers' award ceremony, 1995. In that photo, everyone held hand-shaped plaques. Pammy stood at the edge of the celebrity group photo which included the Duchess of York and Carol Smillie.

'You'll find, Anna, that I'm not an old-fashioned boss. Actually, I like everyone – from Mike, my producer, all the way down to you – to call me Pammy. I like a bit of office camaraderie. But rudeness, laziness, selfishness, lateness, or intolerance are some things that I *won't* accept from my team.'

Her 'team' appeared to include a man Anna knew, and was incidentally horrified to see, who was hanging up his raincoat on the largest unavailable hook. The hook couldn't cope with two items of clothing. Anna's jacket wrestled with the man's raincoat. It was a battle of the fittest, and the raincoat won. Anna's jacket fell to the floor in a heap.

'This is Mike, your line manager,' smiled Pammy, as Mike ignored the jacket, sauntering over to his desk as if he had nothing better to do. His body was built to last, and he was wearing a t-shirt to prove it. *Built To Last*, read his big chest. Muscles moved like worms inside his arms.

In a sudden change of tone, Pammy wailed, 'So. Mikey. Let's have a meeting. Tell us what we're *doing*.'

Anna had already made acquaintance with her 'line manager'. Not only that but she had made an awful, and lasting, impression.

'Er, we've already met,' she smiled, watching Mike as he threw on to his desk a plastic carrier bag bursting with huge, hardbacked books and big fruit. 'Hello again,' she tried, but he ignored her, taking out an American-red apple and biting into it. She felt vaguely embarrassed as he exposed the white apple flesh with his teeth, but, still, she smiled at him, wondering whether Mike was about to remind her, as he had last week, that he was black.

* * *

On Friday, Anna had been having lunch in the canteen with Jimmy Salad. They had been discussing Radio Central's need to increase its share of a listening audience. Or rather, Jimmy had talked, and Anna had listened.

'We need to appeal across the whole *spectrum*. There should be programmes for Asians. Jews. It's ridiculous the way we think only in terms of the ordinary, average . . .'

'And other groups.'

Anna had interrupted, only because she was aware of a black guy staring at them. Mike. Anna guessed that he thought that Jimmy sounded racist. Although Jimmy was himself an ethnic minority, being half-Chinese.

'Well, yeah, other races,' agreed Jimmy. 'The Japanese, for example. I bet you could get *them* listening.'

'And black people. Black *Britons*.'

'I don't *believe* it,' said Mike finally, dropping his fork. 'As if we're *one* group.'

'I don't think Jimmy meant . . .' started Anna.

'Not him. I meant *you*, actually.'

Anna was aware of canteen heads staring at her. Anna, who had always hated to be looked at. Although that had not stopped Don driving her around, throughout her childhood, with a megaphone on the roof. '*Vote Conservative . . . Vote Conservative.*' Anna had sat in the back of the car, pretending that the chanting, and, indeed the fatherly figure in the front, had nothing to do with her.

'I suppose you think I'm about to mug you now? Or, don't tell me, I'm a *schizophrenic* . . .'

'Now, come on,' interrupted Jimmy. 'Slow down here.'

'No. I will not just ignore such blatant, flippant racism.'

She felt as if she must have metamorphosed into the type of woman who had a big, bouffant hairstyle and a blue breasted-blazer, living in a strictly white neighbourhood in Surrey. Yet, at poly, Anna had been on hundreds of marches against apartheid. At school, she had *envied* Pritti Poonjay, who had never been forced to eat school dinners – the ice-cream scoops of lumpy mash. The steel taste of corned beef hash.

'No, I didn't mean . . .,' she tried.

'Of *course* we can't be broken down.'

I am myself, she thought suddenly, *part-Welsh*.

'Well, so what am I? African or West Indian?'

'West Indian?'

'You see,' said Mike, triumphantly. 'You can't even tell the bloody difference. That's the trouble with people like you. It's so bloody ingrained, you don't even know it's there.'

He rose, slamming his tray on to a pile of them. Behind him, the stack of trays clattered, as if in applause.

Anna appeared to be in the middle of a meeting, although she wasn't sure at what point it had begun. It might have begun when Mike had brought over a chair, sitting half in front of Anna. (Now she had a restricted view.) Or when Pammy had said, 'So. Mikey, tell us what you did at the weekend?'

Anna stared at the back of his t-shirt, which read, *Built To Be First*. She hoped that Mike would give her an opportunity, at some point, to explain the prejudice that she might, only after years of social conditioning, and unintentionally, have displayed in the canteen on Friday. Meanwhile, she listened to Mike talk about his weekend; and how he and *Frannie* had taken *Charlotte* to see *Postman Pat*.

Frannie had apparently lost a contact lens in the stalls bar.

Anna sat there, smiling or looking concerned in all the right places until, suddenly, she realised that, from where she was sitting, it might look as if she was eavesdropping.

Surely Anna wasn't entitled to know about Fran's advancing breast cancer, or the botch job the builders had made of the bathroom? She was about to move to another desk, when Pammy said, 'Well, that *does* sound like a fun weekend. So, Anna. What are your feelings about our issue this month? Closure?'

Anna paused, whilst working out what to say.

'Oh, yes,' she said at last, taking out her pen from her pocket, in an effort to appear self-assured. 'I met Sean Harrison in the corridor and . . .' But she had lost her confidence and, when that happened, she found it difficult to speak using whole sentences.

'We're doing Closure today?' she asked, as they stared at her. Pammy moved some photographs around her desk, randomly – suddenly snapping, 'Well, really, if you don't have any *opinions* on the subject.'

There was silence for a second.

'Explain to Anna what we *do* on this programme, Mikey. Anna doesn't seem to know anything about *problems*,' said Pammy, angrily picking up a pile of pamphlets from the right side of her desk. She plonked the pile on to the left-hand side, and muttered, 'Why have they sent me a showbusiness operator? Jimmy *Salad*, for goodness sake.'

'The programme's divided into themes,' said Mike. 'This month's theme is Closure. Last month's was Depression. So if anyone phones re depression, you'll know not to put them through.'

Pammy: 'We did that *last* month.'

Mike: 'Yes. Tell them we covered all of that in August.

69

Lithium, Prozac, amphetamines, suicide, morbid disorders. We've covered it all in depth – sometimes for the whole programme – and we don't want to go over . . .'

'Anyway. Closure, Mikey?' asked Pammy, putting on her glasses.

'Right. September's theme. The ability to shut off an episode in one's life,' Mike said, leaning forward. 'To achieve finality. To be able to move on . . .'

'Blah blah blah,' added Pammy, usefully.

'Etcetera. Yes. *Dr* Sean Harrison presenting with you this month, of course . . .'

'I'm pleased we've got Sean on again,' said Pammy, taking off her glasses. She put the chewed-up arm in her mouth. 'We need more *doctors*. More medically qualified people.'

'What we need is more *black* people,' muttered Mike. 'Anyway, Sean's doctorate's in psychology, I think.'

'Well, even *so*. I do feel he should be with us every month. He can talk about any issue, and I tell you something, the fact that he's so devastatingly good-looking certainly doesn't *hurt* the programme, does it, sweetie?'

'This is radio, Pammy.'

'Radio, schmadio. It's the *millennium*.'

As they paused to digest Pammy's theory, Mike's mouth opened. Moments later, laughter poured out. 'You and Sean were *hilarious*, that time, when that *woman* . . .'

He stopped talking, to laugh some more. Anna kept one eye on her cup of coffee, as liquid seeped out.

'What?' asked Pammy, pretending surprise. 'When? I don't know *when*,' she wailed.

'When that woman phoned up about her genital *warts*. You know she'd left her husband to set up some sort of *women*'s union in Africa. And you said . . . ?'

'What was that? D'you know,' she asked, looking at Anna. 'I can't for the *life* of me remember . . .'

'You said, "Well, darling, if you're going to *choose* to patronise a foreign culture, you can't expect only to bring home samples of the local *cuisine*."'

'Right,' said Pammy, disappointedly. Clearly, she had been hoping to hear something more amusing. 'I remember now. *So* . . . Why don't we have Sean on every month, then? I mean, as we have your approval, Mikey?' she said, winking at Anna.

'No. We've got Wilhelm Grohe on next month. He's going to be the man of the moment when *One Month to Happiness* comes out. Hopefully, *all* our listeners will learn to be happy by the end of that month.'

Pammy laughed and squeezed her knees together. 'Let's hope not,' she said. 'Then *we'll* all be out of a job.'

'Maybe so. Anyway. After Wilhelm, we've got Maurice Stowe to do Death for all of November. And how often do we get a good black guy like Maurice on to the show? *Plus*, he's written some great books on bereavement. *Letting Go*. That was published in eighty-seven. *Smiling Through*. Ninety-two. About alternative funerals. And *Keeping Hold of the Memory*. That was last year's big hitter.'

Anna wondered whether to say something. Anything. She felt that, if she didn't say something now, she never would again. So: 'That sounds great,' she said at last, if only to remind herself that she was there.

But her cup collapsed at that moment, leaking coffee everywhere.

She was not capable of summarising in a sentence her own problems. Yet there Anna was, that Monday afternoon – about to précis other people's. Headphones on, she was

71

sitting nervously in a studio waiting for the programme to go on air. Fortunately, Roo had taught Anna how to breathe effectively.

Breathing in, Anna thought of her lunch with Sean Harrison. There had been no room for the two of them at the 'team' table. So they had sat alone in the canteen, together.

Breathing out, she remembered Sean saying that he often felt like the outsider. He rarely fitted in anywhere. Anna had confessed to feeling the same – although only to fit in with Sean.

Breathing in, she recalled overhearing Pammy, at the 'team' table, saying, enviously, 'Look at the way Sean's homed in on *that* one.'

Breathing out, she thought of Mike's half-heard reply: '. . . likes to play God . . . loves the victim-type . . .'

Now, she listened to Pammy as she ad-libbed, talking about the joy of being able to ad-lib so freely on radio.

'Radio is so *intimate*,' oozed Pammy. 'But my producer is giving me dirty looks. And I'm about to be told off, so I think I ought to get back to the script. Because . . . What do we have here . . . ?'

Anna breathed in again. She could see Sean through the studio glass, loosening his tie. Usually, she didn't like older men, or the way their skin slithered like snakeskin down the neck. But he was movie-star handsome, like a darker, sexier Harrison Ford, and Anna wanted now to unbutton the length of his white shirt. She wanted to touch his neck. His hands would slide the top out of Anna's skirt, and she would . . .

She breathed out, hearing Pammy's voice sing out of the loudspeakers, 'Today, we're going to talk about sadness. We're going to talk about anger. We're going to talk about hurt feelings . . .'

Breathing in, Anna reminded herself to cancel her date with Tom. There were too many signs of compromise in Anna's life without adding Tom to it. The stereo, for example, still lacking a CD player. Myrna as a flatmate, growing fatter every day.

'Well, I have with me, here in the studio, Dr Sean Harrison. Regulars of my show will know that Sean can talk about many things. But Closure is his *speciality*. Hello, Sean.'

'Pammy.'

'Good to have you on the programme again. So . . . this is getting to be a regular thing.'

'Isn't it? People are going to talk.'

Yesterday, Tom had phoned Anna. Did she want to 'do something' soon? Anna had said yes, but only because she wanted dating, like flossing, to become a part of her daily routine; and because at least her mother would approve.

Barbara, for one, had never been able to understand young people. Why did they have to take everything so seriously? Didn't Anna meet young men, all the time, at work? Surely they asked girls to go to the cinema, or out for an ice-cream somewhere? How *else* did they find wives? Why didn't Anna simply allow a young man to take her out for dinner? Was that so very hard?

Barbara could not absorb the fact that relationships had changed since the 1950s. Or that dating etiquette was different now. Anna could not possibly tell her mother that Millennium Woman was required to shag after a date. It was expected; although, for that, Anna blamed the women's movement. In the fifties, she would have been married before a man had asked her for sex. Legally, she would have been in a better position to refuse him. Now, it was more difficult. Women's-liberation organisations had helped everyone, she felt, apart from the majority of women.

Women had seemed happier in the 1950s – at least on washing-powder commercials. These days, they had the burden of a modern, high-flying career. But they hadn't been unburdened of any old-fashioned responsibilities. Anna still had to be attractive, and, to that end, hunt around for the latest in hair-care products.

She had suggested to Tom that they meet for dinner on Wednesday – the most unceremonious, neither-one-thing-nor-another day of the week – in the hope that Tom would see the dinner date for what it was. Wednesday, after all, was an evening for washing one's hair, or for watching the midweek episode of *Coronation Street*.

But Anna had agreed to see Tom before she had met Sean Harrison. Now Anna had seen what a man could be. A man who knew how to loosen his tie, sexily.

'So tell me what closure is exactly,' Pammy asked Sean, with almost absolute sincerity. 'I mean, to the ordinary, average person in the street. Like me.'

'Oh, I wouldn't call you average, Pammy.'

'Well, I don't *know* about that,' laughed Pammy.

Suddenly, she was serious. 'In actual fact, I would like to remind my listeners, at this point, that I am *not* a doctor. I'm not a psychotherapist. I'm not a professional. I suppose, what I am is, I'm an ear. An ear that's here for all of my listeners, short or fat or thin. Ugly, or pretty. Disabled, even. Tall, or stupid, or clever. Well, *there*, I think I've covered everyone.

'In short, I take the tangled strings of people's lives. And I untangle them. So, enough with the introductions. Sean . . . ? Explain to me September's theme of Closure . . .'

'Closure is about putting the past behind you. It's about not allowing the past, and what's happened in the past, to bother you.'

74

'I would add that Closure might be an American word, but we *Britishers*' – she stressed her American accent – 'shouldn't treat it as if it's as foreign to us as, say, American football . . .'

'Cheerleaders.'

'Or McDonald's hamburgers.'

'Well, McDonald's is as British now as our currency, of course.'

'So, go on about Closure here,' said Pammy, tartly. 'If something *bad* has happened, do you put that behind you?'

'Exactly that.'

'And how do you do that, Sean?'

'Well, in a number of ways. Say, you've just come through a bad relationship, you say to yourself, "Fine. That was poisonous. But I'm finished with that."'

The back of Pammy's head was nodding furiously.

'But isn't that hard to do?' she said. 'I have been in a number of relationships, which I've known to be bad. Yet I find I'm calling and calling. You know, I can't keep off that phone.'

'Well, don't laugh, Pammy. You could be suffering from an obsessive-compulsive disorder.'

'Seriously?'

'Yes. It's no joke for those suffering. Often, women with OCD go untreated. They're misdiagnosed and treated like hysterical, silly women, but it's a very real problem, in my opinion.'

Anna was suffering from an obsessive-compulsive disorder.

'And, as with any compulsion, you need to learn how to control it. Actually, I'd suggest that you try going phone turkey for a few days.'

'Phone turkey,' giggled Pammy. 'Honey, I like that.'

'Yes, put the phone out of sight. Remove the temptation. Only take incoming calls. It's the same as giving up anything. You have to say to yourself, "It's not that I've lost the addiction to him. It's just that I didn't phone him *today*."'

'Like they say in alcohol dependency groups?'

'Yes. It's the same with any addiction. Smoking, for example. I always advise smokers to burn up a packet of cigarettes in a mug. Watch that yellow stain build up. Then sleep next to the mug.'

'Sleep next to the cigarette ends?'

Sounds repulsive, thought Anna

'It is repulsive,' confessed Sean. 'But it works. Then, of course, you have to avoid cigarettes completely. But *recognising* your problem – being able to put a *name* to it – is the first step.'

'So, that's fine with cigarettes. But getting back to relationships. How do I forget about a *man*? A man without whom – I can tell you, Sean honey – life doesn't feel worth living?'

'Well, if you just can't let go, I would advise you to list all of the *problems* with that relationship. There must have been some, or the affair wouldn't have finished.'

'Right, of course.'

'Then write that list out one hundred times.'

'Like school lines?'

'Exactly. Like lines. It's amazing what that does. Just seeing all of the problems listed really does help. I mean, it's the sentimental memories which hold you back. Those memories need to be thrown out. The letters. The presents.'

'But I like to hang *on* to them. As a reminder of the good times . . .'

'Well, if you really want closure, Pammy, you'll need to sacrifice a little sentiment.'

'True. Good. Yes. Good advice there from Dr Sean Harrison

. . . And we'll be taking your calls throughout the hour on this subject. Closure. How to move on . . . This, of course, is our introductory programme, but we'll be talking about this throughout September. And you know the number. Freecall 0800 678771.'

Button *One* flashed green.

'Hello, *Problem Call*,' said Anna, pressing Line One.

'Is that Pammy Lowental?'

'No. I'm the operator. Can I take your name and age please?'

'Jackie. No, Jane. I'm thirty-six. Well, Jackie.'

She typed: LINE ONE: JANE.

'We'll call you Jane. OK?' asked Anna, offhandedly. She had been trained not to drain a caller of emotion before they were connected to a presenter. Otherwise, the call could be wasted.

'What is it that you want to talk to Pammy about?'

'Well, I heard Pammy talk about bad relationships before,' said Jane, her monotone more natural than Anna's own. 'I've been in a bad relationship since about March, nineteen eighty-nine. My boyfriend gets drunk, and he beats me up, you see.'

BOYFRIEND BEATS HER UP, typed Anna.

Line Two flashed and she pressed it, saying, 'Can you *hold*, please?'

Line Three flashed and she pressed it, saying, 'Can you *hold*, please?'

Line One flashed again and she pressed it, saying, 'I'll put you through to Pammy now, Jane.'

'No. I'm not finished,' said Jane, sounding semi-detached. It was as if she was silently, and simultaneously, having another conversation. 'So, anyway, I've got these four children, and we haven't got hardly any money . . .'

FOUR CHILDREN. NO MONEY.

'I'll put you through now, Jane.'

Mike walked in, saying impatiently, 'Any calls? It's obvious that Pammy's bored stiff.'

'I'll put you through now, Jane,' she said, trying to keep all emotion out of her voice.

'And I've just found out,' added Jane, plainly, 'that my daughter, who's fifteen, is pregnant . . .'

DAUGHTER, 15, PREGNANT.

'. . . by her uncle.'

'Her uncle?' She could hear her words as they broke down into letters.

INCEST.

'Yes, Pete,' continued Jane, coolly, and as if she was reading from a computer. 'It's Liz's father, Rob. He wants to kill Pete now . . .'

'We need a call, Anna.'

'Putting you through, Jane.'

'And what with Rob just out of prison, I've . . .'

'*Anyone*. God, when I was doing your job, I'd have had four lined up by now. Just put someone through, OK?'

'Putting you through *now*, Jane.'

'What I want to know from Pammy is, should I leave him?'

She pressed *Send*, feeling her face heat up.

Jane's problem wiped clear from her computer, and sent to Sean to resolve, Anna turned to Line Two. 'Sorry to keep you waiting. Can I take your name?'

LINE TWO: POPPY. BOYFRIEND MURDERED LAST YEAR.

Listening to Poppy's voice, Anna couldn't stop her hands from shaking. Although, naturally, Anna read about such crimes every day, still it was a shock to hear the victim's voice.

78

Of course, each day she read news headlines describing such horrors.

Yet, tapping Poppy's problem into the computer, Anna realised that she hadn't thought of the people behind such headlines, sitting opposite her on the tube every morning, or walking past her in the street. One never realised just how many people must have been murderers, dressed up. By daylight – she imagined now – they must turn into shocked newspaper readers, like Anna, terrified to turn their tabloid pages.

LINE THREE: **RAY.** FORMER ALCOHOLIC. BASHED HIS EX-WIFE.

She pressed *Send*, grateful to wipe Ray's problem from her screen.

Until now, Anna had thought that all of the horrors Myrna talked about were in Myrna's terrible imagination. After all, nothing had ever happened to Anna, or even to Myrna.

Every morning, she now imagined, a cross-section of the men and women that she saw on the street, or on the tube, must have wiped any excess blood from their bodies, washed off all of that guilty seminal fluid, and covered themselves up, casually, in smart clothes. As every door closed, something must be happening behind it: incest, bigamy, date rape. Anna just hadn't realised it until now.

LINE FOUR: **STEPHANIE.** BOYFRIEND RAPED HER BEST FRIEND.

LINE FIVE: **DONNA.** FATHER VIOLENT. SHOULD SHE ALLOW HIM TO SEE HIS GRANDCHILDREN?

Now she knew what the majority of people went through when they came home. Their husbands there, to bash them in. Their boyfriends abusing their children to 'break them in'.

Pressing Line One again, she overheard Pammy handing

79

Stephanie over to Sean. 'How can Stephanie stop feeling angry, Sean?' asked Pammy, and Anna panicked on Sean's behalf, knowing that he wouldn't have an answer. There *was* no answer. But, there Sean was, easy with his reply. He made life sound so simple.

LINE ONE: **JUDY**. GUILT. SENT CHILDREN TO BOARDING SCHOOL. HOW DOES SHE GET CLOSURE?

LINE TWO: **PIPPA**. RATS IN FLAT. POVERTY LED TO SHOPLIFTING. HUSBAND SCHIZOPHRENIC. SHOULD SHE GET OUT OF THE RELATIONSHIP?

It was only a matter of time, realised Anna, before her current life ended and a different one began. Until now, she had been clever. She hadn't married someone with a mental disease, or lived, even for a short while, in a high-rise block infested with rats.

She felt guilty putting Pippa through. How would Sean, in a two-minute-maximum soundbite, reply? But he was fine.

LINE THREE: **CAROL**. FEEDING DUCKS IN PARK. MOLESTED BY MAN WITH METAL BAR. LIFE RUINED. HOW DOES SHE FORGET?

Had Anna been in the park, just walking through, that very day, feeding the ducks as she was wont to do, her life, by now, would have collapsed. Throwing wet bread into open mouths, with the hope of meeting the approximation of her ideal man, who would be doing exactly the same, she could be caught from behind by a man with a metal bar. He would force Anna into the bushes. How would she cope as his trousers came undone, and he forced himself all over her, his body filthy beside her own?

Only Sean appeared to have the answers.

LINE FIVE: **ANNETTE**. BROTHER KILLED IN CAR CRASH FIVE YEARS AGO. HOW DOES SHE STOP GRIEVING?

Anna would be buried by now at the bottom of a local paper's page four, had she been caught taking a short cut around a no right turn. Right turn, into the supermarket, easily dead. In the right place, at the right time, she had so far avoided the motorway pile-up, her radio tuned to Heart FM, a lorry spilling its load in front of her, forcing Anna to swerve. Or two seconds earlier, another train could have barged into her own.

At least Sean would be there, to pick the pieces up gently.

LINE ONE: CLAIRE: ATTEMPTED SUICIDE AFTER FIND- ING MOTHER IN BED WITH HER BEST FRIEND.

Each time Anna transferred a call, she looked up to catch him looking at her. And although she knew that he was talking to the callers, it was as if, with each call, Sean was addressing her. It was as if, in fact, he could see clear through her.

'Attempting suicide isn't *Closure*, Claire. In fact, it's the reverse. It tends to open up a whole different set of problems . . .'

Finally, all of the lines were full, and Anna could rest, watching Sean as he moved his flop of a dark fringe out of his eyes. She listened as he took the tangled strings of people's lives and untangled them.

Pammy was saying, 'Well, we've *all* of us thought about suicide, haven't we, Sean?' She sounded sympathetic, poss- ibly because Anna was hearing her through a pane of glass.

'I don't know. Have we?'

'You know, I feel better now,' said Claire. 'Just speaking to you.'

'It must have been very painful for you, Claire, even to . . .'

81

'*Very* painful, Claire,' interrupted Pammy. She now sounded bored. 'But my studio manager's gonna kill me unless we go to an ad break. So . . . Can you hang on there?'

'Yes,' said Claire.

'Well, good. But, ah, no.'

Opposite Pammy, Mike drew his finger across his throat. He pointed to the clock on the wall. 'News,' he mouthed.

'Well, I hope we *did* help you out there, Claire,' said Pammy. 'Because I hadn't realised. We're seconds away from the end of the show. And I can't perform a miracle in five seconds. I need a little longer than that. So, you hang on in there, Claire, sweetie. Remember, life is like *shoe* leather. You need to put the shine back in. Polish it up, or it'll wear you down. And we'll be back tomorrow for another slightly different look at Closure. With my special guest for September – Dr Sean Harrison.'

The after-show meeting lasted for more than three hours, merging, in Anna's mind, with a private conversation Pammy had had in public with Mike about her three current boyfriends. Anna was able to digest it later to her flatmate Myrna, thus:

<u>PAMMY</u>, Presenter – THERE WEREN'T ANY GOOD CALLS. REMEMBER, WE'RE HERE TO ENTERTAIN.

<u>MIKE</u>, Producer – TOO MANY DEPRESSIVES. WE DID DEPRESSION LAST MONTH.

'And you wonder why I refuse to work in an office environment. Graduates, unskilled – it doesn't matter,' shuddered Myrna, eating the last of Anna's Granny Smiths. 'They're all packed into offices and forced to answer the telephone.'

'Mmm,' agreed Anna.

'This Pammy woman does sounds dire,' she said, taking

a bite out of Anna's apple. 'Is she why you went and got pissed with this Sean bloke?'

'No. I went and got pissed because, I tell you, Myrna, the world is as shit as you say it is. I mean, the *calls* we got . . .'

'Yeah, like what?'

'Well, like one woman's boyfriend was murdered last year, and she's still . . .'

Myrna snorted.

'You call that a problem? They should try surviving a *war*, then they can talk about problems.'

Everyone had problems, Sean had said. It was simply a matter of locating them. Sean had just bought Anna another glass of wine, and was looking at her thoughtfully.

Sean had asked Anna, Mike and Pammy to the pub for an after-work drink. But only Anna had said yes.

Mike had had to sort out his bathroom mess, and Pammy had had to sort out her boyfriend mess. Pammy had three boyfriends. She had Bruce. She had Boris. She had Archie. Bruce presented the mid-afternoon programme. It was his job to provoke a discussion. He would regularly pick fights with callers, calling them *morons* if they suggested that Bruce was wrong about, for example, international maritime agreements or the European currency convergence criteria.

'I'm an economist, advising the Government, actually, and I wanted to call in, Bruce, to say you've got it wrong about . . .' That would be Bruce's cue to cut the man off, and to push his taped jingle into the machine. *'I'm a moron, a moron, a bleedin' moron.'*

From the numerous, and detailed, discussions which she had overheard Pammy having with Mike, the studio manager, the programme secretary, and the canteen staff, Anna

83

had gathered that her boss was in a long-term relationship with Bruce. She was in a short-term relationship with Archie, and an on-off relationship with Boris.

Although Anna had seen the ugly Bruce – his red-hot lower lip crouching like a small animal in the nest of his beard – she couldn't help feeling envious of the sheer number of men mentioned by her boss. Pammy had men's names coming out of her mouth. Bruce. Boris. Archie.

Anna's envy was a hangover from her school days, when male names would be listed in red pen, like assets, all over exercise books. Justine's rough books had been a rash of boy's names. Anna's had listed only the names Errol and Leee. But they were both from the eighties' soul band, Imagination.

'No, but *I* don't have problems,' Anna said to Sean, her head swimming with wine. 'Not problems compared with your *callers*. I mean, that Claire . . . And that *Stacey*.'

'Claire?'

'She was the one who found her mother in bed with another woman. And tried to commit suicide.'

'Oh right. And the other one?' he asked, laughing. 'Sorry. I have no long-term memory.'

'Stacey?'

'Yes, what was wrong?'

'Her father had decided to become a woman.'

'Right,' said Sean slowly.

'You see now?'

'The point is, you can't *weigh* problems.'

'Oh, I know. But I do feel as if I haven't got anything to complain about,' she said, unhappily.

'Well, are *you* perfectly happy?' he asked suddenly, moving his dark fringe away from his eyes.

His long legs were almost touching her own under the

table, and either the wine was kicking in or Anna was feeling a frisson of sexual tension. 'Well, *no* . . .' she said. Admittedly.

'The trouble is that most people won't even *hear* the words ethnic cleansing or massacre, let alone talk about it,' Myrna was saying, eating from a family-sized packet of liquorice comfits, and watching a TV programme about pets winning prizes.

'Well, I don't like hearing about it either,' said Anna, half-watching a rabbit winning a gold medal for effort. 'I mean, call me insensitive, but . . .'

'So you're happy just to put your head in the sand, and watch quiz shows?' asked Myrna, watching the quiz show, and biting away the candy casing around her liquorice. They both paused, for a moment, to listen to the studio audience applaud the rabbit.

'Actually, I'm *not* happy,' said Anna who had not realised the extent of her unhappiness until speaking to Sean. 'There is so much that is wrong with my life.'

'So, what's wrong?' Sean asked, bringing her another glass of white wine. 'Is it your career? Finance? Health? Family?'

'No, not really. I mean, I can't put it into a sentence,' she said, worried by Sean's expression. He was looking at her as if Anna was holding back an answer, rather than trying to find one.

Sean was bound to be disappointed to find out that Anna's mother was still married to her father; that she was solvent; and that she was heterosexual. Being an agony academic, he probably had a history of complex, troubled women, and was no doubt far more interested in exploring a woman's mind than her body.

'This job? Some man?' Sean went on, and Anna wondered whether to talk about Him, or about Tom. But, looking at Sean's concerned expression, she decided against it. Boyfriend trouble was so commonplace. If only Anna had had a troubled past. If only, at least, she had a troubled present. Yet Anna spent her life drifting through the days, shopping a great deal, in order to make the time pass more quickly.

'It's more of a feeling. That everything is . . .'

'A bit grey?' he asked, leaning close. He smelled wise – of leather-bound books and silk ties – although that was probably his aftershave. 'Insubstantial?'

'*Yes*,' she said, a touch too triumphantly. He had found her problem. 'That's it. Insubstantial. Everything's just OK.'

'You see? We're that bit closer to finding your problem.'

'Oh, but we can't just talk about me. Anyway, I'm sure you're bored by other people's problems. Let's talk about you.'

'Don't put yourself down. I've noticed you do that all the time.'

Anna stared at him, in surprise. It was as if this tall, dark and hazy man – although that might have been the drink – had been watching Anna for many years without her noticing. Sitting with Sean's legs so close to her own, his knee touching her knee, she felt then as if he fully understood not just Anna, but all women. In contrast, after a party, *He* had found it hard to identify Anna's oldest coat on a bed piled high with them.

'You think?'

'All the time.'

'Do I, really? Maybe that was . . . Oh, never mind.' Anna stopped, looking down at her lap. For some reason, she was on the verge of talking, not about Him, or Tom, but about Sonia, whose flat she had seen on Saturday.

'That was . . . what?' he asked, his eyes all pupils.

'Oh, just . . . Never mind. Let's talk about something else.'

'No. Finish what you were saying.'

'Well, just that I went to see this flat the other day. And it all seemed fine. Sonia – the woman looking for a flatmate – seemed to like me. I mean, I don't think I did anything *wrong*. But, on the way out, I heard her say that I wasn't right. That I had problems, or something.'

'I tell you, everyone has problems,' said Sean, softly. 'I'm sure even this *Sonia* does.'

'Oh no,' laughed Anna. 'You didn't see this woman's flat. Or her figure.'

As Myrna shovelled liquorice comfits into her mouth, Anna fed pasta into her swing bin. But the bin's flap-top, like a dog's jaw, had gorged its fill of disposable cloths and tins of tomato soup. For the last hour it had been dribbling soup from its mouth, like dried blood.

'I thought that other rabbit was better,' said Myrna, switching channels on the TV.

'Yeah.'

'So, did anything happen with this *Sean*?'

'No. Well, not yet anyway.'

Anna tried to squeeze in the pasta, as her bin growled in resistance. She picked out some unnecessary rubbish in order to fit it in, building a tower of soup tins on the floor, which tomorrow she might take for recycling. (She would put it in the other recycling bags, in the living room.) Myrna, meanwhile, was watching two men on television, watching television.

'If those men think *that's* behaving badly, they should meet Gregory,' she said, switching off the TV.

* * *

'Just a classic case of Closure,' Sean had said, finally.

'What?' asked Anna smiling. 'I don't think so, Sean. You've just been working too hard,' she said flirtatiously. 'Writing too many books on the subject.'

'Seriously. You're a classic case. You've got to phone up this Sonia, find out what it was that she objected to . . .'

'I couldn't do *that* . . .'

'Well, otherwise you'll never know, will you?'

'I'm *not* doing that. She'll think I'm even *odder* . . .'

'No she won't. Not if she's as self-contained as you say. That kind of peace of mind doesn't just happen. She's probably been working it through for years – no doubt with a rather good therapist. If you ring her, she'll respect you for it.'

For a while they played word tennis. Anna saying, 'She won't.' Sean saying, 'She will.' Anna hitting back with, 'She won't.' But then Sean stopped playing. He leaned back in his chair, and looked around the pub, as if for other, more interesting, faces.

'Well, anyway. *I'll* have more respect for you if you do,' he said at last, reaching behind for his jacket, slung around the neck of his chair. 'I'm sorry. I've got to go.'

'Oh, OK,' said Anna, stiffly.

'You can't just let things *bother* you, you know. You need to let your feelings out, or they'll grow inside you, like a cancer. I mean, victims are only people who allow themselves to be *victimised*. God, Anna, if you want to win back some self-respect, learn to take control of a situation. Do something about it. That's what I can't stand on *Problem Call*. People phoning up, whingeing on, but if you try and help them . . . If you give them advice, they don't take it. I mean, they won't *listen*.'

'*I* listen. One of my friends is always saying that I listen too much.'

'You need to phone this woman up. Just phone her.' His voice softened to a resigned, 'Look, I really have to go now. You can tell me how the call went tomorrow.'

'Sean has these eyes . . .' she told Myrna, as the tins dripped thick colours on to the kitchen floor.

'*No*. Eyes! Well, I'd go for him, Anna. Sounds as if he's a truly special guy,' said Myrna facetiously, and in an American accent. She switched on the radio.

'Pammy said that he "homed in" on me. I mean, d'you think it sounds – from what I've said – as if that's true?'

But Myrna refused to answer any of Anna's 'silly' questions. (She was too busy listening to a radio programme about the nuclear arms race.) Critical questions, such as, now that she had met Sean, should Anna cancel her recently arranged date with Tom?

Should she – Myrna had asked, ignoring Anna – be frightened of an individual rather than a state-controlled terrorist attack?

Was it rude for her to phone someone after ten o'clock? interrupted Anna.

Should Myrna start to campaign?

Should Anna tell Tom?

Would she, Myrna had said, stop being so frivolous and shut the fuck up?

She had always enjoyed belittling Anna. When they had first met, at school, Myrna had mocked Anna's teenage magazines, referring to them as indoctrination for pre-pubescents. These days, she insisted that Anna wanted a job and a boyfriend only because society suggested that such things were not only desirable, but attainable. She made her feel like a lightweight, although, damnit, Anna thought about global politics too – only not on a daily basis.

'Calm down,' muttered Anna, leaving the room. 'It's only a radio programme.' She went to the telephone in the hallway. But Anna only had the nerve to dial half of Sonia's telephone number. Then, when she plucked up the courage to dial it again, the number was engaged. She put the phone down, and it surprised her by ringing.

Anna was surprised to hear Justine's voice. Could Anna help Justine out?

It had been a long time.

Yeah, sorry about that, said Justine. But she'd been sortofbusy actually. But Anna knew that she was setting up this club night, right? Yeah. But Justine had to persuade a 'panel' that the club night would work.

What did Anna just say? The club's called Stormont. Anna must have heard of Stormont? No, Justine's night's gonna be called Fuchsia. *What* did Anna call it?

Justine had to persuade a panel that the club night would work. Eight o'clock. Thursday evening. It could all go wrong. Now, when she had the right DJ. *The* DJ, in fact. Fuckin' . . . Had Anna heard of the DJ? Justine had to make a presentation. This was *it* for Justine. It was the first time she'd done anything like this. Right, yeah.

She needed to talk to Anna. Out of all of her mates . . . Could Anna come round? To her new place? No, she couldn't do tomorrow. Could Anna come on Wednesday? She was the only person Justine could think of. Who had a proper job. Well, Anna should bring him too. Tom *what*? Did Justine know him? *Whose* friend? *Roo*'s friend? Why did Anna have a friend called *Roo*? Sounds like a sodding squirrel. Who? Well, bring him, because Justine needed

Anna. Oh, please. Be a mate. To show her the flyers, and
. . . Well, after the 'date'.

Whatever.

Anna cringed as she put the phone down. Why did she
feel the need to brag to Justine about her social and sexual
activity? She sounded like a swaggering adolescent boy, for
goodness sake. Why had she said that she was going out on
a 'date'? She sounded like a Californian cheerleader.

And *how* could Anna have mispronounced the name of
Justine's club night? ('It's called Fuck-see-a, right?') Why-
oh-why had she said that Roo wasn't really a friend? And
that her job with Radio Central wasn't even really a job?
Worse had been her description of Tom.

'Boring but a great shag, I'll bet.'

OhGodWhydoIdothat? Anna thought, absentmindedly
dialling Sonia's number once more.

'Hello,' said Sonia, suddenly, shocking Anna.

Prepared to put the phone down, Anna said instead, 'I'm
sorry to bother you. But it's Anna Potter speaking. I came
to see your flat and . . .'

She winced as Sonia didn't speak.

'Oh, *hi*,' she said, as if suddenly remembering an Anna
Potter. 'Did you get your pen OK?'

'Oh, yes. Thank you. But the reason I'm ringing is
actually . . .'

'And I had to give the room to a friend in the end,' she
said, lamely. 'Sorry.'

'Oh, yes. No, the reason I'm ringing is because I overheard
you say on the phone that I just wasn't right somehow and
that I have problems and I wanted to know *why* and whether
it was about . . .'

Anna couldn't believe what she was – albeit in one long
sentence – saying.

'Oh God,' said Sonia, cutting her short. There was silence for a second. Then: 'You heard me say that?'

'Yes, but that's fine.' Anna hoped that, this time, commas and full-stops would jump into her speech. 'I mean I know you'll think I'm weird for ringing but I felt I had to after I heard . . .'

'Right.' There was a nervous giggle. 'Bloody *hell*.'

'I know I sound *odd* . . .'

'*No.*'

'I mean, I'm sorry if I sound . . .'

'No,' interrupted Sonia, firmly. 'I'm glad you called if you heard me say that. I mean, *God*.'

'Well, I *know* I sound ridiculous . . .'

'*No*. I'd have done the same. No, the thing is . . . The reason you weren't right. Oh God. This is . . . I had to give the flat to a friend.'

'Yes, I know that. I just wanted to know why you said I wasn't right. When I was at your flat. You know, you were on the phone.'

Sonia laughed uncertainly.

Anna was desperate for the line to go dead. She felt as if she was fourteen again, and making hoax phone calls with Myrna. Although it had been Myrna who had suggested the phoning, she had always forced Anna to do the talking. As Anna had embarrassed herself on the phone, Myrna had watched.

Often, Myrna had wet herself laughing. Pee had run down Myrna's leg and on to the floor of the phone box. Anna remembered the smells of the sticky, sour breath of previous callers, and her own desperate script: 'I really think you're sexy. Honey, I bet you're good in bed.' Anna had felt it rude to put down the phone then, and she felt it now.

'I see,' said Sonia.

'Look. Don't worry. It's fine, I'll . . .'

'*No*. That's fine, er . . .

'I'll go.'

'No, the truth is. It's OK,' said Sonia, straightening out her voice. 'The truth is . . . What is it? Let me . . . That's it. I thought you were too nice.'

'Too *nice*?' asked Anna, as her anger melted away.

'Yup,' she said. 'Too . . . It's funny, you phoning . . . I mean, I'm changing my mind now. You're probably more like me than I thought. But, anyway, on Saturday, I did think that you were too nice. Yeah, that's it. Really.'

'Really?'

Anna was too nice.

'Yes. Actually, in a really *aggressive* way.'

'Aggressively nice?'

'Yeah,' she said, as if thinking out loud. 'Too nice.'

'Right,' said Anna.

'Yeah. But, it's so odd. Because, I think I got you wrong. You phoning,' Sonia fluttered. 'Well, anyway . . . That's what I thought on Saturday.'

'Well, that's all I wanted to know. I'm glad I phoned . . .'

'You know, as we're telling the truth here. I mean, I actually *haven't* found the right person yet, so if you want . . . Well, maybe, if you'd like to see the flat again . . . ?'

'Oh, right. Oh, was that not the truth? About a friend?'

'No,' Sonia said, giggling conspiratorially.

Anna felt a rush of confidence. A rush that reminded her of that first cigarette of the day. 'Oh . . . Well, actually, I think I'm happy where I am now.' She was taking control of a conversation, and it was a powerful feeling. 'But if I change my mind . . . Well, I'll let you know.'

'Oh, well, OK,' said Sonia. She sounded disappointed.

'But thanks. I really feel *better*,' said Anna. 'Just to have spoken to you.'

'Well, good. I'm sorry if I . . .'

'No, really. Anyway, I've really got to go. But I'll let you know if I think about moving again. Sorry I can't tell you *now*,' she added. 'But you know how it is.'

'Oh, OK. Bye then,' said Sonia, her voice shrinking to a shy: 'Thanks for ringing.'

'No,' said Anna, brightly. After a lifetime of interruptions, she felt as if she was finally having the last word. 'Thank *you*.'

Putting the phone down, Anna was flooded with calm. She imagined that people felt like this as they were about to die. Clearly, Sean Harrison had been right: victims were only people who allowed themselves to be victimised. If Anna wanted to win back some self-respect she should learn how to take advice. She should look for closure.

'You seem happy. Who was that on the phone?' asked Myrna, as Anna went back into the kitchen. 'Oh no – not *Him*?'

Anna bent down to pick up a tin that looked to be having too much fun, rolling around the floor. 'Who's He?' she asked, thoughtfully.

Chapter Five

It was Wednesday evening, and she was on her way to meet Tom. They had arranged to meet at a restaurant in Islington at eight o'clock. But Anna was late. It was ten past eight, and she was fifteen stations away from the Angel, because she had taken a circuitous tube route in order to travel with Sean.

'Are you taking the District and Circle line with me?' Sean had asked her, after they had walked out of the Radio Central building together. 'I'm going that way.'

'Oh . . . er yeah,' lied Anna, so that she could be with him.

The more scenic route, she thought now, sitting beside Sean on the train, separated from him only by an arm-rest. Anna was pleased that she smelled seductive. She had earlier sprayed herself with perfume, although resenting using the last of her Obsession for Tom.

'So, how are you?' he asked, as if genuinely concerned. So, Anna described to Sean her telephone conversation with Sonia. How, from now on, there was to be no more Ms Nice-although-rather-aggressive Guy.

'Good. And I'm impressed that you phoned her. That must have taken courage,' said Sean, as if genuinely pleased. He stretched his legs long across the aisle and said, 'You see, advice can help.'

Anna smiled at her reflection, admitting that Sean's advice had indeed helped, and not simply with Sonia. Certainly – as from yesterday – she was a non-smoker.

Last night, Myrna had watched, bemused, as Anna had lit the cigarettes in her Memory Box, one by one, leaving them to burn, by themselves, in an ashtray.

'What are you doing? The room's going to stink,' said Myrna, coughing excessively and – in Anna's opinion – unnecessarily. 'Smoke in your bedroom, if you have to. Anyway, I thought you were giving up – not taking it up as a competitive sport.'

'Look, I'm doing this to give up smoking, OK?' said Anna. She decided not to add that, since Myrna had begun to make Anna smoke in her bedroom, it had become more of a private, rather than an anti-social, pleasure. 'I'm going to sleep with the fag ends.'

'As if you haven't done that already. There was that neanderthal who'd fought in the Falklands. The Quality Fruiterer . . . Him – the writer, who by day worked in Ryness . . .'

'Don't mention Him any more. The new Anna is going to express her needs and wants. The new Anna knows that He was from a different planet. The new Anna Potter isn't dependent for her emotional security on men . . .'

'The new Anna Potter,' interrupted Myrna, 'is going to start to address herself in the third person.'

'Wow, perhaps I should think before I speak in future,' said Sean, laughing. 'It sounds as if you've taken my every word as gospel.'

'Well, but I felt so good after speaking to Sonia . . .,' said Anna seriously. 'And it really did help. I mean, it felt *so* cathartic, throwing out everything in my Memory Box.'

'Your what?' asked Sean turning to face Anna.

'I mean all my *meaningless* and sentimental keepsakes,' she quickly added, embarrassed to have such a box.

'Like what?'

'Oh, everything.'

Because she had always been a hoarder. She had kept that security badge from her day's work experience at TV-AM. She had hung on to her '*Of course, we will keep your name on file . . .*' rejection letters.

'What were you expecting?' interrupted Sean. 'For them to root you out, and find you? Oh, Anna. Life's not like that. Anyway, why hang *on* to things like that? To upset you, at a later date?'

She knew that now. She was thirty-one, and no fool. So, Anna had dumped the business cards belonging to an ex-boyfriend who had owned a company, manufacturing mannequins for the fuller figure. *Bigger, Bustier, Better*, his cards had read. (Throughout their relationship he tried to re-model Anna as Bigger, Bustier, Better.)

Sean was right – those cards brought back bad memories. She didn't know, now, why she had kept them. But she hated to throw out some of her more romantic mementos. His scribbled: *I love you*.

'And who might He be?' asked Sean. Mischievously.

And so Anna described Him, and their relationship. 'You know, He could end up famous,' she laughed. If His books became bestsellers, she might have to sell stories about His past sexual peccadilloes to the tabloids. *My two-in-a-bed romps with . . .*

'He's an author?' asked Sean.

'Oh yes,' said Anna.

97

Although as yet unpublished, He was writing a novel about the struggle between communism and capitalism, and its effect on the individual. Somewhere in there, He was going to touch upon religion, the problems of power, the experiences of women. Set in Eastern Europe, North America, and the Far East, his novel spanned the nineteenth and twentieth centuries. He had shown Anna the structure, scribbled on the flap of Louis De Bernière's *Captain Corelli's Mandolin*. It was to be a kind of fictionalised history of mankind.

'Sounds interesting,' said Sean, raising an eyebrow, sceptically. 'So, what went wrong with the relationship?'

Anna sighed, explaining that He had dumped her, out of the blue, for another woman. He had refused to answer her calls. Then, late last night, He had 'popped round' to Anna's flat on His way home from a book launch.

'And don't tell me,' said Sean, spreading his legs wide. 'He wanted you back, but this time for *ever*?'

'Well, actually, He said He'd been worried about me.'

'I've been worried about you,' He had said, sitting down, and tapping his fingers on her kitchen table. 'You haven't phoned since Saturday.'

'Yeah, I'm not making outgoing calls,' said Anna. 'At least for the next few days.'

'Why not?' He had asked, moving Myrna's bottle of tomato ketchup to the edge of the table.

'It's called "phone turkey". This guy at work said I use the phone too m . . .'

'Which guy?' He interrupted, pushing the salt and pepper pots together.

'Sean Harrison. He's written lots of books about relationships and he said that . . .'

98

He interrupted with a laugh.

'Please don't say you've gone all psycho-babble on me.'

'That's what I thought, too, at first, but, you know, Sean makes a lot of sense.'

'Oh, come on, Anna. It's all crap. You know that,' He said, taking Anna's hand. 'But, I didn't come here to . . . I wanted to talk about us, actually. Because, you know, I still love you – despite everything.'

She took her hand away. 'Yeah, that's why you've practically moved in with that opera director. And that's why you wanted to sleep with Sonia.'

He looked down at those huge, gentle hands. Then, He said, 'It's not . . . Neither of them are like you.'

'Oh, and don't tell me?' said Sean, laughing. 'They didn't understand Him? Not in the way you do? Well, I'm sorry Anna. But, even to someone who didn't *psycho-babble*, it's all very clear. The man's a wanker.'

But one only had to talk to Him in the flesh! When He talked about Himself, it was different. Then, if anything, He was self-effacing.

'Really, He's shy,' she said. Only most people were unable to see through the tough exterior to the terror underneath. When Anna had pointed this out to Him, this morning, He had been surprised. How had she known? God, He had spent his entire life putting up a front. But, as the Barbaras Dickson and Streisand had sung, she 'Knew Him So Well'.

'That's what He wants you to think. That's what men generally want women to think,' said Sean. 'When will women start to see the difference between love and plain old-fashioned lust?' he asked, rhetorically. 'So, I suppose He asked then if you ever thought about Him?' he asked, wearily.

'How do you know that?' she asked, shocked.

'I'm a man, Anna. I've read the script.'

'So, do you never think about me any more?' He had asked shyly, last night, His fingers wrapped tightly around Anna's salt-shaker. 'Now that it's incoming calls only?'

Anna laughed, feeling the atmosphere tense, as Myrna walked in wearing a long, lacy Victorian nightdress.

'Oh, my God,' her flatmate had said, seeing Him. 'What are you doing here? Twisting the knife?'

'Myrna, don't.'

'Oh Anna, don't tell me you're falling for his bullshit again. All that, "Oh, poor me, I've got to brutally reject you," rubbish?'

'And what's it got to do with you?' He snapped, banging the salt-cellar on the table, for effect.

'Only that I want to have a fry-up. And you're in my kitchen, rearranging my condiments.'

She snatched the salt-cellar from Him.

'Well, wait a second, would you?' He said, staring at Myrna's stomach. He was frightened of Myrna because she didn't make the effort not to eat in front of men. 'Then you can stuff your face.'

That annoyed Anna.

'Why should she wait? It's her bloody kitchen,' she said, feeling protective of Myrna, and on the side of womankind generally.

'Oh Anna,' He said, looking up at her with those eyes. 'Don't be like that.'

'Like what?' asked Myrna, switching on the kettle. 'Look, she doesn't want to see you. And if you don't stop stalking Anna, she'll take out an injunction against you . . .'

'Do you want me to go?' He asked Anna.

'Er, yes,' Anna said, wanting to add, 'for the moment.'

'Because that'll be it, if I go now.' He stood up. 'I mean it.'

'Fine,' said Anna, who had thrown out all memory of Him

anyway. The 'I love you' written on the back of a bus-ticket.
The mug.

'And you're a bitch,' He said to Myrna, by the door.

'Stop treating Myrna like shit.'

'He can't help Himself,' said Myrna. 'He's a shit Himself.'

'And you're ugly,' He told Myrna.

'Well, I might be ugly now, but after cosmetic surgery I'd be a
beauty – whereas you'd still have a fucking terrible personality.'

'Definitely a wanker,' said Sean as the train drew into St James's Park.

'Do you get off here?' asked Anna, as the doors lurched open.

'Yes,' said Sean, but still he stayed sitting, as if confident that the train would wait for him to leave before closing the doors.

Indeed, the doors did remain parted for Sean, whilst he explained to Anna that her problems came from investing too much in her relationships with other people. She should invest rather more in herself, he said.

'Perhaps, *now*, you won't need persuading to take my advice,' he grinned, standing up. Seconds before the doors came together, Sean left the train.

Anna was beginning to regret taking the Circle line to be with Sean; it had taken so long to reach Monument. There, she had changed trains for the Northern line, and now her train was sitting, stuck in a tunnel.

There had been no announcements, or explanations, from London Underground. If it stayed here much longer, no doubt Anna and the man opposite, dressed in women's clothing, would begin to talk. They would discover intimate details about each other. They would die a slow death on a tube together; and, eventually, Hollywood would make a film about their unusual friendship. *Anna and the Transvestite*. It would recall their last moments together.

Not for the first time, Anna imagined her own funeral.

It would be raining, she decided. The clocks would be stopped. The pianos would be silenced, and the telephone cut off. The sun, dismantled. The wood, swept up.

Then the mourners would come, to muffled drum. Amongst them, Anna's father, wearing his orange kagoul – the one that he had always worn during childhood family camping trips, which shrank to the size of a pocket pouch. Above them, aeroplanes would scribble on the sky the message *Anna Is Dead*.

Well, maybe not.

But her father would be crying, and Anna's mother would comfort him. She would put her arm around her husband's waist, as she had, many years ago, during those Welsh camping trips, and would stare at her precious daughter's grave, mouthing the one word, 'Why?'

It would be a question on all of their lips.

Meanwhile, Liz would be listening to a grieving Justine. A suffering Justine who would be saying to Liz, 'You know, before Anna's death, I thought you were just a loud Australian tart. A stereotype, in fact. But, you know, you're so kind. I don't know – Anna always saw the best in people.' And, for once, Liz would say nothing.

There would be nothing left to say.

Mike, however, would be telling Anna's family and friends, 'Wow, did I misjudge *her*. Anna worked alongside me, and, boy, do I feel bad. Actually, I had a row with my boss today – I told Pammy not to come to the funeral. She wouldn't have been wanted here. I mean, she never understood Anna. Not in the right *way*.

'Mind you, perhaps I should have allowed her to pay her respects. You see, I was wrong about Anna as well. You know, I called her a racist. Yet, *how*? She might have been white, but, in so many ways, I believe that Anna Potter was as good as black herself.'

Then, they would all listen to Anna's ex-boyfriend, and, incidentally, think Him extraordinarily handsome, as He read out the eulogy.

'I couldn't convince Anna that I loved her. She wouldn't believe me. But I loved her. Roo loved her. Her god-children, Daisy and Oscar. All children. Men, generally, loved Anna Potter. Well, she was beautiful. She was bright, and funny. Oh, and well-read. She was bright and sunny, and so good in bed.'

Sean would stand there, deep in thought. He would wish that he had declared his love for Anna straight away. He had had the most to lose. He had lost the *future* . . .

The rain would slip-slide down Myrna's grey PVC raincoat. She would regret calling Anna frivolous earlier that evening. Anna was not so much frivolous, she would be thinking, as fun. Deep down, her flatmate had an intelligence and a depth that was extraordinary. 'She was incredibly bright,' Myrna would tell Anna's father. 'And, no matter what you always thought, successful too.'

Dad: 'I can see that now. I only wish . . .'

Myrna would wish that she had been the type of flatmate found in television drama serials – the type prepared to discuss office life and men of an evening rather than, for example, death by nuclear holocaust. If only she had been the type of flatmate to swap clothes, and pore over diagrams of sexual positions torn out of magazines! If only, at the very least, she had kept a full fruit bowl.

Too late, she would think. *Too late.*

The tube started up again, and tears came to Anna's eyes as

she thought of Him saying, 'Anna was my North, my South. She was my East, and my West.' She blinked back her tears. She hadn't realised how sad her own funeral could be. Anna simply had not realised how loved she was, by everyone.

The transvestite opposite her stood up. His lips were too thickly painted, and his eyes stuck together with insect-legs of mascara. His heels were unnaturally tall and thin. (How could he walk in those shoes?) Plus, his chin threatened to grow a beard at any minute.

'Sorry,' said Anna, as the man almost fell on top of her.

Or could he be a woman? Now, Anna could see that the woman had real breasts, pushed out of her bra like two cottage rolls. His legs were shapely. But 'she' had thick, heavy fingers, like her ex.

'Oh sorry,' said Anna, kicked in the rush of people trying to board the tube at Old Street. She stared into the spreading gloom of her reflection in the window, as the train doors fell together.

Finally, she thought happily, *I'm free of Him*. Had the relationship persisted, Anna might have been trapped in a vicious circle, where Tom loved her, she loved Him, and He loved only Himself. Because, before Sean, she would never have had the courage to ask Him to leave.

The train stopped at Angel station, the doors flapping open, and Anna stood up, trying to remember why she had agreed to this night out with Tom.

The ticket collector queried Anna's ticket, turning it over and over. 'Where did you purchase this, madam?' he asked, his eyes all fluorescent-blue lighting as they searched Anna's face.

'Why?' she asked him, pitying him.

'*Because*, madam, you have a ticket here for eighty pence.

This. Ticket. Is invalid.' His face was strung together with red veins.

Fortunately, Anna had arranged to meet Tom at the restaurant. Otherwise, he might have seen her fawning over the ticket collector. Not only fawning, but failing to flirt with him, in an effort to become more valid. Finally, Anna had been fined.

'Ten *pounds*?'

She fumbled inside her bag for her purse. It lay in there somewhere, stained in lipstick, and between the half-eaten sandwich and two self-help books – *How to Solve the Problem of Low Self Esteem*, and *One Month to Happiness*, both by Wilhelm Grohe. She had brought the books home from work. Homework.

Mike had insisted she read them, as Grohe was their next month's guest. Anna had reached the second chapter of *One Month to Happiness*, assuming that Mike would quiz her on it, and had so far learnt that men were like pencils. They liked to get straight to the point. Whereas women were like pencil-sharpeners. They honed their world to perfection.

Finally, there was Anna's plastic purse. She lifted it out with an unstamped letter to her penfriend, Gilly, in America. It had lined her bag for some time. (She only needed to buy a stamp.) As the ticket collector filled in his form, as if all life depended on it, Anna dropped her bag, and out fell her spare sanitary towel and one of her books: *How to Solve the Problem of Low Self Esteem*.

'Well you can start,' sniggered the collector, 'by paying the proper fare. Then you might feel better about yourself.'

'Oh, the book isn't er mine. It's my aunt's,' said Anna, unconvincingly. She stood there, feeling frail inside her coat. Smaller, somehow.

*   *   *

105

Her body needed a cigarette after the ticket incident. As she walked along Islington High Street, her throat opened, her lungs like deflated balloons. She yearned for a Silk Cut to fill them out. But Anna remembered last night's smell of the ashtray on her pillow. The stink of a bowl of dead cigarettes. And she was able – for that moment at least – to resist.

She pushed open the heavy door to the restaurant, spotting Tom at a table in the corner, and feeling suddenly cruel. (Compared with Sean, Tom was merely average.) This felt more important to him than it was.

It was a miserable-looking restaurant. The walls were painted dark wine. The tables were lit up by single candles which wept wax. No one was audibly speaking, and each table was dressed self-consciously, like modern brides in old lace.

'Thank you,' she said, as a waiter with swirling brown hair took away her coat.

As she walked to Tom's table, Anna felt as if she was going on stage. Everybody's focus was on her, and chairs had to be moved out of her way. She hated to be looked at. Yet she was always the one asked by comedians to participate in their act. Anna would smile and think, *But* you *are here to entertain* me.

'Hello.'

'I'm sorry I'm late,' she said to Tom as the stereotypically handsome, and almost foreign, waiter pulled out a red velvet-coated chair for her, saying,

'Mademoiselle.' *(Mademoiselle!)*

'Are you?' asked Tom absentmindedly.

'Am I what?'

'Is that comfortable for you?' asked the tanned waiter.

'Late?' added Tom.

'Yes thanks,' said Anna to the waiter, aware that she had her priorities wrong, in that she would have liked to have prolonged any conversation with the interestingly handsome waiter.

'I think so,' she said to Tom, his skin the colour of chips.

'So, can I get you anything?'

'A menu, thanks,' said Anna, hoping that the waiter would think that Tom was not Anna's boyfriend, but an older, and rather dull, brother. 'And a glass of wine. The house white.'

'We'll have a bottle of that, actually,' said Tom.

'And some mineral water, please.'

'Sparkling or still?' asked the waiter, smiling. (Why did she always meet her ideal men out of context?)

'*Sparkling*,' said Anna.

'I'm afraid I can't stay long this evening,' said Anna, as the waiter left their table.

'Don't tell me – something's suddenly come up?' muttered Tom into his menu.

'I mean, I've got to go round to a friend's – she's having a panic attack about setting up this nightclub. Why, what did you think I meant?' asked Anna.

'Never mind,' said Tom.

She understood him perfectly.

They read their menus, Tom's a laminated wall between the two of them. Anna chose quickly, listening to the couple at the table next to them, who were arguing about their wedding plans. The woman wanted sugared almonds. The man wanted smoked trout. *She* wanted classical music. *He* wanted soul.

'So, how's your new job?' asked Tom eventually, trying to find a place between the cutlery and the silver-plate serviette dispenser for his giant menu. And so Anna told

Tom about *Problem Call* and all the world's problems passing through the computer screen. Of Pammy Lowental, who on Tuesday had reminded Anna of her great responsibilities. Anna was sitting at the coalface of the problem industry.

'Can you believe she used the word *industry*?'

They ordered their hors d'oeuvres. The waiter placed a bottle of wine between Tom and Anna, as she described Pammy. The fleshy, filleted hands. The shallow-carved eyes. The tiny pinprick pupils. The thick pink lipstick that left marks wherever she went. On Bruce. On the studio manager's cheeks. And on Mikey.

'Can you believe she calls a grown man *Mikey*?'

'It's only what I'd expect from a grown woman called *Pammy*.'

Their two orange soups arrived, swirling with cream. Anna realised that she was hungry, telling Tom of the caller who phoned every half-hour with a different problem. Oral fixation. Separation anxiety. Early male menopause. Loneliness . . .

'He asked for my home telephone number. I was half-thinking of giving it to him. He'd get on well with my flatmate, Myrna,' she sighed.

They laughed and paused, so that they could listen in on the neighbouring couple's conversation. That couple was still at odds over the wedding. Because *she* wanted to be married in a church. But *he* didn't want anything to do with God.

Anna picked at the wet wax around the candle. Tom was telling her about one of his pupils, who had said, that day, that Tom was doing extremely well as a teacher. 'Keep up the good work,' the boy had said.

'The worst thing was,' said Tom, 'I was grateful.'

Anna smiled as their soup bowls were cleared away, telling Tom of the time Roo's daughter, Daisy, had said about Anna's trousers, 'I don't think they're fashionable.'

'The worst thing was,' said Anna, 'I changed out of them.'

Tom laughed, as the waiter brought over their main courses. Beside them sat the young couple, now fresh out of wedding plans, and unspeaking. Anna filled up her glass of wine, and Tom asked her whether she would mind him smoking.

'No, no, that's fine,' she said, picking at the hot wax, as Tom lit up a Silk Cut.

'Terrible, isn't it? Between courses, too.'

She couldn't stand the smell of his smoke. 'Isn't that wonderful? Overnight, I've turned into a non-smoker. Sean's right about the actual physical addiction leaving your body quite quickly. God, I feel so liberated.'

'I'll put it out,' said Tom now, looking at his cigarette as if it was to blame for everything.

'Oh no, don't. I want to be one of those ex-smokers who complain all the time about passive smoking and cough unnecessarily.'

She coughed, and he laughed as their two steak dijons arrived. He asked the neighbouring couple if he could use their ashtray. That set them off again. *She* wished that her fiancé would stop smoking. *He* wished that she would stop nagging him.

'You didn't have to . . .' said Anna, as Tom stubbed out his cigarette.

'No, the food's here. It's fine.'

Anna outlined to Tom the joy of life without cigarettes. As Sean had said, she would save money. She would no longer be an addict. Because, why should she be the one to bankroll big, evil tobacco companies? Or sap the ailing

NHS? Finally, Anna would be able to breathe properly. She wouldn't die . . .

'Oh, I don't think Sean can help you there. I'm afraid that death still awaits you,' said Tom, filling up their wine glasses. 'Talking of addictions – how *is* He? Your ex, I mean?'

Oh, Anna was over Him.

Of course, if it hadn't been for Sean, Anna would probably have clung on to Him. But she had closure now, courtesy of Sean. Incidentally, had Tom heard of Sean Harrison? Only he had been on TV. Had Tom seen *The Shelley Show*?

'No,' said Tom. 'I work for a living.'

And so they talked about Sean; Anna admiring his way with words, and Tom admiring the way he had helped Anna to forget about Him. ('Mind you, I wonder how he did *that*?') Anna explaining that he had advised her to draw up a list of His bad points. ('Now, that I would like to hear.') Anna, after much persuasion, showing him her list.

1) How He found it hard, given His mother, to trust a woman.
2) How He found it difficult, in this day and age, to be a man.
3) How He found it impossible, given His flatmates, to invite Anna back to His flat in Kensington.
4) How He had always sounded so clever-clever.
5) How He had been too good-looking.

'Congratulations, by the way,' interrupted Tom. 'I hear that Roo's pregnant again.'

'Oh, I don't think I can take the responsibility for *that*,' she said, somewhat drunkenly. Tom was really quite handsome, she thought, although she did wish that that fact could be verified in some way. If only there was an international committee set up to monitor these things.

'My assistant told me, today.'

'Ah, well, it *must* be true.'

'And is it good news, d'you think?'

'Oh yeah, of course it's good news,' Anna insisted, explaining why Roo's pregnancy was bad news. For Anna. Because her best friend changed after giving birth. She felt a biological urge to whinge about everything.

Roo began to see a purpose in life to kitchen roll. Her face would light up at the sight of another mother. She and this other mother would then complain, for hours, about what an uncomplaining state motherhood was, and how Anna couldn't possibly understand. Anna, after all, had the freedom to live exactly as she pleased.

Roo would act as if Anna's preoccupations with work and money and men were peculiar and pointless, whilst her own obsessions (head circumference, breathing cessation in babies, and supplementary bottles) were a matter of life and death.

Roo could talk for days about defecation.

Tom laughed, as the waiter interrupted them to take away their dishes, Anna's still covered in a jungle of fennel.

'You should eat up your greens,' said the waiter, flirtatiously.

'I know,' she said, suggestively. Although she didn't know quite what she was suggesting.

'Desserts?'

'I don't want one,' said Anna, who did.

'In that case we'll have the bill,' said Tom. 'Because, don't you have to leave early?'

'Oh, right, yeah,' said Anna sadly. Sadly, because, with each glass of wine, Tom had become more attractive. She had not thought of Sean once, during the last half-hour.

'I mean, unless you want coffee?'

'No, I should go. I mean, one doesn't want to keep *Justine* waiting.'

'Oh right. What's so special about Justine?'

'*I'll* pay,' said Anna.

'No, no. You had to put up with my smoke.'

'Well, I'll pay *half*, anyway.'

'I tell you what. You pay next time.'

The waiter opened the door for Anna, and she was hit by the cold. The seasons were on the turn; the sour, bottled scents of summer replaced by the smells of woolly scarves and stiff school uniforms. She and Tom stood there, looking at each other, and shivering.

'God, it's cold out here.'

'Yeah.'

'*So.* You're off to Justine's now?'

'Yeah. And listen. Thanks for dinner. It was lovely.'

'Well, she must be a good friend. I mean, for you to want to go there now. It's late.'

'I don't think I'd dare *not* go. Justine's scary. I wouldn't have survived school without her.'

'Oh no?'

'It was one of those hard inner-city comprehensives. You know? Even the head had a drinking problem.'

'Really?'

'Yes. That was why I didn't get into university.'

'Oh. But this Justine. Surely you're not still scared of her? I mean, you're adults now; you don't have to go. Don't different rules apply?'

He smiled.

Ah, but Justine wasn't all bad. She always had the grace to phone after Anna's parties – if only to explain why she hadn't shown up. Plus, she was Anna's oldest friend. She had invited Tom too, tonight. So, if he wanted to have a coffee at Justine's . . . ?

He did.

Justine's 'friend' was so filthy that he looked as if he was growing out of the brown rug. He clearly felt that he would be giving too much away if he spoke, and so sat smoking a bulky spliff, and grunting. Still, Anna gathered that his name was Jed; that at home he had a huge vinyl record collection; and that he had just had sex with Justine.

Most men, she wanted to tell him, had had sex at some point with Justine.

Jed stretched out his long, skinny legs. A rough, sliced knee poked out of the holes in his trousers, and Anna felt as if she was seeing something she shouldn't. She averted her eyes, smiling at Tom, although irritated by his presence. Why was he there? Had *she* brought him? He seemed even more uncomfortable in Justine's squat than Anna.

Why was he wearing that jumper?

Lined up beside Jed were five huge joints. Fat, like tampons. Jed passed the spliff he was smoking to Justine, and was now busy rolling up a sixth, ripping up Denise Van Outen, who was that month's cover of a men's magazine, into tiny, thick pieces, licking the sticky side of a Rizla paper, and tearing a cigarette in two, to turf out the tobacco inside.

'Bit of Boutros?' Justine asked, passing Anna the joint.

'Boutros?'

'Boutros Ghali,' said Jed.

'Charlie,' said Justine, lazily, as Anna re-lit what she presumed was a cannabis joint.

'Coke, Anna,' warned Tom.

'Right, sorry. I erm don't.' She passed the joint to Tom, who refused it too.

113

'Scared of gettin' into trouble with the *authorities*, Potter?'

'No, of course not. It's only that I have . . .'

It was only that she had a fear of dying. Anna was reluctant even to take the recommended dosage of Paracetamol. One felt fine; it might even, as the packet suggested, hurry straight to the heart of the pain. Two, however . . . Well, that was plain carelessness.

'This place is nice,' lied Anna, looking around Justine's new home. A tall, thin plant was the only sign of life in a room which smelled of elderly people dying inside a charity shop. A futon was rolled up like a homeless junkie at one end, while at the other end lay a kitchenette, its stone walls the colour of curdled milk.

Justine looked around as if she was seeing it all for the first time. 'Yeah, it's all right,' she said.

Fag ends piled up on plug points. Anna felt sick at the sour smell of concentrated cigarettes. She wished that she could jump up and out of the small window, which flapped open, desperate for air, above the fridge.

'So, how's it all going?' She suddenly remembered her purpose in Justine's life. 'I mean, your club plans?'

'That DJ's fucking good. Mind you, he has to be if Just can persuade this club committee,' said Jed, drowsily, and Anna nodded slowly. He spoke so rarely that she presumed he had said something significant.

'Yeah,' agreed Justine. 'Eight o'clock, tomorrow. Load of sad pricks sitting around, making decisions.'

Anna stared at the carpet, and at a black banana skin, which appeared to be wriggling its way towards her, as if she was the one most likely to save it. Chopped up on the floor lay the dregs of what looked like a party – splashes of lager, dried-up parts of a quiche, and stubbles of tobacco –

114

and Anna wondered why she hadn't been invited to any flat-warming.

She would have liked, at least, to have been invited.

'Isn't it only a committee of investors?' Anna asked, gearing up to give an impression of usefulness.

'What, the panel? Yeah, it is.'

'Well, they won't know anything about music, or club-nights, will they?' *Why do I sound like a banker approving a small-business loan?*

'Of course they will. They own the bloody club.'

'Yeah, but that doesn't mean they're DJs, does it?' said Tom. 'Anna's right.'

'Either way, I can't persuade them. I'm shit at all that crap. People sitting behind desks, judging you.'

'So, what sort of music will you play at this club night?' asked Tom. He lit a Silk Cut.

'Actually. I was wondering . . .' Justine looked at Anna, who had decided never to speak again – at least whilst with Justine. (She wished that Tom wouldn't speak either.) 'I was gonna try to persuade you. Is there any chance of you coming with tomorrow?'

'What, to your . . . ? Why?' *Why can't I complete a sentence?*

'Well, I don't know,' said Justine. 'Tomorrow's dead important, and I just know that if you were sitting there, all straight in your suit, they'd be persuaded. Y'know? Here's my notes.' She handed Anna a beige A4 file.

Anna felt the cardboard flap. 'Well, I don't know . . . As you've just made clear, I'm your sad, straight friend. Anyway, I've never even been to that Stormont club, let alone organised . . . What do *I* know about clubs?'

'Yeah you do,' said Justine, smiling, and lying down on the carpet. 'What about the Secret Society?'

115

'God, d'you remember that? We were *eight*.'

'You go that far back?' asked Tom.

'*Way* back.'

Their first day at school, in fact. Itchy uniform, complete with hat. Anna's mother, crying as she buttoned down that white shirt. A draught coming in through the buttonholes. Anna feeling lost in a warm, white vest, thick, leather-strapped shoes and socks as tall as her knees. Still, it was September, cold out there and smelling of dead leaves.

('So, what d'you say, anyway, Potter?' asked Justine. 'Will you come, tomorrow?'

'I don't think it's my . . .'

'Fine. It was my mum who suggested you, anyway.'

'Auntie Elaine?')

They lived at the end of the same cul de sac. Their mothers had organised the street party together for the Queen's Silver Jubilee.

Justine's mother, Elaine, didn't wanted the Poonjays there. 'Auntie' Elaine could take or leave foreigners, but she didn't believe in Bangladeshis. She wasn't a racialist, but she didn't like the look of Vietnamese boat people either.

Don't get Elaine wrong, she liked ethnic minorities, particularly as they seemed now to be in the majority. *Plus*, Elaine made a point of enjoying spicy foods. Gefilte fish and curry. The Notting Hill Carnival was very colourful, in Elaine's mind. (Although she had her own views about the violence.) But coloured people were, in her perfectly valid opinion, equal. Separate, but equal.

Anna's mother argued that, OK, they Brought Down House Values, but it was only for one day. And had Elaine seen the Poonjays' furnishings at Number 13? The new

116

shag-pile carpet, covered to fit the parquet flooring? The Poonjays' huge Union Jack? The biggest in the street, its material flapped about the porch long after the rest of the street stopped celebrating.

('Why did Elaine suggest me?' asked Anna, quickly discarding the Auntie.

'She said you'd "know how to behave".'

'Well, I don't know why she'd say that.'

Justine affected an Elaine-like accent, saying, 'But Justine, Anna's *such* a good friend of yours.')

She and Justine had shared everything, including Anna's lunch-boxes. They had shared a star sign and Justine's detentions, Justine's chicken-pox and Anna's Crayolas. They were good friends, and Anna had the passport photographs to prove it. The two of them in their primary-school uniform; Anna stiff-smart; and Justine's jacket pocket towing away at the seams.

('I did say that we barely saw each other now. But Mum was too busy saying, "This is your big chance, Justine, to make something of yourself. They'll take one look at you and see that you lack responsibility. Whereas Anna can present a CV to show that she's *never* gone off the rails."'

'That's ridiculous.' *I have so gone off the rails.*)

Justine led Anna out of the predictable and to places such as Piccadilly Circus when they were supposed to be in primary school. Anna followed Justine out of the indoor shopping mall, sneaking past the ticket collector, and travelling by tube to Tottenham Court Road. Feeling lost, had it not been for Justine.

117

Feeling lost, on her first day at secondary school. Justine had shown Anna the way through swarms of school-children, rushing from the old school building to the new one. Among red and white stripes of school-kids, Anna might have been crushed had it not been for Justine and her new fence of crew-cut friends, sitting on the steps of the Wimpy, spraying vinegar and singing advertisement jingles.

'Oi,' they had screamed at Anna one day.

The boys had shaved their heads. Second year had started, and Justine had begun to have sex, and to stand in a wedge of friends outside Martins the Newsagent, demanding entertainment with menaces from disabled elderly people. Anna might have been grievously, bodily, harmed by Justine's skinhead friends, sitting on the newsagent's steps, roaring racial abuse and spraying urine, had it not been for Justine.

'*She's* all right,' said Justine, who had begun to wear terrifyingly thick platform sandals. 'Potter's OK.'

('I'm sure Mum thinks I'm still at school.'

'Yeah,' agreed Anna. 'My mum thinks I'm twelve and still in love with Martin Sheen.'

'Then of course there was Charlie Secker.'

'Charlie Secker?' said Tom. 'Another actor from the seventies?'

'Oh no,' said Justine. 'Not Charlie Secker. He was *the real thing.*')

Charlie Secker.

Charlie had had a perfect thirteen-year-old boy's body, actually widening at the shoulders, as the diagrams said, slimming at the hips and fitting, perfectly, a boy's behind.

Anna had longed to be a part of it, hanging off it in some

118

way, like a button, or a girlfriend. But Charlie had been authentic to her only in snapshots. She knew him at school, sauntering along the polished corridor. Or in the Wimpy Bar, playing with the plastic tomato. Charlie, through the front window of his house, watching television. Or on the tube, legs up on the opposite seat. Charlie, surrendering his ticket at the barrier. Looking through the record-shop window.

He was like the fellas in Anna's magazine photo love-stories. She had imagined his thoughts, floating from his head, in bubbles.

Charlie, in front of the TV: *I'm sick of staying in, watching the football.*

Anna, at Myrna's house: *I wonder if that fella will pass by soon.*

Charlie, cheering Anna on at hockey, in school: *That girl looks fun.*

Anna, looking at Charlie, on the way home: *He really does have a way with him.*

Charlie's labrador racing up to Anna: *I might be a dog but I can help to move things on a bit.*

Charlie, saying: *He likes you.*

Anna, saying: *He's cute.*

Charlie, saying: *D'you wanna go for a burger this Saturday, and then on to the disco at the local youth club?'*

Anna presumed that there *was* a local youth centre. All of her teenage magazines referred to them. Or a place where the fellas and their girls got together, to play pool.

Anna spent her Saturday nights with a gaggle of girls outside Sainsbury's, passing around a bottle of alcohol, as if it was poison, before going on to a disco, held in the draught of a school assembly hall. A disco where the female sex dominated, moving self-consciously to chart-topping music, and tittering at the size of each other's breasts.

But she and her friends had heard tell of another type of Saturday night. She knew of the parties, inside people's houses, where there was the possibility of being beaten to a pulp, or being made pregnant.

'D'you wan' to come to Russell Cocker's party this Sat'day?' Justine asked.

'Oh, er, no. I don't . . .' started Anna.

'Only Charlie Secker's going.'

Charlie Secker.

She would risk falling pregnant for Charlie Secker. He had a winning way with him – even in Myrna's opinion. They would dance together and meet up in the park on a Sunday, to stroke Charlie's labrador.

But first, she would have to meet him. Because, for Anna, Charlie barely existed away from the London Underground. And, freed from the tangle of the tube system, would he want to be involved with the pale, uninteresting Anna Potter?

'Yeah, course he will,' Justine had said, at the party, as Anna tried to merge with the shadows dancing around the living-room carpet. 'Just come outside.'

'No, I don't think I can go *outside*.'

She had seen glimpses of the goings-on through the window. Russell, fishing his tongue around Justine's mouth. Paul Mowbray, puking on the rhododendrons.

'Well, suit yerself,' Justine laughed.

Like one of the lads squeezed into a girl's shape, Anna looked ludicrous, trying to be shapely in a ra-ra skirt. Outside, there would be a terrible light. It was early summer outside, and a season which showed her legs to their worst advantage.

'Only Charlie Secker's outside.'

'Well, *OK*.'

('You look miles away,' said Tom.

'She's dreaming of Charlie,' grunted Justine.

'Hardly.'

'What d'you think of my costings then, Anna?'

'I've never costed anything in my life. I won't be any help tomorrow. Really. I honestly don't know why you're asking me.'

'Well, forget it then. I thought you *might* want to be involved. I mean, when Mum suggested you, I thought, "Why not?" You've always been able to talk to people like that. Remember Mr Steel?')

To outsiders, Justine looked hard. She had worn-down skin. Sharp bones sliced their way through her cheeks. Eyes bored holes. She had a cruel look, but she wasn't that way. As far as Anna was concerned, Justine was all right. Justine was OK. *Justine Quealy's gonna be expelled.* Anna remembered that rumour floating around school. Myrna had said, *Don't worry, Anna. She'll be much happier in some youth detention centre.*

Auntie Elaine had had a short, sharp, shock. ('Oh, Barbara,' she had said. 'Do you think if Justine had her father, this wouldn't have happened?') Anna had come home to find her mother's friend sitting in the 'best, guest' living room, squishing and squirming on the plastic-covered sofa.

'Anna, how *are* you?' asked Elaine, looking up, and pretending to smile.

Did Anna know what had happened to Justine? Auntie Elaine had been to see Mr Steel, but he wouldn't listen to her. In his experience, as a headmaster, mothers defended their daughters, no matter what. But if Anna could see him,

121

and . . . *Apparently*, no one had a good word to say for her daughter.

She had started to cry. 'Anna, if *you* could speak to him?'

They had once been good friends, and Anna had the passport photos to prove it. On the first day of secondary school: Anna with Justine – her hair, plaited à la Bo Derek. On their last day of secondary school: Anna with Justine – her hair plaited à la Boy George.

('So you just want me to *be* there tomorrow?' said Anna now.

'You'll come?' Justine smiled, possibly for the first time ever.

'Well, OK.')

Anna was alone, in a train carriage. Two stops earlier, she had been alone in a train carriage with *Tom*, snogging. But now Tom had gone, and at any moment a stranger could come in, and bludgeon Anna with a hammer. She would meet a lonely, painful and humiliating death. Years later, bits of her body would be found, lying flat along the Jubilee line.

Not that that would stop Anna's dad insisting she had died from a smoking-related illness. ('I did *warn* her,' Don would say.)

Anna again imagined her own funeral. But this time everything was wrong with it. It would be a funeral without a body, first of all.

Warren would argue: 'Makes it all seem a bit of a farce, doesn't it?' Typically, a table would collapse, vol-au-vents squashing underfoot. 'Dead embarrassing,' Warren would mutter, sniggering at his own use of the word 'dead'.

Her Australian friend Liz would be upset. She would be melodramatically, shamefully, visibly, upset. Her face would puff pink, exploding into tears, and she would sob like a child robbed of ice-cream. Her mouth would belch bubbles of snot. Her rich foundation would wash away, leaving her cheeks cracking pink like raw pavement.

Justine wouldn't show. She would be too busy making plans for her club-night.

And He would be late, sidling up to Liz, instinctively knowing that she was an easy lay. (All He had ever wanted, He would realise, was an easy lay.) 'Don't be depressed,' He would say to Liz, Liz taking His words to heart. 'Anna wouldn't have wanted that.'

Yes, I bloody would, thought Anna, thinking of Myrna.

Myrna would go out – if only to escape that half-empty flat. Her evening-class tutor would say, 'I was wondering, Myrna, whether you might want to go on to do a PhD in philosophy? You know, you shouldn't mope around, not with your brain. Your friend wouldn't have wanted that.'

Yes, I bloody would, thought Anna, knowing that *Problem Call* would quickly take on a replacement – someone called Susan, who had programme ideas in her sleep. *Susan* would be black, and big in pan-African-American activist movements. (She would know Spike Lee.) She would be given a desk on her first day in the office.

She would rush straight to being friends with Mike, without having to sleep with him first. 'Lunch?' Sean would say, taking Susan down to the canteen. 'Mind if I call you Sue?'

Sue would rush straight to being lovers with Sean, without having to be friends with him first. She would be quickly promoted.

One day, she would spot a coffee stain on her desk. 'Who

123

did this?' Sue would ask, repulsed. And Sean would say, 'Someone called Anna. But forget about a tiny stain, Mrs Harrison – you have a *baby* on the way.'

Sue would be having Sean's baby. But that wouldn't stop Pammy choosing her as the next co-presenter of *Problem Call*. 'Oh Suey,' she would say. 'What did I do before you came along?'

For the life of them, nobody would be able to recall.

After the funeral, Anna's father would pop round to the flat, just to take away the last of Anna's possessions. 'Hope you don't mind, Myrna. My only child . . . This is hard. And you were right when you said that Anna was successful. Why did I find that so hard to see?'

'Don't be silly,' Myrna would say. 'It's important to grieve. Although sometimes I wonder whether death wouldn't be preferable. I mean, at least death puts an end to all that fear of *dying*.' Don would find that interesting.

'Actually, it's going to be the subject of my PhD,' she would say.

'*Really?*'

Myrna would become the daughter Don had never had. Well, she had a fine brain, did Myrna. He would live vicariously through her, taking pride in Myrna's award-winning, published, PhD. And one day, Don would say, 'The irony is, if Anna hadn't died . . .' He would not be able to finish the sentence.

'I know,' Myrna would say. 'I wouldn't have gone back to university.'

'I wouldn't have found the courage – to stand for election.'

'I wouldn't have got my PhD.'

'I wouldn't be an MP.'

'We'd be plain Myrna and Don.'

'We'd be nothing.'

124

'Same as she ever was.'

As for Roo, she would be in that blissful, awful state of pregnancy, thinking only of that new life growing big inside her.

She would read, in a birthing manual, that pregnant women should avoid soft cheeses, shellfish and funerals. 'Oh, don't worry about coming to the funeral,' Barbara would say to Roo. 'If Anna was alive, she wouldn't expect you to be there. Not in your state.'

Yes, I bloody would, Anna thought, comforting herself with the fact that at least her mother would mourn. But only for a month, or until the mid-season sale at Fenwicks. Then she would slip back into 'normality' – as Barbara chose to call her life.

Living with Don, but separately.

Oh yes, everyone would slip back into some sort of a routine. Roo and Warren, finding another godparent for their children. Tom, helping Justine through her meeting, tomorrow.

Tom would do the decent thing and marry Myrna, who would be discovering that the living was easier without all the bickering over her own wet grey knickers, draped around the furniture, or Anna's toothpaste spit, drying around the bowl of the sink.

Anna had never realised how unloved she was. *Life seems more peaceful*, she thought, as her train stopped suddenly at Swiss Cottage, *without me*.

Chapter Six

Anna had lost Sylvia with psoriasis. She was supposed to be on Line One, but there Anna found only *Gloria*; and the problem with Gloria was that her problem was shared by every other caller on Thursday's programme: Are you a Giver or a Taker? 'We don't want another Giver. Lose Gloria,' Mike screamed, in the manner of a futures trader. '*Lose* Gloria. *Get* Sylvia back.'

Sylvia had a sexy problem, said Mike. Not only was her skin addled with psoriasis ('great – straight out of a horror film'), but it was all take, take, take with Sylvia. People were always *giving* to her; they gave her advice and sympathy; they rubbed ointment into her back; they recommended lotions; they all looked after Sylvia.

'She's still in the system,' said Todd, the studio manager, calmly twiddling his buttons. 'Somewhere.'

'Sylvia. We would *very* much like to hear from you,' said Pammy, raising her voice and leaning close into her microphone, as if Sylvia might be hiding inside it. 'I am sorry, sweetie, but we seem to have lost you. *Problem Call* currently has a new operator and she is having *trouble* keeping track of the calls.'

'Never mind. Shall we go to Gloria, Pammy?'

126

'Good advice, Sean. Gloria?'

'Oh hello, yes?' came an impatient, severely grey-haired voice. 'Am I on the radio now?'

'That's right, sugar.'

'Only I've been hanging on for a long time now, and the researcher said . . .'

'The *operator*,' corrected Pammy.

'Can I just finish?'

'Sure, honey,' she said, sending a computer message to Anna which read: *Have you found Sylvia?*

'The telephonist said that I would be on soon.'

'Well, then. How can we help you, Gloria?' she asked, not bothering to correct Anna's job-title this time.

'Well, it interested me, your programme.'

'Good, good.' Pammy's voice oozed insincerity.

'Because I think *I* have a tendency to over-give.'

'Would you like to tell me in what way, my dear?'

'Well, I work for a hospice and in the evenings I run charities. Fun-runs, prison sit-ins, quiz suppers in aid of the Third World, that sort of thing.'

'Oh, what riotous *fun*. Lovely.'

'Well, more often than not, they're *not* fun.'

'I see. I get the picture,' soothed Pammy, as she sent Anna a computer message which read: *Have you still not found Sylvia? (PL)*

'It's just all too much,' snapped Gloria.

'You find you're taking on too much. Is that right, sugar bean?' It was as if she was addressing an extremely small child, who was about to jump from an incredibly tall building.

'No. More that people are asking too much of *me*.'

'I see. *Sincerely*, this is about my old friend, communication, isn't it, Sean?'

127

'Yes, in many ways . . .' started Sean, as Anna received a message from Pammy which read: *HAVE YOU FOUND SYLVIA? (PL)*

'I mean, it's something we can *all* understand. And the point is, sweets, you have to say to people, "I'm not a basket – I can't carry you."'

'But . . .'

'You can't continue to *do* that, Gloria. Otherwise, they'll come to rely on you. If you walk around like a sandwich board, advertising your availability, people will *treat* you like a sandwich board, won't they? Am I right?'

'Well . . .'

'So, why not stand up to these people?'

'Well, I do take pleasure in some of the activities.'

'If you're a traffic light, Gloria, that's always green, people are goin' to go *right ahead* and take advantage of you. You have to say *stop*. Occasionally. Else you're giving out *all* the wrong signals.'

'But . . .'

'Too right you are. Do you have a job?'

'Yes.'

'And what do you do?'

'I work in human resources.'

'Well, good. You see. And I hope that's helped you, Gloria, because, have we found Sylvia? Yes, we've found Sylvia. Sylvia is *back*.'

Sylvia had been sitting – patient on Line Five – for some time.

'Thank you, Sylvia, for having the courage to phone back. It's not *easy* phoning a show with such a steadily growing audience-share, such as *Problem Call*. It's the programme that more than sixty per cent of Radio Central listeners describe as essential listening.'

'Oh, no,' said Sylvia. 'I'm just so happy to speak to you, Pammy. I feel as if I *know* you. I've been listening to your show for years. I'd have called each day, every day, but I couldn't think of a *problem*. Until today when . . .'

Anna stopped listening, and stared at her terminal. She was thinking about Tom, and picturing him standing beside her, in a wedding photograph.

Do you think Pammy will ever let me get a word in? (SHar)

Anna looked at Sean Harrison through the dark glass. He stared straight at her, as if to confirm that the message was from him, and she smiled, she hoped, intelligently.

Had Sean's message not interrupted Anna's thoughts, she would have allowed her thoughts about Tom to reach their conclusion. She might even have been persuaded to have imaginary sex with him. But, now, Anna could forget all about Tom.

Certainly, Tom could forget all about Anna. She was picturing Sean's passport photograph falling casually out of her tube pass. *Oh, just my husband*, she would tell the ticket collector.

I hope Pammy has time for Olivia on Line Five. I've made a point of saying that she wants to talk to you. (APo)

Oh, why that message? If only Anna had waited, spending hours, or even days, perfecting the message, it could have ended up clever, or poetic, or lyrical.

Thanks. As she's last, Pammy'll be too tired to speak by that time. She's yawning now, so you never know . . . (SHar)

Thank you for understanding me, thought Anna.

Is this Cliché Call or Problem Call (APo)

She was beginning to breathe irregularly.

Cliché Call - Pammy says nothing that hasn't been sewn into a tea-towel first. (SHar)

Of course, Myrna had said that romance was nothing but a marketing concept. That, in the computer age, men and women didn't fall in love. Instead, they downloaded their details on to each other's interfaces. But Myrna should have been there, then, to feel the sexual tension. A tension that Anna had not felt with Tom, even in her imagination.

- There's a whole Pammy Lowental language, sweetie . . . (APo)
- Oh yes, honey . . . (SHar)
- Don't advertise your availability, darling. (APo)
- You're my own little sandwich board, sugar. (SHar)
- But don't be a basket. (APo)
- I'm not a basket, I'm a traffic light . . . (SHar)
- Well, I'm green for go . . . (APo)

Oh God, had she sent that?

- You're not so green . . . (SHar)
- Stop! Pammy'll see, sugar-bean. (APo)
- How could she see? She's opposite me. Or have you been giving out the wrong signals? (SHar)

Not intentionally, thought Anna, as Pammy said, 'And now, wanting to talk to *Sean*, we have Olivia, on Line Five,' she said wearily, because an hour's worth of enthusiasm had exhausted her. Olivia, honey. You feel as if people are walking all over you. Is that right, my love?'

There was no reply.

'Olivia? Don't tell me she's lost Olivia too? I think our

operator is going to have to have a spanking . . . Let me see what happens if I press this. Olivia?'

'You've pressed the Shutdown button,' said the studio manager, typically deadpan.

'OK, OK. I'll take my finger away, and la-*la*. Olivia?'

'Yes? came Olivia's small, sweet voice.

'Good. Now you're our last call of the day . . .'

'First-time caller. Bit nervous.'

'Fine and great. On this programme, nothing matters. We're all nervous. Now, I believe you want to talk to our resident Closure expert, Dr Sean Harrison?'

'Yes, I would like to talk to the doctor. Please.'

Anna watched Sean loosen his tie, thinking, not only was Sean Harrison-Ford handsome, but he was clever. He was clever in an old-fashioned sense of the word. He had spent much of his life locked away, studying. Anna knew that because Sean had said as much over lunch, today. She knew that Sean had been on dining terms with psychologists such as Alfred Bluger and Siegfried Hale.

'Really?' Anna had asked, as if such names were familiar to her.

Sean was clever. He had met Carl Rogers (even Anna had heard of *him*) and had written a number of original journals, in the 'Contemporary Anthropology' series, about the psychological analysis of neuroses. His first three books, all published by The Small Press – *Beyond the Id*, *Studies on Illusion*, and *The Science of Symptoms* – had disappeared. But *Orgasm*, which Magnus published in 1996, and *Closure*, published in January of this year, had been bestsellers. They had made Sean's name. 'But only as a schlock psychologist,' Sean had said. 'Trivial rubbish.'

('Er, hmm. Hmmm,' nodded Sean, as Olivia explained that her friends took advantage of her. Olivia wasn't even

131

sure that they were her friends. These 'friends' used her parents' house as if it were a hotel. They were always borrowing money, and fashion accessories, from Olivia.)

After the publication of *Orgasm*, Sean's career took off. He became a regular guest on radio problem programmes such as *Problem Call*. He wrote a column called 'Sticky Sex Matters' with the rap singer Kimm for a teenage magazine. (Sean wrote from the male perspective, Kimm from the female.) He even had a daytime-TV presence – on *The Shelley Show*, which discussed emotional and personal issues in front of a live audience.

Anna confessed that she had only seen the programme once, over Myrna's shoulder, although, naturally, she had read all about Shelley. Hadn't she done the 'In My Bin' column for *Mz* magazine, where celebrities revealed what was in their bin? Shelley, she remembered, had in hers four empty boxes of Cadbury's Milk Tray, and six of last season's kitchen tiles.

Sean started to describe the set, then laughed. It had been built to look like a priest's confessional booth. Guests wanting advice would have to sit in Sean's booth. During one programme post-mortem, Shelley had said that whereas Cilla always wanted a *Blind Date* wedding, *she* wanted a Shelley divorce.

'Filmed live in front of a studio audience,' Sean had said. 'That way you'd know that the laughter was real.'

'That's terrible.'

'Oh, it gets worse. I didn't even leave. I was fired. Or rather, the editor asked me to make way for a newer, younger personality.'

Sean had once had a future in academia. But even he was aware of the stereotype he now fitted: that of a media shock-psychologist. He was one of hundreds prepared to comment on anything, from the mother who hated her son, through the president addicted to sex, to the celebrity who had just committed suicide. And all in under twenty seconds.

He knew that other psychologists, and serious academics, envied the attention – what with all of Sean's television and radio performances, all his lectures and his columns, his tendency to pop up as a soundbite on current-affairs programmes.

But it was not the attention Sean Harrison craved. He did not want to to be amusing; to find himself turning up on daytime television programmes. He did not want to be witty, to be sought by television producers as a first-rate rentaquote, to be good for several thousand short interviews.

Sean wanted the respect of his peers. He wanted to be an original thinker. He wanted to make history, to have changed the course of history, to appear in those heavy analytical tomes as somebody other than a celebrity psychologist and a source of several amusing case studies.

Each time a new book appeared – *Pioneers in Psychology*; *Anthropology and Psychotherapy*; *The Modern Mind*; *Psychiatry in the Twentieth Century* – Sean would rifle through the index. And he would find pages and pages on hysteria; the study of hallucination; David Hume; Johann Herbart; humanistic therapy; Halliday; health psychology; even Sean's dim-witted contemporary, Hawthorne, for God's sake. And there would be two lines, at most, devoted to Harrison.

'I'm what your generation would call a cheap media tart,' Sean said to Anna over lunch.

'*My* generation?'

'Or a sad case. That's what you'd call me. Either way, I'm sorry. I've just bored you half to death.'

'I *asked* you to talk to me, remember? I was sick of talking about Him.'

'*Unfulfilled.*'

That was how Sean had described himself over lunch. The rest of the programme team had left the table, and Anna had been flattered that he had chosen to stay and talk to her, over coffee.

'This is the first time I've discussed this. I don't know why I'm talking about it now.'

'Well, thank you. It's been fascinating.'

'You're just being kind to a disappointed old man.'

'Hardly an old man. No, God, it's nice to meet someone with real ambition. Most of the men I know are just, well . . . *teachers.*'

'Nothing wrong with teachers. Those that can, teach, and those that can't, try and talk about it on the radio.'

'Listen, why don't you go back to The Small Press? Write books that you *value*.'

'Oh God, no. It's too late for a serious career.'

No, there *had* been a young man who had approached him. He had wanted Sean to write a book about wish-fulfilment. But the young man had disappeared, sending him a short note a month later explaining that there was no market, at present, for such a niche interest, or, indeed, for Sean Harrison.

'Why are you friends with these people, Olivia?' Sean asked his caller.

'Well, they live near me. We've . . . We've always been friends.'

'What do they *give* you, by way of friendship?'

'Well . . . Actually, I can't think of any . . .'

'Do they make you feel valued?'

'No.'

'Do you enjoy being with them?'

'I suppose . . . No.'

'Are you sometimes scared by them?'

'I am, yes.'

'But you would call them your friends?'

'Oh, yes.'

'I only ask because you talk about them as if you're doing battle with them. It's as if these so-called friends are actually your enemies.'

'Sometimes they are. Yes, doctor.'

'Call me Sean. I mean, we're good friends.'

Olivia giggled.

'We might have spent one minute on the phone, but I can call you a friend. Why not? You know Olivia, most people would say, if asked to count, that they had around a hundred friends – but how many of them *truly* are?' asked Sean, rhetorically.

'Ten?' guessed Olivia.

Sean changed tack.

'Olivia, how do you define a *friend*?'

'Ooh . . . erm . . . right . . . reliable, nice, good company?'

'Don't ask me – I have my own definition. But I tell you what, why don't you write, on a piece of paper, how you would define a friend? What you expect from them. You could expect very little, and that's fine, but if a friend doesn't meet your expectations – however low those expectations are – I wouldn't call them a friend.'

'Right,' said Olivia, understanding.

'I wouldn't lend them money, or clothes.'

'Yes,' said Olivia, hesitating.

'I wouldn't spend time with them.'

'You're right. Yes, you're right.'

'*Because*, Olivia,' said Sean, pausing dramatically, 'I'm worth more than that. We're *all* worth more than that.'

He sighed.

'These people aren't your friends, Olivia,' he said. 'Unless, of course, you define a friend as someone who *manipulates*, and *intimidates*, and *belittles* you. Robs you of any self-respect.'

'No.'

'No, these people aren't your friends, Olivia. No – surely you value yourself more than that?'

'So, remember Sean's wise words, Olivia,' added Pammy. 'If you don't value yourself, how can others even *begin* to?'

Anna watched Sean sit back in his seat, as Pammy ended the show. She watched him scratch his head, and unhook his microphone. She watched him deflate for a second. And all she wanted, at that moment, was to take the unhappy, unfulfilled Sean Harrison into her arms, and to fulfil him.

Anna still had an hour and a half to go before Justine's meeting in Soho, and was killing time in a late-opening supermarket.

She had just been forced out of the Eight Items or Less aisle. Anna had twelve items. She had hidden her vegetables under the toffee-flavoured ice-cream substitute, but the checkout girl had asked her to join another queue.

A long, straggly queue.

Anna stood at the back, wanting to start her banana-flavoured Mr Happy yoghurt. She was thirsty, desperate for a taste of the ice-cream, which had been a last-minute impulse buy. Anna had given up unrefined sugars, but she had been unable to resist the picture of a block of toffee on the tub's label.

The man in front of her turned round to stare disapprovingly at Anna's ready chopped, and bagged, vegetables. His own trolley was filled with muddy potatoes and dirty, long-haired carrots, and he looked smugly at his veg, as if to say, *Some people are prepared to spend a little extra time peeling polythene bags from the communal roll.*

But Anna didn't have the time to peel potatoes, let alone to bag her own vegetables. Of course, she did eat too much sugar – although for that Anna blamed the supermarkets. They had a monopoly on food retail, and displayed those products with the most fat (these they labelled low sugar) and the most sugar (these they labelled low fat) at the front of the shelves.

What could a poor, ordinary, unassuming shopper do in the face of cover shots of jolly cows and smells of freshly baked bread? Anna was a sucker for the bright colours covering the sugary products. She could almost taste the packaging on her toffee ice-cream substitute.

A woman joined the back of the queue, behind Anna, and smiled. Anna thought of the chapter she had just read in Wilhelm Grohe's *One Month to Happiness.*

HOW OFTEN DO WE FIND OURSELVES FROWNING?

In a study by Wierberschardt (1987), Group A was shown a picture of a woman with a straight face and Group B was shown a picture of the same woman, smiling. Group B attributed the words: 'successful, sexual, interesting, lively, and attractive' to the woman; Group A, on the other hand, described the woman as 'dull, asexual, unsuccessful and short . . .' The same study showed that children smile 400 times a day, whereas adults smile just 15 times a day. Yet people who smile more are happier.

She turned round to smile at the woman, who smiled back.

Anna then smiled even more broadly, but the woman's face opened up to reveal teeth, and Anna tried to compete with such a smile. But she did not have a large enough mouth.

'I hope you don't mind my saying this, but you look depressed,' said the woman.

'I'm sorry?' Anna felt as if she had something on her face, like leftover food.

'You look really *down*.' The woman laid four courgettes and a single kiwi fruit on the conveyor belt. 'Like *I* did, before I found . . .' She tailed off.

Jesus? wondered Anna. *Love? Pyramid-shaped teabags?*

'I'm fine, thanks,' said Anna. *Leave me alone*, she thought. *I am perfectly happy being unhappy.*

'I used to say the same. But, deep down, I was desperately miserable,' said the woman, taking out a leaflet. Her kiwi fruit rolled about the conveyor belt like a ball buffeted round in a pinball machine. 'Look, why don't you come along to our next meeting? At least think about it.' She handed Anna the leaflet.

Is your life empty and meaningless? Are you searching for love? So, why not come along to a Friends of Krishna meeting? You can feel better, with the help of Hare Krishna.

'Thank you,' said Anna, tightly. (Jesus, then.)

Spiritual groups seemed to target her. Jehovah's Witnesses called round to the flat just when some man had dumped her, and she was vulnerable, half-naked in her pyjamas, and alone. She was always being hit upon by Hare Krishnas or missionaries from the Church of Scientology.

Yet if ever Anna was with a friend, they left her alone.

Did she have over a hundred friends, as Sean had said was typical? Well, Roo and Warren she'd count as two . . .

old College friends made twenty-four . . . forgot Myrna, twenty-five . . . old school friends, thirty-six . . . thirty-seven . . . thirty-eight . . . Liz . . .

Yes, but she hadn't counted the friends she had made on her beautician's course. Thirty-nine, forty. Oh, and she'd forgotten all of her Arndale crowd; they all came in couples now . . . sixty-six, sixty-eight, seventy. The friends she had made from her fringe-theatre days . . . seventy-four. Was that all?

Oh and she could count Tom as a friend now – and Him, and all of her ex-boyfriends Bryan and Roger and Danny and Alfonso. And Liz's friends, who she saw some-times . . . and Roo's friends. *Some of them are now more mine.*

One hundred and twenty-two – phew. Those from Myrna's evening course. (She would have made more friends, had she stayed on after the first term.) And, of course, Anna had forgotten her sixth-form drinking posse . . . Karen . . . Jenny . . . Kate . . . One hundred and forty-four. Well, that was respectable, but, hang on – Anna hadn't counted the crowd that included Harriet and Lesley and Lynne. Yes, she hadn't seen them since two years ago, last June. That Club Med holiday! One hundred and ninety-three . . . and then there was the *Problem Call* team, although would she be on any of their lists?

Perhaps not yet.

Wait a minute. She didn't need Mike and Sean; there were all her overseas friends – Franca in Italy, and Bjorn in Norway. Bjorn. How *was* Bjorn? . . . Her American pen-pal, Gilly . . . That made two hundred and twenty-two . . . oh, and there was Pritti Poonjay . . .

Still, two hundred and twenty-three was . . . far too many. It was an ostentatious figure; it suggested that Anna was easy-come, easy-go. Anna Potter would have anyone as a friend. She might as well tout her friendship in the free-ads newspapers.

She had too many friends. One only needed a few. It was the same with soft furnishings: a couple of primary-coloured scatter cushions brightened up any living room; any more, and the same room seemed cluttered. It was all, ultimately, about appearances.

She was now sitting in a café over a cooling cup of cappuccino, as she still had an hour to fill before Justine's meeting. 'You want anything else?' the waitress asked, and Anna ordered a cannelloni. She wished that she was a regular at this café. Three generations of Italians would treat her as one of the family.

'Hello, Anna-lina,' the mother would call out, when she next walked in. 'Ciao, *bella*,' her round husband would say, kissing Anna's hands. His wife would give her pinnied husband a light slap on the wrists.

And then in would walk Vittorio, who for years had had his eye on Anna.

She would marry Vittorio and help to run the restaurant, having five children, befitting the stereotype, and growing fat on pasta and ciabatta.

But she would be bored in the restaurant, and Vittorio's father would tell Anna to 'shut up, and smile for the customers'. He would ask Vittorio, 'Why you not marry an Italian girl?' And that would be when Vittorio would begin to beat her.

'It is a woman's curse,' her Italian mother-in-law would spit.

Still half an hour before Justine's meeting. Anna walked London's dirty back-streets, stopping to look in Wardour

140

Street's shop windows. She went inside a shop that sold kitsch clocks in fluorescent plastic colours.

'Hell-*o*,' said the shop-owner, a little too brightly, and Anna felt as if she was the first customer for weeks. 'Seen anything you like?' said the owner, her hair in pigtails.

'Er, just looking,' grinned Anna, picking up a green clock that had been moulded into the shape of a pear. It came complete with a detachable stalk.

'That's one of my favourites,' said Pigtails, smiling. 'Not a bad price too, for what it is.'

Anna turned the clock upside down; the price-tag read, '£34.99.'

She breathed in, moving quickly away from the pear clock. 'I design them all myself,' added Pigtails, as if Anna had queried that. Anna felt as if she had walked into Pigtails' dream-shop – the shop that Pigtails had had in mind for many years.

And then Pigtails had seen this place for rent. That had made her mind up. She had bought coloured box files, presenting her idea to a bank. Finally, she had been given a small-business loan, to set up this shop, Zany Clocks – *for the people who take their time seriously.*

Pigtails had carefully set out her clocks on the specially made shelves. Brothers, sisters, friends and their fathers had been brought in to help paint the walls orange. There had been a successful launch party. Pigtails had opened her shop to the public, waiting for someone to make their first purchase. Waiting, and waiting, and waiting.

But no one came into Zany Clocks.

Not until Anna, today. Or rather, that was how it appeared to Anna as she moved slowly around the shop, aware of the woman's smile, which followed her, like Mona Lisa's, wherever she went.

Because Pigtails had to sell something. The bailiffs were on her back. She hadn't paid this month's rent, and the bank was about to call in its loan. Brothers, sisters, friends and their fathers were all keeping away. These days, Pigtails was always in a bad mood. Her mother, saying, 'I told you so;' and Pigtails insisting, 'I'll give it one more day.' Today being the day.

It was just Anna's luck to walk in on a young woman's dream. A young woman whose pigtails were starting to droop. Pigtails was smiling now, but unless Anna bought something, that smile would fade.

There was Anna, picking up egg-timers, picking up clocks, watched by Pigtails, dressed in a floral frock. She didn't want the chronometer in the shape of a tree (£46.99), nor did she want the stopwatch that had been melted into cheese (£21.99). Anna had no use for a watch that told the time in Peru (£16.99), and was repulsed by a clock moulded into a dark brown stool (£40.99.) 'Oh yes,' said Pigtails, coming over. 'It looks so *real*, doesn't it? Watch this.' She pressed a switch, and the stool-clock broadcast the sound of a constipated man on the toilet. At least, Anna assumed that it was a man.

'Don't you love the idea of getting two things for the price of one? I mean, a clock *and* a trick, y'know. Mind you, I didn't design this one. My brother begged me to order it out of another catalogue.' Her pigtails were very depressed.

'He thought it was funny,' she said.

'It's nice.'

'*So*. Anything you want?'

So, Pigtails had finally run out of patience with Anna, and with her dream.

'No, I . . . I don't think,' said Anna. Pigtails smiled even more unhappily. 'Hang on. This is nice,' said Anna, picking up an alarm clock that had been flattened to look like a fried egg. 'I *do* like this,' she said.

She was glad. Yes, she was pleased with her egg alarm clock. Anna walked out of Zany Clocks with her purchase. When the clucking chicken alarm went off, the egg yolk ran. It was zany. What's more, it was a clock.

It had cost her £16.99.

But why had Anna bought an alarm clock when at home she had an alarm clock shaped alarm clock, in perfect working order? It was not even as if Pigtails had been happy with Anna's sympathy purchase. £16.99 was not enough to bring back Pigtails' dream.

It was all emotional blackmail. Anna had spent £16.99 too much on a clock. For that, she blamed Pigtails – who should have realised, before she opened Zany Clocks, how harsh the world of commerce could be.

Anna was angry to be walking the streets of London when she should have been at home eating a ready-meal-for-one. She was frustrated to have spent her lunch-hour reading Justine's notes about her club-night when she should have been lunching with Sean.

Anna sat on a bench, watching the traffic of passers-by.

She began to peel off the price-labels from her shopping. Anna did not want her Sudanese cleaning lady to know how much she was prepared to pay for bagged vegetables. Her cleaning lady lived in a temporary hostel with her newborn baby and could not afford toilet paper. Or rather, Anna assumed that she could not afford toilet paper, as she was always stealing Anna's.

Why was she half an hour early for a meeting which had nothing to do with her? It all put Anna in mind of that 'chat' with her headmaster back in 1985.

She remembered Mr Steel's office as an oasis of green

143

carpet, bottles of whisky, and earthy pot plants inside a Victorian monolith of a school. Slits of windows inhaled dirty air everywhere except inside his room. Yet Anna had felt uneasy.

'This has nothing to do with you,' said Mr Steel.

'I know.'

'*Plus*, I didn't think you'd defend drug-taking.'

'Oh, I don't sir. I just wondered whether you could at least let Justine take her A-levels. That's all. I'm sorry.'

'And look as if I condone drug-taking?'

'But it's only another month of school.'

'Well, this is all very *noble* of you, but . . . I wouldn't have thought that you were friends with Justine at all.'

Not only was Anna doing something noble, but she was missing double geography – because she had not been friends with Justine for years. Not since primary school, when they had been forced together. Well, they had lived at the end of the same cul de sac. They had shared everything then, including Justine's bad reputation. They had shared Justine's punishments.

They had both been kept behind after school – after Justine had pushed the foster girl into the swimming pool. Anna had apologised for laughing, later asking for some of the girl's rough paper. But that had been a mistake.

The foster girl had smiled almost gratefully, pulling page after page out of her exercise book. She had gone on tearing, deaf to Anna, who had begged her to stop. Anna had known that the girl would want something in return.

Sure enough after that there had been a series of gifts. There had been that present of a Pippa doll, and the Forever Friends pencil sharpener. The girl had refused to take back her blue Shatterproof ruler. It was, she had begged, a present.

144

From that point on, Anna hadn't been able to join in any after-class activities. Well, these were all at the girl's expense. Pinning abusive signs to the girl's back. Hiding the foster girl's blazer. The foster girl who was now Anna's friend. So, Anna couldn't laugh at the fact that the girl didn't have a proper mum and dad, or a Donny Osmond pencil case.

She had been forced to go to the foster girl's birthday party. Alone. The girl had owned only one board-game. They had had to play Sorry all afternoon. At tea, to Anna's horror, there hadn't been any cake.

Anna sat on the bench, warm with the thought of her two hundred and twenty-three friends, turning cold as she realised that only one of them had sent Anna a congratulations card, to celebrate her promotion to *Problem Call*. (Liz.)

Only fifteen of them had remembered Anna's thirtieth birthday – and of the nine people invited to the birthday dinner, only eight had turned up. A birthday dinner made up of the finest ready-made ingredients from Selfridge's food department.

'Shall we start without Justine?' Anna had asked, between courses. She had stared miserably at Justine's napkin, still rolled up, on the raffia mat.

'Anna, I doubt she's coming now,' Roo had said, gently.

'I can't understand it. She said she'd be here.'

'Why don't you clear away her place?' said Myrna, moving sideways into Justine's empty space.

Anna put Justine's soup on a low heat. She laid out her tarragon chicken on a separate plate. She kept out the cutlery, just in case.

'You never know,' she said, hopefully. 'She might still show.'

'I doubt it,' said Myrna. 'She's probably in a gutter some-where, out of her tiny, empty mind.'

'Oh yeah, couldn't make that,' Justine had said the next day. 'Sorry, Potter.'

Potter. Outsiders might have presumed that a pet-name. But Anna knew better. Her surname, when used by Justine, had always preceded some or other humiliation. Potter enjoys school. Look what Potter's got in her sandwich-box. *Potter*'s friends with the foster girl. Potter likes squidgy cheese triangles. Potter doesn't like sex. Potter's friends with the fat girl. Potter's frigid. Potter's going out with Graeme Lomond. *Potter*'s started her periods.

Anna remembered that one painfully. As she had taken the long walk from the comprehensive's Portakabin to the old grammar school science block, she had left behind a trail of sniggers.

Justine hadn't told Anna about the red stain seeping through her dress. Only the new girl – Myrna from Middlesbrough – had taken Anna to the bathroom, furnishing her with a sanitary towel and a few facts about the miseries of menstruation.

Later, Myrna had gone on to inform Anna of the miseries of life in general.

Anna had arranged to meet Justine at the club at eight o'clock. But it was ten past eight now and Anna's escalator was sliding underground into Piccadilly Circus station.

She would not be at Justine's meeting. As Sean had said, she should stop investing so much in her relationships with other people. She should invest rather more in herself.

A train was due in three minutes, and Anna would be on it.

Anna defined a friend as someone who was reliable,

146

and warm, and honest, and fascinating, and nurturing. Yet, Justine was unreliable. She did not nurture her oldest friend. Rather, she manipulated, and intimidated Anna. She patronised her, and robbed her of her confidence.

The doors of the tube train squeezed shut. Anna sat down, angrily. From now on, she was not going to be treated with disrespect. As Sean had said, people should value themselves more than that.

She took out her print-out of his computer messages. *Yes honey*. Of course she would lose Justine. But Anna would not miss one friend. *You're my own little sandwich board, sugar*. Not now that she had two hundred and twenty-three.

Chapter Seven

Thank God – Friday.

It was the end of Anna's first week, and she was beginning to know her way around the office. Behind Pammy's
desk – the stationery cupboard. Beside Anna's desk – the
communal kettle. (She was always being asked to make the
tea.) In reach of Mike – a library of books ranging from Erge
Frumm's *The Art of Being Content* to Pammy Lowental's most
recent autobiographical self-help work: *How I Came Back from
the Dead*.

The filing cabinets were kept in a back room, every problem filed alphabetically. As her first task for the day, Anna
knelt down at the S cabinet looking for the Single file that
Pammy had asked for. It was needed for the Friday morning
planning meeting.

'Do I come to that meeting?'

'*Nooo*,' said Pammy, outraged, as if she had exposed Anna's
plot to work her way ruthlessly up the Radio Central ladder
until, in a bloody coup, Anna would take her job.

'Right. Sorry,' said Anna. It was only that she had not
know how to fill her time; there was no programme on a
Friday.

'I don't think we're quite ready for that, are we? Shall

we start by you finding me that Single file? Then we can talk about *management* meetings.'

'I only meant if I needed to come . . .'

'Let's try to walk, dear. Then we can run.'

Now in that back room, Anna pulled out the steel tray of S files. Sadness . . . Self-esteem, Self-image, Self-judgment, Self-pity . . . There was nothing under Single, Solo, or Solitary.

Under U, Anna found neither Unmarried nor Unwed – merely Uncertainty, Unhappiness, and Underdog. She looked under Loneliness, finding only a fat file marked Losing, inside which there were various sub-headings – Losing an argument, Losing a husband, Losing a limb, Losing money, Losing self-respect, and Losing the will to live.

Anna tried Bachelor, but such a file didn't exist. What she did find was a section headed Celebrity anxieties; and she simply couldn't resist reading about the sufferings of the rich and famous. The section was filled with smaller files marked Eating disorders, Egotism, Non-prescription drugs, and Self-mutilation. There, at last, Anna found Single.

She shuffled through the sub-divisions, Single and anxious; Single and broody; and Single and desperate, feeling smug as she realised that she herself belonged in the file marked Single and enjoying it, rather than, say, Single and suicidal. Certainly, she was enjoying thinking of the message that Tom had left, last night, on her answering machine. *Anna, it's Tom here. It was nice to see you last night, and I was actually wondering whether you'd be free on Saturday. Erm, yeah. Give me a ring.* She had been pleased to hear his voice. Yet, Anna decided not to return his call, knowing that she almost had Sean.

Pammy came quietly into the room, shaking her head at the sight of Anna, kneeling on the floor, reading a magazine article about the difficulties beautiful, wealthy, celebrated women had finding a suitable date. She took the file marked Cindy Crawford out of Anna's hands. Ever so gently.

'Might I ask what is going *on*?'

'Oh, sorry. I found this in the Single file, which wasn't in the right place. It was in Celebrity anxieties.'

'*So*. You disapprove of our filing system?'

'No, not at all, but everything was in the wrong place. I mean, Death was filed under Emotional issues. I was just confused, that's all.'

'You don't think that death is associated with emotion?' Pammy shook her rose-blonde curls, and Anna half-expected to see them fall, like scented petals. 'I must say, now *I'm* the one who's puzzled.'

Pammy explained that, unlike, say, the Jimmy Salad show, which might file things *logically*, she preferred to exercise her staff's emotional instincts. Did Anna want to take issue with that?

'No, not at all.'

'So why are we sitting here, reading about Cindy *Crawford*, when we should be at the Friday forward-planning meeting. Hmmm?'

'I . . .'

'Err, hmmm. Exactly.' She stood up, her bosom almost toppling her over, and brushed down her powder-blue A-line skirt. '*Up*, young lady, unless you want to sit in here all day reading about supermodels.'

'Am *I* meant to be at that meeting?' Anna felt as if she had asked for a week off work to read up on Cindy Crawford.

'*Yeees*.'

She grabbed the Single file and followed Pammy back

into the main office. A blonde woman – who freelanced from home, answering Pammy's mail – sat next to Mike. Anna had seen her before but couldn't remember where. And there too was Sean. Anna tried to look everywhere but at him. Unfortunately, he caught her eye.

'*Hi.*'

As there was no programme today, Anna had not expected to see Sean in the office. She had dressed down not so much for Friday as for the end of civilisation. Her green jumper, bought third-hand from Kensington Market, had been hand-washed and drained too many times before being wrapped in a rolling-pin and left to crack and dry. Anna was wearing dungarees, for God's sake. She wanted to run home and change.

'*Finally,*' said Mike, as Anna sat down.

'Don't ask where I found *Anna,*' said Pammy now, putting an arm around her charge. Anna prayed that she wouldn't mention the celebrity file on Cindy Crawford. 'I found her reading the celebrity file on Cindy *Crawford.*'

Blonde Freelance laughed, and Anna remembered where she had seen her: at the local municipal swimming pool. Blonde stepping out of the shower, dripping wet and semi-naked, like a star in a soft-porn film from the seventies.

She so resembled a Barbie doll that Anna had been surprised to see that her breasts had nipples.

Anna wondered whether Blonde remembered seeing *her* naked. Anna, shivering, in line for the showers, and trying to cover up with a stolen Trust House Forte Hotel hand-towel. Had she remembered, Blonde would know why Anna chose to wrap herself in so many clothes.

How, she wondered, had Blonde manged to fish out all the beauty from the gene pool, when Anna had to

151

suffer reedy hair and eyes the colour of mud? She always felt that women like Blonde were thoroughly selfish. They sat there smugly as if any woman could make the effort to look that way.

'So. Do we have any thoughts, Anna?' That was Pammy.

'Well, I don't really have any ideas as *such*. But I did think we could discuss the problems that people have when they look like a famous person.'

'You mean, like, say, Cindy Crawford?' That was (bitchy) Blonde.

'It has to be under the umbrella of Closure.'

'Mikey's right. So let's get back to the drawing board here.'

'Anyway, it's hardly going to prompt an interesting discussion. "Hi, I'm Mary from Slough, and I look like Hillary Clinton."'

That, again, was Blonde.

Anna looked at Sean, to see if he was laughing too. But he was half-reading a newspaper, and unaware that Blonde was smiling in slow-motion at him.

Beautiful Blonde, with her American-white teeth, was the sort of woman Sean Harrison would fall in love with. She was the type of woman Anna would describe as secretly ugly. It was only that she was sly enough to fool people into thinking otherwise.

'Actually, the fame thing isn't as black and white as that. There's . . .' Anna paused, because she had seen Mike's expression.

'Do you mind telling me which are the black aspects and which are the white . . . ?' he asked.

'I . . .'

'In fact, don't tell me, let me guess. The awful side of being famous just happens to be the *black*.'

'To be fair,' said Pammy, 'I don't think Anna thinks before she speaks. And, you know, the idea might be naive, but it's not completely uninteresting. Of course, it has nothing whatsoever to do with *Closure*. So we can't tackle it now. But maybe later, OK, Anna? And Mike, if *you* want to talk about the prejudice issue later, you know I'm right here. OK, honey?'

She's unreliable even as my enemy, thought Anna, looking at the pink ribbon Mike was wearing for breast awareness day. ('Well, I think we should all wear ribbons,' Pammy had said. 'I didn't know that it was a particular *day*.')

'Well, anyway,' said Pammy now. 'What *I* wanted to suggest is that we do Being Single,' she said. 'Because that, after all, is what Closure is all about. I mean we *all of us* want to at least end up finding husbands, and . . .'

'That's not true, actually. The majority of western women are now financially and emotionally independent. They hardly need a husband to get by.'

That, surprisingly, was Blonde.

Anna felt as if she was watching a porn-magazine centre-fold break free of her staples, coming to life as a strident women's rights protestor. Anna did not have the courage to stand up, publicly, for the sisterhood – although, for that, she blamed women like Blonde, who were always so catty in a crowd. They ridiculed women who had not yet located their G-spot. They mocked women, such as Anna, who chose to wear make-up.

Women such as Blonde did not wear make-up. They did not need to.

It was easy for Glamorous Blonde. She would not be scared of being dismissed as a frigid bitch who couldn't get a man – as had happened to Myrna in the Swan when she had intervened in a domestic battle. 'No wonder you're on your own,' the woman Myrna had taken to defending had screamed at her. 'Yer frigid whore. He wouldn't fancy *you* anyway.'

'All I'm saying,' said Blonde now, 'is that I'm bringing up three children, on my own, without their father – wherever he is – and *fine*. I mean, I'm solvent. I've got my own flat. My own GTI. I'm independent. Perhaps unsurprisingly, I'm happy.'

Blonde could have been drafting an ad for the personals. Anna imagined her own ad reading, *I'm overdrawn. I rent a dump. I drive an old Mini whose headlights are so battered it looks as if it is crying. I'm dependent on everyone I know. Perhaps unsurprisingly, I'm unhappy.*

'If anything, *men* are the redundant sex,' continued Blonde. 'Women have to break down those myths. One of which is that all women want is a man. These are myths perpetrated by men, and only because we have no *need* of them any more. Well, most of us, anyway.'

She looked sideways at Anna.

'Well, I'm like Anna,' said Pammy. 'You see, I do need a man.'

'I didn't say that,' said Anna, horrified. 'I don't think th . . .'

'I mean, I *am* Ally McBeal,' interrupted Pammy, moving her bulk around her chair.

Anna apologised for laughing.

'Don't worry, Anna,' said Pammy, turning to her, and smiling, nastily. 'It's not *you* we were rejecting, but your idea. Personally, I love the idea of having a whole programme about single people . . .'

'But that wasn't my id . . .' *I don't even have any business cards*, she thought.

'And it's good that you brought out your little file.' She

154

patted the Single file on Anna's lap. 'That shows *initiative*.'

Sean suddenly leaned forward.

'I'd like to devote a programme to Revenge,' he said, wrestling his fingers through that thick hair.

'Yes,' said Anna. *Starting with Pammy.*

'I don't mean revenge for day to day, petty grievances,' he said. 'What I'm talking about here are lifelong grudges. Angry thoughts that turn in on themselves and switch to self-anger and self-hatred. Revenge on people who've destroyed a part of you.'

Blonde looked at him and raised an eyebrow.

'I *see*. Right,' said Pammy patiently, as if the discussion was starting to move too quickly for her.

'Revenge,' thought Mike aloud. 'Yeah, I can see that working.'

'Well, I don't know. I believe we should learn to *re-direct* our anger first.'

Sean did not look at Blonde, who had spoken. To Anna's relief, he lightly dismissed her, saying, 'Well, that's fine in academic La-La land. But here on Earth people's feelings are real. And people feel real anger. Say, at school, they were bullied. Well, what's the point of working that through with your therapist for thirty-odd years? Get revenge instead. Get Closure.'

Pammy: 'I don't know. I don't feel too comfortable about advocating this.'

Mike: 'Well, I like it. It ties in well with Greer Lawton's book, which is out at Christmas. *Get Back*.'

Blonde: 'Surely the best revenge is happiness? Surely, we should be withdrawing such anger from our enemies, and focusing that same energy on the positives in our lives?'

She looked at Sean as if he represented all of mankind. Blonde and Sean seemed to be having a silent conversation to which the rest were not privy – although Anna might have been imagining that.

Sean held his pen as if it was a cigarette, and sighed, saying, 'Well, I disagree. Ever since *Hamlet*, revenge has had a bad press. But, really, revenge is a good thing. *Physiologically*, it's been proven to be a good thing.'

'Well, that doesn't make it all *right*,' interjected Blonde, her voice high-pitched.

'Revenge gets your blood moving faster,' said Sean, ignoring Blonde again. 'Makes you feel warm inside – particularly if the punishment fits the crime.'

'Revenge is such a *male* response to anger,' said Blonde, her voice at an even higher pitch. 'Lash out!'

'No, that's not true. Women swear by it too, although I'd admit that there are differences. Men, for example, prefer their revenge to be brief and brutal, whereas women take a more deliberate and drawn-out approach.'

Anna felt warm inside simply watching Sean breathe. Hearing him use the word *physiologically*.

'I do *agree*,' said Pammy, doodling on her over-sized sketchpad, 'that past experiences can be a real ball and chain. But aren't we in danger here, Sean, of boxing with *shadows*?'

'Well, good. Good to be out there fighting, instead of just sitting there, playing victim.'

He looked at Blonde knowingly. She shot him back a look that Anna was unable to read.

Mike said, unhappily, 'It can be hard to get revenge, though. I mean practically speaking, because say – and I use this merely as an example – the school bully has moved away? Or has become, say, a member of your friendly local constabulary?' (His fingers mimed quotation marks as he spoke the word *friendly*.)

'What I'm trying to say . . . And I know I won't be listened to – being both female and blonde . . . But, what I'm trying to say is that instead of getting revenge, we should be focusing on making amends with our aggressors. Talking about our concerns.'

'Talking has its place,' said Sean, impassively. 'But real anger needs a real outlet. And there's a difference, too, between healthy anger and unhealthy anger. Unhealthy anger turns in on itself. It's unhealthy to blame oneself, instead of – to use *your* example – the school bully.'

'*My* example?' asked Mike looking right and left. 'No. I was using it as a *general* example. I was never . . .'

'You tell yourself, "It's my fault." Which can only be destructive.'

Pammy seemed puzzled. Blonde squeezed the clip on her clip-file.

'Let's not get diverted from the subject,' said Mike. 'Because I like the idea of revenge. And I don't think it will hurt the ratings either. Pretty sexy subject, actually. It would please Duncan.'

'I think we should do it then,' said Pammy. She clicked her multi-coloured pen to green.

'Great.'

'Not because of the ratings,' she added quickly. 'But because *Problem Call* should grasp the nettle . . .'

'. . . of difficult issues,' nodded Sean.

Pammy nodded too, scribbling something illegible on her notepad. Blonde inserted her pen into the clip of her clipboard, as if it was an old-fashioned torture instrument. The pen jammed.

'Great,' said Sean. 'We all of us filter our present through our past. When what we *should* be doing is letting go of it. And what better way to deal with some bastard ex-boyfriend than . . . ?'

'Than by cutting up his suits?' said Blonde, opening and snapping shut the clip. Her voice was smooth as she said, 'Well, maybe I should have done *that*, Sean, instead of trying to deal with an adult situation in an adult manner.'

'Well, why not? Better that than talking about *low frustration tolerance beliefs* over the bloody breakfast table.'

'Oh, I see,' said Blonde, releasing her pen. 'Well, thank you, Sean. I mean, thank you for choosing *now* to express your feelings, rather than when it was appropriate: ie, six months ago, when I wanted to discuss all of this . . . this *inner conflict* of yours.' She was pale pink, but her voice kept steady. 'But, oh no, wait for a professional planning meeting and *then* talk about our relationship. *Now*'s a good time. Just let it all out.'

The word 'relationship' hit Anna in the stomach. She minded not so much that Sean and Blonde had been together, but that she had been blind to it. It was as Wilhelm Grohe had written in *One Month to Happiness: Do you find yourself taking delicate, human relationships and wringing out of them all warmth, and meaning – until all that is left is simply a figment of your imagination?*

Yes, thought Anna. At the age of thirty-one, she still had imaginary boyfriends.

If you answered yes to that question, you might in fact be suffering from Negative Reality Thinking. You will have turned your desires into dreams, with the subconscious hope that they will then not come true. How can they? They are dreams. You think you are safe in the world of make-believe. But are you really? Reality has a nasty habit of intruding.

'I'm sorry, Pammy,' said Blonde, stuffing together her

158

Filofax. She stood up. 'Perhaps it would be better if I didn't come in on Fridays – at least while Sean is co-presenting. As you know, I did think that he and I could work together, but I should have realised that his theories on couple conduct after a relationship – and my own – were incompatible.'

'No,' said Sean, quietly and firmly. '*We* were incompatible.'

'You have a tendency to turn any unhappy situation into a terrible one,' said Blonde, standing up, but still shuffling her bits of paper together. 'You awfulize, Sean.'

She walked out, dramatically.

The meeting quickly broke up after that. Pammy jerked away and began to flick through a pile of faxes. Mike slid his chair smoothly away from the table and muttered something about his wife, Frannie.

Sean leaned back in his chair, and looked at Anna. 'Coming to lunch?' he asked, with a half-smile.

'Oh. Actually, I've arranged to have lunch with this friend,' admitted Anna, sadly. 'Liz. I'm meeting her here.'

'Well, bring the friend,' said Sean. 'I need someone to talk to about that awful ex-girlfriend of mine.'

'How long have you been together?' asked Anna of Sean. 'With the er blonde woman? I don't know her name.' She sipped from a can of caffeine-free Diet Coke, to get rid of the metal taste of her chicken supreme.

'God no, we're not together,' he said, stabbing at some broccoli. 'Haven't been *together* for six months. We should never really have been together at all. Bad enough to have two psychotherapists in the same room, let alone in the same relationship.'

Anna nodded, with understanding.

'Oh please don't be *understanding*,' Sean said, picking up his fork and spearing his asparagus tip. 'For the whole year – twelve months – three hundred and sixty-five days of our relationship, she was so understanding. Patiently, endlessly, brutally, *understanding*.'

Anna was sitting with Sean in the Radio Central canteen, oblivious to the crowds of people around her clattering trays and queueing up for the lasagne, although even she could hear the petty sounds of argument centring around the chicken supreme.

'Chicken fucking *supreme*?'

'Chicken?'

'Supreme?'

'Only chicken supreme?'

The lasagne had run out half an hour ago, and Anna could hear the comforting hum of resentment shuffling along the canteen queue. She heard the customers blaming the serving staff. The serving staff, blaming the kitchen staff. The kitchen staff, blaming the suppliers. The suppliers, blaming management for ordering too much chicken supreme. Management, blaming the kitchen staff for cutting the lasagne into over-sized squares. Kitchen staff, blaming the serving staff.

'Explain to our clients that we are sorry. That we have run out of lasagne,' management muttered to the serving staff. 'And would they like some of the lovely chicken supreme? *Explain*,' management said severely, to complaints from Ada of the serving staff.

Two months earlier, the canteen management had changed hands. Counters had been ripped out. Walls had been painted a leafier shade of green. Old tables had been taken out, and new ones put in. Now, coffee could be self-served from a metal dispenser, which also served hot chocolate.

The canteen had become a *restaurant*, although the same old cans of cola filled a new and fancy fridge.

The canteen's users suddenly found themselves referred to as 'the clientele'.

The same old serving staff, including Ada, were sent on a group bonding week. They climbed the Brecon Beacons, discussing with management their concerns as they endured team-building exercises. They learned to be open with each other about their difficulties, and to use a compass when out climbing a Welsh hillside. Serving staff were trained to say, 'Would you like a piece of fruit with that?'

And, 'Have a nice day.'

But it remained the same old canteen. The old leftover smells remained, as did the contracted catering suppliers. The sugar now came in tiny paper bags to allow more efficient stock analysis. The salad was separated into see-through compartments. But it was the same old Gertie serving it. Only management had changed. The same old Ada was sitting on the till. Same old Ada – still bitter and unpleasant, in her endearing way.

But now she said, 'D'you want fruit wi' that?'

'No thanks.'

'Not a bana'a?'

'No, really.'

'It's good for ya, honest.'

'No.'

'Vitamin C in an orange?'

'No.'

'Well fuck off then and have a nice day.'

Anna heard all this argument bickering around her; she could see the queues of people demanding lasagne. She could hear the shock-jocks discussing Monica Lewinsky, Milosevic and management. But she tried to block it out.

Because she was enjoying an intimate moment with Sean. He had just asked Anna to tell him about her family.

'Why?' asked Anna, coyly.

'Well, only that your relationship with your mother might explain the reason why you let Pammy treat you so badly.'

'She does, doesn't she? But I don't know what to do about it.'

'So, does your mother put you down as often as Pammy does?'

'God.' Anna stopped eating, and looked at him. 'How d'you know *that*?'

'Oh well.' Sean looked sad. 'I've been in this game a long time. Women often have issues with their parents.' He smiled, sympathetically. 'In your case, I knew it would be your mother.'

'How?'

'Well, the way you allow Pammy to treat you. Your attitude to older women generally.'

'Am I that easy to diagnose?'

'Sorry, it isn't my place.'

He looked bored.

'Oh no, please, say.'

'No, seriously. I shouldn't.'

'Honestly. Please. I'd be grateful.'

'Well, I suppose I was right when I advised you to speak to that woman, wasn't I? The one who you felt rejected you, because she let her flat to someone else? I mean, don't you feel better about that?'

'Oh, much better. And I'm still not smoking. I've chucked out my whole Memory Box, even the friendship stuff.'

'Are you still looking for a flat by the way?'

'Well, um, yeah, I suppose . . . Yes.'

'Because I might be able to help you out. A friend of mine

162

– a psychiatrist – is going to the States for six months, and he needs a cat-sitter. Someone to look after his place, rent-free. Do you like cats?'

'Oh yes,' she lied. 'Of course.'

'Well then, I'll talk to Sebastian. But about . . . You know, if there's one thing I've learned, it's that relationships don't right themselves.'

'Mmmm.'

'You should discuss your feelings with her. Your mother, I mean.'

'*No*,' said Anna, lightly. 'You don't know my mother.'

Anna's mother believed that feelings, like bowel movements, should be aired only in the privacy of a GP's surgery. Introspection was 'modern' and, worse still, 'American'.

Ah, smiled Sean, but she wasn't only Anna's mother. What was her name? *Barbara* was also a woman. And unless Anna sorted out her issues with her own mother, she would always have problems with motherly figures, such as Pammy. Did she want control of her life? Well, then, she should talk to Barbara as an equal. Or was Anna enjoying her prolonged adolescence?

His smile stretched into a grin.

Anna laughed, admitting that she was still out to shock both Barbara and Don. By calling them *Barbara* and *Don*, or by changing her religion. (Or at least the denomination, from C of E to Catholicism.) She raided her parents' cupboards whilst visiting their house, and felt it her right to take home all of their belongings. Anna's mother would joke, *Leave behind the silver*.

Was that what Sean had meant?

Yes, grinned Sean. But, seriously. Wasn't Anna behaving like a teenager? Or was that what she wanted? Did she want to be a child forever? To go on and on being dependent? She

163

was beginning to sound like one of Sean's former patients. Soon, she would dream of being strangled by the roots of her family tree. Yes, seriously. The syndrome had been well documented. If a parent was critical, the 'child' would become self-critical too. Feelings had to be expressed.

'It's more complicated than that,' said Anna, thoughtfully. 'I think Mum's scared of the world, to be honest. And, although she doesn't seem it sometimes, she's sort of fragile. If I told her what I actually felt about her, I think she'd fall apart.'

But Anna couldn't protect her mother indefinitely. She was not responsible for the modern world, or, indeed, for her mum. *Barbara* needed to draw on her reserves of strength. Otherwise, Anna would be sacrificing her own sense of self, to shield her mother from reality. That was no good for Barbara, and it was no good for Anna.

It was important for them both to be open.

'Mmm,' she said. 'But, the thing is . . . Mum's actually sacrificed a lot for *me*. Sometimes, I feel as if she sacrificed her *marriage* . . . She and my dad barely talk these days. I don't know. She waited a long time to have me. I'm her life, really.'

It sounded, to Sean, as if Anna's mother was blackmailing her, emotionally. Children weren't there to paper over the cracks of a parent's problems. Whatever was wrong with her mother and father's marriage they should sort out themselves. Anna didn't have to play piggy-in-the-middle forever. She certainly shouldn't feel like the answer to all her mother's problems. That way, insanity lay.

'I suppose you're right,' admitted Anna, thoughtfully.

Oh, Sean didn't pretend to have all the answers either. It was just that the way a family functioned, or did not function, would affect the child's self-esteem. If the mother-child

164

relationship was unhealthy, and left to fester, the dynamics could be hugely damaging.

Often people stayed in relationships only in the hope of someone coming along and rescuing them. But that wasn't going to happen, was it? Anna had to find a way through.

She shouldn't look so worried, either.

Sean knew that it was not his place to interfere. But he did hate to watch the way Pammy treated women such as Anna. He said, 'Your parents aren't always right, you know. All they teach you, is to be like them. Break free from the past, Anna. Break free for your own well-being.'

'I thought we were going to talk about *you* today,' said Anna, smiling.

Anna had arranged to have Liz sent down to the canteen when she arrived, all splutters, and wearing God-knew-what – although she was beginning to regret not standing Liz up.

'Hello there,' said Liz, appearing from God-knew-where.

Her make-up almost matched her face. Sean would barely be able to see the join. Any feature worth lining with kohl, or emphasising with blusher, Liz had underlined and over-emphasised. Well, she had come to London, almost a decade ago, to find a man.

'There are none at all,' Liz had said, 'in Australia.'

Yet no matter how much thick foundation Liz wore, her skin still looked filthy, like the bottom of a just-drained sink. No matter how many layers of lipstick she creamed on, still it wore off. Liz suffered constantly from visible lip-liner.

Right now, the outline of her lips was dark brown, to match her tray of food – one slice of cake and a scoop of coffee ice-cream. She sat down with a splat, but had forgotten a spoon.

'Hold on a mo',' she said, lipstick dripping like brown sauce from the outline of her lips.

'That was . . . ?' asked Sean, raising an eyebrow as, behind them, Liz played havoc in the kitchen. Not finding a spoon, she had gone behind the counter to collect one, and had run into Ada on the way. Ada's screams could be heard echoing out of the kitchen, reverberating around the canteen.

'Bloody hell. Had to wash my own *spoon*,' said Liz now, sitting down and making herself comfortable.

Anna closed her eyes in embarrassment.

'Liz, this is Sean. Sean, this is Liz.'

'Sean. Hell-*o*,' said Liz, as if she had not seen a man for several, solitary-confined years.

'Mind if I join you?' That was Blonde.

'No, course not,' said Liz. 'Plenty of room, if I go beside *Seany*.'

Liz switched seats. But not in a quiet or discreet way.

Blonde sat down, saying, 'It's *Anna*, isn't it?'

'I thought you'd stormed out,' muttered Sean. 'I thought, At last, she's having an honest-to-God, human tantrum.'

'Yes, it's Anna.' Mousily.

'Well,' sighed Blonde. 'That's why I came to find you. I don't think that's the right note on which to end our conversation. Nor is it the right way to deal with our situation. It's important for us both to . . .' But she was interrupted.

'*So*. What's the juicy gossip?'

That, of course, was Liz.

'What do you mean – juicy gossip?' asked Blonde, squeezing a slice of lemon on to her fish.

'How did you manage to get some fish?'

'Oh, Sean. You know I can get anything I ever want.'

'I mean, the gossip about men,' said Liz. 'Any decent

166

ones, Anna, on your new programme? I mean, apart from *Seany*.'

Anna sat there mortified. She felt each of her organs squirm.

'God, and I wonder why my career isn't progressing beyond a certain point.'

'No worries,' said Liz, misunderstanding Blonde. 'I know you and Seany are together.'

'Actually, we're . . .'

'No, there's a guy over there though, looks real cute.'

Looking their way was a man of indeterminate age, with the biggest moustache Anna had seen outside of a First World War photograph.

'Him?' she asked in disbelief.

'Don't look his way. I'm doing The Rules.'

'Which rules are they, Liz?' asked Sean, pushing his plate away. 'Anyone else want dessert? I'm going to get.'

'Nah, that's fine. Take one of mine. I don't want this pud, actually.' Before he could protest, Liz had tipped the iced square of sponge onto his plate, saying, 'Hope that's OK with your chicken remains.'

'Oh, you're not talking about that book of rules for women, are you?' asked Blonde repugnantly, as Sean looked with horror at his sponge. 'The ones which tell women how to behave around men? Like: "Don't accept a date after Wednesday for a Saturday night."'

'After Wednesday?' Anna made a mental note.

'Yeah, those rules,' said Liz.

'The ones which generalise about mankind?' Blonde snorted. 'And patronise womankind?'

'I'm not to look at that guy at all,' said Liz loudly, ignoring Blonde. 'And then when he comes over I'm to act all cordial and genial and stuff until our fourth date, when I can let

167

myself go a bit, and maybe phone him even – although I have to end the call. And then, after a coupla months, we can finally have sex.'

She raised her voice, until she could be heard by people several tables away – including, no doubt, Moustache.

'The morning after sex, I'm to do stretches or something – anything to take my mind off him, so I don't make him feel like he has to marry me. But if I'm a real Rules girl he will *want* to marry me, after about ten months. And it'll be a real-lasting marriage, not just some loveless merger.'

'Phew,' said Sean, sighing, and beginning to eat the sponge.

'I think he could have heard that, Liz.' Anna, embarrassed, tried to think positive thoughts.

'It's all ridiculous.'

'No, you should try it,' said Liz. 'I mean, I was sceptical too, at first.' She looked at Blonde. 'But Seany would propose to you, I'd betcha, if you'd play a bit hard-to-get. Wouldn'tcha, Seany?' She nudged him in the ribs. 'I mean, don't be so pushy-career-woman all the time. Just act a bit cool now and then.'

'You mean, act as you do?' asked Blonde, coolly.

Anna moved her chair away from the table, and from Liz.

'Actually, I find it harder than most to go by these Rules,' confessed Liz, laughing with her mouth open. 'Especially the sex bit. I always want to rip their underpants off and get down to it. Y'know? Straight away.' She laughed loud and long. 'But all the same, I reckon The Rules work. I'll definitely get a husband this way.'

'Maybe. But for how long?' asked Sean.

'Oh, forever. Because they'll have chosen *you*, right, rather than you pursuing the guy. Works great.'

'Tell that to Princess Diana,' said Blonde.

'I'd love to, but she's dead. I cried for hours when she died.'

'And then forgot *all* about her?' sneered Blonde.

The four of them paused for a moment, ostensibly to remember Princess Diana. But Liz was making eyes at Moustache. Blonde was peeling her baby potatoes. Sean's fingers were tapping on the table, impatiently.

Anna, meanwhile, was finding it hard to eat. She was pushing cubes of creamy chicken around her plate, and contemplating a method of escape – although she did want to monitor what Liz was saying.

'Well, Diana hardly lived happily ever after with her husband,' said Blonde, drinking her orange juice. ('Is this fresh?' she asked herself.) 'As soon as Prince Charles realised he'd fallen in love with a woman who liked *disco* dancing and . . .'

'Blondes have it particularly *hard*, I reckon. And, yeah, that's fresh,' said Liz, sniffing Blonde's orange juice.

'And why is that?' asked Blonde, smirking, and raising her eyebrows at Sean, as if mystified.

'Everyone thinks they're stupid, don't they?'

'I suppose it depends what they say. I mean, isn't it the same with *Australians*? Mind you, some people don't even try to break down the stereotype.'

Her eyes cut to slits as she stood up to leave.

'Or that their hair is real,' continued Liz.

'What do they think?' asked Blonde, drinking the last of her orange juice. '(God, this really is from concentrate.) That it comes out of a packet?'

'Yeah,' said Liz, to Blonde's departing back.

A broad grin satisfied Liz'a face. A grin which worried Anna, who turned round only to find Moustache making the long walk from his table to theirs. Moustache, who had a body to match. His hairy chest was visible through his thin, pale-striped shirt.

He walked straight towards them as if he was the star of some seventies cop show, swaggering towards his big American car. Behind him, he left four friends – all of them male, and short, and thin. Anna watched him approach, and felt a sick sense of shame rise in her throat. She sat there pained by her friend's delighted face.

'I'm sorry to interrupt,' said Moustache, his hands gripping the table as if for support. 'But haven't I seen you somewhere before?'

'You might have done,' said Liz, finishing her dessert. 'Do you ever go to a club called Athena?'

'That's *it*. I thought I'd seen you somewhere.'

'Good club, isn't it?'

'Great,' said Moustache, his moustache bristling into a smile. 'Last time, I promised myself that if I ever saw you again, I'd get your telephone number, *so* . . . ?'

'Well, I would, but I'm doing these Rules at the moment. I tell you what, why don't I take yours?' She took out a large black book, which was printed with the gaudy gold words: Little Black Book.

'OK, I suppose that'll have to do,' he flirted, glancing back at his puny mates. He took Liz's pen from her, opening her Little Black Book, and scribbling down the name Marcus, as well as a telephone number.

Liz undid the zip on her sweatshirt top.

'Nice name, Marcus. Why don't you sit down?'

'You can have my seat,' said Sean, standing up. 'I should be going.'

'Or mine,' said Anna. 'Sorry, I have to get back to work, Liz.'

170

'We'll leave you to it, Liz.'

There was the usual musical clatter of chairs as Sean and Anna stood up to leave and Marcus sat down, his moustache active with excitement.

'Nice meeting you, Seany. If it ever goes wrong with Blondie, you should call me,' Liz said.

'Oh really?' said Marcus.

'Yeah, why not?' She smiled at him. 'Who's to stop me?'

Anna and Sean walked towards the exit.

'So, we'll leave your friend there,' smiled Sean. 'Happily breaking all the rules.'

'Oh, she isn't really a friend as such.'

Anna felt more comfortable now that Liz had left. But at the same time, she thought that there might be a stain on the bottom of her dungarees. Or an eyelash on her nose. Something was wrong, but she could not put her finger on it.

Sean, at the lift: 'Awful, isn't she?' *(Yes, that was it.)*

Anna, mournfully: 'Awful. But she's got so many problems – it's as if she needs me. I mean, what do I do? Just ask her to leave me alone?'

Sean laughed, pressing the lift button, and saying, 'I meant my ex-girlfriend, not your friend – although I do see what you mean about Liz. It is hard sometimes, isn't it? To get rid of someone? But if you're so uncomfortable around the woman – well, why be *around* her? Just tell her that you don't need her in your life. Be up-front about it.'

'But that would be terrible.'

'She'll hurt more if you don't say anything. More importantly, *you'll* hurt more. Anyway, what else does one do? Words are the only weapon we have when we want to communicate.'

'I suppose. Yeah, that's true.'

'I don't know why people find it so hard to end friendships – although they run their course, like every other relationship. You just have to lance that boil.'

'Oh, but she's not that bad. I mean, I'm not trying to get rid of her. She's a character, you know? As Myrna always says, characters make life more colourful and, well, what *is* normal? Liz can be so generous. She isn't all bad, honestly.'

'Well, my *ex* is. I wish I could get rid of her. Oh, where's this goddamn lift?'

'I mean, she's not like Justine.'

'Who's Justine?' He looked sideways at Anna, his hands deep in his pockets.

'A friend. Well, *was*.'

And so Anna told Sean about Justine, and about the way Anna had stood her up. Had she been wrong to do that?

Not at all, said Sean. People moved through our lives. Only a tiny number showed up at the beginning and stayed until the end. It would not alter the fact that Justine had been a good, good friend. But that now, both Anna and Justine had changed.

Naturally, Anna felt bad. But nothing stayed the same for ever. If Anna would forgive the Pammy Lowental-type example, she was giving her brain an aerobic workout. And who enjoyed going to the gym? Plus, did Anna know that one burned off most of the calories *after* exercise? The work she was doing now, in ridding herself of Justine – that was the hard part.

'Well done, you,' said Sean, nudging her.

'You think?'

'Yes,' he said. 'Although you really should be working this through with your therapist.'

'But I don't have a therapist.'

'Really?' said Sean, turning to look at Anna. It was as if Anna had said, *But I don't brush my teeth.*

'You really should have a therapist,' he said, as the lift came. *(You really should floss on a daily basis.)* 'I'll give you Eileen Weiszfeld's number. In the meantime, that'll be three pounds sixty for my services,' he joked.

I'd pay far more, thought Anna, smiling.

'I'm going up, I'm afraid,' said Sean, holding open the lift.

'That's fine, I'll get the next one.' The lift doors closed on Sean. 'Oh, you gave me a shock,' she said, as Pammy came up behind her.

'Did I, Anna? I don't know – *did* I?' She said this as if Anna had killed Pammy's mother and had not yet properly apologised. 'Let's sit down.'

Pammy sat on one of the communal chairs in the corridor. Her tight skirt rode up her thick thighs, the lining exposed. Anna sat next to her, looking at Pammy's hair, which would not settle.

'We're away from the office here. We can talk here,' she said, her voice carrying, as people walked past, or stood waiting for the lift. They must all have heard Pammy talking to Anna. She sounded like Joyce Grenfell, patronising a terrible two-year-old in a sandpit.

'I'm sorry about that caller – Sylvia. I promise – it won't happen again.'

'This isn't about Sylvia, is it? This is about us, working as part of a team – you, me, Sean, Mikey, Lena, the freelancers, Todd. You have to fit into a group. I mean, this is very much a group *programme*, and you need to come up with ideas. Mikey needs help if we're going to stay at peak-time in the schedule.'

'I'm sorry. I know I should be coming up with ideas.'

'Well, if you want to progress on this programme.'

'I do, yes. Of course.'

'Then, you're going to have to pull your weight,' said Pammy, still smiling the same smile – it wouldn't leave her face. 'I wanna see an improvement in your performance. *Yes?*'

Anna nodded.

'So, let's have some ideas at Monday morning's meeting, yes?' Pammy patted her thighs.

'Yes, OK,' said Anna, realising that that was her cue to leave.

'Oh, and Annie,' said Pammy. *Had she called her Annie?*

'Yes?' asked Anna, turning round. *If she had, that was a turning point.*

'There's no I in teamwork, is there, Annie?'

'No,' Anna had to confess. 'There isn't.'

Chapter Eight

I am a fun person, she thought.

Friday night, and Anna was sitting on the steps of the Armada Theatre in Piccadilly, waiting for Roo, who was, as usual, late to meet her. They had tickets for a play about Irish poverty at the turn of the century – *Four Poor Women*. Roo was reviewing the play for *Mz* magazine. *But what am I doing here?* wondered Anna. *Generally?*

I am a happy person, she thought, miserably, feeling the hard cold steps through the frayed patch on her dungarees. She had just finished reading the Self-Esteem chapter in Wilhelm Grohe's book *One Month to Happiness*. Grohe had provided a list of positive phrases and affirmations for readers to repeat, like a litany – such as *I love myself* and *I have energy for my personal life*.

It's a small spiritual lift, and should be taken no more seriously than that. However, it works, in the same way that Prozac does – although without any of those nasty after-effects. Express yourself positively. Think boldly. Feel better about yourself.

I am exciting to be with, thought Anna, gloomily. She forced a smile for Roo, who had just arrived.

'Sorry I'm late,' said Roo. But this time Roo had a good excuse – she had been to hospital. Yes, seriously. She had been so sick. *Physically*. No, it wasn't just morning sickness. No, it was far worse than that. Just the sight of a restaurant menu, stuck up in a passing window . . . The merest hint of a TV food programme – its running order filled with fresh sauces . . . The foggiest *memory* of a recipe, rich in whole prawns, or padded, green Brussels sprouts (uurgh) . . . Anything could make Roo retch, her abdomen bungee-jumping through her mouth. No, she hadn't had this with Oscar or Daisy. No, it was *not* typical of pregnancy.

Roo had Maternal Hyperemeses Gravidarum.

'Oh God, that sounds serious. What's that?' said Anna, as Roo sat down on the steps beside her.

'It's an extreme and debilitating "morning" sickness which lasts all day and all night. The worst pregnancy one can have. Oh, God, you've been eating garlic.' She turned her head away.

'Two *days* ago,' said Anna, thinking that it was typical of Roo not to be run-of-the-mill-plain-pregnant, but to be suffering from Maternal Hyperemeses Gravidarum.

She never did anything by halves. Roo might have forgotten the agony of her last pregnancy, but she had not been the one to suffer it. *Anna* remembered every detail.

The agony of the first trimester. The worry of the second. The anxiety of the third. Suddenly, Roo's waters breaking. The bloody show. Roo, suffering more than any Third-World earth-mother giving birth in a field. Oh yes, Anna remembered it all.

Afterwards, Roo had described everything on the phone: the four-day labour rivalling any gulag for its sweat. And all of it without any pain relief.

'Can they give you anything for what-did-you-call-it?' asked Anna.

176

'Maternal Hypermeses Gravidarum. Not really, no. Could harm the baby.'

'Right,' said Anna, marvelling at Roo's sacrifice. The moment Anna conceived, she would order her pain-killing epidural. Well, Anna knew what labour was like. She had been there, over five years ago.

Roo had been at her flat when she was forty weeks pregnant with Daisy. She had been comforting Anna, who had been pining over Bryan.

Suddenly, Roo screamed, bending double with pain. She called for an ambulance, and Anna panicked, trying to recall all of the home births she had witnessed in hospital dramas, notably *Casualty*. She said, 'Remember to breathe.'

Or had the ambulance-man said that?

By the time they arrived at the hospital, Anna was in a desperate state, especially after the forty-minute wait for some attention. Eventually, an agitated midwife arrived. She examined Roo, asked Anna whether she was the birthing partner, and then left her for another hour. Anna feared the worst, until the midwife returned.

'What are *you* still doing here? Come on. Out of that bed.'

'I'm in labour, actually,' said Roo, as assertive as she could be in a sheet-like gown used to intimidate people in hospitals and hairdressing salons.

Anna picked up her jacket to go. Not only was she in awe of the midwife's starched uniform, but she wanted to finish reminiscing about Bryan, who had just ended their relationship.

'You've just left me sitting here for an hour. No one's said a word to me . . .' said Roo, fiercely.

'That's as may be, but you're not going to have a baby. Not today, at any rate,' said the midwife, looking at Roo as if to say, *You're one of those middle-class private patients, aren't you? Well, I don't have to listen to you. I'm not on commission yet.* The woman managed to say all of this with a single thrust of her breasts.

'Well, what was all that pain about then?' asked Roo, looking around as if searching for a higher being, like a staff nurse, or a doctor. 'I'm sure I was in labour.'

'They were Braxton-Hicks contractions. It was false labour.'

You've been faking, mocked the woman's chest.

'What's false labour?' asked Anna, hoping to stop Roo losing her temper, and glad, given that Warren was on a business trip to Hong Kong, that it was all a false alarm. Anna remembered enough of *ER* and *All Creatures Great and Small* to know that giving birth to boy, or girl, or baby calf, could be agonising to watch. More importantly, it could put the birthing partner off sex.

'False labour is like a rehearsal for the real thing. Now get dressed, because we need your bed.' She held up Roo's maternity dungarees. *Well, if that was the rehearsal*, thought Anna, *I can't wait for the actual performance.*

That was Roo. Roo, who took everything to excess, including moderation. Last year she had read that one could avoid heart trouble by practising moderation in all things. So for at least a month, Roo had been a model of temperance, drinking only half a daily unit of wine. She had read no more than four pages of a novel per day.

But she could not cope with being average for long. Roo had always been A grade.

She had turned down a place at Cambridge so that she could run Britain's foremost student radio station – Arndale Community Radio. She had chaired almost every one of the poly's events and societies – from nights of karaoke to marches for the Militant Tendency.

('Shall we go in?' asked Roo, standing up.

My opinions count, affirmed Anna.)

Anna's best was always only ever the national average – whereas Roo excelled at everything, including being a close friend. She had helped Anna into her job, and had set her up with several men. Now she wanted Anna married. Hitched up. Stitched up. If Anna so much as bumped trolleys with a man in a supermarket, Roo would have her married off. If she could find a way to impregnate Anna – well, that would be her job done. A job done exceptionally well.

'So, how's Tom?' asked Roo, still looking sick.

'How should I know?'

'Oh. I thought you'd been out – after my cousin's party.'

Roo sounded disappointed. She had always been more involved in Anna's relationships than Anna had (although only for their duration). She thought that Anna's life was like a long-running soap-opera, and lived vicariously through her 'swinging' single friend's sex life.

'Yeah, but only on a Wednesday.' She felt like telling Roo that she was not a fictional character, and had not been created for Roo's light night-time entertainment.

'Well, give him time. I bet he'll grow on you.'

'No, I've met someone else now, anyway.'

'Oh yeah?' said Roo, suddenly all suspicion.

'His name's Sean.'

They went into the foyer, and Anna introduced Roo to the idea of Sean. They collected their tickets, and Anna described her lunches with Sean. They ordered their interval drink, and Anna bitched about Blonde.

Roo bought a programme, and Anna revealed her trump card – the print-out of Sean's computer messages. *Yes, honey*. But Roo didn't like the sound of Sean. *You're not so green . . .* Not if Sean's ex was still on the scene. Besides, Sean might have been good-looking, in a superficial way . . . He might have been clever, in an arrogant way. But Tom was . . .

'Yes?'

'Tom was *real*.'

Anna sat down, irritated by the red-velvet arm-rest which exacerbated her eczema. 'And I invented Sean, did I?' She should have known that Roo would find fault. Roo, who liked to produce and direct and prompt Anna's relationships, giving herself a Hitchcock-like cameo role in all of her romantic, comedic productions.

'Tom was *there*,' added Roo.

True, thought Anna. The advantage of Tom was that Anna was able to kiss him whenever she wanted, without first having to verify that he found her attractive. All she had to do was to dial his number and he would arrive, like pizza.

He was convenient, like telephone banking and ready-cut vegetables. It was no wonder Roo had approved of him. Roo had every mod con, from a dishwasher to a husband. Lucky Roo, who was able to have sex whenever she wanted. And even when she didn't. Although the sex had to be with Warren.

Whereas Anna had a half-empty, king-sized, double bed.

Lucky Roo, with all that certainty. Anna was bored with the foreplay that went into bedding a man. The removal of any excess hair (Anna was amazed at how much was surplus to her requirements). The washing of the hair on her head. The refusal, for the requisite amount of relationship time, to have sex. And the post-coital time that went into clearing up, after a man had romantically and spontaneously brought Anna breakfast in bed.

A lifetime with Warren, for sex on tap? For *Warren*'s offspring? A lifetime of compromise, of giving up more than half of her bed, for Warren to sprawl around in? Yet, marrying someone like Warren, Anna would be perfectly happy, playing with their wedding presents. The electrical kitchenware. The canteen of silver-plated cutlery.

But then she would wake up one morning beside a husband, like Warren, who had turned to fat, with freckles machine-gunned on to his chest. And she would despise him, his TESSA, and his fixed-interest endowment policy. The way he wrapped himself in more than half of the duvet.

She would look at her compromise husband, and at her canteen cutlery – both of which she hated – and Anna would wish that she had saved up for some fine china herself, leaving the Warren lookalike well alone.

Unlike any fat, freckled husband, most superior household goods could be guaranteed to last a lifetime. Plus, if a food-processor was found to be faulty, it could be quickly replaced, one's statutory rights remaining unaffected. Whereas shopping for a husband was much harder second time around.

'Anyway, you don't *have* Sean yet, do you?' said Roo gently. 'Whereas you *did* have Tom . . .'

'What do you mean: did? Do I not have Tom any more?' smiled Anna.

'Well, would you care?' asked Roo. 'I mean, Tom left a message, didn't he? About Saturday night. And you didn't return his call.'

'He phoned the night after we went *out*,' she said, as if that was unheard of.

'Well, I wouldn't worry,' said Roo, easily. 'I doubt he'll call again. He doesn't think you're interested now. To be honest – and this is a secret – I *believe* he's seeing my cousin on Saturday.'

Now, Anna was interested.

'What do you . . . ? Why? What's the relationship between your cousin and Tom?'

'Well, at the *moment*, all she does is to set up his experiments for him. But there is a bit of a spark between them.' Roo laughed, lightly. 'If you'll forgive the pun.'

'Really?' said Anna, horrified by a world in which even Tom would have a contingency girlfriend.

'Actually, I think they're seeing each other tonight too. The inspectors are in and I think they'll want to celebrate.'

'What do you mean, toni . . . ?' whispered Anna as the safety curtain went up on the stage.

The lights dimmed, and the play began, somewhat insensitively cutting in on their conversation. Anna tried to concentrate on the stage, but there were too many characters and she quickly lost the thread. Too many thoughts cluttered her head. One of which was: how could Tom two-time her with a chemistry assistant?

Albeit, a young and beautiful chemistry assistant.

Tom, who had only the other night kissed her, she thought. Furiously. Surely by snogging Anna, he had implied a lifetime of marriage and children? Suddenly, Anna felt Single and anxious; and Single and broody. There was no denying it – she was Single and desperate. In a couple of years, she would be Single and suicidal.

(Next to her, she heard Roo retch.

'Are you OK?'

'Yes.')

Single and broody, yet she did not envy Roo being pregnant. Anna had seen the way Roo's body had changed. The way it was scribbled with green varicose veins. That chopping-board stomach inflating, and a brown line tattooed from belly button to bikini line. Pink marks, spreading like a limited-service rail map from the abdomen to the groin.

In the last month, Roo would go all pear-shaped. Her hips

182

would flare to seat the baby by the hook-like crook of one's waist. No, Anna did not envy Roo her pregnancies, although she sometimes wished that her body had a purpose other than to attract men.

Anna's body lived in a permanently ante-ante-natal state, as if desperate to burst into motherhood. She had tried to live by her *Mz* week-per-page diary, which informed her about international dialling codes and temperatures in California. But her body had an alternative, monthly calendar. It operated by its own routine, bursting mid-cycle into a tantrum of hormonal spots, for instance, which tended to clash with important social occasions.

There was no getting away from it. Although women were conceiving later, and falling pregnant through all manner of artificial means, Anna was thirty-one, and fast approaching middle-age. *My God*, she thought, as a mexican wave of audience laughter swept up the aisles. *I'm approaching forty. Come fifty, and I'll be menopausal.*

And yet, she did not want Roo's children. Or, truthfully, even her own. She would rather it was all over and done. Particularly the labour itself; the only word in the English language not to have a euphemism. *Must hurt if Roo found it painful*, she thought.

Anna's pain threshold was much lower than Roo's. And, for much of the time, she did not feel maternal. Anna was not the type to peer in prams, or to wonder at the design strengths of a human being writ small.

She was conscious of her body's battling hormonal surges, but Anna did not envy Roo her offspring. She loved Oscar and Daisy. Really she did. But sometimes, Oscar reminded her of a frustrating toy, running low on batteries. Daisy could be ever so cute, especially when dressed as a baton-twirling majorette, but she could also be cruel, withering Anna with looks that read, *Clearly, you are not only in a job that wouldn't befit an even vaguely ambitious teenager, but you don't even have a boyfriend.*

Occasionally, Oscar could irritate Anna so terribly that she longed to remove his batteries.

When Anna left the Hastings household, she was delighted to close the door on a corridor filled with primary-coloured bumper trucks. There were only so many times Anna could be bothered to read *Rosie and Jim*. Or to play piggy-in-the-middle between Daisy and Roo.

Whenever Anna wanted to talk to her friend, either Daisy or Oscar would interrupt. They would want to be fed, or talked to, or watched. Roo would only half-listen to Anna, who could be pouring out her heart about Alfonso, Danny, Roger, or Bryan.

But that would not matter, because Roo was in love. It appeared to be an unrequited love: those two never seemed to give anything back. Roo would look at Daisy, or Oscar, in a way that suggested if she averted her eyes for a second, they might collapse down dead.

Sometimes Anna envied Daisy, because Roo took the time to mould Play-Doh with her. If only Roo would stop doting over Oscar, and pay a bit more attention to *her*.

Roo had talked about motherhood with Anna. But still she could not understand the hold Daisy and Oscar had over their mother. Roo had said that the love she felt for them was overwhelming and contradictory and imprisoning. But how, thought Anna, could that outweigh everything?

Well, children were like plants. That was how Roo sometimes felt. Every day, one gave them food, and showered affection on them, watching for them to grow. It was all a matter of hope and oxygen.

Anna did not have time for plants, nor even flowers. The

patient, three-day wait with flowers, watching them die. The sick lime smell, as they hung around. The vase afterwards, daubed for days, for all the scrubbing, with sticky green stem remains. Anna preferred the smell of roses, fresh from an aerosol can.

'All of my plants die,' Anna had said, thoughtfully. 'I just forget to feed them.'

'Hmmm.'

'Either that, or they grow out of control.'

'Well, *exactly*,' said Roo, pointedly.

The play at last reached its interval. The safety curtain came down, and Roo joined the toilet queue. Anna went to the bar to collect their drinks, and Roo on her return took a sip of orange juice.

That sent her back to the toilet again.

Anna was left with Roo's huge haversack, filled with spare nappies and bottles and bibs. Even when her children were not with her, Roo carried the accessories of motherhood. She did not feel whole without a couple of travel bottles.

Roo had always bottle-fed her babies. She had written, in her *Mz* column, that breastfeeding was old-fashioned.

When women's breasts were shaped like bottles, and they had nipples like teats, that was one thing. But nowadays, women's breasts are not designed for feeding. We find it sensual to breastfeed, but . . .'

But Anna knew the truth. Roo's breasts were strictly ornamental. She did not want her breasts to sag to the shape of bottles. Roo was prepared to suffer the embarrassment of taking out her bottles to feed in public. The odd, shocked glare from women of her own generation. The government health warnings on packets of formula milk. *Studies have shown that breastfeeding is better for babies*

. . . Roo was prepared to put up with all that. Well, if only for the sake of her breasts.

'Oops-a-daisy,' said Roo, coming back from the toilet, and taking her haversack back from Anna. The contents spilled out.

'Oops-a-daisy?' laughed Anna, as Roo bent to pick everything up. Although Anna knew that Roo had been forced to censor her language after a nursery teacher had rung up to reprimand her for Daisy's incessant use of the word 'shit'.

'There has even been the odd "fuck",' protested Daisy's teacher, shocked. If Mrs Hastings wanted to get Daisy into a top-class pre-preparatory, she was going to have to clean up her vocabulary. From now on, it was to be all 'oops-a-daisy, dearie-me', and 'oh-what-a-silly-Mummy!'

'You wait until you have children,' sighed Roo, as if it was only a matter of time. She slumped down beside Anna.

'It's the being pregnant I'd hate more. You *do* look ill.'

'You know what I resent most?' Roo said, passionately, pausing. 'I mean, as a woman?'

The inequality of opportunity in the workplace? wondered Anna. The inadequate maternity benefits? The sudden defining of the sexes?

'The way your figure changes.' Roo looked as if she might launch a campaign against it. 'No amount of working out can help. I mean, look at these tits.' She sat up and stuck out her breasts, which had grown to the size of two Giant Smarties.

'They're huge, aren't they?' she said. 'Practically pornographic.'

'Don't worry,' smiled Anna, 'I don't think you're going to be hunted down by the producers of *Baywatch*. Not *just* yet.'

'You say that as if it's my life's dream to look like Yasmin

Bleeth . . .' smiled Roo, shuddering at the sight of Anna's glass of white wine. 'When you know that it's to look like Winona Ryder.'

Anna smiled. She knew that Roo had said this only to remind Anna that she bore a vague and disappearing resemblance to Winona Ryder.

'So, what do you think of the play?'

'Oh. Not bad. What d'*you* think?'

'Yeah. Not bad. Quite good, actually. I mean, I don't normally like tragedies. Oh, my bladder. God, I have to go to the loo again.'

That was no mean feat, considering the size of the queue. Roo went to stand at the back of it, as Anna picked up the programme. As she flicked through the programme introduction, and the advertisements for Indian restaurants, Anna thought about Tom, kissing Roo's cousin.

She shuffled through to the potted biographies of the cast. The first detailed the only man in the play, whom all four women were hoping to marry. Anna looked at his photograph, deciding that he was not as handsome as Tom.

The two-minute bell rang.

At the age of eight, Erica Dale played Pepper in the Broadway production of Annie . . . Anna studied Erica's photograph for signs of plastic surgery. She had always thought that, if she had the courage for plastic surgery, Anna, too, could look like, say, Erica, or Winona Ryder or, indeed, anyone.

She skipped Georgina Ellis – the play's token plain woman – to read about Rachel Simeon.

Rachel Simeon's TV appearances include Stopping Melody, In Suburbia *and* The Bill. *Stage-work includes* Oliver! *and* Annie Get Your Gun *on Broadway. In 1984, Rachel received the coveted Black Ear award for her performance in* Furtive Secrets.

Anna wished that she had such a CV.

187

She had always suspected that she had talent – although she knew not for what. It troubled her, every four years, that she could have made an Olympic athlete. If only Anna's parents had had the patience and the commitment to organise professional coaching!

But they had never nurtured Anna's talents. Barbara had refused even to let her star in the school play. Had she been trained, from an early age, to ice-skate – who knew? Anna could now be skating like Torvill and Dean. Golf – she could be one of the first famous female golf-players. Anna had always been good at crazy golf.

The minute bell went off. *Ladies and gentlemen, would you please take your seats . . .* Anna read the next programme résumé. *Renata Sorenta has performed with . . .*

Renata Sorenta . . .

Renata . . .

Renata . . .

Roo returned, asking, 'What's wrong? What are you looking so shocked about?'

The curtain went up on four women, one of whom was Renata Sorenta. It could have been another Renata Sorenta. It was such an actorly name, after all – although invented; Renata Sorenta's real name was Rebecca Smith. But Anna doubted that. No, there was no doubt. It was her. The woman who had ruined her life. Anna might still have been an actor.

Had it not been for that woman, Renata.

She had not heard the name for nine years. Not since that fringe-of-fringe production of *Piers the Ploughman.* 1989. Everyone had loved Anna's interpretation of the role of Envy. Even the leading man, Roger Brown, had called her acting 'brave' in rehearsal. He had talked about Anna going on tour in a show produced by a friend of his. She would have to perform topless, he said, but, hey, what the heck. Anna might get Equity membership. She had refused – embarrassed even to undress in a female communal changing room, let alone in public, and for strangers.

Off stage, Roger was full of suggestions as to how they might best off-set each other's talent – Anna presuming that Roger found her attractive. She was twenty-two, and no fool. But she had met his type before, too many times, and was by then bored of such obvious shoulder muscles. As if those knife-like cheekbones meant anything to her now that she was no longer a virgin. It was all just macho posturing. How shallow would she be to fall for him?

It was only packaging. Fine for a fifteen-year-old needing a pin-up. But Anna was twenty-two, and in need of a bit more than tall legs and brown flyaway hair to run her fingers through.

She had known many a man like Roger Brown, on every cast list, in every town. ('Look, we should discuss your role,' he had said. 'Come back to my place.') There was always a man like Roger Brown. Hanging around, looking too long. ('We have to learn how to interact,' said Roger, by his bed.) Still, it didn't take long for Anna to fall – into the arms, and for the lines, and into the bed of Roger Brown.

Their relationship lasted until opening night.

Roo: 'You were brilliant, Anna.'

Myrna: 'Yeah, very good.'

Mum: 'It was very nice, dear. Was it written by a friend of yours?'

Dad: 'It's a good way to spend your free time. But how's the job-hunting going? Maybe Roo here can do something for you . . .'

189

Mum: 'Although, did you have to play *that* part. I mean. Envy!'

Dad: 'I'd love to see you on a good vocational training programme. Get a proper profession behind you . . .'

Mum: 'I mean, you're hardly envious. I've always thought you very happy with your lot.'

Renata Sorenta: *'Why would anyone want to put on a play like* Piers the Ploughman*? It was hardly a crowd-pleaser centuries ago, and this production of it is nothing but a dull, cut-and-paste job. I might have gone to sleep had it not been for some hilariously ham acting. Anna Potter, playing Envy, was particularly infuriating. Whoever led her to believe that she could act was cruel and vindictive. She delivers her lines as if she is serving at a fast-food restaurant, and just as miserably.'*

Renata Sorenta's opinion had been more important than those of Anna's parents, Roo, or Myrna – because her thoughts had been printed in *The Stage*. The review had been read by anyone who mattered to Anna.

Roo: 'What a bitch. Don't worry, if I ever run into her, I'll pour a bottle of wine over her.'

Myrna: 'Don't waste the *wine*.'

Dad: 'Well, you know my theory? That, actually, anyone can act. I mean, we all act all of the time, don't we? I act in the office. I act at home. On the train. Of course we all want to be Hollywood *stars* . . .'

Mum, *absentmindedly flipping through her* Little Book of Soil: 'Don't worry, dear. I don't think anyone ever reads the words in newspapers. They just look at the pictures. I know I do.'

Dad: 'We all want to be Robert Redford. But we just have to knuckle down, in the end, and get on with a proper job. Nine to five like everyone else.'

Roger Brown: 'Oh, *Renata*. Or should I say Rebecca? No,

190

you don't want to take any notice of that hysterical bitch. I went out with her at drama school, and she won't leave me alone now. I wouldn't worry, Anna. This isn't about you. She's written that balls just to get back at me.'

Still, Anna was angry. How could she make it clear to everyone that Renata, when writing such rubbish, had had so blatant an ulterior motive?

Anna was having a hard enough time besides. The play closed after only two weeks. Her relationship with Roger did not last even that long. ('You didn't think it was anything more than . . . ? Oh shit. No, we were just having *fun.*') Through all of it, the name Renata Sorenta stayed in Anna's head. Anna lay in bed with it. She fantasised about setting fire to Renata's house. She imagined herself, up on stage, collecting an Oscar. 'I'm afraid,' she would say, 'this comes with no thanks to the awful Renata Sorenta.'

Newspapers would track Sorenta down after that. The *Mirror* would set up a dedicated phone line asking, 'Do you know the whereabouts of the Awful Renata?' She would be found and publicly vilified for trying to stifle the career of Britain's 'top bit of Oscar totty', Anna Potter.

Anna dreamt of confronting Renata and pulling her hair out, one by bleeding one. With any luck, Sorenta would die, horribly. But not before admitting, publicly, that Anna was a very fine actress. Renata had only written such rubbish because she was envious of Anna's intelligent good looks. She was envious of her continuing hold over Roger.

Or Anna could start a letter-writing campaign to the editor of *The Stage*. A letter-writing campaign that would rival any of Amnesty's. *Are you aware*, she could write, *that the failed-actress Ms Sorenta's so-called reviews are, in fact, vendettas? Incidentally, she is sleeping with your wife.*

Eventually, *The Stage* would let Renata go. Unable to pay

her bills, Renata would end up homeless and starving on the streets of London. Anna would one day walk past Renata, wrapped inside a filthy blanket.

She would refuse to buy one of her *Big Issues*.

Long after that day's newspaper had turned chip-wrapping yellow, Anna still thought of Renata's cruel words. *Anna Potter, playing Envy, was particularly infuriating.* She knew the review, word for malicious word, by heart. *She delivers her lines as if she is serving at a fast-food restaurant, and just as miserably . . .*

Anna stared out all of the females on stage. Never, before Renata, had she wanted to kill anyone. Now, however, Anna had her chance.

At least, to hurt her.

She looked sideways at Roo, who really did not look well. Could Anna persuade her that *she* could write that review? *Four Poor Women is let down by one woman – Renata Sorenta.* Roo was always trying to push Anna into a career in journalism. *I vowed, when writing this review, not to refer to the title, but it seems entirely appropriate – at least with Renata Sorenta. You don't expect to find sub-standard acting on a West End stage. These are West End prices, after all.* All Anna needed to say was that she wanted this chance, to break in. *Whoever led Sorenta to believe that she could act was cruel and vindictive.* Or that Roo was far too ill to review the play herself. *She delivers her lines as if she is serving at a fast-food restaurant, and just as miserably . . .* Besides, Roo could edit the copy afterwards. She would keep control.

Roo always did.

Anna thought of Renata reading her review. Of Renata trying to face her fellow actors, saying, 'It's like an attack,

192

out of the blue.' She would give up acting, as Anna had, saying, 'I feel as if I've been mugged.'

'That wasn't my intention,' said Renata on stage. 'I'm so sorry,' she said – the poor woman – finishing her speech.

You will be, thought Anna, her blood quickening.

'We're back,' said Roo, opening her front door. 'What are *you* doing up? It's late.'

'Daisy wouldn't go to sleep until you were back,' said Warren, appearing, accusingly, in a pinny. 'I had to give her that Kinder Surprise.'

'Surprise, surprise.'

'Mummy's back now,' said Anna, kneeling down to Daisy's level. 'She just wanted *one* evening of drunken debauchery.'

'Although she couldn't face the drink,' heaved Roo, disappearing into the bathroom. She was a leafy shade of green.

'You're so immature,' said Daisy, disgustedly.

Anna looked down at Daisy. 'Where did you learn that word?' she asked. 'Such a clever girl.' But Daisy clearly knew that this was just another bid to win her approval.

'*Mummy*, I was on the island of Sodor . . .'

'Where's the island of Sodor?'

'Where Thomas the *Tank* Engine lives,' said Daisy contemptuously. 'I was under there, and the runaway engines were coming,' she said pointing to the dining-room table. 'Like this?'

Anna sat under the table and inside Daisy's land of make-believe. She was the world's best godmother, peering through the fringes of the tablecloth.

'Yes,' said Daisy doubtfully.

'Come under here, Daisy. Quick. The runaway engines are coming,' yelled Anna, feeling childish – although, for that, she blamed the alcohol.

'No, it's Daddy,' said Daisy, sullenly, as Warren came into the room.

'What the . . . ?' he laughed. 'What're you doing under there?'

'I'm on an *island*. This is *our* island, isn't it?'

She looked at Daisy for support. But Anna should have known by now that a child's love could not be bought like that. One had to give them presents.

'No,' said Daisy, blankly. 'It's a table.'

Roo came into the living room. She sat on the sofa, and Daisy climbed on to her lap. Anna crawled out from under the table, glaring at Daisy, who had returned to baby-mode, assuming the foetal position, and looking not-quite-real.

'So, how were they?' Roo asked Warren.

'Well, number one, I changed three of Oscar's nappies – one of them dark brown, and squidgy, and filled with sultanas,' he said. 'Number two, I gave Oscar his bottles and one of those organic gluten-free rusks. Was that OK?'

'Of *course*,' said Roo happily.

'Number three, I put him to bed, and he screamed, so I gave in, and took him out again. I had to give him chocolate, actually. It was the only way he'd go back to sleep. Chocolate and that paracetamol stuff – Calpol. Number four, I sang to Daisy, whilst the news was on. Number five, Oscar woke up and started crying. Number six, I . . .'

'Hang on, why was he crying?'

'*I* don't know, do I? Maybe he'd just had an existentialist crisis, and realised that life is futile and pointless. That life has no pleasure in it and that we all die – usually in horrible circumstances.'

'Or maybe he just felt sick because he'd eaten so much chocolate?'

'May*be*. Who knows? Anyway, number six, I . . .'

This was a regular ritual with Warren. Whenever he was left Home Alone with the kids, Warren would list all of the things he had done for his children. The Warren who was master of his empire in the City would disappear. Gone would be the Warren who swaggered around. The Warren who ordered people around. The Warren who refused to drive on the left-hand lane of the motorway for fear of anyone overtaking him.

In his place would be a small boy, writ large. His freckles would become more pronounced, and Warren would begin to resemble Just William. A pouting, proud, drunken Just William.

Warren was certainly slightly drunk now. And he had been drunk in April, when Anna had walked in on him.

Roo had given Anna a key, telling Anna to let herself in.

She had found Warren drunk, and lying on the floor. He confided that he might have had thirty-one birthdays – but that secretly he was sixteen and obsessed with women's breasts. He often imagined how female colleagues would look in pornographic films, through Vaseline-coated lenses.

'Issh true, y'know.'

Building-society officials made him feel fraudulent – like a boy drowning in a man's suit. *God*, and sex hadn't been the same since Warren began to have it regularly. Yeah, he drove a big car. But why were women in suits so frightening? Apart from *lisshle* Anna.

And the only men Warren knew now were like him, plastered on to their wives, or dripping nappies in department-store family rooms. Or they had turned into women, discussing careers or uterine contractions. What had happened to all those women in washing-powder commercials? Only *shweesh* Anna was left.

Did she want to fuck him?

* * *

Warren was still listing all of the things he had done for his children in a single evening. Reasons Roo should be grateful 1, 2, 3 . . . Anna looked away and at Roo's bookshelves, dyed-blond wood. They had again broken into a rash of parenting manuals.

She stared enviously at the distressed-pine table, and at the artificial-fur rug. Oh, she thought, to be in a position to buy one's own furniture, rather than having to inherit it.

Anna had inherited all of her furniture from her parents. The collapsing table her parents had been about to dump, ten years ago – until Anna had rescued it from the garage. The table and the rug – stained with all manner of memories from Anna's childhood.

When Warren had asked Anna to sleep with him, she had made her excuses and left. *Sleeping with Warren would have been terrible.* After that, neither of them had mentioned it. *To Anna, he was like a male version of Roo.* But there had been moments, recently, when he had caught Anna's eye. *Besides, what a terrible thing to do.* Warren was not unattractive, given the right context. *What was she thinking of?* Anna had wondered about Warren sexually. She thought she could rival Roo in bed. *It would tear Roo's life apart.* For Roo to come home, to find the two of them. *She would never forgive Anna.* To make Roo lose control, for once.

'Is that it?' Roo asked now, all schoolmarmish. She hid Warren's empty bottle of Scotch behind a cushion.

'Hang on, no. Number thirty, I cleaned the windows. They were filthy.'

'Well, thanks for doing all that,' she said wearily, stroking the sleeping Daisy's hair.

'Oh, that's OK,' said Warren.

He leaned back with his hands smug behind his head,

exhausted by all that self-pity. *And whisky*, thought Anna.

'I don't know why you say it's so hard, looking after two children on your own. They're a real asset.'

'Oh, well I'm glad of that. Wouldn't want them to think they weren't adding anything, financially, to the household.'

'I didn't say they were a financial asset. I mean, *hardly*. So, how was the play, anyway? Is it going to get a good review in *Mz* magazine?'

Anna felt all warm inside.

'I'm not actually writing the review,' said Roo proudly, looking at Anna as if she had shrunk to the size of one of her children.

'Why not?' asked Warren.

'Anna is.'

'Oh, why?'

'Well, why not? Anna writes *well*. She just needs a break. Anyway, I need a break too. I feel *so* bloody ill.'

'I think you're going to have a girl,' said Anna with the same confidence she affected when talking about horoscopes. 'Because Roo was fine with Oscar, but she was as sick as this with Daisy.'

'It *is* going be a girl actually. Because of the illness, I had an early scan.'

'God, they can tell at *this* stage?'

'They saw the clitoris.'

'Can you believe they found it at nine weeks?' said Warren. 'I still haven't found Roo's, and I've been looking for thirteen *years* . . .'

'Thanks Warren. God, I feel so sick. It's as if the foetus is telling me not to eat anything . . .'

'I'm just surprised it can get a word in edgeways.'

Roo looked at Warren, who had slurred the word 'edgeways'.

'What are you *playing* at?' she asked him.

'It was a joke,' he said sheepishly, looking sideways at Anna.

''Cause I don't see anyone laughing. And Anna's *not* impressed.'

Anna felt as if she was a child whose five-year-old friend was being bawled out by his mother. She looked at the sleeping Daisy, wishing herself at home and in bed. Roo's living room made her tired. The carpet, so scattered with playthings, looked like a battleground.

'It was a bloody joke. You have *no* sense of humour.'

'Because I'm amazed Oscar and Daisy are still alive after the way you treated them tonight. I mean, it's more by default than any careful planning. Giving Oscar chocolate! He's eleven months *old*, for fuck's sake. To give in, as soon as he starts crying.'

'I didn't give in straight away . . .'

'No, two seconds *later*.'

'Well, what d'you think I have? The patience of a saint?'

Amazingly, Daisy lay still asleep.

'You're fuckin' lucky to have me. There are so many women out there, desperate for me to father their children.' Warren looked at Anna. 'Women who would fucking wet their knickers to have me.'

'Yeah – *incontinent* ones,' joked Roo.

Anna apologised for laughing.

Warren looked at Anna as if he had been double-crossed, not just by these two, but by women the world over. It was as if he hadn't known, until that minute, that Anna would take his wife's side over his. That, if they were to separate, Anna would, like the children, automatically go with his wife.

'Maternal Hyperemeses Gravidarum. It's all just hormones,' he mocked, as if discovering the key to a woman's mystery. But then he sighed, as if he couldn't be fagged to unlock anything.

Not, thought Anna, *that Roo and Warren would ever split up*. Roo and Warren would always be together. *Unless something happened between Warren and Anna*. In the year 2043, robot workers at their old-age home would still be trying to separate them. *Why that caveat?* They would be fighting in their tapestry-hard armchairs. *Of course, nothing would ever happen between Anna and Warren*. The Hastings would be together because they had grown close over the years, in the same way that wedding rings shaped, after time, to fit the finger.

'If someone thumped me in the street for no reason, he'd say my reaction was *hormonal*.'

'I'm going to bed.' Warren stood up, swaying a little.

'I mean, can't you give me a *little* bit of sympathy? What women have to go through, for Christ's sake. Pregnancy. Labour. I mean, what pain do *men* have? What have you had to suffer, Warren?'

'Only the bloody conception.'

Anna apologised for laughing, again, as Warren slammed the door behind him, and Roo wondered why she ever left her children alone with him. Why Warren had given Oscar chocolate. Why, in fact, did *Roo* refuse Oscar chocolate? Why did she force-feed Daisy her porridge? She wished that well-looked-after children would glow orange.

'I mean, why do I bother? It doesn't show.'

'Oh, it does,' soothed Anna. 'Eventually. If you were a bad mother, they'd end up as drug addicts. Or politicians, like my father.'

She apologised for joking about such a serious matter.

Well, it did *not* work like that anyway. Roo only wished it did. Sometimes she felt too good a mother. She was too

199

close to her son, for example. Roo had seen Oscar with the Barbies, and had thought, *Oh my God*. It was all Roo's fault. Messing around with his oedipal complex. Maybe she loved him too much. One day, Social Services would be sent round.

Everything was Roo's fault. She hadn't spent enough quantity time with Daisy. Last week, Roo had screamed at her for putting Oscar in the freezer. Daisy had threatened to call ChildLine. Could Anna believe it? A five-year-old? Roo wouldn't have *dared* to answer back in her day.

Not until adolescence, anyway.

Roo spent too much time at the office. Even when she was at home, Oscar must have thought her umbilically attached to that telephone. Roo didn't care *how* well the nanny had been trained in Sweden. The way that woman treated Oscar. As if he was a dog, bringing in dirt from outdoors. Helle from Stockholm was the nanny from hell.

Helle didn't believe in working mothers. Roo had found her diary last week. The nanny had stupidly left it out. Of *course* Roo had read it. Well, she had spent all day with a Swedish phrase-book, desperately trying to translate. But Roo couldn't find proof that Helle was the devil.

So she didn't yet have a reason to fire her.

Helle kept the children clean and safe, damn her. Unlike Warren, who simply laid claim to their children's best features. Daisy's whining came from Roo. Her extrovert nature, though? Well, naturally, that was Warren's. The fact that Oscar was walking early he put down to the Hastings genes.

Of course.

Although, frankly, that was only thanks to Roo. Oscar was an early biped because of those bloody co-ordination classes. She had enrolled him. Warren had said that they were unnecessary. Could Anna believe that?

And, on top of everything, Roo was pregnant. Warren acted as if, now that the foetus was here, he might as well keep it. Yes, she supposed that it *was* half his. No, Warren was happy enough *now* with the idea of there being a third. One more reason for him to live. After he had died. The Hastings name, carrying down the line – although what would Warren say when she told him about the car? How they would have to swap it, finally, for one of those family estates? Oh, Roo was so tired. Couldn't Anna just go out with Tom? That, at least, would be one thing off her mind.

That night, Anna phoned Tom, just as soon as she got home.

'So, what have you been doing tonight?' *Out with your chemistry assistant?*

'Oh, typical Friday night in.'

'Oh yeah, and what's that?' *In with your chemistry assistant?*

'Y'know – get the beers in. Friends.'

'Oh right,' she laughed. 'Sorry to call so late. Only I've just got back from the theatre.' *I am cultured, unlike any chemistry assistant.*

'Oh,' he said, unimpressed.

'I was reviewing the play for *Mz* – the magazine.' *I am successful, unlike any chemistry assistant.*

'I *see*. So, while you were out being glamorous, I was in with a steak forestière for two . . .'

'Oh. So . . . You cook then?' *Or did you have some assistance?*

'No, not me . . .'

'I love cooking.' *I've got a very expensive recipe book somewhere.*

'Oh. Really?'

'You'll have to come round. I owe you dinner, don't I?' *I'll buy ingredients like oregano.*

201

'Well, I actually rang. Last night. I forgot you'd be at Justine's meeting. I wondered whether you wanted to do something tomorrow. Saturday.'

'Well, why don't you come over then, and I'll cook you dinner? About eight?' she said, her voice acquiring an urgency.

'Yeah, that'd be good.'

'Have you got a pen?'

'Right here.'

'Well, it's 113B Finchley Road.'

'Finchley Road?'

'Yes, but at the Swiss Cottage end.'

'Great.'

Chapter Nine

Anna's mother had always been old. She had always had grey hair, quietly seething dry at the ends. At parents' evenings, she had often shamed Anna by standing there, small like a grandmother, wearing orthopaedic porous shoes. Other, youthful, mothers had made friends – they had shared the school run. Barbara had stood, grey, at the school gates, collecting Anna quietly on her own.

'Where did I put that box? I had seasoning somewhere. I did . . . A-*ha*,' she said, rummaging through her wallpaper-lined cupboards for a box of herbs and spices.

Other mothers had been full of life, but Barbara had always looked tired. At a school gymnastics display, when other mothers had sat admiring, Barbara had whispered to Elaine, 'I'm sure it can't be good for the body. All of those strange contortions. Anyway, I think Anna's happier just sitting. In front of the television.'

Elaine and Barbara were neighbours, and had been friends for many years, sniping at each other's lives from the sidelines.

'Now, let's see what we have for your dinner party,' said Barbara, taking out a rusting tin box filled with assorted spice jars. She rattled through them. 'Mixed herbs, pepper, garlic powder, vanilla essence . . .'

'It's not a dinner party. It's just one bloke coming for his tea,' said Anna, picking up one of the china eggs that Barbara collected in a bowl on the kitchen table. 'Although I'll have to cook for Myrna too, if she's in,' she said, for the first time irritated that she was being treated like a teenager.

It had never bothered Anna before, being Barbara's baby. In fact, she had taken comfort from the cosy, familiar environment that was her parents' home, retreating into adolescence every time she visited, and adopting childish, petulant tones.

But was that what she now wanted? To be a child forever?

'*So*. Do you still share a flat with Myrna?' asked Barbara, lightly, looking at her china eggs as if frightened of Anna breaking them.

'Of course I do,' said Anna, wondering whether she had always sounded so sulky, when talking to her mum. 'I'd have told you if I was living somewhere else.'

Barbara moved her eggs out of harm's way.

She would never acknowledge that her daughter had moved out of the family home. 'The things you young people do,' she would say, looking uneasily at Anna. When she visited, she would tell her to tidy up her bedroom. A few years ago, she had asked her daughter why she was never at 'home'.

'This isn't my home. I moved out years ago,' Anna had said, confused.

'Oh yes, to your polytechnic.'

'What are you trying to say? That I wanted to get away from you? That, *ostensibly* I was going to poly, but really . . . ?'

Yes, Anna had gone to her polytechnic. Ostensibly. If she *must* use that word. (Well, was it not an obscenity?) But, yes,

Barbara suspected that Anna wanted to get away from her. Well, why go all that way, otherwise? Why go all the way to Arndale? *No* girl, to her knowledge, had moved so far away. Justine, for example, had gone to a college in London.

In all honesty, Barbara did not see the point of further education. Not for a girl. Yes, thank you, she had heard all about Anna's 'feminism'. ('Feminism' when it suited her. Slapping on the make-up when it didn't.) Anna could have earned more money as a secretary in a smart office somewhere.

Of course Barbara understood. She had had dreams of her own. Once upon a time she had wanted to be an air hostess, or a nursery nurse. Oh yes. But, unlike Anna, Barbara had known when to say, 'Enough's enough. Forget *excitement*.' She had had to get a job.

Of course it would be different if her daughter was married. As it was, Anna was 'playing around' in her flat in London. She would come back, mark Barbara's words, when she was hungry.

Whenever Anna did come back, her mother would stop whatever she was doing, to whip up a treat or two. Some Angel Delight, perhaps, or meringues, filled with aerosol cream. Iced cakes, fresh out of a packet.

She would stop whatever she was doing in the garden, and come inside. Barbara's beloved garden was where she spent much of her time, dirty large fork in hand. Yet, despite her best efforts, the garden was still overgrown. She was always having to cut down, cut down.

'Myrna's very clever, isn't she?' asked Barbara, as if that was a very bad thing. She had mud in her fingernails, noticed Anna.

'Yeah. God, what shall I make tonight? Myrna's a vegetarian.'

'Well, that's fine. Just make chicken,' said Barbara, decidedly.

'She doesn't eat meat,' said Anna.

'Oh, well, that's going too *far*.'

She had very definite views. Barbara did not know much about the world, but she knew what she thought. Homosexuality was fine, for example, as long as it was done in moderation. She had read, recently, that all young people were Going Gay, and it frightened her, as did drugs and Arthur Scargill.

'Right,' she said, looking around. 'Recipe book.'

In her day, everyone had eaten meat. Out of a tin, in fact. They hadn't made such a fuss. Now the whole world was into 'health' – as if somehow that was the answer. Pwuh! People, everywhere, were 'working out', and it terrified her – watching women her age taking step-classes, and kick-boxing in leotards.

'I don't understand the point,' Barbara would say, 'of vegetarian sausages.'

She could no longer trust her doctor. One read so many stories about bogus surgeons. Everyone was having sex, or was on Viagra. Why didn't Anna just get married? Or have a career such as Barbara's – something small, in the local library? Why did the supermarket stock thirty-two varieties of yoghurt? She was happy with plain, herself. Barbara did not even enjoy TV now – where were all the variety shows?

It bothered Barbara, this talk about a 'technological revolution'. If only things were as they were, when Anna had plaits in her hair, and murderers were not released, to murder again. Yes, she blamed those in charge. And children's television.

'I'm so pleased that you've started cooking,' she said,

bringing out a recipe ring-binder, and sitting down with it. She flipped through it, to a stool of melted chocolate which had dried onto the fourth page.

'How did that get there? I'd always thought you were happy eating something cold out of a packet.' She flipped over the pages. *Flip, flip.*

Barbara imagined the worst about her daughter. Of course she did. Anna lied about her life in London, but still she knew that Anna did not eat regularly. And, at the back of her mind, it was worse than that. She dreaded to think . . . Certainly, she doubted whether 'dirties' like toilet seats were fluffily covered up in her daughter's flat. (Well, she had seen for herself the filth lining Anna's oven.)

'I can't stay long,' said Anna. 'I've got to cook, and the flat's a mess. I'll have to Hoover before Tom comes round.'

'Tom,' repeated Barbara, thoughtfully, keeping the name – like an unfamiliar taste – in her mouth. 'I didn't know you ever Hoovered,' she smiled, indulgently, as if Anna had just brought up an unusual hobby.

Anna knew what her mother was thinking – that thank God her daughter wasn't like most young, modern, women – inviting men into her home, for sex. She had heard about that. Oh yes.

Flip went her mother's recipe book.

Yes, Barbara knew what 'modern' was – although she tried to distance herself from that sort of thing. Unlike the sixties, 'modern' meant having sex all the time, and with anyone. (Often, for money.) Or stripping.

Well, Barbara was no fool; she had watched those day-time chat shows. *The Shelley Show. I have a secret that I've kept from you, Mom. I have decided to become a man, Mom. Don't tell me how to live my life, Mom.* She knew that there

207

were such daughters around, deciding to become lesbians. Or developing eating disorders.

In Barbara's day, of course, they had had names for such 'illnesses'. Greed. Bad behaviour. Madness. Now it was all 'bulimia nervosa.' 'Hyperactivity.' 'Schizophrenia.' Barbara was having to learn a whole new language, and having Don as a husband did not help. *Flip*. They did not even cross paths much nowadays. *Flip, flip, flip*.

Although Barbara did not like to think about that. So long as they stayed married. Mrs Don Potter. There was no need for them to share a bed. Her husband had, of course, got into the Internet, 'e-mailing' Anna advice about her job. He had always lived through, and for, their daughter. Don always had to be one step ahead. Ever the politician, as Elaine would say.

Oh, and politics! Of course, for that, read *adultery*. Politicians weren't serious any more, of course. They used to take care of things, without shouting. Now, MPs were always smiling on the television, or telling people to take responsibility for themselves. *That's* your *job*, Barbara felt like telling the Government. If only she had dared.

'Women do still *do* the vacuum cleaning, Mum,' said Anna, and Barbara was pleased to hear this. Visibly. She went on looking through her recipe book, smiling with relief. *Flip*.

Meanwhile, Anna studied her mother's face, thinking what a lie she lived, pretending that everything was as it had been, in the 1950s.

Anna had colluded in this lie, pretending that she had no modern-day issues to deal with – contemporary issues for single women, like Careers and Sex. Until now. As Sean had said so rightly, she could no longer protect her mother. She was not responsible for the outside world, and was unable to continue sacrificing her own sense of self, purely to shield her mother from modern reality. That was no good for anyone.

'You know, I used to dream about doing this,' said her mum, staring at a picture of a bowl of brightly coloured vegetables. 'You and me – mother and daughter – sitting together.' She used the phrase 'mother and daughter' as if to affirm that fact. 'Swapping ideas for soups.'

Anna had rarely seen her mother so animated. *Flip, flip, flip, flip.* But it was no good going on like this – pretending that the two of them were in a seventies-style advertisement for washing-up liquid.

She needed to find the right moment to tell her mother what she was feeling. Although, why was that so difficult? Perhaps it was because her mother loathed talking about what she referred to as 'the nitty-gritty'. According to her, it was embarrassing, and all 'just filth really'.

They hadn't talked honestly. Not for ages. Not since that day, years ago, when Barbara had thought about leaving Don. On that day, she had talked about everything. It all flooded out then. How it had taken Barbara ten years of marriage in order to conceive. Ten long years of – whisper it – *sex* with Don.

It was 1980, and Barbara was about to walk out on her husband. Had it not been for Anna, she would have done, too. Her bags were packed and by the door. She had cancelled the milk delivery.

Empty of Don's sounds, the house had been silent. A thirteen-year-old Anna had sat her mother down. She had asked her to explain, please, just what was going on. Anna had set out some biscuits on a plate. She had arranged the British Variety selection in a fan, as her mother had talked.

Amid rivers of tears, dripping from her chin, her mother had quietly confessed everything. Why Anna had been an only child, after twelve long years of marriage. She and Don had been trying to have a baby for six years, before they had even talked to a doctor.

In Barbara's day you waited. But all of her friends were starting families. *She* looked more womanly than all of them. (Barbara had always made an effort with her appearance.) Yet, there they all were, with children – just slung around them, any-old-how – while she and Don were on their own, with no one.

It was not done. Not then. To be on your own. Cars were built, in Barbara's day, for children. Everything came in family packs. Crisps. Digestive biscuits. There were no miracle drugs. Well, she had not been prescribed any. The doctor had told Barbara just to 'keep trying' as if, by implication, she had, until then, been failing. Yes, he had examined her. But only to see if anything was 'obviously' wrong.

'You have,' he had said, 'idiopathic infertility.'

'We're doing it wrong?'

'No,' he had laughed. 'It means that you both appear physically to be fine. Or that we doctors, at least, don't know why you haven't conceived. The secret to having a baby . . .' He had leaned forward, touching Barbara's knee.

'Oh, yes?' (Eagerly.)

'Is to have lots of sex.'

She had been embarrassed. Well, in those days, it was all Benny Hill and sniggering. No one could keep a straight face. Not about a subject like Sex. In her day, you didn't go around shouting about it.

In Barbara's day, women had been competitive. Anna would not understand. It was all: 'How many children do you have?' Cut-throat. Not like now, when women swapped stories about their menstruations – sometimes on prime-time television.

Then, people looked down on you if you did not have at least two. Kids, that is. Bleating, whining, whingeing, laughing: they turned up in the supermarket, or on the bus, or in places where there *was* no place. It was not like today. In those days, children were a part of society, and no one seemed to have trouble having them. No one apart from Barbara. All she had wanted was to create human life. *Was that*, she had asked herself, *so much to ask?*

For ten long years, Don and Barbara had hammered away in the hope of having children. In Barbara's day, a doctor wouldn't prescribe pills. As Don had then said, 'You just put your head down and get on with it.'

In moments of near-madness, Barbara had wondered whether she wasn't, secretly, a man. As for Don, he had resigned himself to a life without children. Although not a religious man, he felt that he must have done something bad in a former life. Something to deserve this. Somewhere along the line, he had made his bed. 'Now, come on Barbara, we'll just have to lie in it.'

Besides, he had his politics.

But, by then, Barbara had lost many a friend, barking at everyone. Yes, 'shy little Barbara'. But the worm had turned. So angry, suddenly. Even she had her breaking point.

She had suddenly snapped. Instead of holding doors open for expectant mothers, Barbara had made a point of letting them go – slamming them into stomachs. Had she had a capable pin, Barbara would have roamed London deflating pregnant women.

(She had laughed, tearfully, as Anna had offered her a Jammy Dodger. 'I'll take one of these,' she had said, accepting a plain one. She liked to watch her figure.)

If only that doctor had been right. If only it had been as simple as simply having sex. Because they had had plenty of that. *Oh*, she had thought, *to stop having sex.*

Barbara had never actually enjoyed it, yet there she had been, having to do it all the time. The regimented nature of it all, coupled with the fact that she didn't like to move about – it might have disturbed the travel of the sperm towards the egg – had put Don off his stroke. After a while, and despite being a man, Don had gone off the whole idea too.

Sometimes, Barbara wondered how Anna had happened at all. But Anna *had* happened; and, of course, after that, everything had changed. Don had moved out, and into the spare room. Well, his role in it all had gone. That was why they had drifted apart – because, for much of her childhood, Anna had slept in Barbara's bed.

She had been safer there.

Barbara had worried that, at any moment, Anna would be taken from her. She was such a tiny thing. Five pounds. Even as a toddler, she'd had skinny, brittle, bones. But it must have been bad for Barbara and Don, not sleeping in the same bed. Bad for any marriage. At least Don had always had his do-it-yourself, and his politics. Give Don a badge and he was away. Whereas she had only ever had her daughter.

Anna watched her mother flip on, through that same, fat recipe book. *Flip, flip.*

She had always felt it her daughterly duty to make her mum happy. Barbara had wanted her for so long. Anna felt that she had to be worth the wait. Plus, during her childhood, she had slept in her parents' marital bed. By

212

doing that, she had no doubt come between Barbara and Don.

In effect, Barbara had given up her husband for her baby.

Now, her baby was thirty-one, but, still, she did not have a husband. Anna felt as if that was her fault. Yet, wasn't this – as Sean had said – emotional blackmail? Children weren't there to paper over the cracks of a parent's problems. Anna listened to her mother's page-turning *flip, flip, flip*. She was not the answer to all of Barbara's problems. *Flip*. That way, insanity lay.

There was so much, thought Anna, looking at her mother, that was wrong with their relationship. *Flip*. Such a gap between them. Mother and daughter. It was not even a generational thing; and, unless Anna sorted out her issues with Barbara, she would always have problems with motherly figures, and be forever bound up in a co-dependent relationship.

Anna needed to talk to Barbara as an equal. As Sean had said, they had to talk openly about the problems. No one was going to come along and rescue the relationship for Anna. If the mother-child relationship was unhealthy, and left to fester, the dynamics could be hugely damaging. Often people stayed in relationships only in the hope of someone coming along and rescuing them. But that wasn't going to happen, was it? *Anna* had to rescue the relationship.

'Mum,' she said, readying herself for the worst. 'Sit down. I haven't come home just to talk about recipes.'

'Oh, what is it then?' asked Barbara, switching on the radio.

'Mum, please. Turn off the radio, and sit down.'

Barbara would say that Anna had been suddenly infected by Don's way of trying to improve her lot. Proving herself –

but for what? *She* had always been happy with a good book, and a bar of chocolate. What was the point of being dissatisfied? It only led to unhappiness, and drink, and drugs.

Barbara switched off the radio, and sat down. 'What is this all about? Is this some sort of a trick?'

'No. I want to talk about us.'

'Riiiight. Why?' said her mother, slowly, and as if Anna had always been slightly retarded.

'Well. I want to talk about our relationship, I suppose. I want things out in the open. You see, you kind of put me down, sometimes. Treat me like a child.'

'Relationship,' said Barbara, rolling the word around her mouth. 'Isn't that an American word? Has it come all that way, over here? Funny, isn't it? I remember, Anna, when you started saying the words "french fries" instead of "chips". It was french fries with everything . . . *Now*,' she said, patting Anna's hand, 'what do I put you down about?'

Barbara would say that she had read about successful people in the newspapers. They ended up divorced. Whereas, she did not have much money, but she had enough. They had had enough, last year, to pay for that nice hotel meal. Hadn't they?

The Garden Court – open to non-residents all the year round. They had taken Anna there for her thirtieth birthday. The service was good. (Even *Don* had admitted that.) They still called you Madam there and gave you a pleasant view, away from the motorway. The waiter had said, 'I can't believe you two aren't *sisters*,' winking at Barbara and Anna.

That had made her happy.

If only Don and Anna had not gone on to spoil it all. Discussing politics in front of everybody. Talking about the

214

'environment' and 'democracy'. As if they were part of all that! What was the point in pretending? Why couldn't Anna be like Barbara? Talking nicely about the hotel service, for example. Or about local hooliganism. Did they have to discuss government and campaigns against genetic food modification? (Was that the right expression?) *She* preferred to be on the outside of those things, uncomplaining.

'OK, forget I used the word "relationship",' said Anna. 'But I still want to talk about the way we are with each other. I mean, I'd like us to treat each other with more respect and consideration.'

'Don't be silly. Is this another one of your Ideas?'

'What do you mean – Ideas?'

'Oh, well, like believing you're adopted.' She smiled, indulgently. 'Or wanting to be a stage star.'

'Well, they're hardly the same thing.'

'Oh, I know *you*,' said Barbara, playfully. 'Something goes into your head and, try as I might, I can't make it come out the other end.'

Barbara would wonder why her daughter could not be like her – with a husband? Yes, one she hardly ever saw. But that made life simpler. Didn't Anna want babies, or a pretty drawstring skirt? What was wrong with ornaments? Did she have to constantly criticise?

She wanted a daughter she could completely understand. A daughter who did things by the book. A girl who got married, and asked for napkin advice. A nice girl, like Justine, who enjoyed painting pictures. She wanted a daughter like herself. A daughter who liked quizzes, and sliced the edges off things, like gardens, and toast.

Perhaps, now, things were about to change. Anna, out of the blue, asking her advice about a dinner party! Perhaps, now, Anna would ask her about men and cutlery.

The questions would come tumbling out. *Should I marry him, Mum? How should I treat those stains on my husband's underpants?* Questions she had asked her own mother, in fact – about Don.

'Oh, I meant to tell you,' said Barbara, going back to her recipe book. 'Far from putting you *down*, as you say, I enjoyed your radio programme this week. *Problem Call*, isn't it?' said Barbara, stopping suddenly at a picture of a chocolate roulade. ('Oh, perhaps you'd like to try this one. I'll mark the spot.')

'You're not supposed to *enjoy* the programme,' snapped Anna, picking up a china basket of china flowers. Garden of Eden Products, it read underneath.

'Not even that one about the man who left his wife because she was having it away with his father? I found that one *very* comical.'

'No,' she said, bitterly.

Anna was thinking how the three of them – the Potters – had never been a family. (No wonder her father spent most of his time, now, away from the house.) Rather, they were a collection of people. It had always been the same. Even on those camping trips, their picnics had been flimsier than other families'. Barbara had wrapped the bread in cellophane, rather than tin foil.

There had always been compromise, throughout Anna's childhood.

The Potters had never had fruit. ('It'll only go off,' Barbara had argued.) On beaches, they were always the family bringing out their own deckchairs. Fraying, flimsy things. Oh, Anna's father had always spent his time trying to update the house. He had done his best, fixing and painting. But, even when it was newly re-decorated, still the family home had looked old-fashioned.

'What's your young man's name again?' asked Barbara, picking an insect out of her flour.

'It's Tom, and I'm not taking that, thanks,' said Anna. 'The sell-by date's four years ago. Look, Mum, I'm here to talk. Properly. About real things. About us.'

'Oh, that flour'll be fine,' dismissed Barbara. 'You don't want to go out buying *new*.'

She was a penny-pincher. Barbara always had been. Well, there had never been much money in the kitty. She had bought clothes from charity shops, nipping skirts in at the waist. (Anna would always remember her mother standing above her with pins in her mouth.) She had bought cheap cuts of meat, cooking up bad smells in the kitchen.

'There's no need to put on one of your black looks. All I'm saying is, don't go buying new when I have everything you need here.'

'Stop changing the subject,' said Anna. 'I want to talk about real things. What's going on *inside*, underneath the . . .'

'Oh, *underneath*,' interrupted Barbara, suddenly understanding. She blushed and lowered her voice to a whisper. 'Have you talked to your GP about that? He could send you to a . . .' Her voice almost disappeared. 'A *gynaecologist*.'

'No, no. What I mean is, I'm not happy.'

'Oh *you* – you're never happy,' said her mum, breathing out with relief.

Barbara had always had low expectations for Anna. It was Don who had invested in that large-piece chess set. Her father wanted people to know that they were cultured. He had bought the block of bound encyclopaedias, so that people would know that they were intellectuals. He had bartered for that African wood carving, on a package holiday to France, so that people would see that the Potters were broad-minded.

217

Don had always been the one who had wanted to improve himself. Barbara had never expected anything of Anna. So long as she kept her room tidy, got married, and didn't cause a fire.

Once, when Don and Anna had had a row, him screaming, 'Don't you want to make something of yourself?', Barbara had piped up, 'Leave Anna alone. She's happy as she is, without some high-flying career. She's happy just sitting in. Aren't you, Anna? She's like her Auntie Pauline in that.'

'Who's Auntie Pauline?' Anna was not aware of an Auntie Pauline.

'*Just* like Auntie Pauline. All round.'

She tinkled with laughter.

'Well, in what way?' asked Anna.

'In what way?' She stood there, apparently thinking. 'Well, she didn't want to be Somebody either. She was always happier doing nothing.'

'I don't do nothing.'

'Well, Pauline did nothing at all, as far as I can *remember*. Oh, she once ran some sort of charity fête. Made a real song and dance about it. But that all went wrong. No, apart from that, she was just happy being herself.'

'So, let me get this straight. I'm just like a woman who couldn't even run a *fête*?'

'Her *husband* had a good job. He set up his own company. Leaflet distribution, I think it was. Of course, they're both dead now.'

No wonder Anna had never expected much. How could she, with Barbara on hand to compare her to all manner of dead relatives? What would Sean say, if he could now witness their embittered, and destructive, relationship?

'What I'm trying to say is, I'm not happy with things the

218

way they are,' persisted Anna. She leaned back in her chair and looked up at the ceiling, as if she might find inspiration there.

'I see,' said Barbara, thoughtfully.

At last, thought Anna, *she's taking me seriously*.

'*I know*,' Barbara said suddenly. 'Why don't you get yourself a new image? Re-style your hair?'

She looked suspiciously at Anna's hair, as if therein lay all her problems.

'What do you mean, re-style my hair? I'm talking about *feelings*. I'm talking about my *life* here, not my bloody hairstyle. You've never been able to understand that there's more to women, nowadays, than them sitting at home, baking their husbands a nice lemon sponge . . .'

'So, tell me what else you've been doing then? And I'd like to see *you* bake a nice sponge.'

'Oh, as if I *haven't* been doing anything.'

'Anna, I don't *know* if you won't *tell* me.' She looked stern, then softened. '*Have* you baked a lemon sponge?'

'*No*. The point I was making was that I *don't* just bake bloody sponges. That – although you wouldn't be interested – I was reviewing a play last night for *Mz* magazine.'

She had never liked success, had Barbara. When she had heard that Pritti Poonjay had qualified as a doctor, Barbara had been dismissive. She had said, 'Well, that's just plain showing off, isn't it?' When Anna had talked about being cast in *Piers the Ploughman*, Barbara had merely sighed, saying, 'Well, if that's what you want to do . . .' She might as well have added, *Then I'm giving up on you*. Learning that Myrna had passed her Oxford entrance examination, she had said, 'I see. Is that good?'

'Of course it is,' Anna had replied. 'It's *Oxford*.'

Right, Barbara had conceded, but wasn't Myrna the peculiar one – and from Middlesbrough? Her family had such odd beliefs. Didn't Myrna's father work for some strange, churchy, religious organisation?

'No, of course not,' Anna had replied, long-suffering. 'He works for the Church of England.'

'*Mz* magazine. Well, that *is* nice,' said Barbara now, without any interest. 'Is that the magazine for elderly people?'

'No, of course it isn't. How can you . . . ?' said Anna, exasperated. 'It's for women who don't wait for life to come to them.' That was what was on the *Mz* masthead, anyway.

'Oh, I'm thinking of SaGA, aren't I? Silly me.'

'Well yes, that is silly.'

She knew she had to stay calm, but Anna was seriously niggled, now.

'I mean, how could you confuse them? You know I didn't want a row. I wanted a serious, adult discussion, but you're . . .'

'Well, don't start a row then. It's not like you, to argue. *I'm* not to know what magazine it was. *So*. Did they ask you to review the play?'

'Who?'

'The magazine people? Or did you do it just for fun?'

'Oh, Mum, please . . . Why should I do it for fun? It was *commissioned*. Well, Roo was commissioned, and I wrote it on her behalf.'

'Is that the Roo you were at polytechnic with?' asked Barbara.

'Yes.'

'The one who likes being in the spotlight?'

'Oh, Mum. Mind you, I suppose she does, yes,' said Anna.

220

Barbara did not trust Roo. She could not understand why Roo would not want to be at home with her children. 'It's hardly normal,' she had said. Don, however, had been Roo's biggest fan. Here was someone with fire and passion.

Here was someone who would, one day, be Someone.

But then he had met her. Roo had been researching an article she was writing about means-testing for state schools. She had asked Don whether it was possible to interview him.

'Fire away,' said Don, looking thoughtful. He liked to be asked for his opinion, on anything. He would stop women carrying clipboards in the street. He would hang around men with microphones, talking to TV cameras. He would start most of his sentences with the words, 'In my opinion . . .' In any group of people – large or small – he would set up an executive committee, standing for the job of General Secretary. 'General dogsbody,' Don would say. Because he was able to laugh at himself.

Roo had wanted an interview with an ordinary, average, middle-class couple. If only, thought Anna, she hadn't explained this to Don as part of her preamble.

Don, who did not feel ordinary, or average. He did not feel middle anything.

Had Roo seen their large, stuffed owl? The metal chess set? The Murano glass they had bought on a honeymoon trip to Italy? It was still intact. There weren't many on the group tour able to afford *that*. What about the china ballerina with the china-net skirt? They didn't come two-a-penny, Don could tell Roo. Plus, what about Anna going to Arndale? Roo had been there too, hadn't she?

Wasn't it now called a university?

Oh, and had Roo seen their bathroom that he had just re-decorated? ('Look at these taps.') Of course, it was all

221

avocado now. Butterscotch was old-fashioned. Come on, he would show her. 'What do you think of these?' he had asked, picking up the seashell-shaped soap. 'The man in the bathroom shop said it would make all the difference. Make the bath look more stylish.' He had handed Roo the lilac-smelling pot-pourri. 'But I don't know.'

'So, that's Roo,' said Barbara, rubbing her hands clean of flour, as if she was washing her hands of Roo. 'She's got six children, hasn't she?'

'Two,' snapped Anna. 'And another one on the way.'

'Right. And how are your other friends?' asked Barbara, her mouth sewn together into a smile. She stood there, trying to think of names. 'How's Justine?' she asked, at last.

'I've made other friends since Justine.'

'Of course, Elaine's parading Justine around at the moment,' she sniffed.

'In what way?' asked Anna, curiously.

'Oh, something to do with a nightclub she's trying to set up. According to Elaine, she's going to be some big impressionist.'

'What do you mean, *impressionist*? Oh – *impresario*.'

Anna was noting down the ingredients for her mother's Death by Chocolate cake. She was determined to try and communicate with her mother, despite Barbara's knack of distorting what she said. After half an hour with her mum, Anna was not able to think clearly.

'As I said to Elaine, "My Anna's happier going out with boys and whatnot. She's like me – she's never been interested in anything financial."'

'No, that's what you'd *like* me to be,' said Anna. 'A housewife and mother.'

222

'*Oh* no. I know what would happen if you had a baby, Anna. *I* know who'd end up looking after it. It'd be just like the dog we had. *Must* have a dog. *Desperate* for a dog. And then, as soon as it came along, you'd lose interest. You'd forget to feed it. There'd be no giving up the boys and the discos. *Oh* no. There'd be no getting up on a cold morning to take it for a walk.'

'Is this the dog we're talking about, or the baby?'

'All I'm saying is, that a baby isn't just for Christmas, Anna. It's a twenty-four-hour operation. You need all hands on deck . . .'

Anna listened to her mother, as she talked on, realising that it was no wonder she had such low self-esteem. No wonder she blamed herself for other people's problems. As Wilhelm Grohe had written, *These are all behavioural patterns set in place by one's parents*. As Sean had said, *Your parents aren't always right, you know. All they teach you, is to be like them*.

From Barbara, Anna had learned how to blame herself for train delays. She had learned how to smile as she left a hairdresser's after a terrible haircut, thanking everyone for their time and trouble. Success was an embarrassment, and to be avoided at all costs. If one was overtaxed, or mugged, one did not make a fuss.

One did not make a fuss.

One stayed on the outside of things, complaining. When Anna had become an actress, Barbara had urged her to stop. Before it was too late. That sort of thing led only to embarrassment. What did Anna want? To be famous! Pwuh! Who did she want to be? Diana Dors? Carol Vorderman? Barbara doubted very much that *they* were happy. With their money and their silicone implants. Why did celebrities *need* such big breasts?

223

'Wouldn't mind them myself,' Anna muttered, increasingly irritated with her mother.

'Well, have a baby then. They'll grow quick enough then.'

'I thought you didn't want me to have a baby. Not out of wedlock anyway?'

'Well, get married then,' she smiled. But that was Barbara's answer to everything.

Now, Barbara was kneeling down, at the fridge. 'Right, what can I give you from here?' asked her mother. But the fridge was full of high-fat milk and cat food. Cat food for the neighbour's cat – and anything useful for a quick salad. Cold processed meats, for example, and bulbs of fluorescent green lettuces.

'Look, don't worry about *dinner*. I think I'm OK, and I didn't come round to discuss that anyway,' she said, determined not to be sidetracked.

'Well, don't say I didn't offer.'

'I won't. I know what I'm going to make.'

'So is *Justine* still doing cordon bleu cuisine?' asked Barbara, standing up, and wiping the dust from her bare knees.

'What do you mean?' asked Anna, caught off guard at hearing Justine's name.

She felt a pang of regret that they were not still friends.

'She used to bring home these lovely apple tarts. I remember Elaine bringing them round in Tupperware boxes, as if they were a gift.' She snorted. 'But, really, it was to show them off.' She looked at Anna, and smiled, patronisingly. 'But then Justine was always ahead of you, in everything. I mean, she had such a quick brain. She was always so good at domestic science, wasn't she? I remember one teacher saying, at parents' evening . . .'

'You seem to have forgotten that Justine was almost expelled. And, anyway, it was no wonder I wasn't academic. It wasn't as if you spent any *money* on my education.' Anna sighed.

'What do you mean? You don't need to *pay* for schools, do you? Not in my day, anyway. Is that another bit of government nonsense? I thought you were very well taught. It wasn't as if you needed to know any more than they taught you there. Boy or girl. Such good pasteurised care. I was glad you weren't clever. It only gets girls into trouble.'

'*Pastoral* care,' corrected Anna. '*Pasteurised* care,' she muttered, irritated. 'And I was . . . I *am* clever. You just don't want to see it. It upsets you.'

'You're clever in your own way,' admitted Barbara. 'You're canny when it comes to feminine intuition.'

'Feminine *intuition*,' repeated Anna, aghast. 'That was an old-fashioned concept in the *seventies*.'

Anna decided to search through Barbara's tin cupboard. She was here on a different mission, but she did still have to think about dinner, with Tom. She found Postman Pat spaghetti in the cupboard, for some reason.

'Why do you buy these kids' foods?' she asked, finding Barbie-doll baked beans.

'Well, I thought you'd like them. They're something new. And you always liked alphabet spaghetti. Oh dear, though. You were *clever*,' she conceded. 'But you couldn't spell. Not for . . .' She laughed. 'At parents' evenings, I . . .'

'Look, I didn't come round here to talk about *parents*' evenings. You're just using it as another way to put me down.'

'Don't be silly. I remember, at parents' evening, one teacher saying, "Anna doesn't shine at anything. But take a look at this," and she showed me a pin-cushion. "Anna's

225

all fingers and thumbs," she said, "but look at the stitching on this pin-cushion. That's Justine."'

'Oh, *please* . . . No wonder I feel so small, all the time.'

'Well, you're hardly very *tall*, Anna.'

She chuckled, like a cartoon character.

'Are you *so simple-minded*? Why can't you bloody well listen to me?'

That shut Barbara up. They sat there, mother and daughter, for a while. Mother, smarting at Daughter's sharp words. Daughter's mouth, decisively shut. Mother looking through another, glossier, recipe book, *Cooking with Sugar*, sponsored by a granulated-sugar manufacturer.

Mother, licking her thumb, and turning the page, licking her thumb, and turning the page. At last, she folded over a page illustrated with an iced bun.

'Is that what you came home to talk about? My simple-mindedness?'

'I came "home" to talk. As we actually did when you told me about your infertility, years ago. You know – the last time we had a proper conversation?'

'It was hardly infertility,' said Barbara, looking pointedly at Anna. She raised an eyebrow, and looked back at her glossy pictures of food. 'What's come over you anyway? It's not like you to scream like that.'

'Well, not infertility then. Whatever it was . . . Your problems with Dad. Either way, it was the last time you talked to me without running me down.'

'Well, if you're going to rake up the past,' said Barbara, tartly. She looked slightly scared, and her mouth was set in a way which read, *I don't want to talk about it*. 'Now, are you staying for lunch?'

'No,' said Anna, quietly.

When she was a child, Anna's mother had always insisted

she finish her mashed potato. If she did not, Barbara had said that she would exchange Anna for a little girl who did. For weeks after that, Anna had thought that her mother was about to exchange her for a child who ate her dinner, lump by lump, and went to sleep at bedtime. Because Anna had not been able to sleep – not for weeks.

She imagined that, if she closed her eyes, her mother would swap her for a child who did not scratch her eczema. A child who did not wet the bed, and wake up screaming in the night. She would send Anna to an orphanage, of the type featured in the musical, *Oliver!* Or to an island for raggedy kids, of the sort featured in *Chitty Chitty Bang Bang*.

Her mother would return with a child out of a picture book, with plaits that were straight. That child would go happily to school the next day. That child would not worry about her mother locking her out of the house, if she was absent for a second.

'That was a terrible thing to do,' she said now.

'What was?'

'I was about eight. And you told me that, if I didn't eat my supper you'd exchange me for another child.' All she had wanted, then, was to be A Girl Like You – as the masthead of her *Bunty* comic had read.

'Oh, *I* remember that,' laughed Barbara thinking that she was back on firmer, more light-hearted, ground. 'It worked too. You were so well-behaved, for weeks.'

Anna had behaved herself for weeks after that, meanwhile suffering terrible eczema on her knees and the cracks of her arms.

'It was a horrible thing to say to a child. Nowadays, it would be considered emotionally abusive.'

'Oh, *nowadays*,' said Barbara, fussing with her hair.

'Nowadays, children get away with murder. I was only saying to Elaine, the other day, when a child broke her arm . . .'

'A child broke Auntie Elaine's arm?' (How could her mother always manage to make her lose sight of what she was trying to say?)

'Let me finish. This child broke the arm off one of her statues, in the front garden. Although, I did say to Elaine, "Well, the statues aren't necessary, are they? They're only for *show*." That threw her.'

'So, tell me something, Mum,' interrupted Anna. 'Why, at school, wouldn't you let me be the queen in that variety show?'

Her primary-school teacher had cast Anna in that starring role. 'She's got a lovely singing voice,' the teacher had said to Barbara. 'And unlike most nine-year-olds, Anna knows the meaning of the word "intonation". But it's a main variety show part, and it *is* going to take a lot of rehearsal. That's why I'm calling all the parents individually. Well, those parents of kids I've picked for the main parts, anyway. So, what do you say? It means three times a week, after school and . . .'

'Well, in that case, I think *no*,' Barbara had interrupted.

Because Anna had Brownies on a Monday and marching band on a Wednesday. She was going for her giftwrapping badge in Brownies, which meant Anna needed to learn how to wrap the perfect parcel. Anything else would tip her over the edge.

'But, *Mum* . . .'

'So, I think no,' said Barbara. And Don had agreed.

It was 1976 and the Potters still made their decisions jointly. Don, saying that it might interfere with Anna's homework. Barbara, saying that there was a small matter

228

of the mothers having to sew the costumes – and Barbara could not be bothered with that. Not for something that would be over in a day – like all of Anna's other interests.

'But, Mum, that's not fair,' nine-year-old Anna had said.

'Life isn't,' said Barbara, making that night's tea. Sausages and beans. 'And come away from the sweetie cupboard.'

And so Anna had had the shame of being cast as a Jumblie in the end-of-term variety show, wearing a green-felt costume. She was sent to sea in a sieve, she was, she was sent to sea in a sieve . . .

'Why bring that up now, out of the blue?' asked Barbara, chopping lettuce for her lonely lunch.

'Because it needs resolving. There are so many things in my childhood which need resolving. That time you hit me with one of Dad's shoes . . .'

'You pushed a child into the school swimming-pool,' said Barbara, slowly shaking her head.

She scooped up the lettuce and put it into a bowl.

'Actually, that was Justine.'

'*Justine*. *You*. What was the difference then?'

'There was plenty of difference . . .'

'The child didn't have any parents, poor thing.'

'I was the one who *befriended* her.'

'I made sure of that. After what you did.'

'So, let me get this straight. All of the good things that happened in my past you take responsibility for, and all the *bad* things . . .'

'I made you go to the girl's birthday party. All of the other mothers thought that their children might catch something. Because, in my day, foster homes were full of germs . . .'

She was slicing a cucumber into thick, even, pieces.

229

'How ridiculous.'

'And I was the same about Pritti Poonjay. She played with you, right throughout your childhood, even *though* she was coloured . . .'

Seeds spat out of the tomato she was halving.

'That's racist vitriol. You can't talk like that about Pritti.'

'Well, you might be friends now, but you said a lot worse then. You and Justine. Making Pritti's life a misery . . .'

She quartered the tomato, looking at her daughter, as if she might – even after all these years – be a stranger.

'That was Justine. She was practically a skinhead, for Christ's sake. And it's in the past, anyway . . .'

'Oh, what *you* choose to be in the past is in the past, but what *I* choose . . . ?'

'You. Ruined. My. Life. That dog you were talking about . . . You *killed* it. You killed the fucking family dog.'

Barbara took another tomato, quickly halving it. She looked sharply at Anna. Why was she behaving this way? If anything, they had always been friends. That was how she described her daughter to Elaine. ('My daughter's always doubled as my best friend,' she would often say.) She tried to steady the tomato. It was her knife, however, that was shaking, slicing her wedding-ring finger. But that did not stop her quartering.

'Your dog didn't die. We sent it back to a home.'

'Yeah, for someone else to murder. Poor unwanted thing.'

'Well, you didn't want it. You wouldn't clean up after it . . .'

'I was a child, for Chrissakes. You were the adult. You should have taken *responsibility* for it . . . And now that I'm an adult, of course you treat me like a fucking child.' Anna was shaking too. She had never sworn at

230

her mother before. 'You know the truth? Sometimes, I despise you.'

Barbara stopped chopping up her apple. She stared at her daughter, the stranger.

'Yes I do, I despise you,' confirmed Anna, watching Barbara with her knife poised, defensively. 'You and your Maggie Thatcher handbag and the way the furniture in your so-called "guest" room is covered up with plastic. I mean, who ever comes round? Auntie *Elaine*? The way you peeled Cornettos in the cinema, when I was a child. It was embarrassing – everyone shushing us. You were always the one with the box of Maltesers, helping yourself one by sodding one. But it's not even just that . . .'

Oh, it was all coming back to her now – a lifetime of stored-up grievances. She needed – as Sean had said – to let out all of her feelings.

'Oh, there's more, is there?' Barbara tried to smile, and failed. She took a beetroot and sliced that, blood pouring from her finger.

'Oh, I haven't even *started*. We could talk about you and Dad as parents. Me playing piggy-in-the-middle with you both, as if you're teenagers. I mean, why you haven't sorted things out now, over fifteen years *later* . . .'

'You know why,' said Barbara, her eyes wet like an animal's.

If Anna did not know her mother better, she would have thought that she was about to cry.

'I mean, why don't you talk about it? Or could that be what the problem is? That you don't damn well talk about *anything*? You've been friends with Elaine Quealy for forty-odd years, and you still won't tell her you hate her guts. Oh no. Just go on, pretending. No one can get through to you, woman. You live in this bizarre, old-fashioned world where everything's as it was. You still wear pleated *skirts*. Even Dad can't talk to you, and he's fucking married to you. If you call it married.'

She felt good, saying all this. It felt so healthy, allowing her feelings to spill out of her. Kept inside, they spread, like a cancer.

'Stop it now, Anna. You're saying things you'll only regret.' All of a sudden, thin tears ran down her face.

'Oh no, I won't regret this. I want to finish this,' said Anna, surprised to see the tears. She hadn't seen her mother cry since 1980 – when she had revealed her 'infertility'.

Anna stood up. She didn't want to watch her mother's face. 'I'm going to tell you what it feels like to have your dog taken away from you, suddenly, out of the blue, as you call it, and to be hit with the heel of a slipper. Why should you get away with it?'

'Have you finished now?'

Barbara wiped her face, but more tears came, sliding down the grooves in her face. She picked up a yellow bowl, dumping in the salad and squeezing on some rainy dressing.

'No, not quite. I want to tell you that we're not a family. That we never *were* a family. That it takes more than having one child to be a family. And that, anyway, the "family" you dreamt about has broken up. And who broke it up?'

'Have. You. Finished?'

Tears were dripping down her face fast, drying half-way down, but Anna could not stop herself speaking. Neither did she think that that would be the right thing to do.

'And don't think you're upsetting me now. I've cried enough in my life, and you didn't care. You lay down these narrow expectations, which are impossible to jump out of.

232

I mean, *I* wanted only to be an actress. But have you ever supported me in that?'

'What've I done to deserve this?' her mother said, quietly, stopping with her salad, and wiping her eyes.

'I'll tell you what you've done . . .' said Anna, angrily. 'I'll tell you, *you* . . . All I can say is, thank God you could only have one child. Because, I tell you, Mum, you've really made a mess of it. No wonder you couldn't have kids. I must have been a . . . a sacrifice. Because God knew you'd be a *fucking terrible mother.*'

Anna stopped, vaguely shocked by what she had just said.

Her mother's tears dried up in a second.

'Don't try to make me feel guilty, either,' Anna said. But Barbara had turned into a stone statue. Anna was surprised to see the stone statue rise, and walk into the room they had always called the family room. 'I'm not going to apologise for telling the truth,' she added, to the back of Barbara's elderly pink cardigan. 'It's all just emotional blackmail.'

Her mother had always looked old, even in black-and-white photographs from the 1950s. That face, pinched in all the wrong places. Eventually, all Potters began to look like each other – even those that had married in. Even Anna's mother: they were all short, and pale, and oddly built. Anna still remembered the Welsh branch of their family, although she had not seen any of them for twenty years. Every Potter initially looked like an Anna, becoming, over time, a Barbara or a Don.

But not Anna. She was going to be different. Different, despite the fact that Barbara had never looked after her daughter's skin, like the women in the Oil of Ulay advertisements.

Anna went into the family room. She sat down opposite

Barbara, who was sitting on an easy chair, her arms folded, and her eyes staring straight ahead.

'Look, I'm finished now. I've said all I wanted to say. I'm sorry if I hurt you, but I feel better for having said it.' Anna smiled, and breathed out.

'I'm glad somebody does,' said Barbara sternly, looking straight at a picture that she had bought in Montmartre, during a holiday in Paris. It showed a dark-haired urchin boy, urinating.

'These things should be said, Mum. It clears the air.'

Barbara did not reply. She just sat there, holding her salad knife.

'Otherwise things fester. You understand that, don't you?' said Anna, feeling, for the first time, as if she was talking to her mother as an adult – although Barbara said nothing. She licked her dry lips.

'The truth is that if this was thirty years ago, I'd probably be married now, with children of my own,' said Anna. 'I'd have my own family. And just because I *don't* . . . Just because women's lives have changed, and we're all more independent now, with careers, that doesn't mean that . . . Well, just because I'm not married, it doesn't mean I'm still a part of your family.'

Still, Barbara sat there, like a deflated doll.

'I'm not a part of your family. You need your own life. With *Dad*. You and *Dad*. I'm not part of that. I'm an adult with my own life. I'm over thirty, and most women my age barely see their mothers from one Christmas to the next, let alone every time they're cooking dinner for somebody . . .'

Her mother's tears had stopped, but her cheeks were wet. Her face looked like a statue's after it had been rained upon.

'And don't sit there like that. It's a type of cruelty, really.

Your comments when they're not bloody asked for. Your silence when I want to *talk*. It makes me hate you, and is that what you want? There *are* women who are friends with their mothers. But, you know, you can choose your friends – you can't choose your family. And I think we should be honest about the differences between us. We're two very different people.

'I'm just not like you. Gardening. Or sitting in front of the television. Swapping gossip with Auntie Elaine. Having the same so-called friend for forty years. It's obscene. Haven't you changed, in all that time? Oh God, I wish you'd say something.'

But her mother still sat there, still the colour of stone.

'I think I should go now.' Anna stood up, and stretched. She was trying to find the right moment to leave. 'And I'm sorry, really sorry that it's worked out this way,' she went on. 'But I'm not a child any more; and your judgments about me, and my life, aren't important. I have the confidence now not to care what you think. You know, I always took your side in arguments. But I was wrong to do that, because at least Dad *cares* about what I'm doing. About *me*, rather than some mythical creature that he thinks is his daughter.'

'Please . . . This isn't fair,' came Barbara's small voice, as Anna put on her coat.

Oddly, hearing her mother speak gave Anna the confidence to go. She paused for dramatic effect and then said, 'Life isn't,' before walking out of the so-called family-room.

The glass in the front door shivered, as she slammed it behind her.

Before now, it had always been Anna's father screaming at her mother. Don had begged Barbara to scream back at him. 'Unlock that bloody face of yours,' he had shouted.

Anna had always gone silently to her mother's side, because Barbara was the weaker one, in any argument. She needed Anna more than Don did.

For a moment, Anna thought that she could walk easily away. But, shaking, she stood there for several seconds, worried. It was only the sight of Elaine Quealy, coming out of her own front door, with a spade, that made Anna head for the train station, repeating, like a mantra, Sean's words: 'Break free from the past. Break free for your own well-being.'

Chapter Ten

They were extraordinarily comfortable with each other. Tom had made himself at home, sitting down on the sofa. Seconds later, they were laughing about something on the television. They had a definite rapport, Tom and Myrna. A match made in heaven, Myrna and Tom.

Anna had cooked for them, buying three ready-meals for two from Marks and Spencer, and adding a sauce. The sauce was out of a Waitrose packet, but she had poured in some red wine, which had been recommended as an Oddbins red wine of the week. She had then heated up the bag of home made soup, from her local twenty-four-hour supermarket. For dessert, she had bought a tub of exotic dairy fresh ice-cream, dropping in some fresh, frozen raspberries at the last minute.

Tom had walked in to a delicious smell of cooking.

'You're a good cook,' said Tom now, helping Anna to clear up. Myrna had gone next door, into the living room. 'I just live out of packets myself,' he said.

'Not last night, though? What was it? Steak forestière?'

'Yeah. Fresh from Marks and Spencer's.'

'Oh.'

She felt a vague sense of disappointment at that.

They had just eaten, but, still, when Tom and Anna went into the living room, they found Myrna there, in front of the television. She was eating her way through a packet of milk-chocolate slimming biscuits. On her lap was a pad of lined letter-writing paper.

'Meal-replacement biscuit?' Myrna offered Tom.

'Oh, yes thanks. What're we watching?'

'It's that music award ceremony,' said Anna, sitting on the sofa between Myrna and Tom. 'What's it called again?'

'Whatever,' said Myrna absentmindedly, her mouth full of biscuit. 'Shit's hit the fan, though. The Best Single Male Artist has just said that he's more important than the Beatles.'

'*Christ*,' said Tom.

'Wouldn't it be nice to be part of all that celebrity world?' asked Anna, dreamily, as glitzy women moved air-kissing through her TV screen.

'Anna reads too many Saturday supplements,' said Myrna drily to Tom.

'It's a bit of an artificial existence,' agreed Tom.

'*No*. We just *assume* that because we're all jealous. I mean, that woman, whatshername, seems genuinely nice,' said Anna, as the Best Single Female Artist went up to collect her award.

'Of course she's *nice*, Anna,' said Myrna. 'She's beautiful, adored, successful and surrounded by free drink, drugs, and adulation. No wonder she's *nice*. I'd be nice too, if I had all that.'

Tom laughed, as Anna thought, *As it is, you're a morbid depressive who brings everyone down*. She wondered whether to express these terrible thoughts. Wilhelm Grohe had said that unexpressed thoughts turned in on themselves. *They spread around your soul, like cancerous cells.*

'I thought you were making coffee,' said Myrna, as the

238

programme ended. The volume rose at an advertisement for exceedingly good cakes.

'No, we were clearing up. After you.'

'Oh,' said Myrna, signing her letter.

Anna was thinking about her mother, and feeling guilty. She hoped that Barbara would take comfort from her garden. Yet, that garden had only ever been a displacement activity. Barbara had taken an interest in plants and flowers only after her daughter had left home.

Oh, but Anna did have to remind herself that she was an adult, and had the right to *leave home, and form her own attachments* – as Grohe had said.

Myrna put her letter down on their glass-topped table. The table was cracked through, like lightning, in so many places. 'Well, *will* you make coffee?' she asked Anna.

'No.'

'Oh, please. I'm so tired.' She turned to Tom for his support. 'I wait on her hand and foot during the week. I'm like Anna's unpaid slave, and it's her job to make the coffee at weekends.'

'No. I'm too much of a yes person. I'm sick of it. I'm learning to say no.'

'Well, that was great,' said Myrna, sarcastically, as Tom smiled. 'Really well done. Now, will you make us a coffee?'

'No, Myrna. Fuck off.'

Tom apologised for laughing.

Anna was suddenly sick of being her flatmate's straight guy. Until this moment everyone had always preferred Anna to Myrna. She had consistently taken the role of Myrna's defender. But Anna now felt as if her role was actually to feed lines for Myrna's jokes. And Tom clearly found their double act highly amusing.

239

'Tom, this isn't the Anna we knew and loved. Before she started working on *Problem Call*, Anna was actually one of life's truly nice people. She allowed her cleaning woman to rearrange her bedroom furniture because she was too scared to say anything . . .'

'Well, not any more.'

'And she didn't used to smile so much, either. You see, she's doing it now. That irritating, meaningless, smile. It's the books she's started reading. All these self-help books – ostensibly for work, but *really* . . .'

'But really for you to take the piss out of.'

'Are these the books where women go on about looking for themselves,' interrupted Tom, 'when actually what they're looking for is a man?'

Myrna laughed, and Anna stared, surprised to see her flatmate having fun. Myrna had not once mentioned war or famine in Africa.

'Too right,' said Myrna.

'They're about coming to terms with yourself, and learning to solve your own problems rather than everyone else's,' said Anna, calmly. 'Actually.'

'She's going to start Feng Shui next,' said Myrna.

'The fashionable way to tidy up,' laughed Tom. 'Talking of neat freaks, how was Justine's meeting?'

'Have you met Justine?' Myrna asked Tom.

'Yeah. Pierced Woman.'

'What d'you mean? Has she had her tongue pierced now, or something?'

'Almost every part of her anatomy, I think. So how was the meeting, Anna?'

Tom did not seem to notice the smell of Myrna's tatty, underfed plants, or the dust covering their every object, like insulation. It was as if he had been sitting comfortably on their sofa forever, just like the rolled-up posters in the corner of the living-room (Anna meant, at some point, to put them up), the pile of books, the hat-stand, and the Safeway bag of tins – still waiting to be taken for recycling.

'You'll be pleased to know that I didn't *go* to Justine's in the end. Partly because of these "self-help" books that you two are sneering at . . .'

'Why should I be pleased?' asked Tom. 'It sounded interesting. Not often one gets the opportunity to . . .'

'Well, I thought you said that I shouldn't go. Didn't you say that?' Hadn't he said that? 'That different rules applied, now that we're adults?'

'Well, that was before I met her. I liked her, actually.'

'God, how could you?' said Myrna.

'But don't you think she uses me? She's always just taken advantage of me.'

'No, I got the impression she valued your opinion. She seemed to look up to you – as some sort of a role model.'

Anna fell silent, as her flatmate sensed the atmosphere and tried to lighten it by singing along to a TV tampon advert: 'It's *my* life . . .'

Anna wondered whether Tom was right. When her mother had talked about Justine, she had felt a pang, probably of regret. But, as Sean had said, *Who said that this would be easy?*

'So, who's your letter to, Myrna?' asked Tom.

'The daughter of a serial killer,' muttered Anna. She was about to apologise for her flatmate's strange behaviour, but Tom said, 'Really?'

'She was abused herself, this daughter,' said Myrna. 'I felt I wanted to do *something*. But the letter's rubbish.'

'I see. Can I read it?' he asked, and Myrna nodded, handing him the pad of paper.

'. . . I am writing to express my profound sympathy. I can't imagine what it must have been like to go through such abuse – being serially raped, drugged, and tortured. It is impossible for me to understand . . .' read Tom, aloud.

'No – this is good,' he said, and Anna was pleased that, at last, one of her boyfriends was being kind to Myrna. Although, was Tom her boyfriend?

'It's shit,' grunted Myrna. 'But everything I write sounds really false or cloying. I can't get the *tone* right.'

'No, it's good. Honestly.'

'She writes well,' said Anna, with some pride.

Last week, Anna had thought of asking Myrna to write Him some letters on her behalf. But then she had thought that, as a result of the letters, He might fall back in love with Anna. Or rather Myrna. Which smacked too much of the plot of Cyrano de Bergerac.

'Anna, this isn't creative *writing*.'

'Well, whatever. You'll get a response, I think.'

'I'm not *doing* it to get a response.'

'Oh, well, why then?'

'Because I'm stupid and I think it might help,' she said sadly. 'You know – the strategically placed letter.'

Myrna wrote many a strongly worded letter. She had written letters to the Department of Health about insidious health rationing; she had written to the Department of Overseas Development about the plight of flood victims in Honduras; she had written to the Treasury complaining about the pittance war widows received. *'So where are all the promised "homes fit for heroes"?'*

Myrna was always referred elsewhere.

'Well, they *do* help, I s'pose,' reassured Anna, remembering the letter that Myrna had written to a train company, and the ten-pound gift voucher redeemable against the purchase

242

of any ticket valid on a Thameslink train, that Myrna had received in reply. 'That Thameslink letter, anyway.'

Dear Sir or Madam,

I am writing to express my gratitude to Thameslink. I used to suffer from panic attacks whenever any train was late, according to the printed timetable. But then I realised that Thameslink trains are always *late! That it is impossible to rely on them or, indeed, anything. As a result, I no longer suffer from stress.*

Thank you, Thameslink,

Yours faithfully,

Ms Myrna Lomond.

'Oh, that one . . . That didn't help anyone. Except me.'

'Well, I'm shit at writing letters, full-stop,' said Anna, to make Myrna feel better about herself.

'God, so am I,' admitted Tom, looking at Anna. (He had clearly said this only to make Anna feel better about herself.)

'Well, it hardly matters now, does it?' sneered Myrna. 'Everyone just faxes. Or *e-mails*.'

Sometimes, Anna wondered whether Myrna had been tricked into living in the modern era, possibly as part of some time-travel-type, big-box-office film plot. She could imagine her flatmate more easily as a governess, in stiff, restrictive skirt, with a servant unknotting the strings of her corsets. Certainly, Myrna's time passed as slowly as in a

Jane Austen novel – her life strung together by events such as Thameslink replying to her letter, or Christmas with her family. Any get-together with her father.

('It's. *My*. Life . . .')

Myrna's father worked for the Church of England – although on the financial, rather than the pastoral, side. He raised funds for a London diocese. He disapproved of damn well nearly everything.

He had terrified the teenage Anna when she had stayed for a weekend with the family Lomond so that her parents could go away together for the weekend.

'How can young people be drawn back into the Church?' Mr Lomond had asked her over lunch. A thirteen-year-old Anna had muttered something about *discos* and *Coca-Cola*, as Myrna's elder brother, Graeme, had gazed at her through his long fringe.

Only a week before, Graeme had telephoned Anna's house. He had asked Anna to a musical production at the church the following Saturday night. Anna had thought his choice of play appropriate. *Grease* drained from every Graeme pore, drowning his neck in a sticky film of red rash. Grease combed through Graeme's hair, pasting his fringe to his forehead. In patches under arms, in spills from green-brown eyes, wept the grease from Graeme's pores.

'I'll let you know,' said Anna, who found it impossible to say no.

One week later, and Anna was trying to avoid meeting Graeme's hopeless, hopeful glances over a Saturday roast. She realised that he was still waiting for a definite answer. (And Anna was staying in his house.) She had left things far too open between them.

'So, do *you* like discos?' he had asked Anna, passing Myrna the potatoes.

The family Lomond sat there, as a unit, waiting for a reply. No Lomond – realised Anna – would understand if she refused to accept that the first-born son was attractive, romantically. 'Yes and no,' she said, afraid of giving Graeme a straight answer at the end of a disastrous stay, during which Anna had upset several bowls of potpourri.

She had upset Mrs Lomond, who was fat in an old-fashioned, seamless way. An out-dated, happy way. Mrs Lomond's job was to cover the family's furniture in tapestries, and to be a doctor's receptionist in her spare time.

Almost immediately, Anna had regretted her decision to spend the weekend at Myrna's, rather than Justine's, house. Even more so now, in fact, as Mr Lomond had announced that they would all visit Blenheim Palace after lunch.

'We are honoured to have such *a pretty* teenage girl join us for our family outing,' he said, smiling at Anna. Anna waited for Myrna to say that they couldn't possibly go to Blenheim Palace, as they had other priorities. (Anna had been about to suggest to Myrna that they go for a walk past Charlie Secker's house. He lived around the corner.)

But Myrna said nothing.

Her father said conspiratorially to Anna, 'Thank you for being friends with Myrna. I know how hard it can be, for you *pretty* girls, to tear yourselves away from the boyfriends and the make-up. Myrna doesn't have boyfriends. Even in Middlesbrough, she didn't have a boyfriend.' He laughed, looking at Myrna as if anxious to re-adjust the features on her face.

Graeme twitched with pleasure at the thought of an afternoon out with Anna, as Anna wished herself anywhere else. She offered to do the washing up, longing to be with her parents, who were on their second honeymoon at a four-star all-in hotel break in Margate. Anna's father and mother had booked the break after Don had had an *affair* with a *candidate* called *Catherine*.

During the tour around Bleinheim Palace, Mrs Lomond referred to Don menacingly as your er father. (Anna's mother had taken to referring to Don as that father of yours.) She appeared to know more about the cracks in Mr and Mrs Potter's marriage than Anna did. As they walked through the palace, en route to the souvenir shop, Mrs Lomond made a number of pertinent remarks:

1) Marriage *Does* Have Its Ups And Downs.
2) Men Aren't Like Women. They Need Almost Constant Attention.
3) Your Er Father Is Really Like Any Man.
4) It's Good For Grown-Ups To Get Away.

'This is so nice. We don't do enough of this, do we, Derrick?' said Mrs Lomond, trying to stop Matthew and Mark knocking artefacts from their stands. They approached the banqueting room. 'I know you were right to make Graeme stay home, Derrick, but . . .'

'He's not the Clever One of the family. If Gray wants to pass exams, he has to study.'

Mr Lomond divided his children up, allowing them each only one characteristic. Mark, therefore, was the Good-looking One, Matthew the Sporty One, and Graeme, the Artistic One. Myrna was the Clever One.

('But only by a process of elimination,' said Myrna.)

'Well, yes, but they're only mock exams,' said Mrs Lomond, about Graeme.

'He's not like Myrna. Graeme has to . . .'

'Shhh. All right, Derrick. Anyway . . . Do *your* parents ever take you to palaces, Anna? On family outings generally?'

'Oh yes. We used to go camping.'

'Well, that's good. You see, we've always made a point of family outings. Every so often. Perhaps with brothers and sisters. Maybe if your parents had . . .'

'*Margaret*,' interrupted Mr Lomond fiercely, as if his wife's name was a well-known word of warning.

'I'm just *saying*.'

'*Mar*-grit!'

'*We* have that dinner service,' said Mrs Lomond, changing the subject. She pointed to a display of gilt-edged plates. 'Don't we, Derrick?'

'I hardly think so,' said Mr Lomond, snorting. 'Even Myrna doesn't eat enough to justify that lot.'

Myrna looked troubled, walking away from the rest of the family. Anna followed her. She was tired of being desperately polite to Myrna's parents, and to inanimate objects. She pointed to a fire extinguisher, and joked, 'Myrna, *this* is nice, isn't it? What period, d'you think . . . ?'

But Myrna was bent double, squealing, 'My stomach hurts.'

'Where does it hurt?' asked her mother, appearing, as if by magic.

'My stomach,' said Myrna, hugging herself.

'*Oh*, my God, Derrick. It's her stomach.'

'She'll be fine,' said Mr Lomond.

'Derrick, *no*,' fluttered Mrs Lomond. 'I will not have your "fines". We need a *doctor*.'

Somehow, they all found themselves in a huge hospital. Matthew and Mark, racing hospital trolleys. Anna, sitting behind a grey curtain. Mrs Lomond, wetly snatching Anna's hand. Mr Lomond, wandering off to look around the hospital shop, as, behind the curtain, men in white coats prodded Myrna's stomach.

Mrs Lomond was muttering, 'Oh God . . . I knew this was coming . . . Mrs Sturgeon. My fault . . . I shouldn't

247

call charity useless. I should have donated Daddy's organs . . .' Behind the curtain, Myrna moaned, as Mrs Lomond clutched Anna's hand harder. A doctor appeared theatrically through the flap. '*Doctor*,' said Mrs Lomond. 'It's not leukaemia, is it?'

'Actually, Mrs Lomond,' said the doctor, gravely. 'Your daughter appears to be constipated.'

The telephone rang. 'I think I'll leave that to the machine,' said Anna, embarrassed that anyone would think Anna at home on a Saturday night. 'I'm trying not to be so addicted to the phone. I use it too much.' She looked at Myrna for support. 'Don't I?'

Myrna ignored her.

The ringing stopped, and the machine clicked on. They heard Myrna's slow-playing voice, 'This is an answering machine. Please leave your name and number after the beep.' Anna thought how strange Myrna's new message sounded – as if Myrna herself was trapped in the machine.

'Myrna, it's your mother here. Are you there? I know you're there.'

'*How* does she know?' asked Myrna, and Anna smiled.

They both knew Mrs Lomond's idiosyncrasies. She worried if her daughter so much as sounded funny on the phone. Myrna should book herself an appointment with a doctor, she would insist. Myrna should persuade him to give her a prescription. She must not be put off. Doctors spent their lives putting people off. If anyone knew that, Mrs Lomond – a doctor's receptionist – did. Her daughter should search her breasts for lumps. Left to their own devices, women developed the most awful diseases. Someone should take a look at Myrna's vagina.

*   *   *

248

'Could you ring me, please, as soon as you get in?' said Mrs Lomond, on the machine. 'It's urgent.'

'Oh yeah,' grunted Myrna, and Anna was relieved to be free, at last, from her own mother's anxieties. Why didn't Myrna talk to her mother about these terrible, incessant, phone calls?

'Did you hear that? She said it was urgent.' That was Tom, looking concerned.

'No, she'll just have convinced herself that I have some fatal *illness* . . .'

'As *you're* always doing,' added Anna.

'She'll have been flicking through her Home Medical Directory.'

'Not that *our* Family Health Encyclopaedia isn't very well thumbed.'

That was Anna, who had decided to play the joker for once.

'I thought she sounded genuine,' shrugged Tom.

'Nah, you don't know my mum. *So*. What are we watching?' asked Myrna, switching through the channels with her remote control.

'This is the best. Stop it there, Myrn,' said Anna at a TV programme that was taking a light-hearted look at contraception.

'The vasectomy one?'

'Yeah. I hope you don't mind us just watching television like this, Tom?' she said, suddenly remembering his chemistry assistant. Although Anna and Tom were enjoying a bit of chemistry of their own, sitting close on the sofa, with only Myrna there to separate them.

'No, it's what I spend most of my time doing.'

'So last night was a break in the routine, was it?'

'What d'you mean?'

'Well, you spent last night with "friends"?'

'No, I didn't. I was in last night.'

'Yeah. "Typical Friday night in", you said. "With *friends*."'

'Oh yeah,' he laughed. 'I meant *Friends*. On the TV. The grown-up Brady Bunch. Those ones.'

'Oh?'

'Three lovely girls and three good-looking guys. A problem a week, solved in each episode. Like *The Brady Bunch*, brilliantly aspirational.'

'Well, what was Roo going on about then?' asked Anna, irritated. 'She said you were out. With her cousin. Your assistant.'

'My assistant?'

'The one who lays out your *experiments* for you.'

'Roo said I was going out with her cousin?'

'Yeah. She said you had a *thing* going.'

'Well, we don't.' He laughed. 'My assistant's about thirteen. And she's been trying for ages to get me together with you. Or rather her cousin, your mate Roo, has . . .'

'So Roo's been lying?'

'Looks like it.'

Anna was glad that someone found that funny.

'Oh, we have a multiple choice,' exclaimed Myrna, interrupting. The programme was graphically listing the arguments in favour of women using the coil as a method of contraception. A) Free from the side-effects of the pill. B) No need to mess around with diaphragms or condoms before having sex. C) A low risk of pregnancy.

'Well, *C*'s shit,' snorted Myrna, who had been born with a coil on her head.

Chapter Eleven

The programme about contraception finished, and Anna tried to create some distance between herself and Tom. But the sofa was too small. Its springs were old, and tipped her towards him.

She was furious with him, not only because Tom wasn't having a relationship with his chemistry assistant, but simply because he was there, that Saturday night, sitting on her sofa, drinking the beer that He had left behind in the cleaning-fluid cupboard. Myrna had brought in the beer. Anna hadn't even known it was there. 'Because you never do any cleaning,' said Myrna.

The three of them became steadily drunk – Anna, all the time, angry at Tom.

But, still, that night, she shagged him.

The next morning, only that was clear. Anna woke late, with a hangover and a vague memory of Saturday night. On Sunday morning, her duvet looked spent, as if, through the night, all life had been wrestled out of it. Anna's pillows had taken a beating. One of them – grey and stripped of its cover – was on the floor beside a squeezed can of bitter which dribbled foam.

She heard Tom, clattering about her flat.

There were wet footprints on the bathroom carpet. He had tramped his smell around their flat. Downstairs, Myrna's plants were scented with the death of his cigarettes. The leaves of her yucca had been scattered with his ash. Yet Myrna still seemed to like him, inviting him to stay for lunch. He stayed the night too, in Anna's bed. (Well, she hadn't had sex since Him.) That night, and the next, finally going home on Friday.

He returned on Saturday (it was now half-way through September), with a change of clothes and some books for Myrna. Before Tom, Myrna's bookshelf had been filled with biographies of Nazi war criminals, books about the Bulger killing, and such novels as *Less Than Zero* and *One Day in the Life of Ivan Denisovich*. After Tom, it was crammed packed with Evelyn Waugh, Jane Austen, and Nick Hornby.

Myrna started reading the Waugh.

Tom began to behave as if he lived there. He became a fixture, in fact, about the flat, fitting in with the fraying sofa. He cleaned their windows and fed Myrna's plants. He fixed the waste-disposal unit and removed any stale food from the fridge. Anna asked Myrna whether she minded that Tom appeared to have moved in. Myrna replied that it benefited them, having a man there to blame for the world's evils, such as war and capitalism.

Plus, she liked him. Finally, Anna's flatmate liked somebody – somebody who wasn't Anna or Gregory. Myrna liked Tom even though he talked when the television news was on. She liked him despite his habit of carrying teabags from his mug to the bin, dripping all the way, and his teasing. His calling Myrna's preoccupation with death 'laughable', and giving her the push to find out about teacher-training courses.

As for Anna, she felt safer, having a man about the house.

252

It was as if Anna had woken up, one morning, to find herself in a situation comedy from the seventies. She, Myrna, and Tom. The three of them sat side by side on the sofa, almost every evening, joking.

He filled their fridge with beer and full-fat milk.

Sex with Tom was the best she had had to date, and Anna's anger at him disappeared, an unexpected feeling of security taking its place. Tom smelled lived-in, like an old-worn, newly-washed, dressing-gown. She liked having him inside her duvet. And he was useful to have around the house.

Tom bought replacement toilet paper and changed the lightbulbs in the communal hallway.

She began to love the fact that, to Tom, the world was wonderful. It was one big science museum, in fact, with buttons everywhere just waiting to be pressed. His world was enlivened by fascinating innovations, all of the time. Pyramid-shaped teabags, for example. How could Anna not love an earth on which there were primary-coloured wires everywhere, just waiting to be earthed?

Anna liked having Tom there. With him, she did not feel the need to fill every silence. With him, she could cover her eczema with blemish concealer, and not feel embarrassed.

There had been times, indeed, in the last two weeks, that Anna had found herself falling for his lines. *'This feels so right, doesn't it?'*, And, on another occasion: *'This is perfect, don't you think?'* But Anna had caught herself, reminded of her close and closer relationship with Sean.

Of course, men like Sean took their time. *Opportunities do not fall into your lap*, as Grohe had written. *They are there all the time, waiting to be taken advantage of.* Men like Sean waited for the right context, and Anna felt certain that, when she moved into Sebastian's flat, there would be the right ambience for Sean to make a pass at her.

Sebastian was Sean's psychiatrist friend; he was moving to New York for six months, and needed someone to look after his cat for him while he was away. His cat and his flat, which was in Chelsea. Sean had put Anna forward for the 'job', which meant living rent-free. Could Anna come round on September 25th? Sebastian had a window then.

Never before Sonia's, had Anna seen such a place as Sebastian's flat. The ceilings rose high, and the carpets sank deep.

Never, had she met such men as Sebastian's friends. It was a Saturday, and his 'gang' were there too – all of them deep, and discussing the meaning of the word 'family' in contemporary Britain. Anna tried to join in, but was too busy staring at such an array of tall men, on such a good-looking sofa.

Ordinarily, these people would have existed only in an advertisement for pure wool, all of them wearing big, warm jumpers, and grinning. Anna wanted only to jump into their arms, en masse. They would catch her in their woollen arms, collectively.

'I love cats,' she said, determined to learn to live with the clawing, sneering creature half-buried in the carpet. 'I mean, I'd *really* like to look after your flat – I mean, your cat – for you.'

She wondered when she would have the chance to tell her flatmate that she was moving out. Myrna's father, it turned out, was seriously ill, and she was staying with her parents. Anna had already asked Tom to take her room. (That way, there would be a smooth transition.)

He had been surprised by Anna wanting to move out, but had said yes. For some reason, he liked 113B Finchley Road.

He liked the fact that the flat had a living room, unlike his own. Plus, the public transport was good.

'Only thing is,' drawled Sebastian, 'I'm going to need you to move in at the end of the week. On Friday actually.'

'Oh. OK,' said Anna, looking at Sean, who was on the sofa, flicking through a men's magazine, to find a mention of himself. She had been dreading Sean's leaving at the end of the week, unable to imagine her workplace without him. Yet, at least, this way, all her fantasies about sex with Sean could be transferred to Sebastian's flat.

Anna felt certain that, there, Sean would sit her down on the deep, creamy sofa. His hand would creep up her top, and undo her bra-strap, and finally he would tell her how much he wanted her. All she would have to do would be to breathe, *Yes*, . . .

'I move out that day,' said Sebastian, 'and I want everything perfect.'

'Oh, that's fine,' said Anna.

She wanted everything perfect too.

Anna had been working a *Problem Call* for three weeks, and finally she knew where to find the photocopier. It was kept in its own room – where she stood now, copying a letter from a married woman who was having an affair with her priest.

The room was cold, and made colder by the programme secretary coming in and leaving the door open behind her. Anna did not feel that she knew Lena well enough to ask her to close it. She smiled at her instead, wondering whether they were about to have a conversation. Anna hoped not. Women like Lena made Anna feel as if she had said something wrong before opening her mouth.

'How long are you going to *be*?' asked Lena, irritably. She looked at her thin-faced watch.

'Oh, sorry. I really won't be long,' said Anna, feeling unclean. She always felt unfeminine around women like Lena: women who wore lacy white blouses and ladies' watches. Pearl earrings.

'Well, could I interrupt? Only I need to copy this directive, for Pammy.' She held up a Radio Central dossier. '*Urgently.*'

'Oh, OK.' Anna moved her letter out of Lena's way.

She was too surprised to react in any other way. Bad manners always shocked Anna into silence. She could not understand how people had the courage to ask for something without saying 'please' or to accept something without saying 'thank you'. When Anna did react to other people's rude behaviour, it was usually too late. Her response, by then, seemed like an over-reaction. Or inappropriate.

'You could have said please,' she muttered, inappropriately, leaving the cold side room for the warmth of the main office next door.

Anna was no longer the new girl. Three weeks ago, everyone had looked at her as if she was a stranger, and as if she was about to pilfer something from the stationery cupboard. Now, she felt almost part of the office furniture. No one looked up when she came into the room – apart, of course, from Sean. He watched her now, as she sat down, and Anna shivered, hoping he saw how professional she could be, sitting there at her own desk, with her desk-tidy and her stack of paperclips.

She tried to look serious, reading through the pile of faxes. There were so many problems in the world that Anna sometimes felt as if she suffered from them all. Seasonal Affective Disorder and Sick Building Syndrome; Substance-

Dependence and Separation Anxiety; Active Negativism and Passive Aggression. She clipped a label to each letter in the pile, sorting out the problems into four shallow boxes.

1) Needs filing.
2) Needs consideration.
3) Needs response.
4) Needs urgent response.

'Any good ones, Annie?' asked Pammy, leaning over her desk, and breathing extra-strong mint breath.

'For anything in particular?'

'Good *question*. Well done you for asking,' said Pammy, crouching down on the thinly carpeted floor. 'Actually, it *is*, my sweetie. I need something for Pick of the Problems.'

'Pick of the . . . ?' repeated Anna, looking into Pammy's face.

'Oh Annie, you really are ol' bug ears, aren't you? Or is it Monday morning syndrome?' Pammy smiled. 'Did you not hear me trail it last week? Hmmm?'

'No, I . . .' Sean had suggested that Anna should treat her boss as she would any school bully – with firmness and pity. She should sound in control. But that was difficult, as Anna's voice was squeaking.

'If you were listening, my dear, you'd remember that I explained . . .'

'I must have been talking to a caller.'

'That I *explained*,' continued Pammy, patiently, 'for the benefit of new listeners – although I *should* have said "for new staff" – how, on the last Monday of every month, we talk about one problem that I pick personally. Do you remember me saying that? Hmmm?'

'No,' said Anna, sounding as if she was about to run from the room, crying.

She was aware that, at some point, she should stand up to Pammy. As Wilhelm Grohe had written: *If you are submissive, other people will be encouraged in their negativity towards you. Feel strong, and that strength will be picked up by others. Their behaviour towards you will change.* But Anna wanted to be liked by everyone – including Pammy. She hoped that, if she continued to be generally likeable, Pammy would, at some point, begin to like her.

'Well, *OK*. Let's think about it now. Is there anything that takes your fancy?'

'Actually, I was wondering about this one as an idea.' She handed her boss the letter she had been about to copy from a woman in love with her priest. Pammy skim-read the fax and handed it back. 'Well, that's not very fashionable, is it? Why should *Problem Call* be discussing something like *that*? Hmmm?'

I value my own opinions, Anna thought. Wilhelm Grohe had written that self-belief was crucial. Without it, confrontation was inevitable, and contentment impossible. *Happiness*, said Grohe, *is not influenced by external events. It is all in the mind.*

'Well, I thought it was an interesting dilemma.'

'*No*. No. That sort of problem would be fine for, say, the Jimmy Salad show. But on this programme, we need something more . . .'

'Yeah, I see,' interrupted Anna. 'It's too . . .'

She was about to say 'downmarket'.

'We need something more *commercial*. Find me the new craze. What's the new craze?' she said, urgently flicking through the faxes. 'What's a problem that's new and . . . ? You know, I've read a *lot* about anal sex.'

'Anal sex?'

Anna felt embarrassed using the words 'anal' and 'sex' together, in the same sentence. Like her mother, she referred to all things physical as 'down there'.

'Exciting, isn't it?' asked Pammy, her smile like pink paste. She had a baby-doll face, but it twisted cruel, as she said, '*I'm* excited, anyway. At *last* we're doing it.'

'What . . . er . . . anal s . . . ?'

With Boris? Anna thought, horrified. *Archy? Or Bruce?*

'Finally we're doing one of your ideas, Annie,' Pammy said, and Anna thought of the Friday morning planning meeting when she had suggested that they do a programme about Ending Friendships.

Ending Relationships had been discussed to death, said Anna, but no one ever talked about the pain of ending a friendship. *The scrubbing out of Justine Quealy's name in her address book* she had thought. *(Her only entry under Q.)*

'I think that's a problem peculiar to you,' Pammy had laughed, but Blonde had been able to see Anna's angle, and Lena, at her first ever ideas meeting, had nodded. Even Mike had agreed. 'It fits in with the Closure theme, I suppose,' he had said.

'And, at some point let's do Bullying in the Workplace,' added Sean, smiling supportively at Anna.

'Wow, yes,' said Pammy, missing the point. 'I'm sure that goes on all the time.'

'Mmm, I think it's good that we're doing Ending Friend-ships,' said Anna, trying to remember that she held her boss in contempt. Pammy was fat, after all, with a blonde mous-tache. Yet, whenever Anna felt any pity for her, imagining her alone in front of the evening television, her boss would talk about 'last night'. Pammy would describe the sex she had had after some showbusiness party, and Anna would

259

remember that she had always spent all her evenings in front of the TV – if not alone, then with Myrna.

Recently, she had been spending her evenings with Myrna and Tom.

Of course, now that she was moving into Sebastian's flat, all that would change. After Friday, she would spend her evenings with Sebastian's friends, drinking iced coffee, and discussing the family and its un-importance in twenty-first-century Britain. Sean and Sebastian's friends would be like family. Family, without the bickering, and the cold beaches, the warm orange squash, and the solitary games of Swingball in clipped, weedy gardens.

'Well, I'm pleased too,' said Pammy now. 'Pleased for you, and pleased to see a woman underneath me. Coming up.'

'Pammy, phone for you,' said Sean, trying not to laugh. He stood there, hands in pockets as Pammy patted him hello on the back. *Any excuse to touch him*, thought Anna enviously.

'Duncan's office,' said Sean. 'I think it's the latest audience figures.'

The colour drained from Pammy's face, and she went to pick up her phone, bending and bowing as she talked to the Radio Central's director of programmes. 'Of course . . . Naturally . . . *Now?*' Above her head there was Anna's signature to the notice, 'I WILL NOT SULK WITH PAMMY AGAIN.'

Anna hated the sight of that statement. She had been led to believe that it was a private emotional contract between her and Pammy. Pammy had used the words 'enablement' and 'trust' before pinning the contract to the office cork-board. When Anna had asked her to take it down, Pammy had refused, using the words 'honesty' and 'esprit de corps'.

'Mikey, we're wanted in Duncan's office. *Now*,' said Pammy, panicking as she put down the phone. 'Could you come too,

260

Lena, please, just in case?' In seconds, the office emptied of anyone important. Apart from Sean.

'Everything OK?' he asked, stopping at Anna's desk on his way out.

'Oh yeah, fine,' said Anna, miserably.

'You don't sound fine.'

'Oh, it's nothing.' But he had a way of anticipating Anna's every anxiety.

And he looked at her, waiting.

'Just Lena, being rude for no bloody reason, and Liz,' she admitted. *And the fact that it's your last week on the programme*, she thought, sneaking a look at Sean.

'Liz?'

'You remember? The loud one? She has this problem, and I've said I'd meet her for lunch today.'

'What's wrong with that?'

'Only that, after last night . . .' She shuddered, and laughed. 'She's the last person I want to see . . .'

'What happened last night?' asked Sean, and Anna sighed.

'Oh, she's so embarrassing.'

Weeks ago, Liz had insisted on booking a restaurant of Anna's choice to celebrate Anna's promotion to *Problem Call*. Liz had money. She would pay; and Anna had been grateful, suggesting that they go to IQ, along the King's Road, as Anna liked its quiet, unfussy atmosphere.

('Good choice,' said Sean, thoughtfully.)

Last night had been the first that IQ had had an available table. Well, as Sean knew, the restaurant had only five tables – so Anna had not known where to put Liz's generous gift. She had had to sit with the yard-high bouquet of flowers on her lap whilst Liz talked loudly about 'Marcus' – the man she had met in the Radio Central canteen.

('Not that man who came up to her in the . . . ?' asked Sean, amazed.

'The very same. Mr Moustache.')

'You'd like him, y'know. He's got a really nice car. And good friends, y'know.' Liz had made this clear to everyone in the restaurant.

'You know, you look *jus'* like my ex,' Liz had laughed, as the waiter took the flowers out to the kitchen area at Anna's request. 'Turn around, wouldya? Yeah, same bum 'n' everything.'

Relieved to see the back of her begonias, Anna had sought anxiously to keep Liz's voice down.

'Why d'you keep shushing me?' Liz had asked. 'Marcus is good-lookin', you know, but his fam'ly lives in Leeds. D'you know it, Anna? I went there when I first came to Britain, touring around. It's a dump, I reckon. So, unless he lives in the bloody *castle* . . .'

('Excuse my Australian accent. Anyway, you can imagine how embarrassed I was, at IQ of all places . . .'

'I suppose you were under the table at this point?' laughed Sean.)

Anna had looked away. She had stared, hard, at the swirl of modern paintings on the wall. Her eyes had hurt, as she tried to stop Liz describing her multi-orgasms with Marcus. How his moustache felt against her . . .

('Yes?'

'I'm not repeating *that*. Suffice to say, it was semi-pornographic.'

'It's all right. Not sure I *want* to hear it.')

Then, Liz had asked Anna about her row with her mother, wanting all the gory details. 'You can't keep it in. Not forever. This is your *mum* we're talking about, Anna.'

'Shhh.'

'I think your mum's great. Just think how your dad, having that affair, would affect her? Y'know. And she couldn't have a baby. You don't even know why, do you? It could be something awful.' Liz's eyes filled with tears, and she wiped her dripping eyeliner on to a napkin. 'Maybe it's 'cause your dad did something to her. Maybe he . . .'

('Serious case of transferral,' smiled Sean.)

Conversations stopped at other tables. Heads turned to stare as Liz blew her nose. They saw her, sitting there, large-breasted, and wiping her face with her sleeve. They saw Liz's eyes, covered in the dripping black grease of eye make-up. They all learned the full story about her cystitis.

('Now, you're exaggerating . . .'

'Well, maybe a little.')

'You'll regret not doing anything about your dad now, Anna,' Liz had said. 'It'll be too late soon, and you'll regret it. *I* did.'

('What did she mean by that?' asked Sean, thoughtfully.

'Oh, Liz has family problems. Real ones – not like *mine* . . .'

'I've told you, Anna,' smiled Sean indulgently. 'You can't put problems on the scales. It's only their *effect* that can be measured. And yours do seem to affect you badly.'

'I suppose. Anyway . . . Liz is running away from something.')

'You're lucky, Anna. Your mum loves you.'

'Well, nothing's that simple. She was undermining me on a weekly basis – it wasn't exactly the healthiest of relationships,' she said, almost convincing herself. 'Anyway, doesn't *your* mum love you?'

'You mean "didn't",' Liz replied.

'Well, what about your father?'

'Oh yeah. Dad *loved* me . . .'

'Well, that's . . .'

'But only when Mum was out of the house.'

Liz would not talk about her past in detail. Anna knew only that at eighteen, Liz had left Australia to tour Europe. Since then, her life had been full of gap years.

She had been in Britain for the last eleven years, finding a courier job and delivering parcels to London reception desks. At that time, Anna had been a Radio Central receptionist. Bored, she had begun to look forward to Liz coming into the foyer. Liz, who would rush in like a cartoon character drawn at speed.

('You make Liz sound like a cartoon character.')

There was more to Liz than her vulgarity – although she could spend hours talking about male genitalia. Nothing seemed important to Liz, except for the trivial. So, why did her mood switch in seconds from laughter to tears?

('I wouldn't worry about it, Anna,' said Sean. 'You can't always take on other people's problems, and Liz shouldn't burden you with hers.'

'Oh, she doesn't,' said Anna. 'Liz doesn't tell me anything.')

Anna knew only that something terrible had happened to Liz's mother. She was either missing, presumed dead, or dead. Anna suspected suicide.

And Liz would never go back to Australia. Well, not without Anna, anyway. 'We'll only go out for a *year*,' she had once said, as if, out of Anna's life, the odd year was neither here nor there. 'And I tell you, Anna, I'd love you to meet Alfred. He's our dog. And Daddy. Seriously. Daddy hardly ever loses his temper now.'

Last night, Anna had asked Liz a simple question.

'What happened to your mother?'

'Oh, that's history,' she had said, going to the toilet to re-apply her make-up. On her way back, she called over

264

the waiter. 'We're ready,' she had grinned.

'Liz Hailsham? Table three?'

'Ready for what?' Anna had asked, as the waiter dimmed the restaurant lights.

('I dread to think what happened next,' said Sean.

'Oh, it was awful,' agreed Anna, shaking her head.)

The waiter had come out, carrying a bright-pink cake, the size of an electric guitar. Anna had wondered, vaguely, why it was being carried towards her. The candles flickered. 'Oh *no*,' she had gasped.

('You're making it up now,' said Sean.

'No, honestly. I wish that . . .'

'Come *on*.'

'OK, I exaggerated the size of it. But she did order a pink cake.')

'Oh *yes*,' smiled Liz, as the cake was set down in front of Anna. 'Blow!' she yelled, as the lights went up, and Anna read her cake in horror: 'Good Luck At *Problem Call*.'

'It's for *you*. I'm so glad you like it. I've had such a hard time keeping that quiet; and the restaurant wouldn't even do it at first. They only did it in the end because it was a Sunday – and quiet. I don' know why you chose this place. I had to persuade the manager, and buy a cake in specially.'

'Well, thank you,' said Anna slowly. 'It's lovely.'

Sean laughed. 'Why didn't you say what you felt?'

'What – that I find her generous gestures embarrassing?'

'Well, perhaps not quite like that. Although you should learn to communicate your feelings more.'

'Well, maybe I will, but not today. Liz sounded terrible this morning. She almost begged me to meet her for lunch. Although I only saw her last night,' she added, irritably.

265

'I thought you'd been practising the word *No*,' he sneered. 'The gospel according to Wilhelm Grohe.'

According to Grohe, Anna had a problem with the word *No*. She had discussed this with Sean – how she found it impossible to separate herself from the thoughts and feelings of others. She over-empathised.

That was why, when anyone asked her to do anything for them, she would say *Yes* automatically. Anna needed to create distance between herself and others. Otherwise, she had a lifetime of hurt ahead of her.

'Well, I did say no at first. But she said she had this serious problem. And it's not like Liz to be serious about anything.'

'Oh, Anna, Anna. You wouldn't allow a man to treat you like this – some emotional battering-ram. So why a friend?'

She had an overwhelming urge to lean on Sean, there and then, asking him to repeat her name, over and over. Anna, Anna, Anna, *Anna*.

'I don't know why,' she said, wishing that the studio manager had not been sitting there, at his computer in the corner.

'You need to start recognising the difference between the authentic and the sham.'

'You think Liz is a sham?'

'I don't know. From the sound of things, nor do you. Despite the impression she likes to give, I wouldn't think she's the most open of people.'

'I never thought of it like that. But you're right.'

Anna was bending a paperclip out of shape. Straight.

'So, what sort of a friendship is that, *Annie*?' he grinned, stressing Pammy's pet-name.

'Well, *Seany-sweetie*, not much of one,' smiled Anna, lining

266

up her straight paperclips. (Oh, how would she cope on Friday, without Sean?) 'I suppose it's not such a laugh any more.'

'Put it this way, d'you miss your nightclub friend?'

'Justine? Well no, but . . .' But . . .

'Well, perhaps, then, it's time to let go. Be straight with this Liz. Don't be cruel. Be direct.'

'And say what?' Satisfyingly, Anna now had three straight paperclips.

'Tell her that the friendship is finished.'

'You mean, *finish* with her?' laughed Anna. 'As if she were a *man*?'

'Well, why not?'

'It's just not done.' She laughed.

'Well, *that's* a good answer. OK. Fine. So be a sheep.'

He looked away, and at the studio manager, who was fiddling with his mouse. As usual, Todd was having a conversation on the Internet. He came to life at his computer. Away from the online chatrooms, he didn't speak much. If Anna asked him a question, Todd would act surprised, as if Anna might be addressing a piece of furniture. Clearly, he did not expect to participate in office conversations.

'But then, why did you suggest today's programme idea?' asked Sean, curious again. 'It's hardly a million miles away from y . . .'

'Well, I wasn't thinking about Liz. I just thought it was a good idea. And I was hoping to find other ways of finishing a *friendship* . . .' She laughed.

'Why? And, anyway, it *is* a good idea. For *all* of us. I just hope you'll get a chance to listen to some of the calls. You never know. You might learn something.'

Anna so wanted to touch him. Last week, Sean had begun to touch her, hugging her after a particularly gruelling

267

programme. She could still smell the expensive wool of his brown jumper. During one rather alcohol-filled lunch, he had taken her hand.

'Why are you hiding your neck?' he had asked her.

'Oh, it's the eczema.'

'Well, you don't need to hide it from me. I'm not going to judge you because of some minor skin complaint.'

Anna felt that it was only a matter of time before he lunged at her, mid-conversation, tearing off her clothes and kissing her hard in small, hidden places. *Surely that was where all this was leading?* Anna asked Roo, on the phone.

Roo said *no*. From the sound of Sean, he would never lunge. He was using Anna for companionship. Their friendship would never be consummated, and the subject of sex would not even come up – unless, of course, it was useful to him. Sean was teasing her. Eventually, he would tire of her.

And if she carried on like this, Anna would lose Tom.

'*Of course,*' said Anna sarcastically. 'Because, doesn't Tom have his *pick* of women? Your cousin, for example? Although, if your intention, then, was to make me blind jealous, it didn't work.'

'So, is Tom moving with you, to your swanky new flat?' said Roo, changing the subject, sharpish.

'No *way*. No, actually he's going to move into my room in Finchley Road. Myrna's away, because her father's ill – which is why I haven't told her I'm moving out yet – and he's going to suggest it to her when she gets back. He hates his own flat; and, for some reason, he loves Swiss Cottage.'

'Why?'

'Well, he loves the local pub, and all those takeaway places. Loves all the things I hate, in fact.'

'You used to like them.'

'Well, he's welcome to them. Sebastian's flat is amazing. It even has a Jacuzzi bath, and all I have to do is look after his cat.'

'Remind me who this Sebastian is again?'

'Sean's friend. But don't bother remembering the name, because you won't meet him. He's going away for six months. As I said, that's why I'm getting his flat.'

'Sean's friend. Ah,' said Roo, knowingly.

She says everything knowingly, thought Anna, angrily.

'Anna, hi. Am I early?' asked Liz, interrupting Anna re-reading the review in *Mz* magazine. *By Anna Potter*.

'Oh no, that's fine. I thought we'd go out today. I'm sick of the canteen; and there's a café round the corner.' She didn't want Liz humiliating her again.

'I was gonna suggest the same,' said Liz, smiling weakly. 'I was scared of bumping into . . .'

'Oh yeah, what was his name?'

Anna went to take her jacket from the communal coatpeg.

'Yes,' said Liz, pulling her pink-plastic jacket shut. 'It's actually . . . Can we go somewhere private to talk?' She pulled out her ladybird earring, and rubbed her ear. Pus had dried like glue around the hole.

'That's not like you. Wanting privacy.'

Liz pulled over a chair and sat at Anna's desk.

'Something shit's happened, Anna. After dinner at the IQ place . . .'

'You two girls off to lunch?' asked Pammy, putting on her big, ill-fitting, camel-coloured coat. She did up the large buttons. 'Well, don't giggle too long. I want you back for the Monday programme, Annie. We're doing Annie's idea this afternoon,' she said excitedly to Liz, who nodded.

'Sean, you coming to lunch with us, seeing as Annie has her little friend with her? You know, I don't know what Annie will *do* for lunch when Sean goes at the end of this week,' she said, as Anna cringed. 'Those two are always popping off together in a huddle. She'll probably never eat *again*.

'*Todd?*' called out Pammy, remembering the studio manager. 'Coming to join the team?'

'Can we just stay here? I don't want to risk seeing anyone,' said Liz, looking around the empty office. The fax machine emptied letters into a box marked Mail.

'Well, OK. But what shall we do for food?'

'I'm not hungry,' said Liz, fiddling with a letter. She sat there, still in her plastic-pink mac, a daisy sewn tight on to the placket.

'God, things *must* be bad. So you don't even want to get a sandwich or something?'

Liz did not reply. She did not laugh, or cry, or scream an obscenity. Something terrible must have happened. Had something gone wrong with Liz's father? Or had they found her mother – at the bottom of some ditch?

'What is it, Liz? Is this about money?'

'No, it's Marcus,' said Liz, flinching at the sound of his name. 'I went round to his, after I saw you. Last night.'

Marcus? *Moustache?* Was *he* to blame for Anna's muttering stomach? She wanted lunch. She wanted lunch with Sean, on Sean's last week. Only four lunches to go. With Sean. Liz had met Marcus all of two weeks ago, in an office canteen. Yet she was upset about a man she had casually picked up.

A man she had met, as Anna's mother would say, two minutes ago. And Anna was *sorry*, but she was sick and tired

270

of listening to Liz. Liz, who still couldn't tell the difference between lust and love. She was thirty, for God's sake. She should grow up.

Was Liz listening?

Liz was bending back Anna's straight paperclips. Liz, who should now understand that Anna had changed. Anna wasn't bored any more, sitting on Radio Central's reception. She was tired – to be truthful – of being nice to everyone. She was sorry if she sounded angry.

Anna would try to say this calmly.

Liz was not a positive in her life. She had thought about her and had arrived at this conclusion. Anna felt devalued by the friendship. Their values were different. Anna had reached a 'choice point' in her life. She was going in a new direction. Lately, Anna had been thinking a good deal about her life goals. She had energy again.

She realised that. She was grateful to Liz for listening to her now. This wasn't an easy thing to say; but Anna felt that they should go their separate ways. They had had fun, but Anna wanted, from now on, to be serious. For too long, she had been drifting. That had to stop. And she was sorry if that meant not seeing Liz any more.

She no longer had time for Liz. She was moving into a new flat at the end of the week. She was thinking of going to auditions again and acting, at least in her spare time. Liz *embarrassed* her, if she was honest. She was loud. And Anna was sorry, really sorry, that she had lost her temper.

She would try to say this gently.

Why was Liz leaving now? Was she not going to say anything? Well, Anna was sorry about – was it Marcus? But of *course* he had finished with Liz. She should have seen that coming. He had such an old-fashioned, caddish moustache.

'He hasn't finished with me.'

'Well, oh. Really? So, wait. What happened then?' Liz could not leave without telling Anna everything.

'One of his mates attacked me,' she said, blankly. 'Last night.'

'Oh my God. Where was Marcus?'

'Watching.'

'Marcus watched you being . . . *Raped?*'

She was confused. If Liz had been raped, how could she be sitting there, undevastated? If Anna was attacked, she would not go out for lunch the next day. *How could Liz risk running into Marcus?* She would be boiling her clothes in the back garden. She would be wearing sackcloth, and looking very unlike herself.

'Depends what you mean by rape. There was no actual penetration.'

Yet there sat Liz, still blank, although looking just like Liz, and dressed as if, at any moment, she might be forced to go on to a discotheque. Had Anna been raped, she would not be able to speak. Her body would have been invaded, after all. She would be seriously contemplating suicide. Never again would she be able to use words such as 'penetration'.

'Well, if there was no . . .' No, she couldn't even say it now. 'What happened?'

'Use your bloody imagination,' said Liz emptily. 'But I don't know why I'm telling you this, anyway. I don't even know why I'm here.'

'Don't go yet. I'm sorry. Look – you should go to the police,' said Anna, shocked at a world in which Liz, who was prepared to have sex with anyone, anywhere, should be raped. It reminded Anna of her twenty-first birthday party when a guest had stolen the last of the party food. She had been just about to put it out on plates.

'See ya around,' said Liz, leaving the door to swing closed behind her.

The fax machine whirred. Anna looked down at her paperclips, twisted out of any shape. *Another bloody metaphor*, she thought, staring into space.

TRANSCRIPT:
Problem Call. Monday, 27 September.

PAMMY LOWENTAL (PL): Well, hello, and welcome
to Monday's *Problem Call*. It's the last Monday
of the month so, later on, we'll be doing our
Pick of the Problems - devoting five minutes
of the programme to one problem chosen from the
countless number we receive every month.

But first we're going to be talking about how
disposable some of our friends are. Should we
work at a rotten friendship, or know when to
end it?

I'm here to take all your calls. A kind voice on
the other end of a phone-line. Of course, some
people aren't open about their problems. Some
people can't phone up a radio station and talk
openly about their problems. Well, I can't help
those people.

But the rest of you - do call in. It's a valuable
exercise.

I don't think I need to introduce myself now,
but I have with me, still, Sean Harrison. It's
his last week in the studio with me, and I hear
you all cry out 'shame'. I know certain people

273

around the office are. But, anyway, welcome
sweetie. Still talking about Closure and how to
get it - Dr Sean Harrison.

Anna was sitting on the tube, as it was sucked into a
tunnel, reading the transcript for that day's programme.
She cringed, remembering the first ten minutes. No one
had called in. And it had been Anna's programme idea.

'We're not getting one bloody caller, are we?' Mike had
said, through Anna's headphones. 'It's ridiculous. I don't
remember this ever happening.'

Sean did. He had messaged Anna to say that he remem-
bered, years ago, co-presenting a programme about shyness.
*Don't worry. No one had had the courage to call in then, either.
(SHar.)* Anna had sat there, listening to Pammy 'filling in'.
Willing the phones to ring. If only one caller had shown
interest in her idea.

PL: While we wait for your calls on our topic
for today - Ending Friendships: How do you do
it? - let's look at some faxes. We've had so
many this week, praising the show. It's always
nice to get feedback because, you know, this
show isn't about ratings or awards. It's about
you, the people, and your lives. And, you know,
you may not think your lives are important, but
I do. Because I've been there. My life hasn't
been so great, you know. I've had three failed
marriages. I'm always finding strange lumps on
my body. I'm in fact just like you, my audience.

Anna could not bear to read the first few pages of the transcript. She had sat there in front of a bank of silent phones,

feeling suicidal, until, finally, Mike had come through the glass partition.

'You're going to have to be one of our callers,' he had said.

'What?'

'Come on, move to that other seat. Don't look like that. I did it myself when I operated – you don't have to worry. Pammy's got her back to you. Come on, she won't have a clue it's you. Anyway, I presume this is a problem you've thought about, or you wouldn't have suggested it.'

'It wasn't my problem, hones . . .'

'So just make up a problem, then type your details in. Go on, make up a name . . .'

Mike had hovered above Anna as she typed,

LINE ONE: ROSEMARY. 31. WANTS A FRIEND TO BUTT OUT OF HER LIFE.

'Good, good,' he said. 'Now, go to that microphone over there.'

'But who's going to answer the phones?'

'I hardly think that's a problem,' said Mike, looking at the row of blank lights. 'But I'll be here, if anyone does ring. It'll feel good to get back to my old job. I was great as an operator. Come on,' he had said, smiling, and sitting in Anna's seat. 'Before Pammy starts singing a medley.'

On the tube, she sat with the transcript in hand, flipping the pages until she reached Rosemary's call. When Anna had begun to speak live on-air, it was as if she became Rosemary. Or, at least, an actress again.

  PL: Hello, Rosemary. We have a caller. Are you
  there, Rosemary?

> ROSEMARY: Yes, Pammy, thank you for taking my
> call. I'm very nervous. I can barely breathe,
> I'm so nervous.

That had been Anna – her intonation perfect. She had seen Sean through the glass, watching and listening, and she was enjoying herself. It had felt to her as if Sean was her audience.

> PL: Oh, don't worry about that, sugar. Tell
> Pammy all about it. You have a friend who's
> upsetting you?

> ROSEMARY: I do, yes. I don't know what to do
> about it.

> PL: Well, let's pass you over, then, to Sean.

> SH: Tell me about this friend, er, Rosemary?

> ROSEMARY: Well, she's always trying to take
> over my life. In big ways and in little ways. She
> tries to control me, and I'm starting to feel
> suffocated.

> PL: So, you'd like her to butt out of your life,
> basically?

> ROSEMARY: Oh, you're so good, Pammy. You know,
> I listen to you all the time; you really know
> how to sum things up. Yes, that's how I feel
> - yes.

Mike had laughed, giving Anna a thumbs up. He had taken over from Anna, as the operator.

SH: So tell me why you feel suffocated by this woman.

ROSEMARY: Well, she's always taken control, I suppose. At college, I was even known as this woman's friend, rather than as An ... Rather than as Rosemary. I didn't really have an identity of my own; and, since then, she's found me jobs, and set me up with boyfriends. Sometimes I feel as if I'm one of her children.

PL: Uh huh, I see. So this woman mothers you with a capital S?

ROSEMARY: An S?

PL: I mean, does she Smother you, sweetie?

Whatever she was saying, Pammy sounded as if she was breaking extremely bad news ever so gently: ie, 'Your mother's trapped at the moment in a hot oven, but don't worry, I'll rescue you.'

ROSEMARY: Yes, all the time. Yes. And she's so successful, this friend. She's always achieving things. I turn my back for one minute, and there she is with another child. Or an award-winning column. I just can't compete.

PL: You know, I'm wondering if this is a self-esteem thing. Am I right, Sean? Dr Harrison? Do you think that Rosemary is suffering from low self-esteem?

Anna smiled as she remembered Sean grinning at her through the glass.

SH: I'd say, definitely. It sounds to me as if
'Rosemary's' opinion of herself is based almost
entirely on the way others see her. So, rather
than finding goals of her own, she's adopted her
friend's ambitions. It's no wonder she can't
compete. Really, she shouldn't be trying to.

PL: Is that right, Rosemary? You know, I wonder
about your name here. I always say that a name
breathes life into people, and I'm wondering
here whether Rosemary shouldn't be shortened
to, say, Rose, or Rosie?

ROSEMARY: Or Roo?

PL: Well, perfect. Now that is a good name ...

SH: I think we're in danger of being sidetracked.
Back to the problem, An ... I mean Rosemary.
I'm starting to wonder whether you're being
too accepting of other people's views of
you. Perhaps this is *your* problem - not your
friend's. As I've said before, if you behave
like a victim, people will victimise you.

PL: That is what I always say, am I right? You
have to think: Stop when you see that stop-sign.

Anna had had to stop herself laughing at that moment.

ROSEMARY: I see what you're saying, Dr, er,
Harrison. But at the same time, I don't know how
to stop this friend treating me like a victim.
How do I ...?

278

SH: In my opinion, it's easier to change than for others to accept that change in you. That's the hard part. If they've been friends with you for a while, they'll want to continue that relationship in the same way, keeping the same old balance of power.

PL: Oh, I see that. I have some friends who try to dictate my path through life. They won't see that I've changed. One of my ex-husbands said, 'But Pammy, you're like the British weather here - changing by the minute.' And I said to him, 'No, Henry. This change is for real. You'd better accept it.'

SH: Yes.

PL: Anyway, should Rosie end the friendship? Because we should remind ourselves that this is what the programme's all about ... although, of course, friendships aren't like broken kettles. You can't take them back to the shop.

SH: I think that Rosie should do or say something that might shift the balance of power in her favour. She should find something that she excels at and hold that up to the friend. Because, otherwise, she might as well accept that the friendship will continue along the same, destructive, path. She'll always feel like the victim.

ROSEMARY: But she's better than me at everything. She's got an amazing career; a great home, kids, money ...

279

SH: I'm sure you'll find something. No one's perfect, not even Pammy here.

Pammy had giggled.

PL: Oh dear, no, not me. I have a lot in common with Rosemary. I myself have always had a self-esteem problem. Part of me is very self-destructive. No, I'm always trying to develop my core identity; to listen to that tiny voice deep inside that says, 'Pammy, you're a good person.'

SH: We take a big chance, Rosemary, when we choose to go through life with broken relationships. They fester inside us and become emotional hurdles.

PL: Yes - you have to tackle the outside in order to reach the inside. But we need to move on now, Roo-sweetie, because the phones are beginning to go mad. I think your call must have inspired a lot of people to ring.

ROSEMARY: So I confront R ...?

SH: Give her the chance to see you in a different way. If she likes the new, successful, happy you, then the friendship stands a chance. Re-negotiate the relationship.

PL: You need to mend that broken friendship, Rosemary. Because relationships are like shoe leather - they do wear out. Anyway, I hope that's helped, because we have to go to

```
another caller now. So, dump the friend, dump
the problem, perhaps? And whilst we're on the
subject of relationships, I should recommend
my own book as material. It's still out in
paperback at the recommended retail price
of ...
```

The train shuffled along and Anna remembered Pammy's
grudging words in the post-programme meeting.

'That was a good programme, Anna. A fine idea. What a
great first caller too. What was her name? Rosemary?'

'I thought so, too,' Mike had said, slowly, staring at Anna,
as if he might have misjudged her. Then his face had broken
up into a huge, comradely, smile. He was clearly deciding to
give her the benefit of the doubt.

'We got a lot of good calls today,' went on Pammy.

'*Rosemary* was the best,' said Mike, firmly. 'I reckon that
the programme really took off after that. Great stuff, Anna.'

'Thank you,' she said, smiling back at him.

She had been scared that Mike might think the smile
patronising. But, after the meeting, he came over to her,
lazing his arm around her shoulders.

'I think I under-estimated you, Anna,' he said. 'Or should
I say, *Rosemary*. More ideas like that, and you'll have to start
doing some research for me. You see, that's the downside to
success, mate. You have to work even harder.'

Mate, thought Anna now, turning to the last page of her
transcript.

```
PL: And that's all for today's programme about
Ending Friendships. We've just time for a Pick
of the Problems, where I choose one fax from the
huge mailbag we receive every day. And today's
```

winning fax is from a Mr Julian Robinson, who
wrote to me about his mother.

Anna had chosen the letter for Pammy to read out on Pick
of the Problems.

SH: This is someone writing in about his mother,
Pammy?

PL: Yes, indeedy. Dear Pammy, wrote Julian
Robinson. I am in my late thirties, and, until
last week, I was still living with my mother.
She wouldn't see me as an adult, or let me live
my life. She treated me as if I was a child. (My
father died many years ago, and I had a lonely
and frustrating childhood.) I knew I had to move
out if I wanted to be my own person.

Anna had sympathy for Julian; she had had to move all the
way north, simply to escape her battling parents.

SH: Well, I think ...

PL: Hold on now, Sean. There's more. He goes on
to say, But my mother now refuses to speak to
me, or to have anything to do with me. She won't
accept the new Julian at all. What can I do?
With Mum, it seems to be all or nothing, and the
trouble is that I miss her. I always ran to her,
and now I don't like my life without Mum in it.
It feels empty.

Anna's mouth went dry. Because, she felt the same.

PL: Well, that's the fax as it came in, from

Julian. Although I've changed the name and
tidied up the grammar. Sean, what can Julian do?

SH: Yes, this is very common. Julian's mother
is, clearly, seeing him as just another part
of herself. And that relationship works fine
when he's a child, and fully dependent. The
problems come when that child - Julian - grows
up. Then the dynamic breaks down. The child has
a separate identity and the mother refuses to
adjust to that.

PL: But Julian misses his mother. Surely that's
the problem here?

Anna missed her mother. It had been over two weeks since
their argument. Two difficult weeks. She had almost phoned
home, three times.

Once, when Pammy was being catty about Anna's leth-
argy with regards to her 'career', Anna had wanted to hear
Barbara's soothing voice. Her mother, who would have said
that a woman would always be judged, not on account of
her so-called career, but on her ability to marry and bear
children neatly – without any fuss. Anna should forget about
her career and rely on her 'feminine intuition'.

The second time, Anna had been depressed. She had
picked the phone up, almost dialling Barbara's number,
wanting her mum to tell her, 'Pwuh. De*pression*? That's
just something they talk about on the television. It isn't
really there. I know – why don't you cheer yourself up?
Go to the pictures, and have an ice-cream afterwards. I'll
pay. I've still got my emergency money, remember? It's in
my sewing box.'

On Saturday – after seeing Sebastian's flat – Anna had

again wanted to call. She had wanted to hear Barbara say, 'Why do you want to go gallivanting off to be a Sloane Ranger when you've got such a lovely situation with Myrna? The grass is always greener in another part of London. That's just nature's way. In my day, you didn't go yo-yoing from one flat to the other. You stuck somewhere.'

Anna felt like crying now, in the middle carriage of a tube, needing her mother there, if only to say, 'Oh Anna, come home. Why sit there sobbing over some silly Pick of a Problem? Come home right now and we can watch a nice repeat on the television – a comedy, set in an office somewhere. I've got Angel Delight. Butterscotch flavour.'

The tears pricking, she turned the last page of her transcript.

```
SH: We all, throughout our lives, form very
strong attachments. And there is no stronger
attachment than that between the mother
and the child - no matter what age the child
is. Particularly when, as in this case, the
mother's husband isn't around. She is probably
using Julian as a substitute for a marital
partner, and that's when the situation becomes
truly problematic.

PL: So, what should Julian do?

SH: Well, really, there is no middle-ground.
He will have to make a choice. And that choice
is between hanging on to that exclusive
relationship with his mother - at the expense
of any other relationships - or choosing
separation. So that, over time, she will learn
to live without him.
```

Sean was right, of course, thought Anna. She would have
to learn to live without her mother.

PL: But, in this situation, won't the mother be
left without anyone? Surely they could try some
sort of family therapy?

SH: Of course that's an option. But, in my
opinion, the problem lies with the mother,
not the family. The mum should make a life for
herself that doesn't depend on Julian.

Anna wished that her mother would make a life for herself.

PL: And how does she do that?

SH: Well, presumably she has friendships of
her own to cultivate. Or hobbies. And there are
plenty of support groups for women on their own.
Julian should encourage her to seek help. But,
really, that's all he can do.

Certainly, Barbara had her garden to cultivate.

PL: That's all? Is that right?

SH: Yes, it's important for him to remember that
he is grown up and independent. That lonely and
frustrating childhood is over. He can now find
fulfilment as an adult. But that's down to him.

PL: Thank you, Sean. So, that's it for today's
show. We really are out of time now. Just

285

remember, Julian, it is never too late to have a
happy childhood. Is it, Sean?

SH: No.

The train pulled into Swiss Cottage station, and Anna stood
up. Reading Sean's words, in black and white, she felt vin-
dicated. Of course, she had been right to cut off contact with
her mum.

It all made perfect sense. She would not be responsible
for her mother. Or rather, Barbara. They shared a last name,
that was all, and, right now, Anna did not even feel like a
Potter. From now on, she would put her childhood behind
her, and find fulfilment as an adult.

Finally, she thought, *I can be free of Barbara.*

Chapter Twelve

Roo even shopped competitively, filling her basket with the most basic of brown ingredients: rice, pasta, bread, nuts, mushrooms, potatoes. Her basket looked as if it was about to be photographed for the food pages of a glossy magazine. Everything inside it was colour co-ordinated.

Anna wondered how her friend had managed to produce such a good-looking basket. She felt the same way when watching TV chefs. Anna knew that they used ingredients such as those in her own fridge, but her ingredients came together to make only a cheese and egg sandwich, whereas Delia's served up cheese soufflé and avgolemono. Shamefully, Anna filled her shopping trolley with ready-prepared meals and cans of sugary drinks.

It was Tuesday evening, and Roo had suggested that they do some late-night supermarket shopping.

Anna now thought that Roo might have suggested such a trip so that she could laugh at the labels on Anna's meals, 'especially designed for the single career woman, rushing from meeting to meeting'. Because, now that Roo was over her 'morning' sickness – or was at least bored with complaining – she was back to being critical. About everything.

Anna shopped unconsciously, filling her trolley with

comfort foods; Roo shopped with a firm conscience, refusing to buy anything emanating from corrupt military regimes. She laughed at Anna's breakfast cereal, saying, 'You're so packed full of preservatives, Anna, you'll last forever.'

'Very funny,' said Anna, beginning to be irritated by Roo's bald competitiveness, and indeed by her ludicrous name. She wanted her closest friend to be called Lucy or Maddy: something stylish, and age-appropriate, that she could call out at a party or in a supermarket.

Oscar sat strapped into the baby seat of Anna's trolley. Roo needed a basket, rather than a trolley, and as usual Anna had had to give up her freedom of manoeuvre for Roo's benefit. Whenever Anna reached for something, Oscar would make a grab in the opposite direction.

Anna was left feeling as if she was in a weak sitcom about a modern, single woman left holding a baby during a supermarket shopping trip.

'You OK with my baby?' asked Roo, claiming Oscar just as an elderly woman approached the pram to admire him. Anna had been about to pretend ownership. And, although she had reached her favourite savoury snacks aisle, Anna was forced to pause with her trolley whilst Roo talked to the elderly woman about Oscar's digestive system.

'Goodbye, plump-cheeks,' said the elderly woman, as their conversation ended.

Roo and Anna walked towards chocolate and sweets together, Roo fuming. Audibly. Because the woman had called her child plump.

Roo hated fat. Just as some women felt that they could judge another's star sign, she spent her life guessing other women's weight. Roo knew whenever anyone had put on a pound or two. She grouped people according to their weight, and did not, for example, like Myrna, who was a size sixteen.

Myrna insisted that her own fat was healthy and made up of wholewheat pasta and natural cereal bars. (Although Anna had seen the empty packets of mallows and Choco Friends squashed behind the fridge.) Anna's flatmate thought that fat-phobic Roo – who doubtless weighed herself before and after a bowel movement – had once been fat herself. Anna did admit that she had not seen a single photograph of Roo during adolescence.

Like most women, Anna herself had a healthy, fluctuating weight problem. Sometimes she would have liked to have been thinner. At other times, she thought about putting on a huge amount of weight, simply to have a real-life purpose in losing it.

But Roo was the only woman Anna knew who was prepared to weigh herself on those 1950s public sets of scales. Anna did not know how she found them; she had thought them extinct, like jukeboxes. Even in pregnancy – with the smallest and most dangerously underweight of bumps – Roo would describe herself as fat. She would starve herself and, incidentally, her foetuses.

Roo had transferred her fear of fat (and every other fear) on to her children. Anna sometimes wondered whether women had children simply because they needed somewhere safe to pour their anxieties. Roo was strangely proud, for example, of her daughter's 'slim hips', and discussed her five-year-old's 'figure' smugly and, more worryingly, enviously. Anna felt sorry for Daisy – having such pressure years before she would be faced with women's magazines.

Anna stopped at the pick'n'mix section. Roo stopped beside her, saying that one could not trust elderly people.

'You never know what's going on inside their heads,' she said.

Roo was often waylaid by pensioners when out shopping, she said. Ostensibly they stopped to admire Roo's children, but then they would ask her, in the freezing cold, 'Should your baby be wearing so many *clothes*?' Or there would be a searing heat, and they would go ga-ga over baby Oscar before coming in closer for the kill. 'He really should' – they would point out – 'be wearing shoes.' Any excuse, said Roo, to poke their heads inside her pram; to give their outdated views.

'It's only because I did the right thing and put him on to proper food early,' said Roo.

At times, she sounded to Anna like an audio-visual parenting manual. Despite Anna's clear lack of need for such instruction, Roo was always coaching her in modern childcare methods.

Anna weighed her party-bag of sweets, not concentrating as Roo discussed the benefits of an early switch to solids. She was thinking instead about Sean's hands, wrapped around a pint of lager. Those hands, gesticulating. His eyes undressing her, and then his . . .

'I mean, I gave him baby-rice at four months.' Roo's voice sliced through Anna's thoughts. 'Some so-called experts frown on that, but I *so* wanted to get him off formula.'

'Is he weaned off milk now, then?'

Anna had never been less interested in anything that Roo was saying, but that did not stop Roo from being suddenly, and unnecessarily, defensive. 'He's only eleven months *old*,' she sighed. 'God, why do people put so much pressure on . . . ? He still needs a pint of milk a *day*, Anna.'

'That's fine. I wasn't suggesting anything,' muttered Anna, trying to think of a new subject of which she knew more than Roo. But none came to mind.

'I mean, he is almost weaned,' said Roo, looking worried.

'Really, he only drinks socially now, and rarely, if ever, from the bottle.'

'You mean, like Warren?'

Roo paused, breathily.

'What do you mean by that?' she said sharply, and as if Anna's words were, at any time, pre-meditated.

'It was a joke,' said Anna, watching Roo squash to death a lazy fly that had landed on the now-sleeping Oscar's stomach. She wondered how a fly could enter so sanitised a place as this supermarket. Even the vegetables looked colourfully scrubbed.

Nor did she know how Oscar managed to switch from awake to asleep in seconds. Anna had watched his head rolling to the left. Sometimes she thought Roo drugged him – keeping him comatose long enough for her to fit in a career advancement.

'So, are you going to do any more reviews?' asked Roo. 'The arts editor loved that one. He said, "This woman *is* bitchy, isn't she?"'

'No, if I give up radio for anything it'll be to act. I really miss the stage,' said Anna, knowing that she sounded pretentious; but she was trying to assert herself about a subject that Roo might be unfamiliar with. If Sean only knew that she allowed herself to be undermined by someone like this, he would lose all respect for Anna. She was beginning to feel, if not equal to Sean, at least less like a teenager with a crush. (She still, however, had a crush.)

'Oh, right,' said Roo, disappointedly.

'I hope I helped you by writing that one, though. You looked *so* sick that night,' said Anna, determined to act on Sean's advice (to 'Rosemary') about her friendship with Roo. From this evening on, she would re-negotiate their relationship, and switch the balance of power. Anna would

291

stop taking the 'child' role in their friendship, and find a way to address Roo as an equal.

'Yeah,' said Roo, looking confused, then changing the subject. 'So, are you enjoying Tom being in your flat?'

'Yeah. I'm getting great sex, every night,' laughed Anna, realising that, although Roo had had a great reputation at poly as an expert in bed, she might well have lost that in marriage. Whereas single relationships focused on the bed, marriages were notorious for focusing on such details as ovens or cots.

'I can have both Tom and Sean. You see, there are *some* advantages to being single,' laughed Anna, lightly, wondering whether to ask Roo if she would mind their stopping off at a chemist on their way back. Anna would say, ever-so-airily, that she needed a packet of coloured condoms.

'What – irregular sex with strangers trying to find your G-spot?' laughed Roo, examining the back of a bar of dark organic chocolate. 'Yeah, *I* remember that. Men you barely know using you for masturbatory exercise.'

'Oh, it's not like that these days,' lied Anna. Lamely.

Anna dropped into her trolley two three-bar packets of a healthy alternative to chocolate. She had been about to talk some more about sex, but was reluctant to use words like 'orgasm' in a public place. She knew, too, that if she continued to talk about that subject as if she was some sort of an expert, Roo would expect her to be familiar with, at least, the correct vocabulary.

'You do know that they aren't even made with cocoa beans?' asked Roo, looking at Anna's chocolate. 'Just sugar substitute?'

'*Yes,*' Anna replied, trying to appear unmoved.

'And that the sugar-substitute coating is made out of insects?'

'No it's not. Now you're being ridiculous.'

'Well, that's what food manufacturers hope you'll believe. That it would be *ridiculous* for them to use insect legs in the process, but it's . . .'

'Oh for God's sake, shut *up*,' said Anna, thinking of Monday's *Problem Call* programme and 'Rosemary's' phone-call to Sean. Two days had passed and she hadn't seriously thought about taking Sean's advice – until now. 'If I want to eat insect legs I *will*.'

Although the thought made her feel ill.

Roo and Anna had always behaved with each other in this mock-nasty, long-suffering way. It was their very British way of being affectionate. They pretended to put up with each other as they would the weather, or war rationing. Secretly, however, they longed to declare their platonic love for one another, perhaps setting up a secret society, and exchanging blood.

Until now, that is. Now, the tone of their affectionate teasing had changed. Anna was in the ascendant. Roo was clearly confused; she was aware that something was different. Although, no doubt, Roo would put that down to her own hormones, or the stress of juggling a career with two children. She would accuse herself of neglecting Anna at a time when Roo knew that she was needed.

She always said this, after an argument, Roo taking the larger share of blame. 'I'm so sorry I didn't call you, Anna,' she would say, 'but I didn't have the time.'

She used their argument post-mortems to run through her achievements. 'I know I've taken on so much. But *you* try dealing with the demands of two kids, a husband, a cleaner, an ironing woman . . .' Roo would then list all of her servants – her list serving only to remind Anna that she had no need of a nanny, an editor, or a gardener.

Anna would be left with the crumbs of self-pity. 'Well, you could at least have *listened* to me . . .' she would crab, too easily, pathetically, forgiving. Too easily forgetting the reason for the argument, Anna enjoyed these dramatic scenes. She hammed them up, treating them as turning points in her plot through life. Plot, plot. If nothing else, she treated them as a chance to soliloquise.

'Are you all right with Oscar?' Roo asked politely, picking up a tin of spaghetti hoops. The label suggested they were cheap and low-grade, and Anna knew that Roo was buying them only to patronise Anna. *Look*, she was saying, *I can eat rubbish too. I can be rubbish like you.*

'Oh, I'm fine, thanks,' said Anna, looking with affection at Roo's sleeping baby. He looked cherubic now; as Anna imagined her own baby would look. Whenever she imagined her own babies, they were always soundly asleep.

'D'you mind if I start using your trolley now?' asked Roo; her basket was full.

'Of course not. We can separate out at the end.'

'Oh, I'll buy it today. Warren's just had a bonus.'

'Are you sure? God, thanks. I'll pay next time we go shopping.'

At poly, they had always taken it in turns to pay – although they had not been shopping together since then. They were only here this evening because Roo had wanted to go out. (Somewhere, anywhere.) At Arndale, they had bought the same type of food, most of it processed.

But things had, of course, changed since 1988. *And not just in a global sense*, thought Anna, wondering whether it was only a matter of time, now, before Roo and Anna were constantly pleasant to each other. Polite – as enemies would be.

'Excuse me,' said Anna, politely.

She studied the range of supermarket soups, feeling suddenly upset. Had it come to this? They had once been so close. Why couldn't Roo accept the new Anna Potter? It wasn't as if Anna was fat.

As Sean might say, she just had more self-respect.

'Excuse me,' said Roo, smiling, as she reached for a bottle of soy sauce.

'Oh, that's fine,' said Anna, able to see Roo's brain working. *What's come over her?* she was probably thinking. *She's changed; she used to be so kind and malleable. Yet I always thought Anna too lazy to change.* But Anna had not changed. She had merely found a way of being herself – as Wilhelm Grohe might say.

'So, will you miss Myrna when you move out?' asked Roo as they reached dairy products.

'I doubt it,' joked Anna, taking advantage of Roo's turned back to return her insect-leg chocolate to a refrigerated shelf. 'I'll have a Jacuzzi bath, for God's sake. Anyway, we've grown apart.'

'God, if Myrna grows any *more* . . .' She eyed Anna's four-pack of chocolate mousses with suspicion. 'So, if this Sean does make a pass at you, will you finish with Tom?'

'No. Why should I?'

'So you'll just string Tom along?'

'No, I like Tom.'

She liked him a great deal.

'But you don't fancy him as much as Sean?'

'*Objectively*, Sean is more god-like.'

'But what do *you* feel?'

In all honesty, Anna did not know. It certainly felt as if Tom had been living in her flat longer than a fortnight. Having him there confused her. Sometimes, he felt like part of her life. (Sometimes, that irritated her.) During the working day, she thought only of Sean, and was obsessed with the idea of having sex with him. But she liked coming home to Tom, and having sex with him.

Anna pretended not to have heard Roo's question, to avoid having to answer it. She knew only that Roo disapproved of Sean because she wasn't able to control Anna's relationship with him. It upset her that Anna could arrange her own affairs without Roo there to create a little 'harmless' competition by, for example, inventing a lusty, busty chemistry assistant.

'Is the little bunny still asleep?' asked the elderly lady, stopping for a conversation again. Anna didn't reply. *What do you think?* she wondered. *That he's dead?*

'He isn't *your* baby, is he? But don't worry. It'll be your turn soon, I'm sure,' said the old lady. Anna felt like explaining to her the way the world worked. That there was no queue for achievements. If the world was like that, *Anna* would have two children, a pregnancy, an upwardly mobile career, a long back garden, and Warren.

She had always had far more patience than Roo in queues.

The woman picked up a twenty-four-hour active daycare cream, sucking in her cheeks as she read the promises on the packaging. Anna heard the elderly woman's false teeth clank and, not for the first time, she wished she lived in a time when women felt that they could let their looks go – at least at that age.

She wanted to grow carelessly old, letting herself spread with thick rivers of veins, hair thick and straggly on her legs. She wanted, at some point, to be able to droop, without schoolboys laughing at her on the street.

Roo was standing beside them now, many weeks pregnant and yet buying Vitamin E skincream to make her more attractive to men. Anna thought how cruel the world was. Even though Roo had fulfilled her biological destiny, she was still forced to keep up an appearance of feminine youthfulness.

Anna read the back of a bottle of a hair serum. Problem Hair Help. She dropped it into her trolley because, frankly, she needed all the help she could get. She still needed to believe in the guarantees given by cosmetics companies. That if she continued to cleanse, tone and moisturise, happiness (or at least a husband) could be hers.

She took the serum, as well as a restructuring skin spray, hoping that passers-by would know that she was only succumbing to the pressure of a society which demanded beauty and youth.

If she were in a Rwandan refugee camp, Anna would have other worries. Although, naturally, she would not have liked to have been a Rwandan refugee, Anna did sometimes wish that she had bigger problems. That way, she would not have time to worry about fine lines and wrinkles.

Anna placed four bottles of red wine horizontally in her trolley, as Oscar started stirring. This always panicked her.

No matter how many times she looked after Oscar and Daisy, she always felt useless around babies, albeit only when they were awake. Oscar opened his mouth to cry. Fortunately, Roo heard him, and dumped an armload of stuff into Anna's trolley before scooping him out.

'OK, Mummy's here.'

Roo loved the idea that someone cried whenever she left the room. Anna, too, was envious of that. She wanted someone – anyone – to love her that much. She wanted the sort of unconditional love that Daisy and Oscar had for Roo. Well, conditional on the understanding that Roo would give them her undivided attention, a range of Fisher Price toys, and food.

Oscar calmed down as Roo stuck a bottle of milk in his mouth. He sucked, as ably as a cartoon character, calm in the knowledge that his mother was doing her job properly, keeping him alive for his next meal.

'I thought you said he was off milk?'

'Anna, please don't tell me how to bring up my child,' snapped Roo.

'Well, that's a bit much, isn't it? Coming from someone who's *constantly* telling me how to manage my relationships.'

She was prepared to be more assertive.

'For *you*.'

'Ah, *I* benefit. And there was I thinking that it just livened up your boring, compartmentalised life. *God*.'

'Believe me, Anna, I don't want your sad, lonely, thin little life.'

'I'd rather sad and lonely than *masculine* and *aggressive*. You live in such a male, Thatcherite way, wanting everything . . .'

The word masculine in particular would upset her.

'I hardly think having children is *masculine*.'

'Well, you're hardly the most womanly of mothers. You leave them with a nanny, for God's sake. What does that Swedish woman double as – your wife?'

Oh dear, had she gone too far?

Clearly so. Roo took Oscar out of the trolley-seat in a manner that suggested she was about to examine him for injuries. Oscar grabbed at the champagne shelf, as if he knew that, in this mood, Roo would give him anything. 'Lovely boy. Are we going to see your sister soon? At home, with Daddy?'

Roo turned to Anna as if ready, once more, to start arguing.

'And what did you mean, earlier, when you said that Warren drank?'

'I said *what*?'

'You *implied* that he was drinking.'

'Well, I don't remember that.'

Neither of them could leave. Roo had too much shopping in Anna's trolley, and both of them were aware of that. Roo eyed her bottles of Scotch as if wondering whether to grab just them and make a quick getaway. But Anna had not finished; she was still smarting at the suggestion that she had a 'sad' and 'thin' life.

They stood beside a basket of beer cans, Anna saying, 'So I have a sad, thin life, do I? Just because I haven't had a big, glitzy, *over the top* . . . ostentatious bloody wedding?'

'Actually, Anna, marriage isn't just a new dress and a party.'

Well, what then? thought Anna, walking towards a checkout.

'Tell that to Warren.'

'What do you mean by that?' said Roo, coming up behind her. She was having trouble holding Oscar; he was squirming in all directions.

'Oh, nothing.'

'No, what the *fuck* did you mean by that?'

The man in front turned round to stare, and even Oscar shut up. He sat still in Roo's arms – the perfect, picture-book baby – as Anna smiled, trying to appear secretive as she built a short tower of tins on the conveyor belt.

'Stop *shouting*,' Anna said quietly, as the conveyor belt moved forwards. 'You're always screaming at someone. Usually poor Warren. You've obviously got too much testosterone.'

'Have you *looked* at your flat tits lately?'

299

'Oh dear, an oxymoron,' said Anna, point-scoring. 'As you – the *review* editor – should know. Although you ruined the flow of *my* piece.'

'Anna, dear, it would have been libellous had I not . . .'

'*Readable* . . .'

'Nasty. Even the fucking arts editor said you sounded cruel, and he's notorious for being the nicest man in journalism.'

They took time out to review their respective positions.

Roo took a Next Customer Please notice and shoved it between Anna's shopping and her own, and they spent the next few seconds dividing up their goods in as aggressive a manner as any soon-to-be divorced couple.

'That's mine, thank you,' said Roo, snatching her Vitamin E cream from Anna's section.

'That's fine. I don't actually need it.'

'Don't *kid* yourself.'

Roo started grabbing items from Anna's section.

'I don't *have* stretch marks. And that's mine,' said Anna, taking back the tin of spaghetti hoops.

'Actually it's not, dear. It's *mine*.'

'Ooh dear. *Stuffed* with stabilisers. Might not live forever.'

That was Roo's cue to look, with disgust, at all of Anna's purchases.

'Cod in Batter and Buttered Cheese Sauce,' she began, her consonants like gunshots.

'Bouquet Garnis for Vegetables,' said Anna, sneering at one of Roo's purchases.

'*Shake* a Cake?' said Roo.

'Root Ginger?' (Because Roo's purchases didn't have as much comic value as Anna's had.)

'Hang on. You've forgotten to buy Sugar in Salt Sauce?'

said Roo, inventing a product. 'It's new out. You'd love it.'

'Well, that's just infantilism isn't it?' said Anna, trying not to laugh.

Anna knew what Wilhelm Grohe would say were he standing there now. Even Sean had argued that language was crucial to communication. Words such as infantilism were useful. *Otherwise people spend their lives over-extending (using one word where ten would do perfectly). Their message is never understood. Life is complicated as a result.*

The man in front finally took out his Switch card to pay. Anna was now at the head of the queue. Oscar started screaming as the elderly lady crept up behind them again.

'I don't suppose I could push in, could I? Only I have nine items, and I'm *loath* to give up one for that silly Eight Items or Less queue.'

The checkout girl looked at Anna expectantly as the man in front walked away. Anna decided to be assertive.

'Well, I *do* mind actually. I've been waiting too.' She wanted to add, *And I don't see why I should be penalised because of your ninth item.* But she felt that that would be going too far.

'*Anna*. You've gone too far now.'

That was Roo. Oscar stopped screaming, sharply, and the checkout girl looked at Anna in disgust. She began to move her items quickly past her scanner. Suddenly, Anna felt that there was such a thing as society. People had finally rallied together, as a community – but only to victimise Anna.

It was too late now to change her mind and allow the old woman through. Naturally, she would laugh about this later, with Sean. But right now, Anna felt embarrassed. Even Oscar looked at her, hard, as if she should be ashamed of herself.

'I'm sorry. You can go in front of me,' said Roo to the elderly woman, taking her products off the conveyor belt.

'No. I couldn't do that.'

Yet you could with me, thought Anna, sulkily. She wished now that she had allowed the old woman through, and felt like a child.

'Please. It's fine,' smiled Roo, as the elderly woman opened a bag of chocolate buttons. *Before paying for them*, thought Anna.

'Not with the little fella. He's so lovely. So *well*-behaved. Do you mind if I give him some chocolate buttons? I know some mothers do.'

At that, Oscar cooed, and Roo, who was just such a mother, nodded, horrified, as Oscar grabbed at the packet.

'But I doubt that you starve him of the good things in life. Oh, he's so *happy*. You must be such a good mother.'

At that, Roo cooed.

'Oh, I don't know . . .' she said, coming over all motherly. 'You can be trouble sometimes, can't you?'

'Such a *tall* boy.'

'Yes, he is tall,' said Roo, smiling, as if she had grown him herself in a plant pot. 'Some people think he's fat, but . . .'

'No,' said the woman, horrified. '*Tall*.'

'I agree with you about *chocolate*, you know. Some women are ridiculous. But I give my two sweets all the time.'

'Only to shut them up,' muttered Anna, as the checkout girl queried the price of one of her items. She pressed a buzzer, which sounded around the store, and held up the unlabelled product. Problem Hair Help.

'Well, babies cry, don't they? As only a *mother* knows.' The woman looked pointedly at Anna. 'Can I have a hold?'

She held out her arms, and there followed a great handing-over ceremony, as Roo forgot that she did not trust elderly people, entrusting her only son to the woman's tiny, fragile arms. She held Oscar as one would a bag of flour. Even Roo looked worried as his head bobbed back and forth. She reclaimed him, anxiously.

'Oh, thank you for that,' said the old woman. 'That's made my day, that has.'

'That's fine.'

'Who does he look like? You or your husband?'

Ordinarily, Roo would have been irritated by the woman's assumption that she and Oscar's father were married; and by the fact that the woman had not automatically seen Roo's genes gathered together, for harvest, in her offspring's face.

She might, ordinarily, have said something.

But Roo and Anna were in the middle of their worst row ever, and she was reminded of that as Anna said, quietly and drily, 'Like a lot of *career* women's kids, he's beginning to look like his nanny.'

'At least I have a bloody career,' hissed Roo.

'Problem Hair *Help*,' screamed the checkout girl, as a man in overalls came over to help. And louder: 'This woman's *Problem Hair Help* hasn' go' a price . . .'

'I'll go an' look for ya,' said the man looking at Anna. He appeared to be amused.

Roo was saying that she could see both her *and* her husband morphed across her baby's face. She said this as if it went against everything nature had intended, and the old woman smiled, as they all stood there, waiting for the man to return with a price for Anna's hair product. Waiting.

'Oh, I have to get to the late-night chemist before it shuts,' sighed the old lady. 'For this month's tablets.'

Anna was horrified to hear this. She might incidentally be responsible for killing an old woman. Yet she could do nothing. Her products had begun to move again, passing quickly along the conveyor belt. She was packing up as quickly as she could, trying to slither open plastic carrier bags.

Predictably, Roo swung into action. 'Well, let's look at your basket,' she said. 'Is there anything in there you really don't need?'

'Why?' asked the old woman.

'Well, the Eight Items or *Fewer* aisle is empty,' she said.

Typical Roo, thought Anna. *Can't resist correcting an old woman's grammar.*

'And my "friend" seems to be taking a while.'

'Oh, I see,' said the elderly lady, and Anna couldn't bear to listen as she listed the staples in her basket. 'Bread . . . milk . . . potatoes . . . I could have got rid of the chocolate buttons. But they're started now, I suppose.'

She looked at them, sadly, as Roo shook another bottle of formula for a whimpering Oscar.

'Well, *I'll* buy them for you. My son's eaten half of them.'

'Oh, I'd give him the world.' She took out a tin of dogfood. 'I suppose I could put this back.'

'I'm nearly finished,' snapped Anna, before the woman had a chance to accuse her of killing her dog. She handed the checkout girl a fifty-pound note. The girl held the note up to the light for what seemed to Anna – who was all packed up – an extraordinarily long time.

'It's my one luxury,' said the old woman, still clutching her dogfood.

'Sorry, no change,' said the checkout girl, handing Anna back some notes and twenty twopenny pieces.

The old woman took out one of her credit cards to pay for all nine of her items, and Anna looked at the wire-cage of a crèche, in which children of all colours jumped inside a box of monster-sized Smarties.

'I suppose you still need a lift,' said Anna to Roo.

'Well, yes, I do actually. I can't exactly take Oscar on the . . . You have no idea what it's *like* to be a mother,' said Roo.

'Well, there were mothers before cars,' said Anna, spitefully. 'Before the invention of the wheel, in fact.'

Oscar sat strapped into the rear car-seat, sleeping, as the point-scoring continued between his mother and her closest friend.

'What the fuck happened in there?' asked Roo, as Anna adjusted her wing-mirror so that she would be able, at all times, to see her reflection. 'Or are we not going to talk about it?'

Roo was back to playing teacher to Anna the schoolgirl.

'Oh, only that I'm not a walkover any more. That I have some sort of emotional *reality* now . . .'

'Some sort of *what*? God, Tom was right.'

'Right about what? What are you going to say? That Tom isn't interested in me? Well, *that'll* work, Roo. It worked the last time you lied about his feelings for me. I don't think.'

'I don't *care* whether you and Tom end up together. Just get me home, for God's sake. And drive properly.'

'Oh, don't tell me. You're the better driver as well.'

'Well, it did take you eight times to pass your test.'

Point to Roo.

It *had* taken Anna eight times to pass her test. But, for that, she blamed one of the examiners – a Mr M. Hards, who had hated her. Anna thought of him every time she did the perfect U-turn.

'Do you want to list all of my other failures? How I

haven't got a husband? I haven't got kids? I haven't got a garden?'

'You loathe everything to do with gardens.'

'Since when?'

'You always say they remind you of your mother's life.'

Roo said this with a smile that patronised both Anna and her mother. It was obvious, however, that she was trying to end their row. Her look said that she wanted everything to return to normal. Roo would take the lion's share of the blame, and they would slip back into their respective roles: Roo treating Anna as if she was another one of her underlings. Anna treating Roo with envy and respect.

But it wouldn't do. Anna wasn't comfortable with that role any more. She didn't even want a best friend any more. As Sean had said, that was a childish way of looking at relationships between women.

'One can't grade a friendship,' he had said.

'Oh, Roo grades everything,' Anna had replied.

Certainly, it didn't surprise her that Roo had the top grade, even as a friend. Sometimes Anna felt closer to Myrna – but Roo wasn't having that. Whenever Anna talked about her flatmate, Roo would say, 'You know, I think of you as my best friend.' She would say it possessively, and as if she could not stomach the thought of being second-best. At anything.

'It was funny, wasn't it, when that woman held up her dogfood?' said Roo, looking sideways at Anna.

'Yeah.' Unsmiling, because she was feeling brave. 'OK, Roo. I'm going to ask you a question,' she said. 'It's something that I've wanted to do for a while actually.'

In Chapter Ten, Wilhelm Grohe had written, *Ask a friend to give you five words that they feel fit your personality.*

'Why d'you want me to do that?' asked Roo, confused.

'I'd like you to give me five words. That's all. Why d'you always . . . ?'

'OK, OK. Before today: shy, erm, kind, warm, easy-going, happy.'

'*Happy?*' repeated Anna.

'Well, what would you rather I said? Deeply miserable?'

'OK, fine,' said Anna.

Decide five words yourself, Grohe had advised; and Anna had settled for: bright, intuitive, ambitious, extroverted, sexy. *Now, work out why there is a gap between your idea of yourself and that friend's idea of you. And work out whether or not that gap can be narrowed.*

'So you don't think I'm bright?'

'Hmm. Well, not in an academic way.'

'Or, say, outgoing?'

'Yes, if you've known someone ten years. Otherwise, I'd say the *reverse* actually. I'm always having to . . .'

'Well, would you say I'm ambitious?'

Roo snorted at this.

If your friend still doesn't see you as you clearly see yourself, perhaps it's time for a rethink. First of all, ask yourself whether your friend's description of you is accurate.

If it is not, ask yourself whether that friend is judging you according to his own rules. Is he merely making a value judgment? To verify this, do my spot check. Ask him the questions on the opposite page. (Remember always to have your own answers in mind.)

'OK, if I was a colour what colour would I be?' (Blue: calm, cool, the colour of a summer sky.)

'If you were a what?'

'A colour.'

'God, I don't know. What are you – a Labour Party focus group? *Green,* I suppose.'

Green? Dull? Earthy? Wishy-washy?

'If I was a country, what country would I be?' (Spain: lively, pretty, cultured.)

'Bloody hell . . .'

'Just answer the question.'

'Canada,' Roo said firmly.

Canada? Cosy? Unimportant? Dull?

'Right. Last one. If I was a season, what season would I be?' (Summer: energetic, sunny, liberated.)

'Well, I don't know where this is leading but . . . spring,' she decided.

Spring? thought Anna. Middle-of-the-road? Irritating? Indistinct?

That did it. Anna had always thought of herself as a summer person. Sipping cocktails in the Spanish sun. She was the sort who was happy in big, floppy sun-hats.

If the spot check failed as well, maybe it is not you or the friend that is at fault, but the friendship. Maybe it is time to question that friendship altogether. Find another friend – one who can meet your standards. Remember: you deserve better.

'I deserve better,' muttered Anna, swerving out on to a roundabout.

'Fuck. Watch what you're doing!'

'Will you stop bloody criticising me.'

'I don't criticise you, Anna,' sighed Roo. 'I don't even know what you're going *on* about with your stupid fucking questions. You'll bring out your *tarot* cards next.'

'Oh, stop making value judgments.'

'Bloody *hell*. I see why you argued with your mum. I'm beginning to side with *her* . . .'

'This isn't *about* sides. Why does everything, with you, have to be about taking a position? You're always on some sort of a ladder. Life isn't a competition.'

'Oh, don't tell me – or a *rehearsal*? Is that what your self-help guru – Sean – said?'

'I tried to tell you about him too. And Tom's hardly going to be the impartial observer, is he?'

'Oh, I forgot. Tom's fucking crazy about you, although he's known you all of three weeks. Although he'd fancy someone else if *I* persuaded him to,' she snorted.

Anna was speechless.

'So, hang on a minute. What are you implying?' She was fuming. 'Tom fancies *you*? Is that what you're trying to say? Is that what you *think*?'

'Well, we speak on the phone a lot now. I was the one who told him to phone you in the first place.'

'You speak to him because you're calling *me*. What, you really think he . . . ?'

'Well, if I was *single* . . .'

'I don't *believe* this.'

'How d'you think I know him? He's my cousin's boss, for God's sake. I spent two whole parties fucking flirting with him. *I* did all the foreplay. *You* only got to fuck him because he fancied *me* . . .'

'And what am I supposed to say? That I'm *grateful*? You are such a sodding bitch.'

She parked, badly, outside Roo's house.

'And it was the same with whatshisname, before Tom. Let's just say He spent His entire time with you trying to get into *my* knickers.' Several points to Roo.

'Well, you're *welcome* to Him,' said Anna. 'And fucking Tom.'

'I don't want them. Either of them.'

Roo knelt on the front seat to unstrap a floppy, still sleeping, Oscar. She picked up her supermarket carrier bag. A bottle of whisky rolled out, unscathed.

'That for Warren, is it?'

'And what's that supposed to mean?' Roo sighed, as she laid the bottle back in her bag.

'Well, I don't blame him. *I'd* drink myself to oblivion every night if I had to live with you.' (Point to Anna.)

'Warren doesn't drink. Much.' She picked up her bag. 'If at all.'

'Funny how, a few months ago, he was out of his head.'

'We all get out of . . .'

'At *six* o'clock. Alone.'

'Well, thanks for telling me,' said Roo politely, picking up her baby. 'Shall we go in and see Daddy now, darling?' She held a bag in one hand and a baby in the other.

'Or will *Daddy* be in bed with another woman?'

'*What?*' Roo slammed the car door shut. 'Fuck *off*,' she screamed, through the glass.

Anna opened the door. 'He made a pass at me that time,' she called out, shutting the door quickly. Roo came back; and was she crying? Roo, who didn't even cry at weepy films? (She hadn't even cried at *Love Story*.) She opened the car door, before Anna had time to switch on the ignition.

'When?' She bit her lip, hard.

'A few months ago.' (Double point to Anna.)

'Are you lying?'

'Why should I? I don't want Warren. He's hardly a prize, Roo. Have you looked at him lately? He really is *fat*.'

(Bullseye.)

Roo stepped back, with Oscar waking up in her arms. Anna strapped herself in, seeing Daisy run out of the house carrying a Barbie. Warren came out after her. 'Well, at last. Helle left hours ago. Where in Christ have you been?'

Anna started her car. *I'll miss Oscar and Daisy*, she was thinking. She could not stop the tears from coming. Although

310

she refused to be manipulated, emotionally. *I'll miss certain things*, she thought. But she would not look back. She would go and find Tom instead, in the pub.

She cried too easily.

Chapter Thirteen

<u>When A Relationship Ends</u>
When a relationship ends, a variety of different emotional responses may be exhibited – anger, fear, and a feeling of rejection being the most common. Much has been written about the grief felt when a relationship terminates. There is no funeral, after all, to signify the death of a partnership; no real outlet for that grief.

Mike read Anna's opening paragraph and hmmed a bit.

'It's good. Hmm. But Pammy doesn't like her briefs to be too depressing. You see, people listen to our programme with a kind of schadenfreude. They only want to hear other people's problems to make their own lives seem gorgeous by comparison. Understand? That's why they switch on – and we have to keep them switched on.'

'Right,' she said.

Anna wanted to impress Mike. Since her fake 'Rosemary' call, his attitude towards her had changed. He no longer seemed to think that she was a racist bigot. Even when Anna had said of a caller, 'She has these black moods,' Mike had simply smiled, saying, 'Well, we all get *them*, don't we?'

'So, d'you think you can be a bit more upbeat?' asked Mike, smiling.

'Right. OK.'

'Start with the premise that people don't always grieve for a dead relationship.'

But people don't always grieve for a dead relationship. As Denvil George wrote in his book, Unburdening *(pub: Revson. rrp £15.99), one can often feel 'liberated'. If you are the one ending the relationship, your reaction to that person's 'disappearance' (because that is what it can feel like) is often relief. 'It can be liberating to end a relationship,' wrote George. 'You now have the freedom to find the right man for you.' And as Stacy Wairing said in* Lies, Damned Lies *(pub: Lissom. rrp £6.99), 'there is no place lonelier than a bad relationship.'*

You may also feel powerful, having been the author of some-one else's misery. It may empower you in other areas of your life: you will focus more on your career, for example. Wairing writes, 'Suddenly, you will have time for yourself: you may decide to pursue a new hobby, for example, taking an aerobics dance class.'

Your friendships will, necessarily, take on new meaning when any sexual relationship ends. Often, during relationships, friendships disappear. 'So, rekindle them,' says Gail Denning in Dividing Men from Women *(pub: Lissom. rrp £9.99). Denning suggests that we forget the benefits that friendship brings. 'Without the sexual element there, to fog understanding, you can connect completely.' Friendships are uncomplicated and rewarding. 'They can endure change far more easily than a relationship.'*

Anna stopped writing to ring Roo.

Her answering machine was on at home. Anna considered leaving a message, by way of a public apology. Given the nature of their row, last night, Anna thought that she might need to apologise to the whole Hastings family. But Roo's voice sounded clipped; it was as if she had re-recorded her message to keep Anna away. So Anna put down the phone.

When a relationship ends, one often feels better about oneself. Either you can surprise yourself with the realisation that some partners are easily disposed of. 'This can lead to guilt feelings,' writes Wairing. 'But one should never feel guilty about feeling happy.'

Or, as often happens, 'you can feel more confident on the outside of that relationship, looking in' (Wilhelm Grohe: One Month to Happiness. *pub: Magnus). Sometimes, a partner can undermine your confidence so completely that you only realise how weak you are when the relationship is over. 'Never forget,' writes Denning, 'that a relationship is made up of two individuals. Individuals who are changing all the time, within – and at the expense of – that relationship.'*

But Anna could not focus, and telephoned Roo at *Mz* magazine, to be told that she was out at a press conference.

'Can you tell her that Anna Potter called?'

'Anna *Potter*,' mused a pipe-smoker's voice. 'Now, where have I heard that name?'

'Oh, well. It's a common . . .'

'Oh *yes*. You're the nasty one.' He laughed gently. A gentleman of the press.

'*What?*'

'You wrote that review, didn't you? About Renata Sorenta?'

'Oh yes. Yes.'

'Well, I suppose they all laughed at Christopher Columbus when he said the world was round,' the voice spoke-sang; and Anna did not know what to say. 'She's up for a Black Ear best newcomer award now.'

'She's *what*?' (Swallowing her words.)

'Certainly is. But don't worry.' The voice seemed, suddenly, to lose interest in the conversation. 'I'll pass your message on to Roo.'

Suddenly, that was not Anna's worry. She pictured Renata, standing on stage to collect her award. 'I'm afraid this comes with no thanks to the nasty Anna Potter . . .' Newspapers would track Anna down. The *Mirror* would set up a special phone line asking, 'Do you know the whereabouts of Nasty Anna Potter?' Anna would be found, and publicly vilified, for attempting to stifle the career of Britain's 'top bit of Black Ear totty', Renata Sorenta.

'You look miles away,' Mike said, coming up behind Anna. He smiled, tapping her computer screen. 'Tomorrow's important; it's the last programme about closure. So, come on. Back to the task in hand.' Anna did not need reminding that tomorrow was Sean's last day. She started writing again, her mind on other things.

As Pammy Lowental writes in Sometimes it's Hard to be a Woman – Especially When You're with a Man *(pub: Magnus rrp £15.99): 'In a bad relationship, the old alley cat often gets better treatment than the woman. Even that alley cat gets fed once in a while, but that does not mean it is loved.'*

Being out of a bad relationship can often restore one's self-respect. It can make you come to terms with your core identity. As Grohe writes: 'You've got to learn to be on your own before you can be in a relationship.'

Mike left the office, and Anna took the opportunity of his absence to phone Roo. Now she needed not just to apologise ('I didn't mean it about Warren; you know he's not interested in me.'), but to hear Roo's soothing voice on the

315

subject of Tom versus Sean. Something like: 'So what that Sean's leaving *Problem Call*? It won't be the last you'll hear from him.' And on the subject of Renata Sorenta, something like: 'Oh, everyone in the arts world thinks Renata's no good. I wouldn't worry about *that*.'

This time Roo answered.

'It's Anna. I want to talk about th . . . ?'

'Just fuck off!' *(Drrr.)*

Again, Anna called. It was important to express one's anger, and any feelings of frustration. She called again, and once more for luck. Only then did she give up, just as Sean stopped at her desk on his way elsewhere. Why did Anna look so distraught? Did she want to come to the Crown for lunch? Sean had Sebastian's house-keys, and they should celebrate.

'I'll just finish this brief,' she said, enjoying his close proximity.

'Doesn't Mike write those crib-sheets?'

But, for what felt like the first time ever, Anna was on a deadline. She wanted to show Mike that she had mastered her brief, and that she now understood every problem that came through the switchboard.

Before now, Anna had never felt much of a purpose at work. Offices felt to her like self-important schools. She had always imagined that she was being given tasks to complete not because they were necessary, but in order to test her ability. She had been a clock-watcher, and as easily bored as Daisy was with Roo. Skirt-tugging: 'What d'you want me to *do*?' She had been a disruptive element in any office. People were always having to find her things to do, to fill her time, from nine 'til five. Until now.

'Mike needed me to write today's notes. He's working on your last programme, tomorrow.'

'Fine.' Sharply.

'But I'm nearly finished. So, yes. I'll meet you in the Crown.'

'Fine.' Even more sharply.

*When one relationship ends, another one can begin. '**Mr Right** won't look at you if you're on the arms of Mr Wrong,' says Denning. 'Separation can be painful, but what if there is no togetherness?' asked Molly Leverton on an earlier* Problem Call *(transcript: 12/12/93). 'If the man is dull, don't accommodate that. The habit of being with someone isn't necessarily a good one.*

'Ask yourself whether you're with your man out of habit? Does he make you tingle? Does he tell you he loves you? Or say sweet things about the way you look? If the answer to those questions is No, No, No, perhaps it's time you asked yourself why. Perhaps it's time to find someone who makes you shout Yes, Yes, Yes.'

It is important to remember that when one relationship ends, another one cannot begin straight away. There needs to be a period of recovery time. As Caroline Rice wrote in an article entitled 'Love is only a state of mind' for the periodical Anxieties Quarterly, *'If one zips from one relationship to the next, all one is doing is taking the pain and hurt and bewilderment from the last relationship and pouring it all into the next one. One is trapped in a cycle of bad relationships.' Ultimately, one cannot achieve true closure by jumping from one emotionally involved relationship to another one.*

Mike came back into the room and read her work on the computer. 'This is great. Fantastic, in fact,' he said, looking at Anna, as if he had lifted from her face a white veil. 'You're good at this, aren't you? Hmm. *Just* . . . D'you mind?'

317

He took her keyboard, typing another last line: *As Pammy Lowental wrote, 'A relationship isn't a rollercoaster, it's a relationship.'*

'There. Always give Pammy the final word. Otherwise she'll fire you. And that would be a shame,' he smiled.

Wilhelm Grohe's recipe for a happy mind.

☼ Eat brain food, such as pulses, brown bread and organic potatoes.

☼ Avoid sugary foods.

☼ Try happy foods, such as kiwi fruit and nuts.

☼ Stay away from unhappy foods, such as chocolate and chips.

☼ Avoid salt.

☼ Always say no to alcohol.

She had never, properly, felt a part of pub culture. Even in a pub like the Crown – which strove to be women-friendly – Anna felt as if, at any moment, someone might notice her sex and tell a smutty joke against women.

She felt out of place and, for that, Anna blamed her father. He had never introduced her to the whole pub concept. Instead, Don had taken her politicking. While other parents had given their children a taste of British culture – sitting them, shivering, at picnic-tables outside pubs, with bags of salt'n'vinegar crisps – Anna had been taken door-to-door canvassing and to annual Conservative Party conferences.

Don had never been a beer-and-telly father. She remembered him once saying that he did not understand why people wasted so much time in pubs, simply sitting in snugs, starting fights. If young people felt so angry, why didn't they try to get on in the world?

He had had ambitions, then, to be Norman Tebbit.

'Thanks, mate,' said Sean, paying for their drinks. He was wearing a scarf, the silky variety suitable for wearing indoors. Anna knew it was the type of accessory that Tom would call pretentious and unnecessary.

Sean sat down and raised his pint of Guinness. 'So, here's to you moving into Sebastian's flat. I'm very pleased.'

'I just wish my *flatmate* wasn't away,' said Anna, her hands around her glass of tomato juice as if it was a hot drink. 'I don't want to tell her on the phone. Not after ten years together. And her father's so ill.'

'There you go again, Anna, thinking too much . . . *Duncan*.'

He stood up to talk to Radio Central's outsize programme controller – nicknamed the Fat Controller – and Anna felt uneasy again, sitting on her own.

She thought of her mother, who had once asked Anna what she *did* in pubs. 'Drink, of course,' Anna had replied. But Barbara could not, would not, understand that. She had never been able to see the attraction of a place which, by and large, served only alcohol.

Her disapproval had led to Anna spending most of her evenings, post-puberty, in the Bell, sitting with her group of friends, drinking snakebites and smoking.

'Sorry about that,' said Sean, sitting down again. 'But you know *Duncan*.'

'So, what are the pubs like near Sebastian's flat?' Anna asked, quickly changing the subject, because she did not know Duncan.

'It's your flat now,' said Sean, taking out some keys, and dropping them on the table. 'I don't think Sebastian spent much time in the pub.'

'Why not?' asked Anna.

'Well, he didn't have much time, what with the book, and the series.'

'Oh, right.'

She couldn't be bothered to ask about book titles and TV channels, and nodded as if she had enough information about Sebastian to be going on with.

'So, listen.' Sean leaned forward and took his glass in both hands. 'How have they got you writing briefs for our beloved Pammy Lowental?'

'Oh, I don't mind. I mean, I enjoyed it, and Mike had masses to do.'

'But Mike's paid more than you.'

That was true.

'What are you saying? That I should have said no?'

'Well, you know what I think. They take *advantage* of you. I mean, this can't be what you really enjoy doing.' He looked at her, as if summing her up.

'What d'you mean?'

'Well, being pushed around by Pammy and used as a dogsbody by Mike.' He bent a coaster sharply in half. 'I hate to see it.' He shook his head, disappointedly. 'You're young. You should be out enjoying yourself – "larging it", or whatever your generation says . . .'

'So what were you saying about the pubs, near Sebastian's?'

'Well, there's the Coach, I suppose.'

'And what's that like?'

'Very like this one, I think.'

She looked beyond him. The Crown was all wood-panelling and smart, glass ashtrays – although no one smoked in pubs such as this. There was just the occasional stalwart cigarette, refusing to give up, its smoke wafting its way through. Most of the regulars here were City types who fitted in a lunchtime drink after the gym. There were none of the smells of her local, the Swan: of rich-red carpets, smoke, and damp, dirty coats.

The Swan smelt awful, but it felt like a local – largely because of Tom. He had been living at her Finchley Road flat for just three weeks, but was already on first-name terms with the new pub landlord. Stewart. Stew. Anna liked to feel that she knew the name of her landlord, although Stewart was only on a short-term contract. She was also moving out of the area on Friday.

'Anna!' Stewart had said, last night, as if she was suddenly part of the worn-down fabric of the place. 'I'm not used to seeing you so late, on a week-day. It'll be last orders soon. You looking for Tom?'

'Is he here?' asked Anna, still shaky, still recovering from her argument with Roo. It had been less than an hour ago.

'Oh yeah, he's about somewhere. So, what's new?'

So, what's new? Tom had helped her to reach this stage. Anna herself would have been too shy to reach this sort of intimacy with bar staff. She had never been able to work out how people went from ordering pints to revealing intimacies from their personal life.

'Oh, nothing much. Er, an orange juice please.'

'I'm glad you're here,' Stewart smiled, clicking the lid off a bottle of orange juice. He poured the juice into a glass. 'You can calm Tom down.'

'Why – what's he been doing?' she asked, paying for her drink. She felt better now, determined to be strong, not thinking about Roo.

'Oh, all those discussions about politics,' he said, long-suffering.

Anna had found Tom next door, talking to some old men

about the 1984 Anglo-Irish agreement. She had felt as if she was back at school, and at her father's Conservative Club.

Don had known that Anna had no interest in politics. And so, last night, had Tom. He had quickly changed the subject, introducing Anna to John, Andrew, John, and Donald. Anna had been surprised to be introduced to them as 'regulars'. In all her years drinking there, she had never seen John or Andrew, Donald, or John. Or, indeed, anyone she recognised.

Yet they must have been there all the time, because John knew the history of the place. Donald knew all about Anna. 'You work on the radio, is that right?' one of them asked; and she, surprised, had thought of telling them all about *Problem Call*, and her bitch-from-hell boss, Pammy Lowental. Anna had watched *Coronation Street*, and knew the form.

They could discuss Myrna's father being ill, and have a whip-round for him. John or Donald would be nominated to pop in and see Myrna, with cakes. Ostensibly with cakes, but really for the gossip. Anna watched *EastEnders*. They would want to know all about her row with Roo, or Don's affair with that candidate in 1980.

But, shy, all she said was, 'Yeah. Radio Central.'

'So, you've come to take Tom home then?' one of the Johns asked.

'In here all the time, isn't he?' said Donald.

'Yeah,' said the other John.

'He *should* be doing his homework,' smiled Anna, cheered up.

'Are you a student?' John asked Tom.

'No,' she laughed, at the very thought. *Younger than that.*

Living with Tom made Anna feel as if she had an adolescent son. Tom left food lying around on plates and smoked out of the window. (She had had to make it clear to him that

322

they were now a non-smoking household.) Anna had even had to remind Tom, twice, to mark Year Ten's homework. The headmistress at Tom's school had had to speak to him about his written work. The head had said, had it been up to her, Tom could conduct experiments all day long. But they all – all of them – had to remember that there was now a national curriculum.

'I'm a teacher,' said Tom. 'You not drinking?' he asked Anna.

'No. I've given up alcohol.'

Tom, John, John, and Donald looked at Anna as if she had just announced an intention to take her own life. 'I'm sure there's a helpline number for that,' smiled John. Donald shook his head and stared at the snooker table.

'Why?' asked Tom.

'I think I'm allergic to it,' she said, knowing that people were loath to argue with an allergy.

'So am I,' said John. 'I come over all drunk.'

'It's eczema,' said Anna, silencing John, John and Donald. But not Tom.

'You're allergic to Sean,' he said. 'One lunch-hour with him and you come out in a rash of anxieties.'

'*Sean* drinks,' said Anna. 'This has nothing to do with *Sean*. It's about health, as Wilhelm Grohe says. Holistically.' (Pompously.)

'Drink's good for you,' said John, urgently supping. 'In moderation.'

'It's not even about physical health. It's about mental energy,' she said airily.

'Oh God, what are you?' said Tom. 'A government leaflet?'

'Fancy a game?' said Donald, picking up the snooker cue. The Johns rose, as if anxious to avoid any argument.

'Tom, I need to talk to you,' Anna said, as the last John left them. 'I need to know something. Do you like Roo?'

323

'Of course I do,' he said.

'I mean, do you *like* Roo?'

Sean stared at Anna as if imagining her with different clothes on.

'You should wear brighter colours,' he said, at last.

'Really?' She had waited a long time for someone to tell her how to dress. Usually she took her cue from chain-store fashions.

'Yeah. The trouble with buying from chain stores is that they use cheap fabrics. You can spot a mass-produced item a mile off.'

'Oh.' She had waited a long time for an attractive man to advise her about important things such as accessories. But now that it had happened, Anna felt uncomfortable, desperate now to run home and to bin all her clothes.

'You should develop more of your own style, I reckon. You wear too much black. Black, brown and green. It's as if you want to disappear.'

'So, what do you think I should wear?'

'Well, the important thing is to feel comfortable. I see you in brighter, summery clothes. You're outgoing enough to cope with reds and yellows. Yellow would look good on you, yes. Yellow, or white.'

'Yeah, I was thinking of going shopping today. But I had to write this brief for Mike.'

'I don't see why *Mikey* couldn't do his own work,' said Sean, irritably.

'Well, he was working on tomorrow's programme.'

'My last programme.' Sean sighed.

'I know,' Anna said, flirtatiously. 'Work won't be the same without you there.'

To exchange computer messages.

324

'We can still e-mail,' smiled Sean. 'I'll message you from *The Shelley Show*. Did you know I was doing another stint there?'

'Well, I hope I'll still *see* you,' said Anna, suddenly afraid. 'I mean, you'll come round, won't you? To Sebastian's – my – flat.' Because, although she had two hundred and twenty friends, none of them had called lately. Except Pritti, who had wondered whether Anna was free for dinner in December. She did not have a window until then.

'Sure,' said Sean making Anna feel, for the first time, unsure. Of Sean. Weren't they on the brink of a relationship? Wasn't he waiting until she had the keys to Sebastian's flat to make his move?

She feared the moment when Sean left.

She hated it when *any* work colleague went, feeling betrayed. Just as Anna was comfortable with them, swapping gossip and office stationery, they would up and leave, all uppity, talking about their grand new job.

She always took it personally, feeling left behind and bereft, gossiping about them in their absence. 'You know, she's making a *mistake*,' Anna would say, shaking her head. 'This new job's just a dead end. I don't know *why* she left the Salad show.'

But what did Anna know? She had been the last one to leave Jimmy Salad's team. She had gone into work one morning to find the office full of bright young things, all of them with blunt haircuts.

They had all been born after 1972. Blunt Haircuts knew more about radio than Anna did. They knew more generally than she did. To compensate, Anna had exaggerated her knowledge of office equipment. She had comforted herself with the fact that she, and she alone, knew how to change the toner in the photocopier.

Roo had persuaded Anna to apply for the job at *Problem Call*. 'It's almost drive-time,' she had said, as if Anna had always, secretly, wanted to work for a programme that was drive-time.

'It'll be funny to think of you still slogging away at *Problem Call*,' said Sean. 'Day in, day out.' He grinned. 'Pammy grinding you down. Day after day.'

'Yeah. I don't know how I got the job. Even at my interview for *Problem Call*, Pammy made it clear that she loathed me. On sight.'

'You seem to know a lot about showbusiness,' Pammy had said. 'But what use is that to us on *Problem Call*? We deal in emotional *reality*.'

But Pammy must have been overruled by other executives at Radio Central, because Anna had got the job, coming into work one morning to find a note from Jimmy Salad, congratulating her. 'We'll go to lunch,' he had said. 'To celebrate.'

Just you wait, Anna had thought. *Without me, the photocopier will break down. No one will clean out the coffee mugs.*

'Pammy is awful, isn't she . . . ?' admitted Anna. She stared at him for a second, wanting to record his face forever in her mind.

'She bullies you. Even my ex agrees,' said Sean absent-mindedly.

'You were talking about me?' *Was Blonde jealous?*

'Yeah. We were wondering what makes someone like you go on and on working for someone like that. I explained about your low self-esteem, and how that would . . .'

'You told her that I had low self-esteem?' she said with a healthy, rather than unhealthy, fury.

Anna had, over the last few days, completed many a psychology book (she had read Denning, George and Wairing,

326

and had nearly finished Grohe's huge *One Month to Happiness*), and she knew that she had a self-esteem problem; still, Anna did not like to be labelled.

'I'd rather you *hadn't*.'

She had been more assertive lately. She knew that she had come a long way, simply by recognising her inner conflict. From reflection came growth, and Anna had been thinking about her life a good deal lately. She was defensive about labels such as 'low self-esteem', certainly. But, at the same time, Anna knew that nobody had defences unless they needed them. She had tried to explain this to Tom, but he had said that it was 'all shit' – which was, frankly, typical of Tom.

'Why? Believe me, *her* self-esteem was at rock-*bottom* when we met.' Sean laughed at the memory. 'She was a car saleswoman then.'

'You're kidding?' (Blonde: a car saleswoman? Anna couldn't imagine it.)

'I kid you not. Desperately unhappy. Working for the biggest *bastard*. A real lazy bugger – made her do everything. Kept talking about promoting her, but nothing ever happened. Anyway, she's happy now. Re-trained as a psychotherapist.'

'Wow. Didn't that take years?'

'Five years. But worth it, she says. She'd have left earlier, but needed the money.'

'Really?'

'Well, she had three kids when I met her.' He looked worried for a second, but smiled. 'So, what's *your* excuse? Or are you happy doing Mike's work for him?'

'Mike was working on tomorrow's programme.' Anna excused herself. 'You know what Pammy's like, and she wanted him to summarise all the themes to do with Closure.

On two sides of A4. She's happy to *blame* . . .'

'Two sides of A4?' nodded Sean. 'Come *on*. That's hardly a lot of words – and worthless anyway. Whatever he's been telling you, presenters always ignore those briefing notes. No, I have to think about tomorrow, actually. Not *Mikey*. I need to think of a way of pulling everything together – everything I've been talking about. So, another orange juice in there?'

'Yeah.'

'What d'you want to drink?' Tom asked, last night, in the pub.

'I want to talk about Roo,' Anna said, sulkily. 'That's why I came to find you.'

'Well, I want another beer. So, Anna – half-empty lager for you?'

She could not help but smile.

'No, seriously, I told you I want to cut down on my units. And when you come back, I want to talk about Roo.'

'Oh, God,' he mumbled.

'What?

'Not sure I know where this conversation's going.'

'Well, I'm not sure where this *relationship*'s going, Tom.'

'Anna. Really, you need to cut down on the word "relationship". Trust me – you're starting to use it in everyday conversation.'

He grinned and left her, sitting there, watching a game of snooker. One of the men potted the black just as Tom returned with his spilling pint of bitter.

'OK, so what's this about Roo?'

'I want to know – are you going out with me just to get to her?'

'*What?* First of all, she's married . . .'

328

'Ah, so that's all that's stopping you?'

'*No*. I can assure you, I don't find Roo attractive. Whatever she's been saying.'

But Tom had also said, during various conversations, that he did not find Marilyn Monroe attractive – or even Kylie Minogue. Anna figured that men like Tom always denied being attracted to pretty women, as if their denials made them more attractive to plainer, more attainable, women. Like herself.

'So, Roo's *ugly*, is she?'

'I didn't say she was ugly, Anna.' (His opt-out clause, just in case Kylie ever turned up to make a pass at him.) 'Of course Roo isn't ugly. It's just that I only have eyes for you.'

'Well, that's not true.' She had seen his eyes during *Baywatch*, unable to keep up with the running blondes in swimsuits. 'You haven't got a romantic bone in your body.'

'Why d'you say that?'

'Well, come *on*. Have you ever even said that you *liked* me? You've practically moved in and . . .'

'Have I moved in? I thought I was moving in at the end of the week.'

'Well, why is all your stuff at mine?'

'Because that's where your bed is,' he said, amused.

'Oh, look. You haven't *once* said anything nice about the way I look. Even.'

'God, OK. You've got eyes like pearls. Lips like cabbage leaves . . .'

'There's no need to be facetious. The fact is, I know what you think about almost every TV programme, but I don't know what you think about important things – like marriage and children.'

'We've only known each other a month, Anna. What d'you want?'

'I meant, *in principle*. Do you, *in principle*, want to get married?'

'It's a matter of great principle with me,' he said soberly.

'Really?' Perhaps if they talked properly about their relationship, discussing all their problems one by one, they could work it out, the two of them.

'Mmm. Marriage is a *great* idea.'

'*Really?*'

'Well, if only for tax reasons.'

'Do you have to be funny about everything? Some things are *serious*. I mean, we never talk about anything important. We never talk about my career, for example.'

'I thought we were always talking about *Sean* and his theories.'

'I don't even mean *Problem Call*. I mean, the career I *want*. Acting.' Anna did not want to talk about Sean, in the same way that she did not want, generally, to talk about her sexual fantasies. Some subjects were best left alone.

'You want to be an actress?'

'*Yes.*' Goddamnit.

'But that's ridiculous.'

As a rule, men were impressed by Anna's ambition.

They were able to forget her humdrum job and imagine that, one day, she would be a star of stage and screen. All of Anna's men – Alfonso, Danny, Bryan, even Him – had understood that while Anna waited to be discovered, she needed a day job. Because they had had their ambitions too. He had wanted to be a writer. Alfonso had dreamt of being a lifeguard.

'And just why is it *ridiculous*?'

Tom didn't answer. He seemed to be searching for the

right words to let her down with, and so she sat there, staring at the unopened packet of original-flavoured McCoy crisps.

It was always the same at the Swan. The evening would begin with stiff pints of lager, perched lady-like on bar tables. But, then, the props loosened up: crisp packets were burst open, half of them mashing into lumps with the drunken, spilled lager, or crushed underfoot. Anna's thoughts would go out of focus.

My life shouldn't be like this, she thought, looking at Tom. *I'm probably not even having the right orgasms.*

'There you go,' said Sean, coming back with another orange juice for Anna. A waitress followed him with the two plates of salad that they had ordered earlier. Bits of foliage served up, daintily, with dressing. 'Croutons?' she asked, laying down two sets of cutlery wrapped in clean serviettes.

'Not for me, thanks.'

'No.'

The waitress carried away her tiny silver bowl of croutons, and Sean started to eat. After one mouthful of salad he wiped his mouth with his serviette.

'So, are you staying with Pammy because you have ambitions in radio?'

'God, no. I want to be an actress,' Anna said, pausing for him to react.

'Really?' Suddenly interested. 'What have I seen you in, then?'

'Did you catch my *Piers the Ploughman*?' she asked, smiling. 'Off-off-off-the West End. Well, Acton actually.'

'No, *seriously*. Is that what you want to do? Acting?'

'Well, yes.'

'Well, why aren't you doing it then?'

'Well, because . . . D'you know how *hard* it is?' Although at least he was taking her seriously.

'How hard can it be? You'll be living rent-free soon. Give it a go.'

He said this as if he was suggesting Anna take up a hobby such as aqua-aerobics.

'Tell Pammy where to stick it.'

'Oh no,' she laughed. 'I *couldn't*.'

'Life's short, Anna. This is only a *job* we're talking about. Don't be so melodramatic.' He smiled, realising he had said something semi-humorous. 'Or at least get paid for it.'

'You should have seen the one review I got . . .' She was about to repeat Renata Sorenta's words but changed her mind. Sean might think that, because the review had appeared in print, it had some truth to it. 'Mind you, it was written by someone with a grudge against me,' she added.

'Oh yeah? Well, you know what the best revenge is, don't you?'

'Yes, but I've tried that.'

'*Success.*'

'But you said . . .' It was not what he had said.

'Achieve all you can. That's all I'm saying. Do the *maximum*.'

'I just can't see you as an actress,' Tom had said, at last. He smiled, adding, 'You hate people looking at you.'

'Well, that shows how long you've known me.'

'Oh, come on, Anna. You can't be an actress.' He had laughed, trying to make light of it. 'You have a hard enough time just being yourself.'

'Well, thanks for the encouragement.'

'OK, being serious . . .'

'Hallelujah.'

'I know I haven't seen you on stage, Anna. So I can't . . .'

'*Exactly.*'

'All I do know is, you've got a good job, and it sounds like they're starting to give you some responsibility.'

'One programme brief.'

'To be honest, I can't imagine you pushing yourself forward. You're not pushy enough. And that's one of the things I loved about you.'

'Boom, boom,' she said, because he was joking.

'Actually, I meant that.'

'We've only known each other a *month*,' she said.

'I know.' He drank some of his beer. 'Or rather . . . OK, whatever.'

'You don't even *know* me, Tom. Not like Sean.' There, she'd said it.

'Oh *well*, I can't compete with Sean. A mere mortal like me.'

'Well, you don't have Sean's drive. That's all. You have no . . . spontaneity.'

'I could be spontaneous,' he said, sadly. 'If you gave me time to plan.'

'I don't think it's working,' she said, soberly. 'I mean, us, as a relationship. You don't even like the *word*, so there's no hope of you discussing our future together. To be honest, I don't know why you can't talk about your feelings. *Sean*'s able to, and he's hardly unmanly.' Anna measured her words carefully. There was no point in their having an argument. 'This isn't the Victorian age, Tom. Men and women talk to each other now. They have partnerships, and draw strength from those partnerships. Because a relationship of real *value* – real, intimate value – takes work. Intensive, *hard* work.'

'In other words, you want "closure"?' Tom asked, holding his beer glass tight.

'That's right.' Was he laughing at her?

'OK, fine.' He reddened, and said, angrily, 'OK, fine, I'll be *serious*. *Seriously*, I loved you.'

'You . . . ?'

'Yeah. I wasn't going to tell you. It sounded too strange, after only a month. But maybe that's how it's meant to happen. To be honest, I wouldn't know, because I'd never been in love before. But, well, there you go.'

His face hardened.

'But, now . . .' he said, finally. 'You know, you're a selfish bitch. God, it's taken me this long to realise it. Well, you're not worth *feelings*, Anna. In fact, you're worth fuck all.'

He was really angry. *Unhelpful anger*, she thought, as he drank the dregs of his beer. If Anna hadn't known Tom better, she would have thought that he was about to leave her, all alone, in a strange pub.

'You *love* me?' she asked, realising that no one, outside of her family, had ever loved her before.

'Love a bitch like you?' he asked, standing up. She could not see his face. 'No, Anna. I don't even like you very much.'

'Well, what were you saying before . . . ? Are you going? Don't go . . . I want to talk about . . .' she stuttered, confused.

'No, I was telling you how I felt. But I've changed my mind since then. My prerogative, don't you think? Now that men are so in touch with their feminine side,' he sneered. 'Go to Sean, Anna.'

'Well, let's talk about this,' she said, feeling suddenly scared.

334

'Ah, but you want closure. So, good*bye*,' he said, directing all of his useless anger at her, and walking away.

'Hang on a minute . . .'

She had more to say.

'Hey, you've given me an idea for tomorrow's programme,' said Sean. 'Because, you know, this is what Closure is all about. *Change*, for God's sake. Growth.'

'You know what's great?' Anna said. 'The way you take my ambitions *seriously*. You don't just dismiss them as . . . ridiculous.'

'Well, they're not ridiculous, that's why. Who does that?'

'My ex-boyfriend, as of last night.'

'Ex-boyfriend eh? So, why is he ex? What went wrong?'

She felt safe mentioning Tom to Sean, now that Tom had gone.

'Well, that was the trouble. There was nothing wrong. I was only with him because I felt comfortable. But then I realised that I only felt safe in the relationship because I knew it was going to fail.'

'And how did this "boyfriend" respond to you breaking up with him?'

'He won't talk about his feelings. I tried, but he wouldn't listen.'

Sean sighed.

'Yeah, that often happens,' he said. 'One person takes all the responsibility for a bad relationship.'

'I did resent the way he wouldn't listen to me when I told him that I wanted to be an actress.'

'Well, you know, it seems to me that you live for other people's approval.'

'You think?'

'Yes. It's as if you're having the life you think you're

supposed to want, rather than the one you do want. For example, why is it so hard to leave a job you loathe for one that might make you happy? Acting could be your vocation.'

'Yes, I think it is.'

'So, go for it.'

'No, you're right. And I will give up *Problem Call* soon. But I've only been there a month, so . . .'

'No better time.' He finished his greenery. 'Seriously. Live a little. You're not stuck in a rut like some. So, leave. *Now*. Leave when I do. *Yes*. Leave with me, tomorrow.'

She laughed. It felt as if he was asking her to elope with him. In a recurring fantasy, her young man in wet breeches said the same. But the fantasy man was not, naturally, talking about career opportunities.

I've got to give three months' notice, she thought. But she could hardly mention contractual obligations. It would be like introducing the subject of a washing-up rota in the middle of a passionate love scene.

'Your trouble is, you think too much,' Sean said. 'Just hand in your notice, for God's sake. How hard can that be? I bet you haven't even rung Eileen yet.'

'Eileen?'

'The therapist I was telling you about.'

'What would she say? That I should drop everything to become an actress?'

'I think she would say that you should stop living for other people.' He was speaking slowly, as if measuring each word for its effect. 'I think she would say that you are defining your world too narrowly. That change isn't just about overcoming a fear of, say, flying.'

'She seems to know me well, this Eileen.' Anna was afraid of flying.

336

'Well, really, what's the point of being in a flight simulator? Go for the real thing. At least then you'll have some hope of getting somewhere.'

'Oh, I *will* give up work soon,' she said dismissively. 'I mean, I *want* to . . .'

'Anna, just declare the date and the intention.'

'OK, fine, I will. Tomorrow then.'

'Tomorrow.'

'Bloody *hell*. What will my dad say?'

'I won't even comment on that.'

'I know. You're right. I'll resign.'

'Tomorrow?'

'Tomorrow.'

'We'll go out with a bang.'

'Yes.' *I certainly hope so*, she thought – because, sometimes, she loved double entendres.

'Here's to achieving Closure,' Sean said, raising his empty pint-glass.

'*Closure*,' Anna agreed, as Pammy appeared, wanting to know why her 'star worker' was taking so long over lunch, and congratulating her on writing 'the perfect brief'.

'Now, stir yourself,' Pammy said busily, bustling. 'Mikey wants you back in the office, Annie. Lena's going to operate the programme today. I need *you* in the studio.'

Anna smiled at Sean, grabbing her coat and bag, following Pammy out. She felt like a child who was being collected by her mother. 'I'm not *that* late, am I?' she asked, as they left the Crown.

A draught came in through her buttonholes. It was September still, cold out there and smelling of dead leaves. She was without her coat. They went inside the warm glass tower that was Radio Central, past Maura, sitting on reception.

'No, but this is an important programme for you, isn't it?

Mikey's given you real responsibility. Yet I *knew* I'd find you in the pub, Annie, mooning over Sean Harrison.'

Gossipy Maura.

'I wasn't mooning over anyone,' Anna said, helplessly. She began to draft a letter, in her mind. *Dear Pammy Lowental,* she thought, as they reached the lift. *This is a letter of resignation . . .*

'When I was your age I didn't waste my time chasing after men,' said Pammy, pressing the lift button, impatiently. Pressing and pressing.

'I do not chase . . . I'm thirty-one,' Anna replied, sulkily. *I am having to leave because of your attitude towards me. Although I have been working at Radio Central for eight years now, I can no longer cope with . . .*

'And you can stop that sulky voice, which I've talked to you about. I thought we had a "contract", but obviously that hasn't helped your attitude . . .'

The lift came and they went inside. The door shut.

'I didn't realise that our "contract" would be put up on the office noticeboard . . .,' started Anna. *I can no longer cope with your constant undermining of me. I had hoped that we might be able to sort out our differences, but I was wrong.*

'Well, you'll be pleased then to hear that Mikey's taken it down.'

'Yes, I am pleased.' *I have enjoyed working with the rest of the* Problem Call *team and will be sorry to leave them, but, unfortunately . . .*

'Well, anyway, you wrote a *very* good brief today. One that showed you had more to you than I thought. Mikey's *very* impressed, and we've even talked about promoting you.'

They reached their level, and the doors fell open. They walked along the corridor, and past a woman who waved her Snickers bar at Anna as if she knew her. 'Ah, I must pop in and see Sarah,' muttered Pammy. 'See how she's doing now, on those new drugs. You go on ahead.'

Anna walked on, thinking.

Unfortunately, promotion is often talked about, but nothing materialises. I cannot go on working for a woman who has no respect or sensitivity for the feelings of her staff, and I hope that, in years to come, you will recognise the hurt you have caused me. No, that wasn't right. She did not want Pammy's pity. *I hope that, in years to come, I will have reason to thank you. You gave me the push I needed to pursue my dream.* But why should she thank Pammy? *But this comes with no thanks to you. I only hope that you will one day regret . . .* No, no. *I regret the fact that you did not see fit to use the years of training and radio experience that I brought to* Problem Call. That would get Pammy into trouble with the Fat Controller. *I cannot help but see it as a waste of valuable, human resources.*

Yours sincerely,

Ms Anna Potter.

Chapter Fourteen

All she had ever wanted out of life was happiness. Yet there Anna was, unhappily switching on the computer. Her yellow screen-saver read SMILE. Anna saw the date on her monitor, and she was suddenly overwhelmed by self-pity. *Thurs 11.08 am, Sept 30.* Sean's last day at work.

'Are you all right?' asked Mike, pulling faxes out of the machine.

'Yes.' Anna was using the time before today's programme started to look up her name on the Internet. *No,* she thought.

'No, she's not all right,' said Pammy, coming in from the studio next door. 'How can she be all right? Sean's leaving today. We must all bear with Annie.'

'I'm fine,' said Anna, thinking that there had been times in her life when she had been extraordinarily happy – but only in retrospect. At such times, she had worried that she was at any moment about to become miserable.

'I don't need anyone to bear with me,' she said, tapping her keyboard in an effort to appear usefully occupied. She had found several hundred mentions of 'Anna Potter', although none of them, naturally, referred to her. But then, what had Anna achieved?

'Today, Annie,' said Pammy, 'I want a man.'

We're not starting all that again, are we? thought Anna.

'So, Lena,' Pammy had said to the secretary, last week, 'what do you think I should do about Bruce and Boris, now that Archy's for once made a decision, and left me? D'you think I should commit to Boris? Or should I force Bruce with an ultimatum? Otherwise I just know Bruce won't commit to me. Oh boy.'

Lena had opened her mouth to respond. But Pammy was too quick for her.

'It is *so* good to talk to a woman like you, Lena. Someone who has endured just as many failed relationships. Someone who knows the meaning of the word *depression*. I spend too much of my time with high achievers. You see, women of my generation, they all have five kids and a place on the board. But, hey, don't tell anyone about Archy.'

Lena had had no need to tell anyone about Archy. They had all known. When Archy had ended his relationship with Pammy, her staff had suffered. For example, Pammy had sent Mike a memo which asked him, in the sweetest of ways, why he was making such a hash of things.

I'm worried about you. Is Fran's mastectomy troubling you? You've been making a lot of serious mistakes lately. I know a lot of men stop finding their wives attractive after such an operation. Do come and talk to me about Fran, if that's what's bothering you. I need a producer who is on the ball at all times. Best, Pammy.

She had saved this memo in a general office file that anyone could access.

All week, Pammy had hovered around Anna's desk, waiting for her to make a mistake. Then she had pounced.

'You're plain incompetent,' she had said on Tuesday, swooping on one of Anna's mixed metaphors. She had taken out her anger on various unsuspecting male callers, during the programme.

'Well, can I just say, Euan, that "men" like you – with serious *commitment* problems – really get my goat. It's time that man, as a species, grew up. And, I'm sorry, because the big hand is pointing to the hour, and that's the end of today's *Problem Call*. But don't switch off, because I shall be leaving you in Bruce the Juice's big and oh-so-capable hands for tonight's *Drive-Time* programme. His hands are *firmly* on the wheel . . .'

On Wednesday morning, Pammy had gathered everyone together in the office. She wanted to make an announcement. 'I think you all know by now that Archy is no longer a part of my life.'

She took a deep breath.

'You've all been a real support to me.' The programme secretary took her hand. 'Thank you, Lena,' Pammy said. '*Thank* you. No, I want you all to know that, from now on, I'm going to give my all to Bruce. I'm going to put all my eggs in Bruce's basket.'

Anna had had to apologise for laughing.

'We're meeting for lunch today,' said Pammy, glancing sharply at Anna. 'And I think, finally – cross fingers, all of you – Bruce is ready to commit.'

But, no. Not beyond Pammy's lunch with Bruce, anyway. By then, he was telling her that he needed the freedom to see other women. He loved Pammy, really he did. But only in the way that he loved all women.

She would make him pay for saying that. That afternoon, in fact.

'Well, that's it for Wednesday's programme,' she had said

yesterday, on air. 'And now I hand you over to *Drive-Time* for Bruce's aggressive, take-no-prisoners, me-me-me view of the world. So stay tuned in to Radio Central – if you can stomach it. Otherwise, why don't you just switch off the radio, and write me – Pammy Lowental – a letter instead?'

'You want a man?' asked Anna now.

'I want *men*. Generally,' specified Pammy. 'I mean, on my programme,' she wailed. 'Duncan sent me a memo today saying we need more male callers. For the insurance advertising.'

She stopped. Her face screwed up with worry, and then rage.

'Well, if we want to keep this time-slot. Because otherwise we'll be moved to some mid-morning housewives' slot. And we don't want *that*,' she spat, as if suddenly noticing that Anna was there. 'Do we?'

'I'll see what I can do,' said Anna, who had been under pressure, in her last job, to choose only women callers for the Jimmy Salad show. 'Although, men don't seem to like talking about their feelings.'

'Well, *make* them,' fumed Pammy, walking back into the glass-walled studio.

Mike sighed, muttering, 'Don't you sometimes just feel like leaving? Just walking out and resigning?'

It was proof of how much their relationship had changed that Anna almost told Mike about her resignation letter, which sat on Pammy's desk upstairs. However, the phone rang, and Mike was forced to take a complaining call from a campaign organisation, Prejudice Against Disfigurement. On yesterday's Ending Relationships programme, Pammy had said that emotional scars were always 'far more disfiguring than the merely physical'.

'I knew that would happen,' Mike said, coming off the phone. 'No matter how many times I tell that woman, she . . .'

'She what?' said Pammy sharply, coming back into the room, and filling it with an expensive perfume. The smell made Anna feel faintly nauseous. 'The programme's about to start, so if you wouldn't mind *coming through*?'

Anna had lined up three callers before the programme began.

Her screen read:

THURSDAY, SEPTEMBER 30: FINAL PROGRAMME, CLOSURE.
LINE ONE: **FAY:** WANTS TO THANK PAMMY FOR SORTING OUT HER PROBLEMS WITH HER HUSBAND. THEY ARE NOW 'BACK ON TRACK'.
LINE TWO: **JENNIFER:** BABY DROWNED IN FOUNTAIN IN UNDERGROUND SHOPPING CENTRE. HOW CAN SHE STOP THINKING ABOUT IT?
LINE THREE: **COLIN.** GENERALLY UNHAPPY.

Of course, not one of the three problems were what Pammy would call 'good radio', but she had asked for male callers, and Colin was almost certainly a man. Plus, Pammy liked calls from women such as Fay who were grateful to Pammy for solving their problems. That was why Anna had prioritised Fay's call.

She was no fool.

Sean smiled at Anna through the pane of glass, and she smiled back, sad at the thought that this would be the last time they would be so close.

More importantly, she was afraid that, beyond this glass, they would never see each other again. She would never hear that smooth, soothing voice – unless she watched *The Shelley Show*.

The fear had only started this morning, but it had taken hold of her, and now Anna was panicking. They had not made any particular arrangements to see each other. Anna had stupidly assumed that Sean would be as frequent a visitor to Sebastian's flat after Sebastian had left. But why would he want to see Anna in any domestic setting?

He had not once invited himself round to her flat in Finchley Road. They were work colleagues, first and foremost. Yes, they had been to the pub next door to the office. But the Crown was very much a work pub. It behaved as if it was a pub in its own right, but the beer pumps and the wall-mounted stags' heads seemed excessively ornamental. It had the atmosphere of an office uncomfortably dressed up in seasonal decorations.

I'll miss messaging you, messaged Sean, and Anna comforted herself with the fact that, had he planned on not seeing her again, Sean would not have sent such a message.

A month ago, Anna might have kept the printouts of his words as a souvenir. This one would have been a perfect reminder of their time together. *I'll miss messaging you.* It was so perfect that Anna decided not to ruin the moment by replying.

Besides, their relationship had moved on – it now involved real-time conversations.

By the time she had changed her mind, deciding to reply, they were on air, Pammy saying, 'Well, hello and welcome to the last *Problem Call* concerning Closure. This programme comes to you courtesy of DoorSeal, the DIY glue that really can Do It For You.'

She played the DoorSeal jingle. 'Shut that door. Close it tight. Oooh, shut that door with *Door*Seal'.

'Right – *welcome*. You all know the freephone number – 0800 678771. And we're going to be getting a heavy sackload of fan mail from the *surprisingly small* proportion of female listeners. Because our own Dr Sean Harrison is finally getting his Closure. This is his very last day. Hello – or should I say goodbye – *Sean Harrison*.'

'Hello, for now, Pammy; and I've enjoyed my time here. All I can say is thank you for having me. Your listeners are a loyal lot, and I've had some lovely letters from . . .'

'Yes, loyal to the last,' interrupted Pammy. 'And that is what it is. *Aw*. Shame. The last programme. Although I think we've covered the Goodbye theme. Didn't I say that saying goodbye was just as important as saying hello?'

'Yes, as part of the Saying Goodbye programme.'

'Still, tell us what you're going to be covering today?'

'Well, I was having a conversation with a friend, yesterday. A friend who was stuck in a job that she hated, and working for a boss who seemed hell bent on destroying her confidence.'

'Mmmm. Mmhmmm.'

Anna worried that she was the 'friend'. Listening backstage, she felt vaguely exploited. She was still not used to sharing her problems in public. She knew, as Gail Denning had advised, that people should offer their anxieties 'like gifts' to other people. But, at the same time, she had read Stacy Wairing's *Lies, Damned Lies*, and was worried that she was an 'over-confider'. Wairing had written that confidences had turned into a modern commodity. They should be given away sparingly. People should be made aware of the value of their secrets. *Emotions are expensive*.

'She wasn't happy, and had a dream anyway of being an actress.'

'She had negative feelings about herself?'

346

'Oh yes – stuck in a life she didn't want.'

'She was just filling up her empty life. Is that right? For show? She was exteriorising? Dr Harrison is nodding here. I'm just sorry this isn't *television*. And what was your advice?'

'Well, my advice to this friend, and my advice to anyone in her predicament, is to take a different view of life. She should forget what is expected of her, and realise her own intrinsic value. In other words, she needs to confront her fears.'

'Sincerely? You think that this is about her lacking the *courage*?'

'Well, I don't think I'm the first person to say it, but living your dream means exactly that. Confronting your fears. Pursuing your own path.'

'I see, sweetie. I see. You have to face that charging bull. And this is all about Closure?'

He was right, of course. Or rather, Anna was right to leave *Problem Call*. She thought about that resignation letter, on Pammy's desk.

'Indeed. If you're starting again, with a whole new way of life, there's no *clutter*. You have real Closure.'

'*Appreciated*. Appreciated. And I guess that the worst words in the whole world are "if only".'

'Well, I wouldn't put it quite so simply. But, yes, I believe so.'

'OK, and we'll be taking your calls on this subject – Starting Again – as well as on all of the other subjects we've been covering in this month's topic – Closure. *Fay*. Can we help you?'

'Oh, Pammy,' came the breathless voice of Fay. 'Thank you for taking my call.'

'Well, sugar. Thank you for phoning *in*.'

347

'I wanted to phone to say thank you. You've changed my life.'

'Well, thank you for taking the time to say thank you. I often feel – and perhaps any radio controller listening out there should take heed of this – that we are more than entertainment here. We are something of a public service.'

'Well, you helped me, Pammy,' said Fay. 'You saved my marriage.'

'And how did I do that, sweetie?'

'Do you remember? You told me to try anger management.'

'Well, good. And it worked?'

'Well, it made me see that you can have a good marriage without living together.'

'Yes, because you have to tackle the outside in order to reach the inside.'

'That's what I tell my husband . . .'

'And he doesn't *agree* with that?' Horrified.

'He's not the agreeing type, Pammy. But we're working on that together, and the children stay with him at weekends . . .'

'Well, good. Good. I just love happy endings. Call me old-fashioned, but I like my stories to end well. Good. Thank you for that, Fay. And now we'll go to an ad break. Remember, this programme comes to you courtesy of DoorSeal, the number one DIY tool for fixing doors that won't shut.'

Check the story out properly before you send someone through. That was not the call I thought it would be, Pammy messaged Anna.

'Jennifer. Over to Jennifer on line two. Jenny, sugar, how can we help you?'

'Hello? *Pammy?* I've been waiting to talk to you for years . . .'

'Well, I hope my operator's not *that* bad,' Pammy laughed, to Anna's fury.

'Do go ahead, Jennifer. What is your problem?'

There was the sound of someone breathing in, and then Jennifer said, 'It happened so many years ago, Pammy. But it's only now I feel I can . . .' She stopped, to breathe.

'You take your time. Enjoy this. Try to relax.'

'Well.'

But Jennifer started to cry.

'Relax, Jen, honey. Remember, life is not an emergency. We're not in *ER* – although that would be very nice.' She laughed, clearly hoping to sound sexy. 'I wouldn't mind a meeting with George Clooney myself.'

'Yes,' snivelled Jennifer, trying to laugh herself. 'Well, this goes back years. I have three children now, but I did have four. I . . .' She started to cry again.

'Did you come to the telephone with a tissue? *Always* come to the phone with a tissue. I always say that. There's no point otherwise,' Pammy said, irritably. 'We waste valuable time while the caller is leaving the phone to find a tissue.'

'I'm back now,' said Jennifer, blowing her nose.

'OK, honey. You talk in your own time.'

'Thing is, I had a baby – February the eighteenth, 1992 – and she died at three months. I was at one of those all-in shopping centres and I just put my shopping down and my baby, Jemima, on the side of the fountain . . . Oh, I can't talk . . . Even now.'

'She drowned?' asked Pammy gently. 'Is that right?'

'She died, yes, she drowned, in seconds. There was nothing anyone could do. No one did anything to help . . .'

'These feelings are still very raw?'

'No, it's just that we don't talk about it now. It's taboo in our house.'

'OK, I'm going to give you my advice. First, let me say how brave you are to phone up today. That shows you've come a long way, *emotionally*. Second, you should know that Rome wasn't built in a day, and neither is faith built in a day. What you need is faith in the future, and that doesn't come on the one-oh-one bus, now, does it? *No*.'

'Can I just come in here?' asked Sean, gently. 'Because I'd like to know whether Jennifer has had grief counselling.'

'I did when it happened. But the woman went on about my dad, trying to bring up all this stuff from the past . . .'

'See your GP,' said Pammy. 'That's important. You have to look to yourself, not to the bus conductor.'

'Yes,' half-laughed Jennifer.

'This is like a traffic jam of the mind.'

'I do think that Jennifer needs to talk to an expert about this.'

'Yes. If you begin to see the problem, that's half the problem solved. Now, do you have a job?'

'Yes, I'm a clerical assistant.'

'Well, that is marvellous. So that fills your time, am I right? Stops you thinking?'

'Dare I say,' dared Sean, 'that Jennifer can only help her problem if she discusses it. It won't just go . . .'

'Dr Harrison is right, of course, Jennifer, honey. You have to work from the bottom up, rather than the top down. And – as they say in the theatre – we'll go to the interval now.'

Pammy faded Jennifer's voice down to a murmur. A commercial faded up for quality kitchenware at half the retail price. Calls came in, and Anna put her headphones back on, trying, again and again, to pack a five-year troubled history into one line for Pammy Lowental.

She could hear, on the Tannoy, the off-air conversation next door. Pammy, ridiculing Jennifer for leaving her baby to drown at the edge of a shopping-centre fountain. Lena, berating Jennifer for her sheer stupidity. Mike, wondering whether they should put out a warning about the hazards of indoor shopping centres. Todd, not wanting to get involved.

Anna felt as if she was listening to her own family squabbling.

All of Anna's lines were full as they were back on air. 'Welcome back to the programme that puts you first. Because I don't believe in the cult of the radio presenter. This programme is about *you*, not me. Colin, what can we do for you?'

'Well, Pammy, I'm just generally unhappy,' said Colin.

'Unhappy? And what is the root of your unhappiness?'

'To be honest with you, I just don't know,' Colin said, as if faced with a genuine conundrum. 'I do know that I don't have a great life. In that, I mean it doesn't have any real depth or meaning.'

'Well, you do know, Colin, that in order to tackle the inside, you have to start on the outside? Hmm? So let's start with this. Do you *have* a job?'

'Yes. I'm a managing director of a medium-sized firm catering in special-sized lingerie for the larger lady.'

'A *good* job,' exclaimed Pammy, satisfied with that.

'But are you satisfied with this job?' asked Sean. 'Is this what you imagined yourself doing?'

'No and no.'

'Well, let's look at this,' said Pammy. 'Because, you know, happiness doesn't exist on its own, Colin. There is probably

351

an underlying root cause. Do you feel, for example, that you love yourself *unconditionally*?'

'Well, no, there's always been conditions. I don't like the fact that, no matter how much I work out, I have a slight paunch. Nor, incidentally, does my wife. Although she works on a beauty counter herself, and looks are everything in that world.'

And in this world, thought Anna.

'What would you like to be doing?' asked Sean. 'Work-wise, I mean.'

'Well, silly as it sounds, I've always wanted to be a juggler. I mean, I've been on courses and . . .'

'Well, we all want to run off and join the *circus*, Colin, but . . .' sneered Pammy.

'But some of us *do*,' said Sean, interrupting, urgently. 'Some of us do run off and join the circus, if that's what we really want to do. It's not so far-fetched, Colin. There *are* jugglers in the world.'

'Maybe so,' agreed Pammy. 'But do they juggle for a living?'

'I'm not suggesting that Colin should just up and leave his business . . .'

'Oh, I couldn't do that. There's people rely on me for the work. Immigrants. They can't get a job in the normal way. Illegals, some of th . . .'

'Fine, fine. Let's put this on the scales. And when I say scales, I don't mean weighing scales. I mean the type that slimmers use to weigh the amount of food they're eating . . .'

'I was thinking more of juggling as entertainment,' said Colin.

'Well, there *are* talent contests,' said Sean, with enthusiasm.

'And let's remember, before we say no to everything, that

no is what happens on the way to saying yes . . .'

Sean: 'For real Closure, you need to wipe the slate clean. If the job is making you unhappy, think about changing it . . .'

Pammy: 'Now, come on, Dr Harrison. Colin has a good job. He just needs to . . .'

Sean: 'I would say that he needs to *sift*. He needs to discover what's important to him. Of *course* he should prioritise. I'm not saying otherwise. But one doesn't lie on one's deathbed saying, 'I should have remembered to sort out my audits.' If Colin has ambition . . .'

'OK, fine,' snapped Pammy. 'Thank you, Colin. I hope that's helped. Remember, from Monday, we'll be having man-of-the-moment, Wilhelm Grohe, in as co-presenter to talk about his book *One Month to Happiness*. Perhaps Colin would do better to phone Wilhelm Grohe, because Sean Harrison and I are mere amateurs, by comparison.' She tinkled. 'Certainly, when it comes to the subject of *happiness*.'

'You're not happy?' asked Pammy, puzzled.

She had brought Anna back into Studio B so that they could privately discuss Anna's letter of resignation. The letter of resignation that Anna had re-drafted several times, purely for the pleasure of it.

'I must say, I was surprised to receive this letter,' said Pammy, exaggerating a look of surprise. 'I thought that you were enjoying the job.'

Anna was sitting in Sean's usual swivel seat, and she felt his ghost. The microphone was in front of her as if to amplify everything she said. She felt that, if she said yes, she sometimes enjoyed her job, Anna would be double-crossing Sean. She could hear his patient voice, saying, *No, Anna. You'll only be double-crossing yourself.*

'Well, that's part of the problem,' said Anna. 'I don't think you realise just how undermining it is – the way you behave towards me. It's bullying, if you'd admit it, on a daily basis.'

She looked up to see Pammy reading her letter. Anna felt oddly annoyed at that, as if Pammy had no right to read her private thoughts. Because, more than a resignation letter, it read like a suicide note. Anna had written it as if it was her last chance to tell the world what she thought of it before jumping. But she had not banked on Pammy reading it in front of Anna. That felt plain intrusive.

She was too much of an over-confider. Anna would have to work on that. She was too generous, regretting her generosity almost instantly, and feeling resentful. Denvil George had crystallised all of these feelings for her in *Unburdening*. George did not like to bracket himself with other self-help gurus. But he really had helped Anna. More and more, she was beginning to understand the cause of her unhappiness.

'You think I bully you?'

'I think you patronise me, yes. All the time.'

'And this is the reason why you're leaving?'

In all honesty, now that Sean was leaving, there was not much reason to stay. But Anna would not admit that, of course.

She did wonder whether she was resigning purely for the show of it all. Well, she was finding courage from somewhere. There was a lot that was pleasurable about sitting in a radio presenter's seat. The microphone wasn't switched on, of course, but she felt its presence. It made her resignation scene feel like a performance. Anna had not realised the power that one could feel as a voice dislocated from a face. She felt that she could say anything without feeling responsible for the effect of her words. Somehow her voice did not sound like her own.

'I think you misunderstand my motives,' Anna continued. 'I think you devalue my work. You exaggerate my mistakes . . .'

'Well, you're right,' Pammy said, surprisingly. (Small voice.) 'I know I'm guilty of that. Perhaps – I don't know – I've been a bit envious of you.'

'Of *me*?'

'Well, you have this way with men. I've seen you with Sean. I've never had that, partly because of the sheer size of my big breasts, and partly –' She paused and leant forward. Anna smelled the expense of her perfume. '*Partly* because of my background. I don't know if you *know*, but my father tried to kill my mother. And I was verbally abused. That's what led to the suicide attempt.'

'Mmm. I read *Pammy, Unabridged*.' Anna could not bring herself to sound sympathetic. One thing Anna had learned, during her time on the programme, was that no one problem was worse than another. Anna had a right to be heard without interruption from Pammy.

'Oh, thank you sweetie. For buying my book. Thank you.'

Anna did not mention the fact that she had borrowed it from the public library. There was no point, now, in upsetting anyone. She would be leaving in three months. Three. Months.

'So, will you accept my apology?'

'I will accept your apology, but my decision stays the same. I want to leave.'

'It's such a shame,' said Pammy. 'I really was about to create a new position on the programme. Mike and I discussed it. We need a researcher.'

355

'But who would operate?'

'Well, to be truthful, I've *always* wanted Lena to be doing the operator's job. I made no bones about it when they wanted to appoint you; and I might have given you a hard time because of that, at the beginning. But, you know, we're all human,' she said, looking anything but.

'You, of course, are *way* beyond Lena in terms of experience, but that's why I would want you to be a researcher, rather than an operator. You have a good brain. You seem to have grasped our issues very quickly. And coming from a showbusiness background, that's impressive.

'Anyway, I'm still waiting for an OK from Duncan's department, in terms of *funding* this new position. But he was pretty pleased with last month's audience figures, although the breakdown will always upset him. Too many women. Not enough men.'

Generally, thought Anna.

'Generally,' smiled Pammy. 'Well, OK,' she sighed. 'If I can't convince you to change your mind?'

'Sorry.' Anna shook her head. Although why was she always apologising?

'Well, I'll talk to Lena about filling your shoes.'

Anna's mood lifted: she knew that no one would be able to fill her shoes. It was a myth that no one was indispensable. Anna had gone back to the Jimmy Salad show, to collect some books, and she had seen the state of the photocopier, its door swinging open and a sign advertising the words *Copier broken*. Anna knew that all it needed was a change of toner fluid.

'Well, we have three months left to use you,' said Pammy, shifting about in her seat. 'That's your notice period, isn't it?'

'Yes, I think that's right.'

'Don't worry, I won't show your letter to anyone else.'

'Oh, thank you.'

In truth, Anna had written the letter with the hope that it would be made public at Radio Central. She had gone so far as to include criticisms of the recent dash-for-ratings culture at the station; of the new regime under the Fat Controller; and of Radio Central's treatment of canteen serving staff such as Ada.

'What are you going to do with yourself?' asked Pammy, putting Anna's letter back in the envelope, as if it was best forgotten about.

Anna had known that she would be asked this question. Pammy took every opportunity, on her programme, to stress the importance of working full-time. She advertised it as her 'philosophy'. Pammy had written about the need for people to work – she felt that it filled up their time.

'I'm going back into acting. It's what I've always wanted to do.'

'Oh, really? For stage or television?'

'Oh, anything.' Anna was surprised and pleased to learn that she had a choice.

'Well, that sounds great,' said Pammy. But she was looking concerned, as if Anna had written not a resignation letter, but a suicide note. '*Good*.'

Good, because she clearly could not work up the energy to do anything about a member of staff committing professional suicide, particularly if that happened out of office hours.

'I'm looking forward to it,' said Anna, to assuage Pammy's conscience. She was looking forward to being away from work and all the chemical smells of office equipment. She had long known that she was too creative to stand the restrictions of gainful employment. Every day, pressing those same buttons

– A6 for coffee, then a squirt of milk, and an avalanche of sugar.

'Perhaps we can go out for lunch some time?' said Pammy.

'Yes, if you want. That would be nice.' It was always a surprise to see Pammy stand up. Her body was so spongy that it appeared as if she might bounce back down again.

'Because I'd *really* like to pick your brains about Bruce.'

Was that Sean, leaving the building?

Ahead of her, she saw someone, tall and dark and carrying a box, escape through the Radio Central double doors. She ran behind the figure, apologising for bumping into the Fat Controller's stomach on the way. Anna was irritated that other staff were making a leisurely exit from the building, sidling out, just as Sean was leaving her, perhaps forever?

'*Sean*,' she said, at last reaching his side. She sounded slightly breathless. 'I thought it was you.'

Of course, he had said goodbye. But that had been a general farewell, to everyone in the office. Sean had thanked everyone, formally; he had hoped that Pammy and Mike would have him back, as guest presenter. Then, he had added, 'And not forgetting the *support staff* either. Lena, Anna, Todd – thank you.'

'You're not leaving now, are you?' she asked him now, making an effort to sound nonchalant.

He smiled, and ruffled Anna's hair. 'Well, it is going-home time, isn't it?' he asked, looking at his watch.

'Yes, but . . .' She bit her lip, feeling suddenly like a favourite pupil chasing after her teacher on the last day of term.

'School's out for summer,' he said, as if reading Anna's mind. He stretched his long body out. One of the buttons on his shirt was undone, revealing a small patch of white chest, and Anna was suddenly aware that people, passing by, were looking at them curiously. She wished that she was in a position to ask him if they could go somewhere private, and personal, to talk. Preferably, to make love.

But, after just a month, their relationship wasn't strong enough.

'Well, I'm moving into Sebastian's flat tomorrow night,' she said.

'I'm glad that worked out,' he replied, looking over her shoulder. Anna hoped that he hadn't seen someone important, someone he had to talk to.

'Oh, so am I,' she said, about to enthuse.

'He was desperate for someone to look after that sodding cat for him. And it's a good address,' he added, quickly. But it was too late; he had dampened her enthusiasm.

'Yes, you'll have to come round,' she said, realising that he wanted to get away. She was desperate to clutch hold of the cuff of his shirt.

'Oh, er, yes,' Sean said, surprised. 'Yes,' he added, a touch too politely.

'I've just handed in my notice,' she said, trying to engage him.

'Good,' he said, absentmindedly. Then, he took a half-step away, saying, 'Look, I wish you well. *Genuinely*. And, remember, go and see Eileen.' The therapist he had recommended. 'You'll need a lot of support if you're really going to decide to change. Goodbye now.'

Naturally, by that, he must have meant professional support. Anna was still going to be supported by their relationship – wasn't she? Her voice, as she thanked him, shrank smaller and smaller. By the time Sean said goodbye, she was almost whispering.

He turned, and winked, and she saw what might have

been lust cross his face, but was more likely, and knowing her most recent luck, to be fatigue. She tried to smile, as Sean had – as if she had not a care in the world. But, unfortunately, she did care. Anna now realised, from all her reading, that she was one of countless Women Who Care Too Much.

Chapter Fifteen

Until now, Anna had thought that flats such as theirs, filled with damp patches, half-squeezed bottles of self-tanning lotion, torn wallpaper, remote controls, takeaway-food cartons, compilation CDs, and piles of old, curling, listings magazines, were standard living accommodation for single thirtysomethings. But now the junk merely looked infantile.

Myrna, back from her parents' house, and depressed: 'Bloody public transport.'

Anna, disgusted by the family bucket of fried chicken, unopened, on Myrna's lap: 'Why are you in your pyjamas?'

Myrna saying *shit*, the chicken was all over her fingers; Anna saying *yes*, and she had smelt it outside in the communal hallway.

'Yeah, well, I need the calories,' said Myrna, comfort reading *What Katy Did Next*. Whenever she was depressed, she would read children's books. *Claudine at St Clare's. Blubber. Are You There, God, It's Me, Margaret?* She would eat takeaway foods too, bringing home boxes wrapped in white plastic bags. Afterwards, she would leave the empty cartons scattered like Christmas presents around the communal wheelie-bin.

'How's work?' asked Myrna.

'Depressing,' said Anna.

Without Sean in it, the *Problem Call* office seemed empty. Every noise, magnified. All day today, Anna had been irritated by everyone. She had asked Todd to stop typing on his keyboard so heavily. During the Friday morning planning meeting, she had said that Lena's idea was ludicrous. Blonde had agreed with Anna.

Anna had been glad to see Blonde there. Glad, because Blonde had a vague connection with Sean. Perhaps she even shared Anna's grief, now that Sean had left the office?

They certainly seemed to share an admiration for October's guest presenter, Wilhelm Grohe. His *One Month to Happiness* was in the shops, and Grohe was hot property in the media. He was being interviewed everywhere – from the news pages of a national newspaper ('Psychologist discovers new way to happiness') to the features pages of *Potato Weekly* ('Happiness Man likes his potatoes boiled'). Anna was only sorry that she had missed Grohe's daytime TV appearances. She and Blonde were surprised that such a guru in the self-help world would agree to guest-present *Problem Call*.

'Oh, *Wilhelm*,' Pammy had said, dismissively. 'He'll do anything to get on the radio.'

Anna presumed that Pammy was envious of Grohe's media attention. She was excited at the thought of meeting him. But, still, she was mourning the fact that Sean had left *Problem Call*. Sean, with his silky scarf. Sean, with his floppy fringe. All day Anna had thought, *Thank God I'm leaving soon, too.*

'How's your dad?' she asked Myrna, uninterestedly.

'I don't know, to be honest. I'm going back to the madhouse tomorrow; I just came home for some stuff.'

'What exactly is wrong?' asked Anna, impatient because Myrna was always having some sort of a family crisis. She was too attached to her childhood memories, and seemed not to realise that, as an adult, she was grown-up enough to have crises of her own.

'Well, I know it sounds pathetic, but I'm not really sure. No one's answering my questions,' said Myrna. 'Graeme even tried to talk to Dad about it, but . . .'

'Graeme was there?'

'Oh, the whole lot of us. We were *summoned*. Except no one can find Matthew. Last heard from in Bangladesh.'

'Why Bangladesh?'

'Matthew's on his world tour.' Wearily.

'Didn't he go with Mark?'

'No. Mark was home being . . . *Mark*.'

'Oh.'

Anna was surprised to hear that the Twins had two separate identities. Myrna had always talked about them as one. The Twins. They were identical. They had gone to the same school, and to the same university. Matthew and Mark. It was as if it had taken Mr Lomond's illness to differentiate them. Mark and Matthew.

'It's terrifying,' said Myrna, her face soft and pink, like a dessert.

'So it really is serious, then?' confirmed Anna, doubtfully.

Doubtfully, because something serious was always affecting one or other of the Lomonds. One family member would catch a cold and another would suffer the complications. An aunt in Africa would die and Myrna would worry about hereditary conditions. Illness spread like an infection through the Lomonds. There were so many of them. Myrna had thousands of relatives scattered across the globe. They were always reuniting for one reason or another – if only to pass on a new illness.

Anna had only her immediate family. Her mother occasionally mentioned dear and dead, or dreadful and distant aunts, but they were no more than that. Her father had recently cut off his Welsh side. They were all common, he had said – the Potters and the Joneses. Don would use any excuse not to get in touch. He liked none of his sisters. He did not approve of the way they brought up their children or their grandchildren.

'Well, my father wanted us all to go home and stop cluttering up his house,' Myrna continued.

'That sounds more like your dad.'

'Hmmngh. Yes. But I said something about his golf-club collection and he didn't say anything. And you know what he's like. If everything was OK, he'd have said something about my "stupid clever comments".

'Basically, there's something Mum isn't telling us. So we've all been walking on eggshells . . . I've even been trying to be *feminine*, to please Dad. Well, I've been spending a lot of time in the kitchen. Making sandwiches. And we've all been acting as if sod all's going on. Somehow, Dad's illness has become an unmentionable, even though that's why we're all there. Ridiculous, isn't it?'

'Yes,' agreed Anna, firmly. 'I'd say you needed to sit down, as a group of individuals, and talk about it. Discuss your concerns as adults.'

Myrna laughed, long.

'I thought you *knew* my family. Dad's always going on about Graeme's emotions as it is.'

'Well, perhaps that's only because he's unable to express his *own* emotions.'

'No, he just thinks Graeme's feelings are, in some strange way, connected to his sexuality.'

The fact that Graeme was gay bothered Anna. He had been the only male, ever, to have fallen for her in a fantastical way, pursuing her throughout those awkward years. (Thirteen to thirty.) His crush had given her confidence. She had felt like a femme fatale – at least to one man. Until Graeme had come out, last year. Then Anna had merely felt like a gay icon, a suburban Judy Garland.

It had crossed her mind that, had she not rebuffed Graeme, they would be married by now, with two children. Happy. Until, one day, Graeme would tell her, during a trip to a garden centre, that he had always been gay. The absence of breasts on Anna's body had led him to believe that she was, in fact, male. Now, what would they tell their four kids?

'Why don't you go back tonight?' Anna suggested, because if Myrna was out of the way, Anna's move would be less painful – for everybody.

'You are *kidding*? There is no way I'd put myself at risk like that, going on the tube in the dark.' Because the trouble with public transport – according to Myrna – was that it was open to members of the general public.

'By the way, your dad phoned.'

'Yeah, he's helping me move out.'

Her words hung in the air, almost visible.

'He's helping you do *what*?'

'Mmm.' Myrna didn't miss a thing. 'I was about to tell you. I mean, it happened while you were away. I've got this great flat in Chelsea. Rent-free, actually. A friend of Sean's wants a cat-sitter for six months. It's a whole flat,' Anna said. 'One bedroom, or I'd . . .'

'Oh right,' Myrna said, surprised.

365

'Yeah. It's really lovely. You'll like it.' Why was Anna being made to feel as if she was having a secret affair? She would start saying, soon, that Myrna could have half her cutlery collection.

'Sebastian's got most of what he needs in New York, so I'll leave you all my crockery,' she said, instead.

'*Sebastian?*'

'And, if it's all right by you, I think Tom wants to move into my room here.'

'Oh yeah, that'll be fine.' Although Myrna sounded as if Anna was abandoning her to any unknown terrors. '*Sebastian?*' said Myrna, again in disbelief, and as if she didn't know that such aristocratic names could exist.

'He's so beautiful – you wouldn't believe it. So are all his friends.'

'So, Tom doesn't want to move in with you, then. You, and all your "beautiful" new friends?'

'It's not an option.'

'Not pretty enough?'

Clearly, Myrna had not seen Tom today. Otherwise, he would have said that he was moving into Anna's room. He would have explained that they had ended their relationship, almost amicably. They had both moved on. Anna would, no doubt, soon start sleeping with Sean.

Tom would eventually find happiness too.

Anna wondered vaguely whether Tom would find happiness with Myrna, and felt uncomfortable at the thought. She changed the subject.

'I'm er actually moving out tonight. Actually. He's left the cat . . .' She had every right.

'And were you planning on telling me?' Myrna shook her head, repeatedly. She started to read *What Katy Did Next* again, with a new passion. It was as if, between those

366

pages, there lay a moral code she could understand. Katy would never betray Clover in this way.

'Of course I was. I had to take it now, that's all.' Did Myrna not understand that Anna could not go on like this: sharing a kitchen, a boyfriend, and a microwave oven? Having to listen to Myrna's radio programmes for minority audiences. Checking whether Myrna wanted to watch the other side before settling in front of the television. She had never liked the way Myrna stacked the dishwasher. Higgledy-piggledy. The knives in the glass holder.

'Well, my dad'll be pleased,' said Myrna at last, trying to laugh.

'Why?'

'Well, I'm finally living with a *man*. Although, naturally, Dad'd prefer it to be in *sin*. He'd think it more feminine. Maybe I'll lie and pretend that Tom's my boyfriend – bring him back with me. Mind you, knowing my father, he'd manage to find something wrong – even with Tom.'

'Yeah. He'd say Tom was common.'

'Tom's hardly *common*.'

'Anyway, I'll still come round all the time. If you'll let me in.' Anna laughed, knowing that this flat, with its peeling, papered, walls and its brothel-like double beds, had let anyone in. Even the quality fruiterer, and Bryan-with-a-Y.

'You can come here for sex with Tom,' said Myrna, thoughtfully. 'And supper.'

'Yeah,' Anna said, convincing no one. 'I mean, the only real difference is that I'll have a Jacuzzi bath and clean carpets.'

She was making light of it. Yet Anna hoped that her life would change inside Sebastian's flat. She hoped even to find a new set of friends to match the cream sofa. 'And an egg basket,' she added, sounding more serious. 'And an ice dispenser.' *Sean*, she was thinking. Absorbed into Sean's life, Anna would have no further need of her own.

'Well, I suppose things can't stay the same forever,' said Myrna.

'No.'

'Although I've never been able to work out why not.'

'Yeah, it's been fun,' Anna said, knowing that they had never had 'fun' – as flatmates should. Exercising, say, in front of the television, or discussing one's career concerns over cookie-dough ice-cream.

Fun for Myrna lay in realising that she could be 'a lot worse off'. She had often comforted herself with the fact that she could be holed up in some Bombay brothel, for example, or kept hostage in Lebanon.

Myrna had a way of accentuating the negative. Grohe had written in Chapter Fourteen: *Surround yourself with driven people. It can only rub off on you. Negative people have a negative effect*. That was why Anna was moving out. That, and the cream carpets and the Jacuzzi bath. Sean.

Sean and Anna could have sex on that deep carpet. Although they would have to be careful about spillage; the sex would need to occur without any exchange of bodily fluids.

No, they would have sex on that narrow bed, piled with pillows and foreign bedspreads, like some exotic, raspberry dessert. Certainly, Anna could not imagine Sean in her bed at 113B Finchley Road. He was far too clean to lie there, amid those greying, stained sheets. He would look altogether incongruous in this flat, like Harrison Ford walking in on a Mike Leigh film-set. The living room was stained with nicotine. The carpet did not even match the curtains.

Sean would be a mismatch too far, sitting there, sex

itself. What would he have to say to Myrna? His own friends formed such a good-looking group – all of them with educated accents. No trace of northern, à la Tom.

'I suppose I ought to go and pack.'

'It's only that this all seems so hurried.' Myrna looked suddenly worried.

'Yes, I'm sorry I couldn't let you know sooner. But, you know how it is . . .'

'Of *course*,' Myrna said politely.

'I hope you're not too upset.'

'No, I'm fine,' said Myrna, holding her bucket of chicken like a hot-water bottle against her stomach. 'Thank you.'

Her father found the steps leading up to Sebastian's house difficult, what with his back and Anna's heavy stereo equipment. He had had to stop for breath, and it was then that he saw a woman at the window of her basement flat, gesturing.

'Ah, your new neighbour, Anna,' said Don, unzipping the front of his jacket in case they were introduced. The woman appeared outside and Don smiled, wiping the sweat from his hair.

'What's happening here?' It became clear that the woman thought they were stealing stereo equipment. But, with a quick flicker of the left eye, she took in Anna's possessions and knew that there was nothing there worth stealing.

In that case, what is going on? her right eye said.

'Everything's fine, thank you,' said Anna, with some assertion. 'I'm moving into Sebastian Landsman's flat.'

'On the ground floor?' It was clear that the woman did not approve of Sebastian. She nodded, without smiling, and disappeared seconds later.

Don said that that was a pity: he was sure that he recognised the woman from the Southern Region Policy Committee's steering group. Her father seemed to shrink into his soft-leather jacket at the woman's snub. Even as they moved the last of Anna's boxes into the flat, he was still saying that the woman should have given him a chance to introduce himself properly.

Don liked the feel of Sebastian's flat. He admired the books that Sebastian had left, lined up on the shelf. He liked the fact that they all, all of them, appeared to have been read. Don picked up one of them – *Emotional Intelligence* – and flicked through, as if deeply interested. Yes, he liked the sound of this chap, Sebastian.

Very few of Don's books at home had been read. He had always hidden Barbara's Danielle Steels and Mills & Boons whenever anyone 'important' visited the house. Anna remembered one embarrassing incident when a Conservative Party chairman had wandered out of the guest living room, finding the TV room and Barbara's stack of romantic novels, shoved down the back of the sofa. 'Your sort of book, Don?' he had asked, coming back in with one of them, and breaking out into loud, windy laughter.

Anna eyed the cat. It had crept in from the other room, the bell around its neck tinkling.

Don put the book back in its place on the shelf, slowly, carefully. Anna had seen him behave like this in the homes of important, so-called friends. He acted like a boy just out of short socks, admiring. It was as if someone might find out, at any moment, that his father had been a builder, and his mother a cleaning-woman.

'Anna, your mum's in a bad way.'

'Mum?'

Usually, it was Your Mother, and then only to complain

to Anna about the money Barbara spent on unnecessaries, such as fancy cakes. Could Anna tell Your Mother that he was retired and couldn't afford to finance her knick-knacks? Barbara was always quick to retaliate. Could Anna tell Your Father that he made too much noise coming in from the Conservative Club?

'Yes,' said Don, drawing a dramatic amount of breath. 'A terrible way. Apparently you had words.' He sat down gently on the sofa, as if he had no right to be there. 'She isn't feeling . . .'

'And you *care*?' Anna asked with a sneer, because he had not cared – not since Anna was under-age, and on camping holidays. No, it was all Your Mother, and then to complain about the way she spent his money on luxuries such as chocolate éclairs.

There had been a time when they bought things together. Murano glass, for example. Anna's Raleigh bicycle.

But Anna had failed a) to pass her cycling proficiency test and b) to save her parents' marriage. The day she had failed to cycle straight through hoops was the day Anna had come home to discover, from her mother, that her father had been having an affair with *Catherine*, the Conservative candidate.

Since then the relationship had gone downhill. Anna's parents had tried to start again, with a second honeymoon, but two years later, Don had moved into the spare room.

He had made that room his sanctuary. It had started to look, in fact, like his constituency office, with maps and signed, framed photographs of Margaret Thatcher, staring down at Don through glass. Barbara's room, by contrast, began to look like a fifties teenager's bedroom, with flowered divans and limited-edition dolls fluffed out in frilly dresses.

Anna had started sixth form at secondary school. Don had begun to spend a lot of his time at the Conservative Club. Barbara had said that she didn't mind *where* Don ate, as long as he funded her librarian training. But by then, she had started to see that there was more to life than washing her husband's underpants.

That was when she had taken an interest in the garden. After Anna had left home, to go to Arndale. Barbara had said that there was not enough to do, otherwise. Don had retired, in order to spend more time with his party. He arranged rallies and dinner dances, never tiring of telling Anna all about it, years later, over lunch at Radio Central. Barbara, Anna only ever saw in the home.

Don saw the family home as a 'project'. He would spend all his time in the house, either in his own room, or up a ladder, re-decorating. Whenever he was in the house, he was 're-modernising', ripping off wallpaper, and painting, or scraping off paint, and wallpapering. There were always jobs to be done; cupboards to paper, and screws to inject.

By the time Anna had finished at Arndale, her parents shared very little. They shared their home, of course (although Don cared only about the house, and Barbara about the garden). They shared Anna; and they shared their finances. Or, rather, Don's savings. He had cut his wife's housekeeping money. Well, he ate out all the time anyway – at the club. And Barbara earned enough from her job at the local library to buy what Don called 'frills'.

Yet despite all of this, her parents had remained committed to the concept of marriage. In Barbara's day, as she never tired of telling Anna, one did not divorce purely because a marriage had ended. One stayed married. In Don's opinion,

372

as he never tired of telling Anna, a marriage was for life, not simply for one's salad days.

So, they shared married life. *If you call that life*, thought Anna.

'I do care,' said Don, thinking for a moment. 'Of course I care,' he confirmed, seconds later. 'We were together more than forty years. Living together in Llandudno Cottage, anyway.'

He said 'Llandudno Cottage' with such sadness. Anna was surprised to hear him use the name that was on the peeling wooden plaque, half-hanging from the basket of flowers in the porch. Her parents had named their home thus after a shop, where they had bought supplies during a camping holiday in Wales.

But Anna had not heard her father use the name, Llandudno Cottage – not in years. He had always said 'Number 6' or, if he felt it was in need of re-decoration – which was most of the time – 'that house'.

Don breathed in heavily, and looked around Anna's living room as if glad that his daughter was, finally, making something of herself. He himself appreciated the finer things in life. Cut glass from Murano. Carved wooden birds.

'If you call that living together,' Anna said, cruelly.

'Well, we're not living together any *more*,' said Don, as if making a point of fact. He coughed, lightly.

'What?'

'I'm living with Catherine, actually. In her flat. Your mum should have . . . Just days.' He cleared his throat. '*Ahem*. Yes. Catherine.'

Anna loathed that name. *Catherine*. It conjured up images of stiff, middle-aged women in suits having sexual relations with old men like her father. Women who made speeches

373

saying that there was no such thing as society. Preaching that all mothers should stay at home with their children. Meantime, making off with their fathers.

'Catherine?'

The name made Anna think of cycling proficiency tests and days she would rather forget. Days when she had returned to find her home ransacked, her father's important papers flying around her mother's garden. She had not heard the name mentioned since then. But she had heard it enough during that period to last her a lifetime.

'Not *her*?'

'It's best this way. It's the answer to our problems. Silly to . . .'

'You mean, all this time you've been with *Catherine*?' Since Anna had turned teenager? She felt white.

'No.' Slowly. 'You know I made a promise about that. It was only when you moved away, to that poly.'

'That was your chance, was it?'

'I admit there didn't seem much reason. To be at home. Your mother had her own interests, anyway. The garden. Elaine. All those years, trying, keeping up a show . . . Once you'd left home . . . it didn't feel worth it any more. Your mother's menopause.'

'You're blaming Mum's menopause for your typical, fucking, *male* . . .'

'No blame, Anna. No blame.' His hands raised in surrender. 'I don't think your mum blames me *or* Catherine any more. Malcolm. No one's to blame.'

'Who the fuck's *Malcolm*?'

'Catherine's ex-husband.' He thought for a second, visibly cheered, and said, 'You'd like him, actually. He works for British Telecom.'

'I don't *want* to like him. Oh, so Catherine was married

374

then, was she? No wonder you couldn't run off with her when I was a kid.'

'That *wasn't* the reason. I had no intention of leaving Your Mother for Catherine. I didn't even think of leaving her until last week. I didn't *want* to leave, even then.' Such soap-opera language. He would announce soon that she had an illegitimate brother called Sean Harrison.

'I didn't know she was married.'

'Well, that was why there was all that *hoo*-ha, Anna. That was why Catherine was deselected. Fine for a man, but . . . You see, *there*'s your feminist principles for you.'

'So, did you have to get rid of Malcolm first? Where's Malcolm now? Under some patio somewhere?'

'A joke. Good. A joke,' Don said, sadly. 'No, Catherine moved away after all that business. She's only now starting to work her way back up the party.'

'*Worm* her way back in.'

'She gave up a lot for me. Everyone knows she could have been another Maggie. Or at least a Gillian Shephard.'

'Well, what a *waste*.'

'All those years apart. She missed the party.'

'*And* you, presumably?' Sarcasm, sarcasm.

'Not as much, no. But we neither of us had anything. I hadn't had anything with Your Mother for years.'

'By that, I take it you mean sex?' She noticed that Don was back to Your Mother.

'Sex. Conversation. You.'

She felt uncomfortable. Did he have to place Anna so near to the word 'sex'?

Don clearly felt uncomfortable too – at his daughter confirming her savvy of the word 'sex'. He stood up and walked again to the bookshelf, running his fingers down the spine of *A History of the Conservative Party*.

'It's not as though we didn't try. We had that second honeymoon, and the third. One after that. Always arguing. She devoted her life first to having you, then to being with you. It's not natural, Catherine says.'

'I think you'll find it *is*,' said Anna, wondering whether she had always been the glue, sticking her family together. Once she had argued with her mother, the three of them so naturally fell apart, falling into different families.

'No. She'd have you in her bed. We'd never . . . Talk. Although you can do without even that after a while.'

'But what about Mum? Did you think about her in all this? I doubt *she* wants to separate.'

Her mother needed to be married, Anna knew that. She could not let go. She was like that; she hated to throw anything away, hanging on to old dishcloths until they shrunk and stank and dissolved in the sink. She had kept Anna's baby-clothes warm in the hot-press, folded and ironed. She had in her cupboard foodstuffs that were years past their sell-by date. In suitcases, in the spare room, Barbara had stored almost all of her daughter's fashion mistakes, including Anna's red leg-warmers, the purple puffball dress, the bright blue pixie boots, the tan needlecord trousers.

Barbara could not bear waste, and had kept hold of a husband for decades, despite his intellectual arrogance, his obvious irritation with her, and his other, cleverer, woman.

'Well, things couldn't go on forever like that,' said Don, and Anna thought *why not?* knowing that her mother was happy. She was happy with her library job, and her gossiping with Elaine, her garden, and her husband, far away; and that Don, too, was happy – with his politics and his home, which he had 're-modernised' himself, presently in magnolia and lemon.

376

'But why move out *now*? I mean, why not five years ago? Why not years ago?'

'Because, when I went home last week, after you'd left, I heard your mum crying. Crying. Yes.' He cleared his throat. It was as if Don was ill-prepared to say the word *crying*.

'I was about to go upstairs,' he said, 'because you know I'm – I *was* – putting in some new strobe lighting upstairs . . .' He stopped and looked bereft for a moment. It was as if Don was wondering where he was.

'Anyway, I couldn't bear that. I went in, and stood by the door, and Barbara kept on *crying*, which isn't like her, is it? Always that stern face. You know, ever since . . . She's hated to show weakness in front of me; and I don't blame her really.

'She sat there, in tears, and said, "I'm a terrible mother, aren't I? It's the only thing I've ever wanted to do . . . It's the only thing I've ever done, and I'm bad at it."

'Well, I couldn't *bear* that,' went on Don, playing with a zip on his jacket. 'Because, if anything, I've always been in *awe* of the way Barbara was with you. You *always* went to her. It was you two against me, and me trying to show you my world.' He paused, and digressed: 'You know what I'd have loved? If you'd have wanted to be in politics. Been a Maggie type, wanting to please her father, and good at education . . .'

'*Dad*,' she said, because Anna was able to articulate her feelings now. 'Please don't try and realise your dreams through me. I can't . . .'

'So, I listened to Barbara going on like this,' interrupted Don. 'And I couldn't bear it – her saying, "She dislikes me, you know. It's as if she's finally seen through me and realised something that I've known all along . . ."'

'What was that?' asked Anna, dully.

377

'Oh, that she didn't deserve a child. That God, or whoever knew about these things, had made a mistake and had given her a baby by accident. A child that she couldn't look after . . .'

'She should view things in the proper perspective,' said Anna, trying to think of Sean's response, presented with this situation. 'A child isn't a gift. I was a *person*, with needs and feelings of my own.'

'Well, we talked,' said Don, firmly. 'And it all came out. She told me about you. Walking out like that. You being her life. I said you'd be back, and we discussed everything. You. Me. Catherine.'

'Well, that's good.'

It was good, and even if it wasn't, Anna was not going to respond to her thoughts. *Why can't you be happy together, like Myrna's parents?* She allowed that thought bubble to float away.

'I'm glad you're finally talking openly about your problems,' said Anna, soberly.

'Of course, Barbara said that she'd known. About Catherine. For over a year now. Put it out of her mind, like she does. Elaine saw us together, laughing.'

Anna could imagine Elaine Quealy passing on gossip like that. 'I saw them *laughing*,' she would have told Barbara. 'In broad daylight.'

'I think that, once she'd admitted that she knew about *Catherine*, something had to happen. Your mum's a proud woman,' he said, proudly; and then he looked sad again. 'Once she'd said that she knew, the marriage was over. It couldn't go on. Not now that *I* knew that she knew, if you know what I mean. I said I'd tell Catherine that our friendship had to end. But Barbara said no, she wasn't having that. It was as if she'd seen the light, she said.'

'You see,' said Anna, trying to make sense of her own emotions. 'My *conversation* with Mum might have been painful at the time, but it made her strong enough to tell you that she'd had enough of . . .'

'But she wasn't strong,' said Don, helplessly. 'It was as if she'd fallen apart, Anna. I didn't know her, not at all. It wasn't just the crying. It was as if the bones had been taken out of her body. She looked . . . *empty*.'

'But you talked?' persisted Anna.

'She stopped crying, and we talked . . .'

'You see, you talked. Good.'

'Yes, we talked. She was all cold, and hard, saying that I had to move out, although I was in the middle of that lighting job. But she said she wanted a divorce. I argued against that, of course.' He drew himself up. 'You know my opinion about marriage and family. I'm a member of the Conservative family campaign group, you know.'

'I know,' she said, wearily. Suddenly, he looked as if he might cry.

But he didn't cry, swallowing hard, and smiling.

'But I couldn't argue with . . . She was so different, that day. She's been so different, ever since that day. She even emptied my room out. All of my important memorandums, and party information, into a suitcase. *Boxes.* I was so angry then, it felt as if it wasn't just me being thrown out; it was all *memory* of me . . . And I moved into Catherine's.'

He looked away, as if trying to control any tears.

'I've had to sort out all of that stuff now, anyway. I've thrown most of it away. It did make me realise that a lot of it was useless . . .' He smiled, weakly.

'Why have you had to throw it away?'

She wondered why her father wasn't happy, even now.

'Well, Catherine's is a bit of a squeeze. She lives in a tiny

379

space, but we'll see . . . And there's no room for improvement, at all. Catherine said that, and I agree, of course.
Nothing to be done, not even shelves put up, because it's
all quite, sort of, perfect. You know, she has three children
of her own. All grown-up, like you. I don't know if it'll
work out. I think I get on her nerves actually.' He laughed,
miserably. 'Even after a week. Well, we're none of us young
any more, are we?'

'Well, I don't know about *you* . . .' Anna joked. (She was
able to joke.)

Happy people are always laughing, wrote Wilhelm Grohe.

She looked at her father and at his soft tan leather jacket,
with long pockets and zips in unexpected places. 'Aren't you
going to take off your coat?' Anna asked him, realising that
at least he was talking to her. She was all grown-up, and no
longer a burden. No longer a problem.

Anna had learned enough about people, in the last few
weeks, to know that Don had found the solution to his own
problem: what to do with his first family. Indeed, without
Barbara on his mind, he seemed easier, breezier. He even
wore his shirt open at the top.

Anna knew that he would not have undone those two
buttons lightly. No doubt, Catherine was behind the shift
in style. 'Undo your top button, Don,' she would have said.
'And wear that casual jacket we bought. Appearances are
everything in politics.'

('Oh yes. Forgot I was wearing this,' he would have
replied.)

Her parents' marriage had been over years ago. Her mother
and father had just to accept that now, as fact. As Grohe had
said – and in this he was supported by Denvil George – it
was simple to distance oneself from a situation. All Anna
had to do was to remember that she was no longer a child,

still at school. To remember that she had problems enough of her own.

'Are you happy now, Dad? With Catherine?' asked Anna, determined to sound adult.

'Oh, happy? What *is* happy?' he asked, irritably. And, suddenly: 'I miss Llandudno Cottage. I liked living at Number 6.' He sounded like a spoiled child who was about to kick out, at the furniture. 'I was doing a lot of re-modernising there, as you know. And I think I upped the value of it . . .'

'And couldn't you have worked out a way to stay?' asked Anna, in a sugary voice, aware that she sounded like Pammy. But she was trying to distance herself from what was essentially (surely?) her parents' problem.

'Well, once we'd talked . . . Apparently, you'd told Barbara that it was better to talk, to bring things out into the open . . . ?'

'Well, yes. But what are you trying to say – that I was responsible for your marriage breaking down . . . ?'

'Well, hardly, Anna,' said Don, amused by that.

'I mean, for you leaving?'

Don sighed, deeply. 'If you could go and see your mum?' he asked, changing the subject. 'Catherine's worried she might have a nervous breakdown. She saw Barbara shopping. Buying expensive ready meals. She looked – Catherine says – as if she was about to faint.'

'Well, there are organisations that can help her.'

The world was in fact full of publicly funded bodies, set up specifically to support people in need. It was only a matter of Anna's mother finding the right telephone-helpline number.

'If she's lonely, she should call Home Alone,' decided Anna. 'They help people like Mum – people who made the mistake of devoting their lives to their children rather than having a life of their own. She can get the number from her local authority Social Services division.'

'I can't imagine Barbara phoning an organisation. Barbara's too shy to complain about service in a restaurant.' Don laughed, warmly. 'That's one of the reasons I fell in love with her, all those years ago. D'you know that?' he asked, as if surprised himself. 'She was so shy. Always apologising, for being alive. I loved that,' he said. 'That modesty.' Then, Don rallied himself, clearing his throat. 'Catherine, of course, says that women like Barbara make life harder for career women, like herself. You know, she finds Barbara irksome.'

Only her father would use words such as 'irksome'. He used redundant words such as 'irksome', 'beverage', and 'beaker'.

'Well, if she wants support, there are organisations out there,' said Anna, briskly. 'Anyway, I'm glad you've sorted things out. I'm going to look round the flat,' she said, standing up, and trying to remember her excitement.

Indeed, the flat was still bright, but each room was different without Sebastian's things.

The bed looked bereft without Sebastian's Indian-red bedspread, studded with glass eyes. It seemed strangely naked, trying to cover itself up with a slip of a sheet. Without those pillows, piled high, it could just as easily have been one of her parents' beds. New, and as if the plastic had recently been ripped off. Without Sebastian's bedspread and pillows, the bed bounced firm. It was as if it hadn't seen any movement for near-on thirty years.

Anna could not wait to see her new clothes hanging in that wardrobe. The floaty, white-linen skirt. The tight yellow tartan trousers. The red slip of a dress. As Karl Benson had written, *You don't wear your clothes. Your clothes wear you.*

The bathroom was the same, thank God. Sterile and clean. Spitting foamy water with the Jacuzzi tap turned on. Anna had brought with her only a handful of bathroom products. They were in one of the black bin-bags.

She had left behind the 'lilac meadow' body-spray which stank like a flower-patterned bedsheet in an old people's home. She had binned those dried-up moisturisers. The disposable razors that she had been using for years. The deep-cleansing shampoo, designed to give back hair its natural body and salon bounce. Because, despite regular use of the product, Anna's hair had very little body. Rarely, if ever, did it bounce.

Back in the living room, she silently thanked Sebastian for leaving behind his books. They gave the place some atmosphere; and Anna could not help herself – she opened the cupboard, to check that the TV was still inside.

She switched it on but found it difficult to watch, its picture obscured by the swinging doors, desperate to shut. What a disappointment. Even the stereo did not look the same without his CDs, all of them still in their boxes.

'I'm a fanatic about that,' Sebastian had said.

He had left just one behind. Beethoven's Piano Sonatas. Anna pushed it inside the CD tray and went into the kitchen, surprising her father, who jumped back from the waste-disposal unit. There was an empty fridge and several wire egg baskets. (There were no eggs.) 'I'd offer you a cup of tea, but I forgot to bring anything . . .' Anna said, opening a cupboard to find it full of cat food.

'Just having a look,' Don said, straightening up. 'It seems to have the works,' he added, unnecessarily. She looked back to find a full-length mirror, oddly placed against the kitchen door. It made her appear grey. Washed-out.

'Don't worry,' said Don, catching her expression. 'You don't look like that.'

They heard music coming from the living room. The Beethoven CD began. 'This is nice. Very good as background,' said Don, although Anna could not help but think it the sedative sort of sound that would be played in a high-security mental institution.

It hid the noise of the boiler, however. Anna had not previously noticed that *burrr*. With Sebastian, and Sean, and friends, and wine, all she had heard was laughter, and the delicious sound of Sebastian's bread machine kneading.

'I'll just take a look at that sound,' said Don, who was good at fixing things. 'I'm sure it's nothing,' he said, as Anna led him to the utility room, which contained one broken-down washing machine.

Inside the boiler cupboard was a can of beer, dribbling foam, and a discarded cheese sandwich shaking with shock on top of the boiler. 'Not very happy, this one,' said Don, inspecting the old-fashioned water-heater. 'Hmmngh,' he said, looking at some switches next to it.

'I expect you'll be all right tonight,' Don said, at last. 'But I'd call someone tomorrow. It might need changing.'

They went back into the living room. Anna was afraid that Don would say that he was going. She didn't want to be alone in a new flat with an angry boiler. At any minute, it might explode.

'Well, I'd better be . . .' Don fingered the collar of his leather jacket.

'Oh, please don't go . . . yet,' Anna said, kneeling beside a cardboard box. He hesitated, perhaps remembering the damage he had done to Anna in her childhood.

384

'OK,' he said, as if aware of his responsibilities.

She felt dependent again. Outside this house, Anna had felt so adult. She had achieved this flat without any help. How happy she had been, staring up at the sheer height of her townhouse-to-be. Well, as happy as one could be, lugging heavy boxes. She was to live among the best that money could buy. Thick carpets and picture-rails.

Now she noted the dark stains where furniture had been moved. Anna felt as if she had failed.

She had often wished that there was an outside body like the International Monetary Fund that could determine whether an individual was a success or not. She now realised that there was indeed such a body – and it was called Don Potter. Don, who was looking at her as if she had failed him.

'It'll feel more like your old home with everything unpacked,' he said, disappointedly, sitting down, more comfortably now. He had always been more comfortable around failure. 'Those stains won't show when you've got your own things out,' he added, just in case his daughter thought that she had fooled him into thinking of her as a success.

The cat smiled, curling up against the television cupboard.

'I'm glad we've talked,' Anna said, unhappily.

'Oh, so am I.'

'It's good that we're talking as two adults.'

'Oh? Oh yes.'

'That – as adults – we have a right to make and live with our own decisions.'

'Good. Absolutely.' He shifted about, uncomfortable again. 'So, how's work then, anyway?' Something that interested him.

'I'm leaving *Problem Call*,' Anna said, trying to breathe naturally.

'You're leaving *Problem Call*?' He leaned forward, eagerly. 'Well, that is a . . . What are you going on to? I *said* that that would be a good move. A *stepping* stone . . .'

'Well, no. Actually, I've decided to go into acting again.'

'Acting?' Had Don misheard? Might Anna have actually said the Foreign Office?

'Yes.'

She had dreaded the moment.

Don had a habit of arranging everyone he knew in a hierarchy. He would place them on a ladder, in order of importance. Actresses and suchlike fell at the bottom of his career ladder. The market was everything. Most so-called actresses didn't earn a decent wage. Waitresses, the lot of them. Not what Don would call decent, anyway. As far as Don was concerned, there was only room for one Judi Dench. The rest were all former pornographic 'stars'. Prostitutes, the lot of them.

Anna had dreaded seeing that look of disappointment on his face. That look that clouded her every career move. Don had risen above his background: why couldn't Anna? His father had been a minor clerk somewhere. Whereas Don had been a civil engineer. In his spare time, he was an agent for a major political party. Was Anna intent on dragging them back down again? Back down to the Joneses of this world?

'You want to be an actress?' he asked, as if the idea might only just have occurred to her.

'That's right. I've handed in my notice.'

'So, why did you say . . . ?' (Low, shallow breaths.)

'I'll go to open auditions. There's one I've seen advertised in *The Stage* for a play that's going to the Edinburgh Festival.'

'I haven't heard of . . . Did you say *The Stage*?'

'Yes.'

'Or these festivities?'

'Festival. You must have heard of the Edinburgh Festival . . . ?'

'So, what sort of *acting* will you be doing?' He seemed to want to cry.

'It's something I want to do,' said Anna, feebly. 'And you should respect that.'

He paused, struggling for words.

'No, I'm sorry, Anna,' he said, at last. 'But I can't let you do this. It's a competitive world out there, and you're giving up years of experience for something silly.'

'I'm not listening, Dad. I'm sorry that you feel unable to support me in this. But this has always been my vocation. And I need to start living out my *own* fantasies, rather than those of other people. I'm happy for you to move in with Catherine. If that's what makes you happy, then I'm pleased for you . . .'

Don looked anxious.

'I worry about this,' he said. 'I don't think *acting* will make you ha . . .'

'Well, I don't think you should be worrying about me any more.' Gently. 'Full-stop. I'm thirty-one, and no fool. My decision is my decision. It shouldn't affect you, or my mother. It shouldn't affect *anyone*, except me.'

'But you'll be losing all you've worked for, at Radio Central.'

'Maybe, but I've never been happy there, Dad. Was I? Really? I'm not happy.'

'We're none of us *happy*.'

'Dad, I have very low self-esteem. This is my way of confronting my problems head-on. If I am doing something I want to do, I will be . . .'

'What are you talking about? You have a solid CV. Your boss said that you'll be able to do some research, didn't she? All you have to do is . . .'

'Dad, *please*,' she interrupted, clearly and firmly. 'I'm not listening.'

She was too tired to unpack, although Don had left an hour ago. Boxes sat there, hestitating, as if undecided as to whether to go or stay. Anna still had not made herself comfortable. Instead, she had used the time usefully – to finish Wilhelm Grohe. *Happiness is more than just a state of mind*, he concluded, *it's a whole new way of life*.

She thought of her inconclusive conversation yesterday, with Sean, and decided to ring him. Anna had taken his home telephone number from the card index at work, where Sean Harrison had been filed under Closure.

Well, she wanted hers.

That was what Anna thought as she dialled his number. That, and that a single, tiny phone call wouldn't hurt anyone. Except perhaps herself. The receiver had crumbs on it. She heard Sean say, 'Hello?', and realised that he sounded busy, and as if she had interrupted him working or, worse still, in bed with Blonde.

'Is that Sean?' Anna asked, confidently and calmly. In control.

'Speaking.'

'Oh, I'm sorry to bother you, but it's Anna. I've just moved into Sebastian's flat and I was wondering . . .'

'*Anna*,' he interrupted, at last. But it was as if he had only just realised who she was. 'Anna the Operator?'

'Well . . .'

That threw her. She did not like the sound of herself. Anna the Operator. Was *that* how he saw her?

'Anna the Actress now,' she smiled, hoping that the conversation could be salvaged. She half-kicked off her right shoe. It dangled from her foot.

'Is everything OK with the flat? I thought you'd sorted everything out with Sebastian. Oh, for *God's* sake. I hope he's not messed you about. I haven't got the time to go acting as Sebastian's landlord. Why the *fuck* doesn't he get his life straightened out? Pissing off to New York and leaving a mess with women. And now the flat . . .' He tailed off.

She scratched her eczema, wondering whether to tell Sean about the old boiler.

'No, I just phoned for a chat,' she said, unhappily, hoping that that would straighten things out. Sean's voice could return to normal. Their relationship could resume where it left off.

'Oh.'

'I thought, as we're *neighbours* . . .'

'Oh dear. Listen . . .'

'I really need to talk to you about my father, to be honest. I've just confronted him with . . .'

'Anna. I'm *very* busy. I'd love to talk to you at length, but I'm starting at *The Shelley Show* on Monday and I need to think about my script. So . . .'

'I'm sorry. I just wanted to . . .'

'Well, there's no need to apologise. It's *only* that I'm busy. I *know* that you read too much into casual relationships . . . Look, do talk to Eileen about your father. Really, she doesn't charge much by the hour. I honestly have to go. I need Monday to go well. I just don't have the time to talk, what with Shelley and . . .'

'I thought you loathed everything about the *The Shelley Show*?'

'They've improved the format and introduced more . . .'

But I don't need to make excuses to you, or to anyone. It pays my bills.'

'You're kidding, aren't you?'

'Please, Anna. I'm really very busy.' He lowered his voice to a whisper. 'And my *girlfriend*'s here.' (Blonde?)

'Oh, fuck you.'

Now she wanted a cigarette.

Chapter Sixteen

The therapist had a strong New York accent, which did not help. Anna felt as if she had turned up in a Woody Allen film by mistake. She would have flashbacks at any moment. Either that, or one of Myrna's relatives would appear, writ large, in an image on the ceiling.

'*So*,' said Eileen Weiszfeld. 'Thank you for being so clear. I appreciated the full and frank way you explained your feelings about Sean Harrison.'

'Yes. But that all happened months ago. As I said, I haven't seen him since – only his girlfriend. She works in my office.'

'That must be *very* painful for you,' said Eileen, concerned.

'No, not at all. Or rather, it was at first. But I don't feel like that now. I mean, I know that they were useless, childish emotions. As Sean actually said – although I wasn't able to understand, when he said it – I read too much into casual relationships. But, since then, I've been trying to distance myself from people.'

'Good, good,' said Eileen, absentmindedly. 'Well . . . This first session is actually now over, but we can talk about that next week – should you decide to continue. That, and your relationship with your parents. Which, incidentally, I do feel is the key.'

'Do you think you can help me?'

'Well,' said Eileen, sighing, and crossing pretty hands on her lap. 'I don't pretend to offer you a *panacea*. Therapy can't do that.'

'Thank you,' said Anna, picking up her pen. She would not return.

What she wanted was a panacea.

It was Christmas, and cold. Only the shops were warm, and selling everything ready-wrapped. 113B looked seasonal enough. Snow-spray, fresh from a can, melted on some window-panes. Smoke rose from a patch of black rubbish on the grass. It was the season to burn household rubbish. Empty takeaway cartons piled high, gift-like, around the green dustbin. From a distance, Anna could hear the sounds of small children. *Fuck you, shitface.*

The house had been sloppily painted brick-brown. There were drips everywhere, stalagtites under window-sills.

Anna rang the bell for B, which now read *Myrna and Tom*. She winced. They sounded so right together – Myrna and Tom. Reading their names, coupled like that, confirmed one of Anna's fears: that, surely, her ex-flatmate was sleeping with her ex-boyfriend?

A voice came through the intercom, saying, 'No – I don't need anything.'

'Myrna, it's Anna.'

'Potter Anna?'

'Yes. Let me in, it's freezing out here.'

The front door buzzed off its latch. Anna stood in the warmth of the communal hallway, waiting for Myrna to unlock the door. The sounds of those street-children had justified their installation, last year, of three locks, clipped to the door, like the ones on Myrna's bras, and just as impenetrable.

Anna hadn't been inside this hallway in months. For old times' sake, she rifled through the post, and found four bills addressed to her, as well as a pile of loudly coloured junk-mail, just as the door opened. Myrna appeared, a mess of curls, like Stig of the Dump.

'Did you forget something?' Myrna asked. Politely.

'I've brought your hat-stand,' said Anna, putting it down. It was heavy. 'Apparently, you wanted it.'

'Oh, thanks,' said Myrna, picking up the hat-stand as if it weighed nothing. She took it inside, leaving the door open.

Anna followed her through, hearing the tranquillising sounds of daytime television. Shelley, saying, *'Some people would say that couples always argue. What makes this particularly good television, sorry, interesting, sorry, awful is that it's . . .'*

'Oh, *The Shelley Show*,' she said, enjoying being back in the living room. Anna had missed the smell of the old sofa, and Myrna's plants, huge and unruly. 'So, what's the new format like?'

'Same old, same old,' muttered Myrna, snuggling back in her seat, under her duvet. Anna sat down, too, and picked up a leafy-green Christmas card.

Dear Myrna, Thank you for your letter. Seasonal greetings. Love . . . (Love, the daughter of a serial killer.)

'And who's Shelley talking to today?' asked Anna.

'A woman who's tired of being used like a puppet by her husband. Or can't you read?' said Myrna, tartly. The strap-line below the TV woman said, *Charmaine – tired of being used like a puppet by her husband*.

'I'm glad you're in, anyway,' said Anna, smelling old smells. 'That hat-stand was hard to carry across London.'

'Well, I'm sorry you had to come north,' said Myrna, tartly. 'Although, when am I ever out?'

'Weren't you going to be doing a teacher-training course . . . ?' she said, trying to meet Myrna's eyes.

'Not until September. Next academic year.'

'Oh, right.'

'I thought you were *acting*?'

'Mmmm.'

'Or is that only out of office hours?'

Anna had gone along to one audition – on the evening of November 5th. The sky had been full of fireworks, adding colour to Anna's route along Vauxhall Bridge and into an old hall packed with youngish, hopeful, women like herself. *Actors (F) wanted to play part of thirtysomething woman for play going to Edinburgh Festival.*

They had been kept waiting for some time.

The waiting room smelled of old chips, but the women looked groomed. They smiled at each other nervously and feigned solidarity. One held a large photograph of herself, face up. *Flash teeth*, thought Anna. But, in the flesh, the woman was disappointing. There were traces of hardgraft on those health-farm manicured nails. *Stubby, yellow fingers*.

Another did her breathing exercises. Aaah. Aaah. Oooh. Oooh. Ah, ah, oo, oo.

The woman sitting beside Anna sniggered. A pretty woman, Anna noticed. She looked like a young Elizabeth Taylor, jumping from a horse in *National Velvet*. Black ringlets.

'They're keeping us waiting, aren't they?' said Velvet.

'Yeah, I know.' Anna's voice came out too loud.

'What's your name?'

'Anna.'

'I'm Madeleine. They shouldn't keep us waiting like this,' she said. 'It's late.'

A fattish man came out, at last, from the other room. He was wearing a shiny, purple shirt, which stretched every button. He introduced himself as Peter the Director. Would they all be so kind, darlings, as to wait while he auditioned them, one by one? Anna tried to breathe evenly, but she was furious.

'Don't you think it would have been easier to give us all separate audition times?' she began. 'I mean, we've been waiting for half an hour already.'

There was always one woman making a fuss. Speaking up. Pushing herself forward. Anna had always preferred to wait in line, loving those ticket dispensers in delicatessens, and in Job Centres. *Please take a ticket and wait for your number to come up*. Until now.

'You. What's your name?' asked Peter, stroking the beginnings of a beard.

'Anna. Anna Potter.'

She would not normally confront people like this (it was important to choose one's battles carefully), but Anna was angry on behalf of all the women waiting in this room. And on behalf of women, everywhere. It would be dark by the time the last woman left. Unsafe, out there.

'Anna *Potter*. Interesting name, darling,' he drawled. It was as if he was using his body like a machine to pump out each word. Anna could see his diaphragm working hard at each intonation. 'Well, Anna Potter, why don't you let *me* run my audition? I think I have more experience than you.' He raised his eyebrows at the other women, taking Anna's CV, and glancing through it. '*Piers the Ploughman*?'

he mocked. 'Oh, listen to this, darlings – *A Woman of No Importance*.'

All of the other women looked down at their laps, en masse, a sudden, collective, interest in the paperclips clasped to their CVs.

Of course, Anna should have left then. But she still had faith in her self-help books. *Many feel that they will be discriminated against if they stand up for what they believe to be right*, Greer Lawton had written. *But the reverse is true: it is important to send out the right signals. If you believe in yourself, others will too.*

'Well, that was brave,' said Madeleine to Anna as the director left them.

'I know. I'm shaking.'

'Oh, look. I'm sorry I didn't say anything.'

'That's OK.'

The other women, who had been looking at Anna as if she was a curiosity, started to make the usual smoking, whispering, snickering sounds of waiting.

'It's just that I really want this play,' said Madeleine, quietly. 'I haven't worked for months – not even profit-share . . .'

'Madeleine Buchanan?' interrupted Peter, appearing at the door.

'Good luck,' whispered Anna.

She was the last one led through those swing doors. By that time Anna had read four out of the five magazines lying on the table. One of them carried a piece, in its nightclubs section, about Justine Quealy's club. 'Fuchsia Girl.'

Happening new night at Stormont. Of course, everyone's pronouncing it Fuck-See-A Girl but, no doubt, that's just what hip-chick Justine Quealy intended when she set up the night that looks all set to rival Dead – CF.

So, Justine had received the go-ahead, with or without Anna.

Without Anna, she had been given the go-ahead. It reminded Anna of Justine's strength. A strength that Anna had, many times, relied on. She was put in mind of Russell Cocker's party. That toilet. When Charlie Secker had screamed, 'Anna Potter's a virgin,' and Justine had screamed back, 'Yeah, and you'll be *dead* if you don't stop tellin' lies about my best mate . . .'

Charlie's voice had slunk away.

Justine had stolen Charlie's tie and cut it to shreds. Anna had taken a slice of it home for safe-keeping. She had kept it in her Memory Box, binning everything, weeks ago – the passport photos of Justine and Anna, the Crayola crayons, and the Secret Society membership badges. *Happening new night at Stormont,* she read again, wanting to tell someone that they had been best friends, in more exciting times. Justine and Anna. (They had been best friends.) But she no longer had the photographic evidence.

Anna's name was called, bringing her back to the present.

She went through to a room that reminded her of a school assembly hall, swept with familiar draughts. At one end was a raised platform.

'Right, darling. Up on stage. Let's see you channel all that attitude,' said Peter, camply. He leaned against a school desk on which sat two takeaway cappuccinos and half a swiss roll, sweating in its cellophane.

Anna stood up there, facing Peter down. She believed in herself. She could play anyone – putty in any director's hands – and felt certain that he would admire her pre-prepared soliloquy. It was a scene from *The House of Bernarda Alba*, which she had rehearsed hard.

'Mmm,' he said, as she finished. 'Let's see your improvis-
ation.'

He asked Anna to laugh, but she couldn't – not on cue.
'Come on, this is pathetic,' said Peter. 'I'm only asking you
to fucking well *laugh*, sweetheart, not give birth to William
Hague. Fine, go *home*. Go on, I'm tired.'

Anna bent to stuff her props back into her bag. The black
armband, the pearl ring, the tissues. She left the stage, trying
to remember all of the actresses out there who must have
heard the same words in their early careers. Judy Garland.
Judi Dench.

Perhaps he saw the tears coming then, because Peter
called her over to his desk. He softened, and looked at her
almost kindly, saying, 'Can I give you some advice . . . er
. . .' He looked down at his sheet of paper. '*Anna*.'

'Yes,' she said, watching his friend spoon sugar into Peter's
cappuccino. 'I mean, yes.'

'How many d'you want, Peter?' asked the friend.

'*Later*,' he said to the friend. 'Two spoons, darling.' He
sighed as he saw Anna, still there, watching his sugar drowning in the crack of the cappuccino. 'Right, my love.'

That was to Anna.

'You know, I've had a *lot* of women audition for me,'
he began. 'I've seen some great actresses – fine actresses.
I've also seen some appalling ones. But, you know, in this
business, even the *fine* actresses don't work for months on
end.' He stopped to grunt, and to pick up a digestive biscuit.
'Do you understand what I'm saying, sweetheart?' he asked,
dunking the half-biscuit into his coffee.

He sighed.

'You don't have much on your CV, do you, Anna?'

'Well, I'm just starting really. I've been working in radio
for almost ten years.'

'Well, why are you giving *that* up then, love?' He asked the question gently, but biscuit crumbs snowed from his mouth.

'No. This is what I want to do, even if this part isn't . . .'

'Well, I'm going to tell you what I think.' He selected a biscuit from the box of British Variety, and breathed out. 'I don't think you've got it. Seriously, darling. I'm sorry to be the one who has to tell you, but put yourself in my shoes. Should I let you leave this job you've got – and for what? For what? Because you won't get work, my love. No – and I'm not talking Hollywood either. Girls *sixty* times better than you are lucky to get a week's work in rep. Why put yourself through that? Do something in amateur instead. Just my opinion, sweetheart.'

His emphasis, as any actress could have informed him, was all over the place.

'So have you been going to lots of auditions?' asked Myrna, without interest.

'*One*. But the director had some sort of a grudge against me, after I . . . And there aren't many open auditions. You have to be a member of the trade union before they'll even see you.'

'So, join the trade union then,' she said, dismissively.

'If only it was that easy.' Anna smiled. 'You have to be a professional actress first. Either that, or a stripper. But, I didn't come round to . . . How *are* you?'

'Why, do you give a damn?'

'Of course I give a damn. What d'you mean?'

'Well, call me *sensitive*,' said Myrna, dramatically. 'But after phoning you thirty-two times, I just plain gave up.'

'You phoned me that many times?' asked Anna, knowing that Myrna had phoned, persistently.

At first, she had avoided Myrna deliberately. What was the point of living in the centre of London, if she was still in contact with a woman like Myrna, who lived on the city's northern fringes? An unemployed woman like Myrna, with a weight problem.

A month passed, however, and Anna had begun to miss her. Myrna, and Tom. That was when she had begun to think of the two of them together. Well, they were sharing a flat. What was to stop them sharing a bed? Certainly, Anna was not there to stand in their way. It was a natural progression, surely? They would be drunk one night, and Myrna would say something witty. Tom would say, dreamily, 'You're so clever, Myrn.' He would take her hand. And the two of them would . . .

She had stopped herself thinking of them, then. Myrna, and Tom. It pained her, to think of them together. But she could no longer think of them apart.

'You were screening your calls, weren't you?' asked Myrna, as Anna looked around the living room, seeing traces of Tom everywhere. Tom's textbooks. Tom's empty beer cans. Tom's scribbled ideas for 'inventions' to patent. She had forgotten how bright he was. Ideas, all the time.

'I kept hearing "Sebastian's" posh voice,' said Myrna. 'So I assumed you were out partying with the beautiful people.'

National 'Madeleine' Velvet had telephoned. Did Anna want to go for a drink? They could talk about Peter, the Director.

They met at the Stag's Head in Soho.

But Madeleine turned out – once Anna knew her – to be plain old Mads. Ringletless. She was loud, in an embarrassing way, and admiring of Peter, who had invited her back for a second audition. She reminded Anna of Liz, but without the laughter. Mads was Liz without the infectious sense of humour. But, unlike Liz, she was the sort to wear high-heels with her trousers. Mads was the type who said Take Care when what she meant to say was Goodbye.

Anna had not imagined her new life, in Sebastian's flat, without Sean playing a part, visiting. Whenever she had thought about herself, sitting in the Jacuzzi bath, Sean had been there too, semi-naked.

She had been wrong to believe in Sean. Anna knew that now. He was only human, after all. Anna knew that she had a tendency to pour all of her desires into one man. As Caroline Rice had written in the now out-of-print *Discovering the Difference*, no man needs a woman who needs him: *These women are guilty of 'splitting'. They choose one man, and throw on to him all their ideals. They want to believe that that man is clever, and charming, and can do no wrong. All of those negative feelings go somewhere else. Usually, to their family and friends. As the Heinecker-Billows study showed (see Index iii), women with the most negative feelings were usually the ones with only a small circle of friends. Women with a large circle of friends were more easily able to focus on the positive.*

Anna had telephoned what seemed to be almost all two hundred and twenty of her friends to leave her new Chelsea telephone number. But after an initial mad rush of people popping in to see Sebastian's flat, or simply to catch up, Anna was left alone in the evenings. Alone, and ignored by her own four walls. Lonely.

The living room began to look like her mother's best guest room. It appeared, from the way everything was placed *just so*, that Anna was anxious for visitors. She felt empty.

She felt empty without Roo, and decided to visit her old friend's house in Tufnell Park. She stood outside, not ringing the bell.

Anna did not have the courage to ring the bell, especially as she could see Warren through the window. She remembered what she had said about him making a pass at her, knowing that Warren would have denied everything to Roo. Not only that, but he would have said that Anna was imagining things. He couldn't possibly fancy Anna Potter. No, not even after *several* bottles of whisky.

She stood there, feeling small and bereft, wanting her friend. But she could see Roo, now, through the window, and did not want to disturb the scene that came into focus before her. Warren, sitting down beside Roo and laughing. Roo, crouching down on the floor to pick up Oscar.

Warren, offering Daisy a sip of his beer.

Oh, Anna knew that, behind that closed door, they were probably screaming at each other. Roo, telling Warren not to give Daisy alcohol poisoning. Warren, telling Roo to stop turning his son into a 'nancy'.

But she could not, of course, hear them speak; and the four of them looked pretty, as in a family portrait.

She left the house, her eyes springing with tears; and was tempted to call Liz, just for a laugh, just for old times' sake, but remembered their last conversation. Ever. Anna needed to talk to someone – Justine, anyone.

She needed to talk to one or other of her parents. But she felt uselessly sentimental, so she rallied herself, and called Pritti instead.

Pritti did not have the time to see Anna. Only after further pressure did she give in to her old friend's pleas, taking one hour away from her demanding, if fulfilling, job as GP and mother to Monika.

Her visit was interrupted by a man coming to fix the boiler. Anna showed the man through to her utility room.

Pritti followed them.

402

'Well, let's start by moving that sandwich, shall we?' said the man. But even Pritti was afraid to pick it up. He shook his head, unable to believe Young Girls Today, and moved the cheese sandwich himself – ever-so-gingerly – to the kitchen bin.

Anna offered to make coffee, by way of a thank you, and so that he would not be tempted to overcharge her.

'I'll make the coffee, Anna,' said Pritti, ever-helpfully.

'Well, you can start by telling me its history,' said the man, patting the boiler – calming it down.

'Oh, but I've only just moved in . . .'

'How d'you like your coffee?' asked Pritti.

'Is it important to . . . ?'

'Black, of *course*,' the man hur-hurred. He leered at Pritti.

Anna stared at him.

'I can't *believe* you said that,' she snapped. 'I don't think you even realised that it was a racist remark.'

'Oh no it wasn't . . .'

'What did he say?'

'You think that because you can *bung* some racist comment into a casual conversation that makes it OK?'

'Now, hang on a moment, young lady, I didn't mean . . .'

'Anna, what *is* this?'

'I suppose you think Pritti's just some servile Asian babe, don't you? Because she was nice enough to offer you a coffee? Well, she *happens* to be a doctor. So before you start on your stereotyping . . .'

'Anna, *please*.'

'I think I'd better go,' said the man to Pritti as if they were in some sort of a conspiracy.

'No you can't just *leave*,' said Anna, as the man zipped up his bag.

Pritti looked at Anna.

'Well, that was embarrassing,' she said, after the man had left. 'Embarrassing, and unnecessary.'

The cat smirked. It reminded Anna of Daisy. It looked at her in that same prescient way, and kept guard of the television. It curled in front of the TV cupboard all evening, and if she tried to move it, it clawed. Anna had the scratches to prove it.

'Yeah, they look nasty,' admitted Myrna, examining Anna's arms. 'I think that Sebastian should be paying you to look after – is the cat's name Daisy, did you say?'

'Yeah. I re-named it after my god-daughter.'

'Did you have a row with Roo then, as well?'

'As well as whom?'

'Well – your mother for one. Did it piss you off that I asked her to call you? Only you wouldn't return *my* calls.'

'How did you get this number?' Anna asked Barbara, who had phoned.

'From your friend, Myrna.'

They paused, to see who would be the next one to speak.

It was Barbara. She said, 'Don't worry, I won't be on the phone long.'

'That's all right,' said Anna, softening. She felt that it wouldn't hurt her, to take one short phone call from her mother.

'I'm phoning on Myrna's behalf,' said Barbara, efficiently. 'She wants her hat-stand back. Apparently you took it with you, when you left.'

'Why did you call my old flat?' asked Anna. Hard.

'I needed to forward you a letter, from your old polytechnic.'

'Oh. Well, don't bother sending that. It'll just be junk.'

'That's what Myrna said – that you wouldn't be inter-ested in anything to do with the past,' said Barbara, her voice flat.

'How is Myrna?' said Anna, because she did not want her mother to say goodbye. Not just yet.

'Well, she was in a terrible state, obviously.'

'Why?' asked Anna, thinking, *I know full well why. It's because I moved out, that's why*. But she wanted to hear her mother say it.

But: 'About her father dying,' was all Barbara said.

'Myrna's dad died . . . ?'

'Yes. Didn't you know?' she asked, curiously.

'No.'

Anna wondered how Myrna would have coped with that fact. Then she remembered that Myrna would have Tom at home, to support her. Tom would be very good in such a situation, comforting Myrna. Remarkably good.

'We're not in touch any more,' she said, coldly.

Anna wondered whether – had she still been friends with Myrna – she would have anyway been made welcome at the funeral. There had been bad feeling for years between Anna and Mr Lomond. He blamed her for his son's homosexuality. Myrna's father had been furious that Anna would not, even once, go out with Graeme. That might have been enough to persuade his son to give marriage a go. But no. She had stolen Graeme's chance of ever having children.

'I'm worried about you,' said her mother, interrupting her thoughts. 'Don said that you're leaving your job.'

'Oh, it's Don now, is it?' sneered Anna. 'Not Your Father Who Art at the Conservative Club.'

'Please, Anna . . .'

'Why don't you stop worrying about me, and start to worry about your *own* problems?'

'But there are so *many* . . .'

Barbara's voice broke into a sob.

'Please don't cry,' said Anna, softening. Her mother had rarely, if ever, cried. Now, it was as if she was crying all the time.

Perhaps it's best to let the tears out, decided Anna, as she realised that she too wanted to cry.

'You don't know the problems *I've* got.'

'Oh, what problems could you have?' said Barbara.

'Oh, you don't know. You just don't know,' said Anna, indulgently. She felt as if she was crawling back into her mother's arms, like a child, but would that hurt? It was only a short phone call, and even Wilhelm Grohe believed in open emotion, especially when it came to one's birth-mother.

'Anna, I *know* you,' sniffed her mother. 'This giving up your job is all some *fantasy*. It was the same with that boy at school. What was his name? Charlie Sucker?'

'Secker.'

'You have a *lovely* little job. Why give that up?'

'Mum, remember I'm not so easily put down, now, by your value judgments.'

'It was the same when you wanted to be a dog-breeder.'

'I was *seven* . . .' she said, trying to sound serious.

'*And* a beautician. Do you remember that? It was your *dream*, you said.'

'Well, I was young,' said Anna, who had begged her parents, after poly, to pay for her course at the London School of Beauty and Fashion.

The brochure advertising the course had made it appear so simple, showing pretty pictures of beauties cutting hair and manicuring slender hands. It had glossily shown students sitting around in cafés, sipping cappuccinos. But Anna had not realised that beauty could be so academic, with lectures and essays and modules. In reality, she had had to go home with piles of textbooks illustrated with women suffering skin complaints. On her first day there, the course had erupted in hives, boils and adult acne.

She had left after one term.

'It was what you'd *always* wanted to do, Anna.'

'I was young, Mum,' she said, trying to stop herself slipping back into her old role, as child, to Barbara, who was playing mother. (Failing.)

'Your *dream*,' said Barbara, but not unkindly. 'You couldn't live without it. You wanted to be a beautician-to-the-stars, in Hollywood.'

'I'd forgotten that.'

At that point, Anna began to smile.

'So Dad's moved out?' she said, sitting down and pulling her knees up to her neck. She was a child again, and enjoying the feeling.

'Yes, but I didn't call to . . . Let's talk about happier things,' said Barbara, brightening.

'How d'you feel about the divorce?' said Anna, hugging her knees.

'Well . . .' Her mother's voice seemed to fail her. 'Why talk about this?'

'Only that I know how much you valued your marriage – in principle.'

'Well, then you'll know that I didn't want a divorce. But once we'd talked . . . It's very difficult to unsay things. And the trouble with Don is that he doesn't know when he's happy. He won't *settle*. Although for that I blame the Conservative Party. They drum ideas into people. It was the party that made Don think he needed things, like pleated curtains. And Catherine. It's all in his head, though. I know Your Father. He won't be happy with That Woman.'

407

Anna wondered whether to invite her mother round to her new flat. She wanted Barbara's opinion of it, knowing that, at the very least – and despite herself – her mum would have been impressed with the exterior.

'But he wasn't happy before, was he? Neither of you were happy,' she said, instead, remembering that any decent psychologist would tell Anna that she was inviting her mother's criticism. *And why do that?* she could hear Sean Harrison's ghost say. *To confirm your low opinion of yourself?*

'Oh, *happy*,' Barbara said, as if she was repeating an obscenity. 'Let's not talk about that. Let's talk about Christmas. What will you be doing? Will you come here, as usual?'

'Well, if it's a choice between you, and *Catherine* . . .'

'Then, better the devil you know.'

Anna heard her mother smile at that.

'Does *Problem Call* go out over Christmas?' Myrna asked Anna, as Shelley hung some tinsel, by way of commiseration, around Charmaine's neck.

'Oh yes. Busiest time, Christmas. Now's when we cash in – what with all those families not functioning, and suicides. Our audience figures go right up. It's great. We get really sexy calls about people dying.'

She looked at Myrna, and remembered.

'Oh my God. I'm sorry. Look, I'm so sorry . . . About your dad.'

'Well . . . Wasn't a big surprise.'

'I know.'

'I mean, he *was* mortal.'

Anna paused. She had rehearsed a speech about dying, but it did not seem appropriate now that she was back in her old living room. Myrna, anyway, quickly changed the subject.

'So, what's it like being at *Problem Call*, now that you're leaving?'

Anna had felt, at first, as if her colleagues were making arrangements for her funeral within her earshot.

They were all shocked to learn that Anna was leaving, gazing at her in wonder. Mike took it personally, pleading with Anna to stay.

Yet, after a week had passed, they all began to behave as if Anna had suddenly gone all uppity, leaving them all behind for something grander. She found the team in small huddles, whispering. 'You know, she's making a *big* mistake . . .' As they saw her, they all smiled. Secretively. Her leaving lent the programme a real esprit de corps. Finally, Anna felt as if there was such a thing as society – although she had opted out of it.

She had felt the same when Princess Diana had died. Anna could have enjoyed the day, had she been in the right place. But she had had a bad view of the back of Westminster Abbey. She imagined that people in bomb-hit London had felt the same during the War. They too could have enjoyed the Blitz spirit, if only they had been in a shelter somewhere in a pretty, rural area.

Anna was tempted to tell Pammy that she had changed her mind, and to stay on, until she had confirmed her first performance dates.

But Pammy had already made practical arrangements for Anna's replacement. Lena whooped when she was given the operator's job. Then she saw Anna, and fell silent again. From where Lena sat, Anna's new life seemed blank. Purposeless. Why was she leaving the security of an office job?

Life went on, anyhow. Wilhelm Grohe had joined as

co-presenter. Anna had been anxious to meet the man who had led her to believe that she was worth something. But it was difficult for her to associate the weaselly figure in the co-presenter's chair with the man who had written the groundbreaking, life-changing, *One Month to Happiness*. He was a mite of a man with a child's drawing of a beard – different lengths of brown hair sprouting out of his chin – and an asthmatic rasp of a voice. His nostrils gaped open and, sometimes, so did the fly of his trousers.

Fortunately, Anna had begun to read writers such as Greer Lawton, Lesley Schroder, and Caroline Rice – all of whom argued that Wilhelm Grohe's theories were flimsy and easily dismissed. She no longer took Grohe's word as gospel. She was far more interested in the work of Gertrude Salamand, and Denvil George. As Salamand had said, Wilhelm Grohe's books were mere pop psychology – learned journals re-packaged for the masses. Besides, Grohe irritated Anna.

He was not happy with Mike's briefing notes.

He was not happy with Pammy as presenter. He was extremely well-known in parts of Germany and Scandinavia, and had done an old friend – *Duncan* – a favour by giving up a month of valuable time to promote his book exclusively for Radio Central. He was not impressed with the operator, Anna. And he did not like Lena; she was disrespectful.

Blonde was too strident.

The production team began to ignore Wilhelm. The core staff sat at a lunch table with space reserved for – *Sorry, Wilhelm* – just the five of them. Pammy, saying that she was tempted to cancel Wilhelm's contract. Mike, admitting that he had never met anyone so lazy. Lena, saying that she had never come across anyone so ungracious. Anna, trying to connect Wilhelm the man with Wilhelm the writer. Todd, mumbling that he didn't want to get involved.

November began, and Wilhelm Grohe left, muttering.

'I feel as if I'm able to breathe again,' said Mike, as Maurice Stowe joined the programme. That month they were doing Death.

Stowe did not stop smiling. 'Life's too short to be so miserable,' he said, queueing up behind Anna at the coffee machine. But December was looming, and Anna fretted. Her leaving had become a taboo subject. No one discussed it now, and she was scared. Actresses sixty times better than Anna were lucky to get a week's work in repertory.

By then, Maurice Stowe had left. Christine Tait took his place, to co-present a month about Xmas Stress.

Anna was terrified. She was leaving in January but no one gave a damn. She was opting out of office life – for nothingness.

No one cared what Anna did next. Except Pammy. She asked Anna to read Gerald Stope's book – *Self-Destruction* – which examined, over 500 pages, why people gave up a lifetime's work on a lunatic whim.

She called Anna into a spare studio, so that they could discuss the book and the 'issues it raised'. Did it strike a chord, at all, with Anna?

'Well, to be honest, I can't remember much of it. I did *read* it, but I've been reading so many of these books lately. They're all starting to merge in my mind. Why?' she asked, curiously. 'Do you you want me to prepare a brief for you?'

'I wasn't planning a programme about the subject, Anna. I thought of it more as personal reading for you.'

'Right, I see.'

'Although, it sounds, sweetie, as if you're taking too much

work home with you. No. I lent you that book because I wanted you to think about your decision to resign.'

'I don't want to leave,' confessed Anna.

Pammy's bosom heaved with relief.

'You know, Duncan's just agreed a bigger budget,' she said. 'You'll have to be interviewed for the researcher role. And I can't promise anything. But I think his department owes me one after that debacle with Lena. I'll see what I can do.'

'Thank you.' *Thank you.*

'I'm not leaving,' said Anna to Myrna. 'I'm the programme researcher now. *So.* Hardly glamorous, but it'll please my father.'

'Which is what life is all about,' said Myrna, emphatically. 'Even after they're dead.'

'Oh God, I'm sorry I missed the funeral.'

'Oh, don't start all that again.'

She missed Myrna, snapping. She realised that now. Anna missed Myrna's face about the flat – always a mess of bones, dark eyes and wild, curly hair. She was such a state. At school, her blazer had had creases striking the back, like lightning. Her skirt puckered, like the surface of the Earth. Myrna's father had called her The Great Unwashed.

Anna wished that they could have an emotional reunion, with lots of hugging, as real flatmates did, on television dramas. Myrna would say, *Oh Anna, you're the best friend I've ever had.* Anna would say, *Oh Myrna, no wonder Tom prefers you to me. You're cleverer, and funnier, and clean of eczema.*

'Don't start what?' asked Anna, instead.

'Being so *understanding.*'

'What's wrong with showing people that you care?'

'Oh God, Anna. Listen to yourself. Since you've been

412

at *Problem Call*, you've been so understanding. Patiently, smilingly, irritatingly, understanding. Can't you, for God's sake, see that?'

'Yeah, I suppose I was a bit . . .' Anna smiled.

'Shhh. I love this bit.'

Shelley stood at the bottom of a *Gone With the Wind*-style staircase.

'Well, you've listened to my guests, and to their problems. Now it's their chance to take their concerns to Him Upstairs. Come on Kerry, Becca, Charmaine – follow me up the Shelley Steps . . .'

Shelley stood, half-way up the steps.

'Keep up, Becca – at the back there. This is what I like to call my moment of truth. You've heard what my studio audience thinks about your marital arguments. They voted anonymously *– and 66% of them thought that you'd be best off separating. Can we see that up on the screen there? 32% thought that you should stay together. 2% were undecided. Now, let's go on up those steps.'*

She reached some cardboard gates studded with pearls.

'OK, it's judgment time, Shelley-style. Behind those pearly gates sits Sean Harrison – our resident psychologist. He's been listening to all of the issues raised in the programme and . . . And are we having a problem *with our pearly gates today?'*

'They're always having a problem with their pearly gates,' said Myrna, as, at last, the 'gates' opened to reveal an unembarrassed Sean Harrison.

'*No*,' said Anna in disbelief as she saw him, sitting on a Shelley throne.

'You're not taking this *seriously*, Anna,' joked Myrna.

Anna apologised for laughing. 'I didn't realise Shelley was so entertaining,' she said, scratching the eczema on the back of her hands.

'Yeah, well I'd rather watch couples arguing than go into work any day.'

'I suppose . . .'

'Shhh – Sean's giving us his verdict.'

My advice to Kerry, Becca, and Charmaine would be to treat their marriages as working partnerships. Of course their husbands aren't perfect. But life is pretty damn imperfect too. Isn't it?'

'Well,' said Myrna, as Shelley thanked Sean, and the pearly gates shut. 'That's as good a moral as any.'

'Although hardly *subtle*.'

'Tom'll be sorry he missed *Seany*. I usually have to tape Shelley for him.'

'How are you two getting on? Has anything happened? I mean, romantically?' she asked, lightly.

Please say no, she thought, spotting one of his jumpers, slung over the armchair, any old how.

'What – with Tom?' said Myrna. 'You're joking, aren't you? He's far too posh for me. I'm from Middlesbrough, remember. You know he went to public school?'

'A very minor one.' Happy to hear that she had been mistaken about *Myrna and Tom*, Anna began to waffle on about Tom's father, who was big in the Labour movement. He had been against the idea of private education, but Tom had been offered a full scholarship to Wesleydale. Tom's mother had insisted he take up his place. His parents had separated. He had hated school and school dinners.

'You sound like a quiz-show contestant,' said Myrna, interrupting her monologue. 'Tell me everything about Tom in thirty seconds, starting from *now*.' She smiled. 'Don't worry, Anna, if you know enough about him, I'll give you him as first prize. Tom, on a plate, next to one of those heat 'n' eat meals that he eats every night. Just as you do.'

Anna said, 'I haven't eaten a ready-meal for months'.

'Mind you,' went on Myrna, 'he really shouldn't have told me about Wesleydale. Yet another reason to rip the piss out of him. It's not as if he doesn't give me great ammunition, anyway – what with all that pseudo-socialism, and pining over you.'

Pining over me? thought Anna, startled.

Myrna said, 'He uses the word "love", to cover up for the fact that, like most men, he has an unhealthy obsession with sex. I mean, you were only together a . . . Talking of *whom . . .*'

She stopped, as Tom came into the room. He was holding two packets of Silk Cut.

'You talking about your secret desire for my body again, Myrn?' he said. And then he looked at Anna as if she had sat on the sofa with the sole purpose of surprising him. 'Well, this is a blast from the past. Hello.'

It was a sexy voice. Plus, Tom looked rough in that jumper. Rough and cuddly. Anna liked the way he dressed, smothered in warm jumpers.

'Have you broken up for Christmas already?' asked Anna of him. She was looking at the slices of eczema covering her hands and wrists, and thinking them pink-ugly.

'No, I took a sickie. My throat hurts.'

'Her Majesty's Inspectors are in school today,' said Myrna. 'So, Tom was too shit scared to . . .'

'Have you *met* Myrna's boyfriend?' he interrupted. '*Gregory*. She met him at an art class . . .'

'Are you back with Gregory?' asked Anna, enjoying being back in conversation with Myrna and Tom.

Tom sat on the armchair opposite the sofa. Facing Anna.

'Oh God, you're not going to start talking about "relationships" again, are you, Anna?' asked Myrna, embarrassed. She pulled up her legwarmers, which had long ago lost their elastic. 'Because, if you are, I'm going to water my plants. I'll leave you two to *talk*,' she said, standing up, and

415

Anna swallowed, scared at the thought of being left alone with Tom. She remembered their last conversation, which had not been pleasant.

The room felt big, without Myrna in it.

'You haven't given up, then?' said Anna, roughly, as Tom lit a cigarette. She wished she could stop sounding like an adolescent boy, whose voice was breaking.

'From tomorrow. These are my final fags.'

'Where have I heard that before?' said Anna. She tried to laugh lightly. But the laugh came out over-loud and long.

'True,' said Tom, narrowing his eyes, and scrutinising her. '*So*, I see Myrna's got her beloved hat-stand back. Is that why you're here? To return the thing?'

Anna looked into his narrowed eyes. Tom did not appear to be someone pining over anyone, least of all her. 'Yes, that's why I'm here,' she said, coldly, pulling herself together. She needed control, remembering that Tom had called her *a selfish bitch. You're worth fuck all,* he had said.

Tom looked at the blank screen of the television, and said, 'Have I missed your boyfriend on *The Shelley Show* then?'

'What?' she said.

'The Boyfriend. Or is Sean Harrison too old to be a boy-friend? I mean, the man must be in his forties. That's *old*,' he said, grinning with one side of his mouth, and tapping ash into a stray mug. 'That's fucking old.'

'He's not my boyfriend,' snapped Anna.

She picked up a newspaper from the side table, and they sat there, silently for a moment. Anna read about water contamination in Wales.

'I'm glad to hear it,' said Tom, allowing the grin to spread, full across his mouth. He tapped his cigarette again, 'The man's a charlatan.'

'But good entertainment value,' said Anna, softening.

'So, was I just for your entertainment, as well?'

'No, I demand better entertainment than that.' She was joking. It was an avoidance tactic; Anna knew that. Of course, it was important that they talk about their relationship. But she was not sure how to express her feelings, frankly.

Obviously, neither could Tom, who stubbed out his half-finished cigarette. He stood up and went to the old-fashioned mantelpiece, ostensibly to pick up a political quarterly magazine, but clearly to avoid having to say anything.

She sat there, reading blurring newsprint. Surely, after months of training at *Problem Call*, Anna could communicate to him just what she was feeling, setting out for him the direction she wanted the relationship to go in? Her desires? Tom would then feel valued, and understood. He could be honest with her about his own concerns.

But Anna was afraid that, if she began to talk, it would all blurt out. She would sob, and tell him how lonely she was. They would then rush straight to having sex, without having a much-needed, adult conversation first.

So, she stayed silent, as did Tom, until Myrna came back into the living room with a jug of dirty water, dripping everywhere. She put it down, on top of the television, and sat in the armchair which Tom had vacated.

Tom looked annoyed, and sat on the sofa, beside Anna. He stretched his legs out, flipping through the magazine.

'So?' said Myrna, leaning forward, smiling. Facing them. 'Are you back together then?'

'*Myrna*,' said Anna, mortified.

'Oh, *sorry*,' said Myrna who was all innocence. She sat back. 'Did I not give you enough time, just now, to sort out your differences? If you could *find* any differences. I tell you, Anna, living with Tom has been just like living with you. He leaves toothpaste spit, drying around the sink, as well.'

'For God's sake, Myrn,' said Tom, wearily.

'For God's sake, *Tom*,' was Myrna's response, pretending to scold. 'I'm sure if it was *Sean* here with Anna, he would have been able to sort out the entire relationship in a matter of seconds. They would have discussed all of their feelings. Everything would have been laid bare. Including Anna.'

'I can assure you,' said Anna, firmly. 'I do not want to be naked with Sean Harrison.'

She read her newspaper, feeling Myrna staring. It was as if Myrna was assessing her for some anthropological study.

'So, *Anna*,' said Myrna, at last. 'Do you miss living here? Want to move back in?'

'Well, yes. I mean, Sebastian's coming home soon,' said Anna, looking up, suddenly hopeful. She had not realised that there was the option of moving back in, with Myrna.

'So, you want me to go?' asked Tom, looking up from his magazine.

Anna glanced sideways at him. He was staring at Myrna in surprise, as if he was being betrayed, not just by Myrna, but by women the world over.

'All I'm saying is, that's a double room you're in, Tom,' said Myrna impatiently. 'I could get two people paying rent in there. A married couple, who argue nicely all the time.'

'What are you trying to say, Myrna?' he said.

'Just that I think you should share that room.'

'What d'you mean?' he asked. Irritated. 'Who with?'

'I thought you said I could move back in?' asked Anna, quietly.

'You *can*,' said Myrna.

'Hang on a minute . . .' That was Tom.

'But you'll have to share it. I mean, you're the one, Anna,

who wanted a king-sized bed. But it's going to waste – lying there, half-empty. So, share it with Tom. Otherwise, I'll get another couple in.'

Anna sensed his fingers, almost touching her own. There was a long pause. '*So*,' said Myrna, ending it. She stood up. 'What d'you both say?' Hands on huge hips.

'I don't mind sharing,' said Anna, at last, to which Tom said nothing. But he took her hand.

Myrna saw this, and smiled. She picked up her jug, and went over to pour water into her yucca pot. 'Well, I'm sorry to get in the way of such an emotionally charged scene, but this one's dying, so . . .' She muttered something about life, as the yucca stretched and breathed.

Yet another bloody metaphor, thought Anna, hoping that Tom wouldn't feel her eczema.

The Simple Life
Lauren Wells

Would you swap the company BMW for a third-hand van? Your Manolo Blahnik mules for a pair of wellies – and not even green ones, at that? Would you know what to do with a vegetable that's covered in earth instead of clingfilm?

Laurence Langland would. He's had enough of office politics and fifteen-hour days. He wants out, to a simpler, better life. And Isobel, his wife, a woman whose gold-plated key-ring says 'Born to Shop', has her own very private reasons for wanting to escape, while eight-year-old Jacob is thrilled because it means leaving his horrible boarding school. Only his elder sister Dory needs persuading - until she realizes that there are boys in the country, too. And so the Langland family become 'down-shifters', exchanging cosy suburbia for the pleasures – and the pitfalls – of rural life. Making the decision was the easy part. But can they cope with the reality?

An hilarious and touching novel about what happens when you have it all – and then don't want it any more.

0 00 649966 X

Working it Out

Alex George

Johnathan Burlip – a man with a redundant 'h', a legal career that's on the skids and an unfortunate way with animals

Tormented by his soon-to-be-ex-girlfriend, his dysfunctional family and petulant colleagues, things get even worse for Johnathan when he loses his fat-cat corporate job and finds himself struggling to survive in a dodgy legal practice in North London. There he is introduced to psychotic Spanish restaurateurs, well-manicured mobsters, and star legal exhibit, *Eddie* the tarantula.

Johnathan's PC parents are desperate for him to be gay, whilst Johnathan is desperate to go out with the unpredictable and alluring *Kibby*.

Morty, the heroic hamster, meanwhile, is desperately trying to keep himself afloat in a toilet bowl. When life repeatedly kicks you in the groin, you can either go down screaming, or work out what's happening and take action . . .

0 00 651332 8